GREAT BLACK HOPE

GREAT BLACK HOPE

ROB FRANKLIN

Summit
Books

London · New York · Amsterdam/Antwerp · Sydney/Melbourne · Toronto · New Delhi

Summit
Books

First published in the United States by Summit Books, an imprint of Simon & Schuster LLC
This edition published in Great Britain by Summit Books, an imprint of Simon & Schuster UK Ltd, 2025

1 3 5 7 9 10 8 6 4 2

Simon & Schuster UK Ltd
1st Floor
222 Gray's Inn Road
London WC1X 8HB

Simon & Schuster Australia, Sydney
Simon & Schuster India, New Delhi

www.simonandschuster.co.uk
www.simonandschuster.com.au
www.simonandschuster.co.in

A CIP catalogue record for this book is available from the British Library

The authorised representative in the EEA is Simon & Schuster Netherlands BV, Herculesplein 96, 3584
AA Utrecht, Netherlands. info@simonandschuster.nl

Simon & Schuster strongly believes in freedom of expression and stands against censorship in all its
forms. For more information, visit BooksBelong.com.

Hardback ISBN: 978-1-3985-3992-1
Trade Paperback ISBN: 978-1-3985-3993-8
eBook ISBN: 978-1-3985-3994-5
eAudio ISBN: 978-1-3985-3995-2

Printed and Bound in the UK using 100% Renewable Electricity at CPI Group (UK) Ltd

for my family

GREAT BLACK HOPE

I.

Out East

In the grand scheme of history, it was nothing. A blip, a breath. The time it took Smith to pocket what might have looked like a matchbook or stick of gum to an unwitting child but was, in fact, 0.7 grams of powdered Colombian cocaine—flown in from Medellín, cut with amphetamine in Miami, and offered to him in Southampton by a boy whom he knew from nights out in the city; 0.7 grams heavier, he loped back through the crush of rhythmless elbows and cloying perfume which wafted up and dissolved in the damp and sultry night—the very last of summer.

Looking around, he realized it was really just a restaurant. By the front door, at least fifty people huddled, breathing down each other's necks as they shouted names they hoped would capture the doorman's attention, while in the backyard were hundreds more. Dozens of tables now shook with the weight of dancing, bodies lit with the particular mania reserved for the end of East Coast summers, when one becomes aware of the changing season, the coming cold. But for now, it was silk and linen, the expensive musk of strangers. Every face appeared familiar—some because he actually knew them while others only bore a suntanned resemblance, the pleasing symmetry of the rich. These were the faces which seemed to populate the whole of his young life: colleagues and one-night stands from the clubs called cool downtown. These faces had appeared at bars, brunches, birthdays, holiday soirees at which black tie was optional—and, before New York, in freshman seminars and frat parties, and, before that, on teen tours or tennis camps, where they'd been acne-spotted, their original forms intact. And here they'd all come, every one of them, to escape the inhospitable heat of Manhattan and enjoy a seaside breeze.

Picture him, stumbling. Six feet and three inches, he towered like a tree, bark brown and quietly handsome. Picture him crouched in a corner as he snorts from a key, the metallic taste of his tongue. The night gleamed back into clarity as he steadied himself to return—when out of the crowd, two men emerged, stern-eyed and square-jawed, barking orders he could barely discern. Calmly, he followed—he didn't wish to make a scene—out through a side exit and onto the street, silent but for the bass of a bop that had reigned on the charts all summer.

Here is where the night splits open along its tight-stitched seam. The realization, arriving at a tan vehicle marked *Southampton Police*, that these men in khaki polos were not the club security he'd assumed at first they were. The night bled surreally. Smith watched himself be searched as if from a perch above, watched his limbs grow limp and pliant as they bent behind his back. The rotated view of girls in wedges; their clothes wrong, the stars wrong. Yes, the greater sense was not of shock, but unreality. All of this was staged. A prank, a punk—the actors in the front seat, too handsome to be cops. The men were swift and practiced. After he'd handed over five hundred dollars cash from an ATM upstairs at the station, they brought him down to be printed, ID'd, and photographed. They were done in twenty minutes, after which he was handed a paper slip and his things in a plastic bag, then sent back into the wounded night. He called an Uber. On the curb, Smith watched phosphenes blinker in the darkness, a chorus of cameras flashing. He'd worn, in his mug shot, a vintage Marni gingham shirt, loose-fit linen trousers, and a gently startled expression.

CHAPTER ONE

Smith awoke in a twin-size bed in an otherwise empty room. For a moment, he kept his eyes closed, allowing himself the simple peace of chirping birds, warmth. Then the memory of last night settled, darkly, and he opened them.

He had to get out.

Already, through the emerging fog of a hangover, he felt panic slowly filling his lungs. He rose and, immediately, began tossing his things into an open weekend bag: his swim trunks and linen, the Isherwood he'd neglected, then the clothes he'd last night worn, crumpled in the corner where he'd shed them only hours ago, arriving home. Smith checked his phone: 6:13 a.m. Carolyn wouldn't be up for hours, but her grandparents would be rising soon—Ann to muddle paints in her open-air studio; Ed to take his café crème and recline with a Proust by the pool—and the idea of greeting them with any air of politesse, of attempting conversation over eggs over easy, filled him with a blood-thinning dread.

Yes, he had to get out.

Toting his suitcase, Smith cracked the door and took a tentative step into the hall—where, through the skylight at center, a sunbeam hung. It was silent in the way of all houses large enough to obscure small, human sounds. Smith slunk, quiet and cattish, down the half-turn staircase and through an Eamesian study, its walls lined with books beyond a wide cream sofa, two emerald ottomans, and, through an open window, the just visible crest of a Corten steel sculpture made copper by sun. Only after he'd called a car from the porch and watched it wriggle down the narrow stone drive did he look back on the house, this place where he'd wasted a year's worth of weekends, drunk by the pool amid the wafting chat of elder bohemians, cozy in the cover of other people's wealth.

This section of Southampton was not the Southampton of raucous parties, of the Real Housewives browning to leather beyond the pools of McMansions, but a more modest enclave, peopled mainly by artists who'd bought property cheap when such a thing was still possible. Wealth whispers, someone once said, and at this hour was silent—the Audi zoomed mutely under a canopy of fluttering oaks. The only others on the road were two Lulu-clad mothers pushing prams at an athletic pace. In other houses, people slept. Soon, they'd wake in observance of brunch reservations and barbecues and the whole town would come alive with the spirited hum of the occasion: the last day to wear white. So Smith was unsurprised to find the train platform empty; just a few harried-looking financiers in pastel polos moving markets from their cellular phones.

The landscape blurred abstractly as the train sped into motion. Smith closed his eyes and tried to think of anything else, but the night returned in smarting flashes. He'd never had so much as a detention in high school yet now had a felony arrest. It was almost funny, brutally ironic in the way of stories he'd heard about other people but had never had to tell himself. It *had* happened, though, he knew. Faintly, he could still detect the red abrasions where the cops had cuffed his wrists. Still ebbing was the Tobacco Rabanne stench of their station. And, as if to confirm it wasn't all some illusory dream, with the terrified wonder of Dorothy thumbing her ruby slippers, he reached into his pocket to find a folded sheet: information for his arraignment in two weeks' time.

An adrenal rush filled his veins and pooled in his throbbing temples as the train made haste down the length of Long Island. He pictured throwing himself to the tracks like some tragic Russian heroine; it seemed a lesser agony. The news alone would kill his mother on impact, he imagined, proving right a threat of which she'd tried to warn him all his life. He hadn't listened, sustained instead by pleasing illusions, ones he was ill-prepared to break. Suddenly, the answer seemed obvious. *Tell no one.* To pay for a lawyer, he would liquidate his Roth IRA at significant penalty, or he'd represent himself in court, brushing up on legal jargon from reruns of *Suits.* Crazier things had happened. It would be, in a matter of weeks, resolved in a quiet way that didn't complicate anyone's idea of him, his promise.

The decision curdled the instant he considered the opposite outcome: The billboard lawyer he could likely afford, 1-800-GET-U-OFF, some nitwit who'd rob him blind, then defend him with the approximate prowess of a rabid baboon, more or less guaranteeing conviction. He looked out at the disappearing nowhere towns as the expanse of his life narrowed to a series of parole hearings and rearrests, flesh thinning like fruit from a rotten tree.

Outside, at Penn Station, the late-summer air was dense with the kind of heat that shimmers, rising from car hoods with warped paint and refracting off plastic heaps of garbage. But it was evident, also, in the exhaustion on every passing face, those left behind in the city of asphalt, concrete, metal. If the news could be trusted, some would collapse from heatstroke in their dank apartments; others would crowd cooling stations on Convent Ave. But out east, the lucky few who remained would gaze through curtained windows and remark that it was a *perfect day* for the beach.

Despite the weather, Smith couldn't stomach heading back to his apartment, so he stalked the yellow glare of Eighth Avenue, past the fetish shops and bistros in the Village. In recent weeks, he'd found it necessary to roam the streets for hours, so that, arriving home, he was so exhausted, so wrung out and nearly dead, that he could slip into a dreamless sleep. On these walks, he was careful to route himself away from places of particular meaning. He preferred the blank reaches of outer boroughs, swaths of the city with which he had no association at all but which could still surprise him—sights as simple as the patterned scarf on a woman's head or a particular brand of Parisian cigarette blinding him into a fugue that disappeared the day's remainder. Hours passed this way, days, adrift on the brook of memory. Veering east on Bleecker, subsumed suddenly by a swarm of buttercream fiends outside Magnolia, Smith considered the residue of experience, how it accumulated like an inky film around an antique object, a sensation that lately felt freighted. And if that accumulation was already so painful at twenty-five, he wondered what it would be like at forty-five, or fifty—or, if those feelings fade, as they were said to, if that would be more unbearable still.

A text jolted in his pocket. Carolyn had woken and, finding him gone, texted *you left* without punctuation. A statement as much as a question—evasive in her way, so that any emotion could be read: confusion, anger, or both. She was the one snag in his plan to keep things quiet; already, he'd told her about the arrest, well, sort of, waking her at four a.m. to weep at the foot of her bed—a confession of gasping inebriety. He wasn't sure she'd even understood how the night had devolved in her absence, her early departure somehow permitting his narcotic spiral. But she'd held him as he wept, then brought him back to bed and tucked him in with the assurance that they would sort it all out in the morning, as if his were a minor error, a shattered vase.

Lately, people had been quick to excuse his behavior, whatever it was; whether he got drunk and mean on a Tuesday afternoon or was sullen and remote for days, his friends and colleagues forgave him gamely, now that he'd been marked by tragedy. Though *tragedy*, that seemed the wrong word, at once banal and melodramatic. Inapt to describe what felt like a rift, a rupture—a pit into which he'd poured all sorts of stuff, booze and sex and quotations from the Bible, but found blacker and more cavernous still. He remembered *before* vividly but found himself grasping for an *after*.

It had been three weeks and four days since August 8, an otherwise unremarkable Thursday. Just as the manic city woke, joggers circling the parks and workers shuttling in by bridge and tunnel, a girl was found on the banks of the river, up near Soundview Park. The waves had licked her clean. Rushed to the hospital by paramedics, she was declared dead on arrival, then identified by a nurse as the daughter of a neo-soul singer, news of which was swiftly relayed to a tabloid that printed it by noon. Smith had been at work, in the middle of an investor meeting, when the vibrations began in his pocket. They halted, resumed, then halted, resumed. So insistent, it seemed as if the whole world were attempting to reach him. Excusing himself to stumble into a stairwell, he clicked the texted link and watched an image of his best friend render.

Socialite Elle England, Dead at 25

Strangely, Smith's first instinct upon reading the headline had been to refresh the page, as if it were a technical glitch, literally impossible, this girl found many miles from where he'd seen her last, hours prior,

at a party downtown for her twenty-fifth birthday. The calls kept coming and didn't stop for some time. Early reports cited lurid and conflict-
ing information—it was cocaine laced with fentanyl, no, heroin; she was
found alive, no, dead. Seeking answers, some friends leapt into action to
reconstruct a timeline, hour by miserable hour, from restaurant to club,
puzzled by reports of the anonymous man with whom she'd allegedly left,
headed where and why they did not know, sustained by the hope that their
search would find her whole. The tabloids would print retractions. Apologies. Others had more morbid questions, and one in particular: Who had
supplied that lethal dose, then left her there to die?

Within hours, it seemed that everyone in the city, including and especially strangers, had heard the somber story, reprinted in every tabloid and
sump of celebrity gossip, mounting pressure on the NYPD to "uncover
the truth of what happened to the daughter of a music legend." The chief
himself declared they sought to do so "swiftly and with discretion," interviewing the disparate characters who appeared in the evening's footage,
still extant in Elle's Instagram story. Dinner at Locarno, followed by dancing. There was no time for grief, nor were they exactly suspects. None had
records, and all had sent themselves home by the time the doorman said
she'd exited the club in the company of an *unidentified man*. Rather, they
were necessary informants, coauthors called upon to fill in the gaps, not
only in the evening's timeline but in her life, her person.

It had been a long night as they trickled into the Fourth Precinct station, a group who'd gathered not twenty hours prior in utterly opposite
circumstances. In lieu of espresso martinis, they were handed bottles of
tepid water and led one by one to a windowless room. Coming out, some
were angry: How *dare* they be called upon in the throes of early grief
to indulge such insensitive questions, about her sex life and history with
drugs; others, in shock, were nearly nonverbal; some had wept in that

dim waiting room. But Smith, still suited from his meeting, had answered all of their questions about the years he'd lived with Elle, her personal habits, and the glamorous masses referred to by police as her "known associates," with a cool and polish that startled even him. And—after being released with the instruction that they might need him, and *specifically* him, to return—as the others headed off to a bar, to trade notes or envelop themselves in the shared wound of grief, he had headed home alone.

And on the last day of that scorched and merciless summer, he took the same route home, through the trash and oil slick downtown, across the river, into Brooklyn's frenzied music. Smith walked until his shirt was rank and floaters filled his eyes, the afterglow of arcs from open hydrants. He scaled the dingy stairs. Moving in three years ago, he and Elle hadn't so much *decided* on an aesthetic as forced their things together in a bright collision of street-salvaged chairs and hand-me-down luxury: a cracked Hermès ashtray, a print of Warhol's gun. Across the room, her door still stood wide open. He hadn't closed it, he thought, for the same reason he hadn't left the apartment. The room was just as she'd left it, a characteristic disarray of tangled linens and clothing strewn across the floor, as if she'd been in the middle of a task, a sentence, and had been called away. It had the effect of all magical thinking, allowing him to remain in the illusion of *before*. *Before* the sleepless nights; *before* the papers and police and patronizing smiles; *before* that summer soured into a haze of curdled days through which he'd stumbled, endless and without a destination beyond the quiet of a tattered mind.

In an instant, he strode across the room, closed her door, and it was *after*.

CHAPTER TWO

The next morning, emerging from an elevator bank into his office, Smith registered the cool observation of colleagues glancing up from their desks. He was late again, and there was no hiding. Sleekly designed, the office was a place of glass walls and communal tables, of polycarbonate and Lucite, built to mimic and uphold the company's foremost value: *transparency*. Spelled CNVS but pronounced "Canvas," the start-up was in the business of disrupting the brick-and-mortar art world with a direct-to-consumer model. What had happened already in industries from eyewear to health care now seemed an inevitability in art: tech usurping the gallery gatekeepers, with their stranglehold on taste. It was a romantic, populist notion, advanced as always by the graduates of Ivy League colleges, along with Sotheby's MAs, ex-bankers in boot-cut denim, and software engineers in Yeezys. A representative assemblage of the corporate creative class, selected, as everything in the office's open plan, for both their form and function. Smith slipped into his mesh office chair and, with a pair of formidable headphones, entered a world of silence.

He had meant to be a poet. It wasn't so long ago he'd spent his days on sun-drenched collegiate lawns, scanning verse; nights in smoke-stale basements where anemics from the English department put on sparsely attended readings. A whole vibe he'd more or less retired on graduation. At the time, it hadn't felt Faustian, this bargain. *Poet* was not a job, while *content strategist*, apparently, was. Even the scorn of others didn't faze him. At a party senior spring, a red-haired actress from family money had said offhand that she was *disappointed* in him for selling out, going the route of their spineless peers, rather than reinterpreting Brecht in a Tenderloin trap house or whatever it was she planned to do, and when he'd replied that he had to pay off his student loans, she'd immediately gone white—well, *whiter*. *Of course*, she'd said. *Yes, of course.* He'd smiled. It was a lie; he hadn't any. Rather, he'd found, like so many young people, that a casual interest in art-making and leftist politics came suddenly at odds with a desire for creature comforts. And so he'd landed here, at CNVS, where despite the Scandi-chic aesthetics, his role amounted to that of an analyst anywhere: an endless interpretation of data, indexed and transposed to reveal patterns on consumer preferences, what they read and bought and when, what they liked but claimed they didn't, and how they spent their most intimate, aimless hours. It was his job to impose order on these currents, and most days, he enjoyed it. The white walls and clean lines and the neatness of an infinite grid; a life he'd carefully crafted, yet felt increasingly compelled to set aflame.

"Smith," he eventually heard through the noise cancellation. He looked up to find his boss, Blythe, grinning in a way that suggested she'd been saying his name for some time.

"What's up?"

"I'm looping with Hemlock today at six and want to at least have a blanked deck to walk them through ahead of Maxime and the content leads tomorrow, so can you shoot over last month's KPIs before EOD?" Smith took a second to parse the sentence, one typical of her speech in that it referenced a number of proper nouns and acronyms spoken at such a velocity he could barely extract its meaning. She'd hired him, in part, because he'd displayed in his interviews a command of biz-school speak, which he'd learned to parrot from friends in consulting and the single "design thinking" course he'd audited in undergrad. A shared language, she assumed, implied a shared mentality, dispassionate and rational, which would make him a useful ally in the office.

"Sorry, what?" Smith asked curtly. A colleague caught his eye and snorted into her latte.

Blythe proceeded to repeat the exact same sentence with the same intonation and none of the words changed, then added, after a pause, an apology "for the fire drill." Nonetheless, this time Smith understood. "Yeah, of course," he answered, though he knew that the deadline would require his skipping lunch.

"Fantastic," she said as she swept her drape of jet-black hair down her back. "How was your Labor Day, by the way?"

Smith felt his stomach lurch. Her large, dark eyes had a knowing look. Was it possible she knew? In a terrifying instant, he assessed the probability—being arrested in a small town meant small-town rules, police blotters in local papers so desperate for news they'd elevate DUIs to front-page status—but decided that it was unlikely. "Uneventful," he answered.

But the anxiety lingered. Smith stumbled into a bathroom stall, googled his name, the location, and the date of his arrest, then scrolled through an infinite picture book—mug shots, the "mugs" in them rightly named, ugly and wrenched with disdain. He saw none that resembled him and, for once, felt grateful to have inherited such a common name. In New York alone, there was a David Smith serving twenty-two years for ditching a pound of weed from an SUV window. Another David Smith serving fifteen for vehicular manslaughter. And another, eight for rape. The fact that these stories, in their poorly reported legalese, had nothing to do with him was of no comfort to Smith, who returned after a bout of dry-heaving to his desk. He felt the unbearable weight of the unsaid, and it was growing.

"Can I call you back," Nia asked when she answered the phone in a breathless whisper. Smith pictured her just as she was, seated in the Harvard Law Library amid hunchbacked hordes of the similarly studious. When he'd visited his sister last winter, he'd found that the gothic environment suited her. A hurricane of focused intensity, she'd zipped from home to class to her desk at the *Law Review*. Others, mid-December, looked sleepless and sullen, but she was enlivened. Asked over break if it had been "difficult," as 2L was said to be, she'd answered quickly, "Yes," then, "Well, no, not particularly."

"I'd rather talk now," said Smith in a leaden voice. He'd stepped out to the balcony of the twenty-eighth floor, where the afternoon air had the feel of wading into a lukewarm lake, his body instantly sheathed in sweat. "I need to tell you something." His change of heart had come swiftly, and he was fearful that even an hour's delay would reverse it.

"Okay," she breathed. "One second." He heard the yawn of a wooden chair as she took her stack of casebooks into the hallway, then out into the buoyant afternoon. Amid the brisk thrill of early autumn, Smith could picture lanyard-necked freshmen splayed out on the Cambridge Common, their laughter filled with dumb, essential optimism. Nia had always been the star, the sun, the firstborn, and setter of the mark to which Smith attempted to measure. And though they'd gone to the same schools and taken the same classes, she alone possessed a gravitas that earned respect from any room—which, lacking, Smith had learned to substitute with charm. "What's up?" she said, returning.

"I'm gonna say something, and I need you to not speak until I'm done," he said. She agreed, and he drew a labored breath before beginning to recount the night in question: From the group dinner with friends of Carolyn's to the nightclub carousel of odious hellos, he detailed each exhaustively should anything prove relevant—he'd chosen to tell her in part because, though she had yet to take the bar, she could still dispense legal advice illegally. And as he told her, he was aware that he could be seen, if not heard, through the glass that separated him from his colleagues, who, if they looked closely, would discern from body language that the words caused him both pain and relief. He knew that once he spoke them, they would become a known quantity, a problem to be managed rather than something ineffable, unuttered. Words were a way to make meaning, but he distrusted them, also, not naive to how they could be spread, warped, weaponized. Recalling his body bent over the hood of a cop car, he gave into that submission. Nia would do what needed to be done. She would tell their dad, who would tell their mom, who would tell their uncles, aunts, and country cousins—an elaborate prayer network of scarcely known kin—breaching the many barricades he'd built around his solitude.

That evening, the heat wave broke. A pause, then panic, as the sky fell in an iridescent sheet all across the rush-hour city. Droplets struck the hot concrete and sent sighs into the air as workers thundered home, making umbrellas from whatever they could. Newspapers, backpacks. They huddled under awnings that offered relief. It was right, Smith thought, drenched and shivering on a subway platform, the train delays and traffic, the collapse of basic rhythms that allowed them to move through days of illusory order. They were not gods but warm, wet bodies in the grip of surrender.

*　*　*

Later, when Smith learned that his mother, upon hearing of his arrest, had collapsed to the floor of her kitchen, he thought to himself, *That is so like her*: the stagy dramatics, in contrast to his father's stern composure. Nia relayed that their dad had been silent when she told him, "transcendently calm," and had asked just one question. That, too, was typical. David Smith Senior was a man of well-chosen words. A man whose adolescence, on Chicago's South Side, had endowed him with a street-weary sangfroid that cropped up in odd ways in his present life as a retired university president; he could be unforgiving about a speck of dirt on the carpet but often shrugged in the face of catastrophe.

His question was this—"What now?"—and by noon the next day, they had all shifted to it. On the phone, Smith could identify the background noise on each line: the street sounds of Nia's surroundings, the ticking clock in his father's home office. His mother's voice sounded strained, from either observation or unexpressed anxiety. Lying awake the night prior, Smith had sensed her insomnia—her desire to call, scold, comfort— but figured Nia would have warned her off each of these with an insistence that nothing was to be gained from such an emotional autopsy; it was still too soon. So Nadine spoke in a tone reserved typically for the diagnoses she most dreaded delivering, vivacious women learning of seropositive tests or cancerous masses, treating it not as a moral failure but a clinical fact.

"The immediate concern," she said, was "to retain a lawyer"—an effort to which they could all contribute. She herself would solicit the recommendations of her mother, a criminal attorney who'd defended dozens of similar cases throughout the years; Nia would hang back after two of her classes, Facts and Lies and Capital Punishment in America, to furtively consult her professors; and Smith would ask the Astleys, Carolyn's grand-parents, if they knew of anyone local. Tasked with this, Smith didn't have the heart to confess that he had no such intention and had, in fact, already forbidden Carolyn to tell her family (or anyone else) what had transpired that weekend, fearful that the revelation would irreparably shift how they saw him. One's reputation was a thing of glass. Still, he made a mental note to ask if there was some way she could subtly extract the information.

The first lawyer, Jordan Blackwell, came highly recommended for his charm and killer instinct. Even his photo on the law firm's website—mocha skin beyond a wry white smile—radiated an alluring intensity. Joining the call, Smith heard his father's voice booming and bright with the memory of some last laugh, which petered out before he asked, "David, is that you?" Smith confirmed that it was. "So, Jordan," Senior continued, taking command, "it'll just be the three of us. I figured that would be best, and we can relay the information to my wife and daughter afterward."

"A family affair," Blackwell joked, though gravely. He spoke without embellishment, breathless gaps between his sentences as he explained that he didn't typically take on low-level drug crimes but, because they'd been referred by his favorite professor from Harvard Law and because he was familiar with Senior's work at Whitley College—he himself was a How-ard grad—he was happy to make the time. "David, you still there?" Smith confirmed that he was. "Great. Now, tell me about this arrest."

Smith found his directness disarming, especially given that his parents had, in recent days, taken to calling it "the incident," as if their very texts were a part of the record they hoped to have expunged. "Well, basically," he began, "I was out in Southampton last weekend. And we were at this party or whatever, at a club, and—"

Blackwell interrupted. "Let's try that again. If I'm going to help you, I need all the gory details, play by play, of the entire evening." Smith's retelling, then, became a collaborative exercise. He recounted what he could, approximating some details—the dinner and who had attended it—and, when pushed, essentially invented others, like the exact quantity of cocaine he'd had in his possession at the time of his arrest. All of this was punctuated and pushed along by Blackwell's own incisive questions, which occasionally betrayed his motive, the pathways by which he hoped to have the case dismissed. Hearing that Smith had been searched by plainclothes police only once they'd brought him to a *public* street seemed especially of interest, prompting an aside—"That's how they got Skip Gates"—to which Smith did not respond, unsure why the detail was relevant; Skip Gates had committed no crime, while he, admittedly, had. And after he had finished, Blackwell paused for an agonizing beat, then, with a certainty that teetered on arrogance, spoke. "I've defended my fair share of clients in the Hamptons; I had a felony rape out in Quogue last summer. And the thing about these Hamptons courts is, they're used to two-bit local lawyers, so when a real city lawyer comes out, they know— forgive my language—not to *fuck* with us. Hearing the details here, I can say with utter confidence that I'll be able to get this handled and have your record sealed."

Smith heard his father's long exhale. The man's aggressive competence had put them both at ease; he seemed familiar, a *killer* whose rote precision was the product of a lifelong tightrope walk that left no room for error. And when he gave his word—"I'd fight for you as I would for myself"—Smith believed him. He listened as his father ran through a few technicalities, cost and timing, then ended the call with a mention of the upcoming Howard-Whitley game, which Blackwell confirmed he'd be attending. You could hear his gummy smile. "My man," Senior said, reclaiming the back-clapping fraternity with which the call had begun. "We'll be in touch."

Though they were mostly decided, the David Smiths agreed in the interest of diligence to keep the next call on the calendar. The second lawyer, James Walsh, had come on the recommendation of a friend of Carolyn's from East Hampton AA; his sole qualification seemed to be the successful defense of a reality star of whom she hadn't heard. He answered the phone in a cascade of *Hello*s and *How are you*s. "I'm sure it's hot down south this time of year," he said, laughing affably and with a charm that contrasted Blackwell's greatly, more relaxed and yet endowed with a salesmanship better suited to the trade of used vehicles. Smith pulled up a picture of the man as he spoke. Fifty-something with a good-old-boy grin and a careful quaff of blondish hair, he seemed determined to exhaust all conceivable small talk before arriving at the issue at hand. "All right, then, David *Junior*. Why don't you tell me about your big night?"

Having dry-run the monologue with Blackwell, Smith littered his account with the agreed-upon details—which were appreciated, or at least granted safe passage without interruption, until halfway through the story, when the first cop appeared. "And did you get his name, this officer?" Walsh asked. Smith, obviously, had not. "Well, what did he look like?"

"Tall," Smith said. "Shorter than me, but, yeah, tall. Brown hair, good-looking."

"That was probably McClatchey," Walsh confirmed, if only for himself. In truth, it would never have occurred to Smith that either of the cops had names, at least not ones useful to him. In his mind, they were faceless drones, Dementorial in their joyless authority. But Walsh seemed distinctly interested in names, in faces and exact locations. He was, or at least pretended to be, familiar with not only the arresting officer but the night-club and even the side street to which Smith had been taken—"Behind a big blue house, correct?"; his familiarity with the shape of the scene added texture to the memory. The grass recovered its green and the night air its music, the cuffs clamped again around his wrists. "Well, it certainly matches the fact pattern of a lot of cases I've seen out here, plainclothes police manning the bars and clubs during high season to crack down on drugs and DUIs. May I ask, how many others were in there with you at the station?"

"Just one," said Smith, recalling the only other detainee, who'd been brown and curiously pantsless—and all the others he'd seen, in the bath-rooms, on the dance floor, carrying on without consequence.

"*Huh*," Walsh said, and for the first time on their call, he seemed sur-prised. "Usually it's a real party in there on a holiday weekend, especially Labor Day; that's like their Super Bowl. They can get a bit antsy toward the end of the season with the weekenders headed back to the city. It's big business, these arrests," he said, his voice warm and remorseless. "So which judge did you get?"

Smith paused, and his father stepped in. "Judge Harrelson. You familiar?"

"Yes, I know Lisa well. My uncle was in the DA's office with her for decades. She's, well, she's tough," he said bluntly. "You know, really, I would've wanted to hear Lambert or even Donaldson, but *okay*. We got Harrelson."

Senior cleared his throat and attempted a casual, golf-game patter. "So, James, what would you say are the odds of getting this thing tossed out altogether?"

The man sighed deeply. "Well, let's see. I've defended a whole bunch of these possession crimes in the Suffolk County courts, maybe a few dozen, and with a young man like David—college-educated, no priors, parents at his side—he's *likely* to get off with a little community service, drug counseling. And of course, you'll have to pay the county fine, there's no getting around that. But yes, in all likelihood, I'd say he walks without a record."

"*How* likely, would you say," Senior pushed, clearly hoping to hear something along the lines of the *100 percent or your money back* guarantee that Blackwell had all but offered.

"I'm not a betting man," said Walsh, laughing coyly. "But, look, as I said, I've known Lisa a long time. And she's sharp as a whip, but tough. If it were Lambert, it'd be a different story, but Harrelson? Sometimes she likes to make an example out of kids who come out from the city and bring drugs into the community, but again, I know her and, of course, the DA personally, so my word goes a ways." He paused. "May I ask who else you've spoken to?"

Realizing his function in the conversation was at this point entirely ornamental, Smith eyed the street below, its distant, ant-like frenzy. "We had a conversation with another lawyer yesterday," Senior answered. "Man named Jordan Blackwell."

Walsh made an unintelligible sound halfway between a grunt and a chuckle. "Haven't heard of him. City lawyer?"

"Yes, he's in Manhattan."

"I'm sure he made you a bunch of promises, huh?" he asked, accepting their silence as confirmation. "City lawyers tend to think they can bulldoze their way in here, not understanding the nuances of the local courts. Look: If this were, say, a murder case, I'd recommend you go with whomever you think is best. But given what it is, which is something that could go *really* bad for you or, you know, could *basically* disappear, what you need is what I like to call 'local color.' Someone who knows the courts and the parties involved, and that would be me."

Satisfied, Senior asked him for his rate, then typed the five-digit figure into an empty spreadsheet cell—a new car, a Rolex. And then, just as
quick as it began, the conversation ended, again with the promise to be *in
touch*, though this time spoken with a stiff formality. They would never
know this man beyond his immediate function. Still, Smith knew—even
as they hung up the call and entered another, where, with Nia and Nadine,
they debated the merits of each: the hard power of a cool command of the
law versus the soft and all the more insidious power of network—the answer was obvious. Pretending otherwise was a waste. They would go with
the second lawyer, who'd refused a guarantee but had called the judge by
name. Of course they would. He knew.

CHAPTER THREE

"We're going with your guy, by the way," said Smith during a lull in conversation. Across from him, at a table in the sun-slant corner of a packed restaurant, Carolyn arched her eyebrows. "The lawyer," he clarified. "The one you suggested."

"Are you serious?" she asked, her mouth open in awe, which spread across the rest of her features as he nodded. She grimaced. "I would hardly say I *suggested* him."

"Well, yes, I know," he confessed, though the fact had become slightly muddled in his mind, undergone the redesign of all good lies, which take on the veil of truth in their retelling. But her expression (was it anger? Concern?) recalled fully his recklessness. "We did our research, though," he continued. "We talked to him, and he seems like the best bet. My parents agree. My sister, grandmother, everyone. It's done."

"Huh," she said, glancing down at the menu. That day, she wore a cream duster they'd found together last spring in a consignment shop off Bedford Ave. Bunching like a robe in her chair, it gave her the look of a virginal bride in some Catholic pueblo, head haloed by a mass of blond hair.

"Anyway, sorry if this is *boring* you."

"Not at all," she snapped, her eyes pools of blue. "I just really hope that's the right choice. You know I'd feel *devastated*, and maybe even partly to blame, if—" Their waiter arrived just then with a carafe of sparkling water and, pouring it, asked if they'd had enough time to look over the menu. They had not, but nonetheless each ordered a latte and one of the restaurant's six takes on eggs. The man repeated their words back to them, eager to prove his attention, then carefully pronounced the phrase *Excellent choice* before leaving.

"Thought he'd never fuck off," she said quietly. "What was I saying?"

"Just that you'd be *devastated* if I went to prison."

"Hamstrung, suicidal even," she decided. "Don't even joke about it."

Since he'd fled her grandparents' house the weekend prior, the two had barely spoken. A few texts, a missed call. It was a significant silence, given their usual cadence. But he'd pictured her daily waking up to find him gone, overcome with fear and perhaps even guilt. Of course, now thirty days sober, she hadn't supplied the drugs nor suggested the party, and indeed, at the moment of his arrest, she had not even been present, having sent herself home before midnight. Rather, summoned from sleep into his tearful confession, she hadn't had the words. And Smith could sense her regret for that ineloquence, that inopportune aphasia, because all her life, in some sense, she'd been learning the language of addiction.

As a dancer in the early eighties, her mother had defected from a ballet company in London to train with Trisha Brown in New York but soon found herself routinely snorting blow between auditions before a slew of rehab stints introduced her to not only Carolyn's father, a then minor downtown gallerist, but a redemptive second act. Now a behavioral psychologist, she studied the mechanisms underlying addiction, its early signals, and as a mother, she'd pointed them out to Carolyn, echoes of her own history—charisma wielded to allure and obfuscate, drawing people into her orbit even as it increasingly devolved to chaos. Still, Carolyn had never known moderation. As a child, she'd had a real problem with picking scabs until they bled, often to the point of infection. With drink, with drugs, with sex, with love, she was the first to call herself a glutton, and so she'd always known she would have to eventually stop, as had her mother when life became unmanageable. Yet it hadn't been some squalid rock bottom but Elle's death that finally made her try.

Their lattes arrived, and as they sipped them, they found their spirits leavened by caffeine, sunlight, and the petty gossip Carolyn had gathered up the road at her morning AA. She glanced around for her sponsor. "I figure if I'm going to do this, I may as well pick the most intense bitch in there," she explained, outlining the woman's infamous diktat: to attend ninety meetings in her first ninety days *and* check in, in person, afterward. "I'm literally three minutes late the other day and she spends the better part of an hour scolding me, saying how tardiness implies I think my time is more important than hers. She called me a selfish twit." Smith laughed loudly and for a longer time than intended, like an abstinent back to bingeing. He hadn't had cause to laugh like that in weeks, so the outburst loosened them both, relieving their earlier tension. "Oh my God," she continued in a whisper once he'd quieted. "I haven't even told you what happened yesterday at Dmitri's."

For the past year, she had worked as the studio assistant to an interior designer named Dmitri Petrovna, known for re-outfitting the homes of Manhattan's rich in post-Soviet austerity. His rooms were unmistakable, a minimalism so arch it became avant-garde: Tribeca lofts and West Village brownstones utterly devoid of satisfactory seating. Carolyn despised his work but enjoyed the job's many perks—invitations to glamorous parties, discarded gifts, and weeks-long stays at the Chateau Marmont whenever she accompanied him to Los Angeles. Yesterday, she explained, Petrovna had asked her to deliver a gift on the occasion of a good friend's opening. This *friend* was a chef and restaurateur of enough renown that even Smith, whose ambivalence about fine dining had long been a joke between them, perked up when she said it. She'd arrived at the restaurant around noon, when his assistant had said he'd be there consulting on the prix fixe menu for opening night. The restaurant, Inducio, was a pan-Asian blend that would become known in a matter of days for serving a duck-egg fetus so rich it would be described in a rave review as "an experience of indulgence not unlike Tantalus's first doomed taste of ambrosia." These duck eggs, among other otherworldly delicacies, would be served in the cavernous dining room that Carolyn had entered, which could seat three hundred across a third as many tables. It recalled other colosseums of downtown dining, which evoked both the scale and the inconceivable wealth of the city they inhabited. And into this theater of excess she'd walked, hands grazing the velvet that dressed every booth, confidently toward the man.

Explaining that she was Dmitri's assistant, she'd watched his face bloom with the memory of their last interaction, months before, through which she'd stuttered charmlessly, undone by two days without sleep. But a month's sobriety had restored to her face a placid beauty. It was thin, clear, angular, and gazing upon it, in comparison to its lesser twin in his memory, he'd actually said the word *Wow*.

Seeing where this story was headed, Smith insisted she pause so that he could google the man. In the portrait preferred by the internet, he wore a chef's hat and apron, his stature cropped by the edges of the pass through which he'd been pictured. He was Asian, perhaps half, with a brush of thick black hair and an evenly brown complexion. Though now in his fifties, he'd managed to maintain the boyish allure that had earned him the nickname "Tomcat à Toque" in an article detailing his romantic exploits over the past quarter century.

He'd quickly ended his meeting—the 1,200 banana leaves ordered for their opening week's mok pa would be plenty—and joined Carolyn in the next booth, asking if she wanted a tour. "Obviously, I agreed," she said, taking a bite of her Benedict. He stood five foot eight, barely clearing her shoulders, but his honey skin and mean, narrow eyes were a draw; she'd eaten her high-school prom dinner at one of his uptown restaurants. He'd beckoned her past the bar, where a hidden door opened into a den-like room with sunken floors. She was complimenting the decor when he placed his hand on her lower back, stared at her for a second—the awkward half-light catching a bead of sweat on his forehead—then leaned in and kissed her deeply. Startled, she kissed him back ("It seemed rude not to"), then, after several minutes of tongues entwined, excused herself and left the restaurant swiftly.

"I called my sponsor right after," she told Smith, describing the thrill and guilt she felt then, slipping out of the restaurant onto Eighth Avenue. Like a relapse without touching a bottle, a powder, a pill. "I told her everything, for some reason. I suppose I was craving absolution, and I figured she was going to yell at me or call me a twit again, but she just sighed into the phone and said, 'Of course your desire for chaos will long outlast your desire to drink.'" The *chaos* to which she referred: Carolyn knew that Rune was married, had just had a son. His wife was a design editor, profiled often by publications who referred to her as their "girl crush" or "style guru," mused adoringly over how she "got it done." The two had even met once, at a party. "Still, I didn't give her a single thought in the moment."

Smith appreciated this quality of Carolyn's, unapologetic about what she desired, even when it teetered on narcissism. She moved through life as one hopes to move through any party, a frothy champagne whisper, never in any one place long enough to grow dull. "I do think my sponsor was right, though," Carolyn considered, peering out the open window. "About the chaos. If I'm not going to drink, I need to at least do *something* interesting."

"So you're going to see him again?"

She shrugged. "I don't know. He's been texting." She pulled up the three messages he'd sent that morning, which joined two unanswered ones from the day prior to construct a thoroughly one-sided conversation. Not just *u up*s and *hru*s but the kind of florid odes to her beauty that men in their fifties favor. Smith knew that she *would* text him back, eventually, providing the excuse that she "just saw this," as if her phone were some funny cipher that didn't deliver messages immediately on receipt but at its leisure. He knew that even if, or perhaps *because*, she liked him, she would affect disinterest with the goal of renegotiating her relative power, which, while middling in the structural sense, was clearly immense interpersonally, and that this would work because it always did.

From her, Smith had gleaned many of the strategies that allowed one to move through life with an air of apparent ease. It was easy enough to sink ships if you dealt charm and coldness out in equal measure, made good jokes all through dinner, then left before dessert. He remembered so clearly the night they met, at a kegger their third week of college; she'd caught him by the arm to compliment his white pants, and he'd allowed his eyes to widen, pretending to have just noticed her, though he'd seen her walking in, looking expensive and bored, and had observed the subtle libidinal shift that always arises in a room when a fresh object of envy enters.

Still, years later, he sometimes caught himself watching her like that, as a character on-screen. He wondered—as he often had with the heroines of his favorite books and films—what it would be like to be his own aesthetic opposite, to have his body so tethered to the age-old markers of beauty, class, and desire as to be the default center of any room.

Tuesday night, at the opening of Inducio, Smith gasped upon entering the room. A majestic cathedral but in service of sin, it was packed with hundreds of congregants—lounging in booths or drifting through tables to kiss the cheeks of forget-me-soons awash in gauzy light. The air smelled of bergamot and spice—turmeric, cumin, sweet basil, anise—then sweat, a spritz of your neighbor's perfume, her teeth already dim from red wine. Arm in arm, Smith and Carolyn sidled through the darkened silhouettes of gowns and tailored suits. The few cool kids who'd forgone the dress code packed into booths, picking at plates of hors d'oeuvres and drinking free booze with abandon. Smith caught eyes with one, who tugged a vape from her quilted bag and began to puff it openly. From one such table, they heard Carolyn's name, then turned in that direction to find a slender, disembodied arm waving. The girl attached to it stood and unruffled her dress, the neckline of which plunged to her abdomen.

Smith's stomach fell. While he'd found Fernanda mildly inane since Carolyn had introduced them, what had once been merely unpleasant now felt freighted by the fact that he'd last seen her on the night of his arrest, though not just *the night* but at the very moment. As he was being escorted out by the plainclothes police, he'd spotted her dancing on a table in the distance. He wondered if she'd seen him also. If she had, she gave no indication as she beamed a smile of hygiene and American money, her silken plait falling serpentlike down her back. She beckoned them to her booth, where she sat with three others: her boyfriend, Laurent; a French friend whose name Smith could never recall; and a plump, tan girl who introduced herself as Katerina. Her spectacular nose gave her a haughty, feudal look.

Fernanda was a fixture of a scene to which Smith was often Carolyn's plus-one: a group of kids who'd grown up mostly in New York or European capitals and, as a result, spoke several languages apiece. Deeming finance, tech, and real estate pedestrian, they dedicated their not-insignificant faculties to careers at luxury brands and Chelsea galleries—and, with the rest of their considerable time, to the obsessive curation of their days. They seemed to live entirely by what looked best in retrospect; a picnic in the park was incomplete without a tuft of bundled peonies, a sketchbook casually strewn. Though he had nothing to offer in the way of weekend houses, Smith understood his cachet among their kind—girls like Fernanda would always spend some portion of their time in his presence vying for approval. Being wealthy and white had, of late, become unfashionable, at least without the veneer of multiculturalism. One could not seem worldly if one's *world* constituted only the boarding-school set, so they looked to Smith—as to the other brown, queer interlopers who passed through their parties—as a guide to an exotic landscape.

Smith kissed Laurent's cheeks and, greeting the others, claimed the seat next to Carolyn. "How was dinner?" he asked, observing the graveyard of soiled napkins tossed on their table. It must have been a near-impossible reservation, opening night, and Smith sensed it had been Fernanda to wrangle it. A native New Yorker, she was both connected and dull enough to construct her self-image almost exclusively from such instances of consumption. Of course, a desire to have *been there, done that* before anyone else and to be dubbed a "tastemaker" as a result was not unique to her but an increasingly common mode to engage with "experience," a set of jeweled objects to be collected.

"*Divine*," she answered.

Katerina chimed in, flaring her powdered nostrils. "My Wagyu was overcooked but everything else——" She nodded to Fernanda approvingly, and Smith thought to himself that she was likely the kind who considered it a mark of class to order her beef still breathing. "Did you two just come for the party?" she asked, looking mildly concerned. A test. To her, it was the lesser invite—conferred upon micro-influencers and their hangers-on, the perennial attendees of envelope-openings everywhere.

"We're just stopping by to give Rune our love," Carolyn answered. With her words, she implied that their attendance was more a matter of obligation, which Smith supposed it was; Rune had texted her thrice to insist that she come. Still, her phrasing displayed expertise in a subtle linguistic game, every bit as bred to play it as Katerina, who asked, after a sip of champagne, "And how is it you know him?"

Carolyn glanced at the crowd as if she hadn't heard the question, so naked in its attempt to discern her social stratum. Proximity to a powerful man was itself a commodity, though, improperly wielded, it could also seem tawdry, desperate. She replied with the contemptuous smile of someone who's already learned and forgotten your name. "We're old friends."

Just then, a man approached, balancing a tray of coupes in one hand. The waiter—who, like the rest of the staff, was of Asian descent—wore a white mandarin-collared shirt, black tuxedo pants, and a tiny monastic cap; old New York with an "Eastern flair." It was unclear if the outfit referenced any culture in particular or if it took a more Wes Anderson–ian view to the continent, an aesthetic cleaved from both context and history. Laurent flagged him down and ordered another bottle of the champagne presently bathing in a bucket at center. It arrived with pomp and two glasses, which joined the four on the table, and as it was poured, Carolyn placed a hand over hers in refusal.

"You don't drink?" Laurent asked, bungling the English slightly. He'd meant "You aren't drinking?" but ironically, in his error, had come closer to the truth.

"No," Carolyn confirmed, "I don't." Fernanda took a nonplussed expression, a reference to the fact that, actually, Carolyn *did* drink, often to the point of having to crash in the spare bedroom of her Tribeca apartment. Carolyn continued, "Since August, remember? I told you last week in the Hamptons."

"Oh, you did," Fernanda confessed reluctantly. Smith examined Carolyn's face, attempting to parse her expression; he wondered if it thrilled or annoyed her now to carry on conversations with people who'd barely remember, to be the sole reliable narrator of any night out. "Still, I must've thought you meant just for the night or, like, the month. I didn't realize you'd stopped altogether."

"Yes, I have thirty-three days," Carolyn said with a look of both pride and grim significance. She and Smith had never openly discussed the fact that the start of her sobriety was the day of Elle's death, but immediately after, she'd begun refusing drinks and referring often to her meetings—a resolve to make good of all that bad, which had been a small comfort to him in recent weeks. And though it was not her first try at sobriety, he hoped, given its cause, that it would be the one to stick. "I'm about to start my fourth step," she continued. "A *fearless moral inventory.*"

"Really?" Fernanda exclaimed, clearly stunned. With a pause, she weighed the information like a scientist, deciding whether or not to let this discovery recontextualize everything she knew, or presumed she knew, about Carolyn: a party girl, yes, but one of manners, intelligence. She surfaced, unconvinced. "But that wasn't a problem for you, drinking. Not *really,*" she said, intoned as neither an accusation nor a question—mere conjecture.

"Well, *yes*, it was," Carolyn answered in a voice that confirmed indisputably that she took some small pleasure in inflicting this realization. "I was on the death arc to be sure."

Shortly after, they stood, bade the others goodbye, and continued to mix among the party. In the darkness, blinding flashes flared, lighting manicured faces. Smith recognized a few: a graffiti artist who'd reinvented himself as the owner of a matcha café; a club kid named Kofi, whom he swerved to avoid; a few models, artists, as well as a glut of money people who appeared alternately annoyed and aroused by the mounting youthful frivolity. Overwhelmed, Smith could feel his stamina wane. He'd promised himself he'd stay sober, less in solidarity with Carolyn than because he couldn't afford any more fuckups with his arraignment fast approaching. In fact, he thought fleetingly, it was time to go, and he was just about to say so, when: "Look," Carolyn whispered excitedly, tugging him by the crook of his arm.

The chef was even smaller in person, the height Smith had been at twelve or thirteen, but with the kiss-the-ring confidence of any boy-king as his illustrious guests stooped to greet him. Still, his allure was evident, not just in his handsome face, his Tom Ford suit, perfectly tailored, but in the fanfare which enveloped him now and had likely for decades. Praise and accusations of genius, they seemed to have cemented him in time. He turned and, seeing Carolyn, stepped away from the admiring throng. "My girl," Rune rasped, kissing her cheek. "I'm sorry it's such an older crowd. So many corporate cunts for me to greet. Not your usual scene, I'm sure, but the after-party will—"

"Don't be ridiculous," Carolyn replied. "It's spectacular." Smith registered, twenty feet on, a woman in mauve staring at him—almost a relief, as

Rune himself had yet to acknowledge his existence. "Meet my best friend," Carolyn said then.

With her introduction, Smith became real to him. He smiled an impish grin that spread lines about his craterous eyes. "Pleasure," Rune said, shaking Smith's hand before grazing the small of Carolyn's back, which invited even more attention from the woman in mauve, now openly glaring. Having seen enough, she began her approach, a languid stroke through the undertow, and, arriving, placed one jeweled, skeletal hand on Rune's shoulder.

"*There* you are!" he said with feigned delight. "Meet my wife, Amy." The woman was, at a distance and in a certain light, attractive. But proximity betrayed her. Notably, though not quite enviably, thin—her features were glitched out of proportion to her face, which itself was too large for her body, giving her the top-heavy look of certain birds and discount brands of Barbie. Her hair had been bleached into submission, brittle to its roots, and a funereal look had just begun to set along her wintry eyes. Side by side, it was really no contest. Carolyn looked alive in a way that this woman perhaps never had and now never would. Her body was a sun-warmed beach, her skin kept color.

Having introduced them, Rune stepped aside to greet the widow of a fascist media mogul whose dress was a lurid garden of floral print and tufted sleeves. Smith was surprised by his ease. He seemed calm, unbothered, as he left his wife and new mistress to get acquainted.

"So, how do you two know each other?" asked Amy, her overplucked eyebrows arched.

"Me and Smith?" Carolyn asked with a smile that belied her evasion. "We met in college."

"I meant—"

"Oh, *Rune!*" she conceded. "Through my boss, Dmitri."

"Dmitri, of course. You're his assistant?" Carolyn nodded. "*We* love Dmitri. Is he around?"

"He's in LA but sends his love."

By this, the woman seemed satisfied, if still slightly wary. She asked Carolyn what exactly she did as an assistant, clearly pleased to find her adversary in such a humble position. Carolyn answered with self-effacing charm, explaining that she was still "figuring it out," having graduated Stanford with "a useless degree," and Amy nodded, the whole time conveying an air of amused disbelief. Like, *Oh, you manage brand partnerships, you little whore?*

Smith kept quiet and refused another drink.

"We love Dmitri," the woman repeated, perhaps to underscore her close friendship with Carolyn's employer, a clever but ineffectual strike. There was no reason she should've known that Carolyn couldn't care less about the job, would've quit tomorrow were it not a nice enough way to pass time. "We'll have to all have dinner when he's back," she continued, the invitation stumbling as it emerged from her mouth, revealing its shoddy sincerity. That matter sorted, she pretended to notice the time, a few minutes to midnight, and announced her early day tomorrow. She said goodbye and, after lingering another minute close by, headed for the coatroom and out of sight.

"Come, you two," said Rune, reemerging from the crowd into which he had disappeared like a motherless child. He announced, proudly, that the after-party had begun, then led them through the storied stealth door. Inside was bedlam. The room trapped a smoky miasma through which they sifted, passing a marble card table surrounded by a flock of swannish models who arched their slender backs; a bald man laughed lavishly beside them and swished his drink, wetting one, who scowled, stood, and wandered off. Ambiently, a techno track played, scoring other vignettes. It was all a seduction—conversations teetered just on this side of sex. The ever-elusive cool party, yet Smith felt outside of it still, like a ghost in the corporeal plane yearning to be embodied.

There was a perceptible difference in this room and the next, two spaces of equal exclusivity, distinguished instead by milieu. In the main dining room, the remaining press corps snapped photographs of the uptown set, the few critics remaining. They were the ones who could afford the restaurant, who would return and rack up bills with bottles of vintage champagne, but it was the kids in the back who would fill it with life—who would keep it from losing this initial flash of cool to become a mausoleum of consumption and commerce.

Rune's eyes lit up as he watched Carolyn disappear into the arms of a rakish acquaintance.

"Your friend is very sexy," he said to Smith. And because Smith wasn't sure how to respond, he didn't. Instead, he stared for a moment at a drink on the bar, the white orb of fruit iridescent in its vodka bath, then picked it up and sipped it deeply, thinking that it was the single best thing he'd ever tasted.

Without a word, Smith left Rune and began to roam. In the room's animal heat, he felt himself start to sweat, to sway. He bummed a cigarette from a handsome man in a cashmere sweater who insisted he stay, introducing him to a table of stylish strangers, who laughed at his first joke (*It's giving Dark Room, by Halston*) and continued to laugh—Smith remembered he was funny, was fun. He remembered that he was a delight at parties, loved parties even, a fact which, taking another drink from a passing tray, he said aloud, a statement so earnest it might've put off these posh cosmopolitans but tonight touched on something they'd all quietly felt.

A pop song played, and they stood up to dance, Smith whisking around the boy whose friends called him Adam, attempting a swing move that, performed successfully, would have made them appear to come undone like a plait but unsuccessfully left them tangled and breathless and howling with laughter at the edge of the room. Adam's breath, when they kissed, smelled of lychee and spearmint.

Smith had a fourth drink, a fifth, then slunk to a corner from which he was plucked promptly. "Come save me from these white people," said Kofi, breathing crème brûlée vapor into Smith's open mouth. A poreless thirty-something who'd spent the last decade in nightlife, seemingly against his will, he had a penchant for bringing up topics ill-suited to dance floors, eager to prove his intellectual depth. Tonight, it was Elle's case, the shroud of silence surrounding it. He hadn't seen any updates and was desperate to know *what exactly went down that night*, his lupine features aglow.

Smith invented an excuse to leave, then drank his sixth drink in line for the restroom, which, trickling forward, revealed another function inside. At least twenty in attendance, themselves across the gender spectrum despite the door's demands—*passé*; besides, no one was pissing. The stall walls barely shielded the hunched-over cokesters, sniffing and snorting in chorus, while others adjusted their hairdos and half-tucks in the mirror. One lank-haired gauntling shoveled something more antisocial into her nose, an opie look in her eyes. Smith couldn't help but tally, by approximation, the jail time's worth of substances passing in and around these stalls. He headed straight for the sinks and saw, on his own face, a woozy expression. If he had a bump, one bump, he could keep up the night. Another hour, at least—he could waft through the crowd, swapping jokes, swapping spit.

Wordlessly, Smith left the bathroom and reentered the party's soft moan. Bodies shifted in and out of focus as he searched for Carolyn to tell her goodbye, to thank Rune for having him—overcome with the sudden sensation that if he didn't leave now he would never. Not finding them, he veered for the door, past the bar where a throng of men danced. He shrugged off Adam's hand on his shoulder, turned to offer a smile, then left him in the eager darkness.

The light in the dining room was incredibly bright, phosphenes like embers, as he paused for his eyes to adjust. It was empty now except for staff, a few dozen, dumping plates of hors d'oeuvres into garbage bags, their translucent gray skins bulging with discarded remains. Half-drunk coupes packed ten to a tray sailed toward the industrial kitchen. And across that sea, in the opposite corner, he saw them: Rune and Carolyn, mere inches apart. Her hair fell like a drape across her bare shoulder, framing the heart of her face, now flushed, as she took a sip of something amber. Her expression desirous, delirious; it was not the uncaring performance she'd mastered. The way she hitched her body to his, the way she indulged him; it was awful to see her like this, so nakedly wanting. And even as the room shimmered in his own drunken vision, Smith recognized the core of his feeling—seeing her forfeit her latest bid at sobriety, their unspoken pact, for the fleeting thrill this flirtation offered—was rage. He felt an urge to drag her screaming from that room. Instead, he passed through the laboring bodies and left.

CHAPTER FOUR

Homeowners and year-round residents of the Hamptons will often refer to September as its best month. After Labor Day, the symbolic end of East Coast summers, the weekenders return to the city, this time for good, leaving Coopers and Georgica and Sagg Main empty but for the geriatrics in weathered coveralls who stagger still through lambent air, heavy with the sunblock scent of last week's beauties. Seasonal cottage industries—surf lessons and Jet Ski rentals—return their equipment to storage, while others, dance clubs that revealed themselves by morning to have merely been wedding tents in parking lots, collapse altogether, offering the illusion of an actual change in topography. Fading as seen from above. Those same restaurants packed from May until August go quiet at noon, their white-shirted waiters roaming, attending urgently to water glasses half full and folding napkins with the somber resignation that shifts will soon be cut in accordance with an ever-dwindling pool of tips for the take. But as one drives through Bridge, through East, and marvels at the vast and pristine mansions, one can glimpse beyond hedges the lucky few left lounging on the decks of their pools, soaking in all that's left of the season's sun.

The David Smiths encountered no traffic whatsoever that Wednesday, September 18, as they drove from Brooklyn to Southampton, so arrived in just under two hours, a sigh after sunset. They'd spent the trip in silence but for the monotones of the local NPR. "Where are we going," Smith asked as they passed the entrance to the inn.

"We should get some food first," his father answered. Of course, they could've ordered in, but this being his first time in the storied haven, Senior wanted to see what all the fuss was about. His interest in luxury stemmed from his having been raised in its resolute absence, six kids across a third as many rooms, so he had always made a point of exposing his children to the fine dining and international travel his youth had sorely lacked. They turned onto Main Street and Senior coasted down a block of dark and shuttered shops, polo-clad mannequins so bored they could die in their quiet windows. "Ghost town, huh," he either asked or observed, turning up the radio to fill the eerie silence.

"You ready for tomorrow," Senior asked as he eased into a parking spot outside a boutique grocery, the last lit storefront on the block.

"I guess," Smith answered. "There isn't much to be ready for." On the phone the day prior, Walsh had been brief: *Wear a suit, comb your hair, and I'll do the talking*. It was only an arraignment, a time for Smith to show, as the lawyer had said, *the whites of his eyes*. No deals would be struck, no sentences levied. It would be but the formal beginning of a legal proceeding that might extend for some time.

"But how do you feel?"

Smith couldn't recall ever being asked this question by his father so plainly. "I don't know. Scared," Smith said. "What about you?"

"Yes. *Scared*."

* * *

Their phone alarms rang in unison at precisely eight a.m., though they didn't need them. Neither had slept, dreams deferred by the dreaded morning. Smith rose and, in the white-tiled restroom, turned the water on hot. He brushed his teeth, hair, and then, as his father performed an identical routine, got to work ironing the charcoal suit he had hung in the closet. By eight thirty, they were both dressed sharply, carrying their overnight bags to the rental car, and after a brief checkout—during which the concierge, looking at the wrong room's incidentals, tried to charge for pay-per-view—they set out for the courthouse. Pulling up, Smith recognized the building faintly, as a face in a dream. It was the same place, he realized, to which he'd been brought on the night of his arrest, where he'd been printed, photographed, and held for thirty minutes. The courthouse sat atop the station, a synergy which struck him as strange, small-town in a way that laid bare the alliances less evident elsewhere. Here, the judges and cops shared a parking lot, an electric bill. They were, indisputably, colleagues.

The courtroom had peeling linoleum floors and the caustic light of all bureaucracy. It was the size of a lecture hall, its front third cordoned off by metal bars to protect the judge's bench, which stood sandwiched between a stenographer's desk and a door to an unseen chamber. The back two-thirds contained chairs, bisected into two regions. "If you have a lawyer, sit here," instructed the policeman who'd escorted them in, pointing to the nearer section. They took their seats in the third row of the otherwise empty area, shortly joined by one other suited defendant, a crew-cut teen who'd blown a 0.14 on a recent drive from Montauk. Smith looked across the aisle at the other section, the unrepresented, in which ten were seated. Beyond them, a line stretched the length of the wall, snaking around the chairs to form a sharp angle. At the front of the line, or, rather, at the other end of it, was a squat man with a reddish pallor who wore a genial smile as he spoke with a woman in a shapeless smock. "Speak English?" he asked at a preachy volume. She confirmed that she did, though hers was halting and paired with an expression of utter bemusement as he read aloud the particulars of her case: a speeding violation which would cost her three hundred dollars and add three points to her record. He offered her a deal—"I'll drop the seat-belt charge if you plead guilty to the moving violation"—and immediately she agreed.

He made a note and, as she was shown to her seat by a bailiff, quickly moved on to the next, announcing his name and crime as an item up for auction. Indeed, that was what he was: an auctioneer bartering fates. As he spoke with each defendant, by himself or with the aid of a Spanish-language interpreter, he negotiated the extremity of the sentence, often offering to drop some charges in favor of a guilty plea, bargains that greased the wheels of this antique court—with some, he spent less than a minute—and revealed additional, perverse incentives. It seemed evident that in the field, the officers would pursue as many violations as conceivably possible, in turn allowing the district attorney to strike one or two minors in favor of securing a more major conviction, the penalty of which was most sizable. It was an obvious grift but conducted with such naturalism and flair that the lawyerless often expressed relief or even gratitude at being shown an iota of empathy. They agreed to whatever and moved on. No need to bring in a public defender. *Suspended license, going once.* After all, the stakes, in these small-town courts, weren't total. No life, no death.

Dressed in designer suits, the Smiths stood out like two middle fingers in a sea of thumbs. They could feel the scrutiny of the others wondering what they'd done to land here, not just up against the wall, where ignored traffic lights and public urinations resulted in fines the price of Senior's tie, but in the lawyer seats, gussied up as if seeking grace from God Himself.

It must've been bad. Smith looked at his father, whose face was slack and meaty, signet rings adorning the hands on each of his knees. He'd never seen him look small.

Finally, Walsh arrived. Wearing the same navy suit and indigo tie from his photograph on the law firm's website, he resembled a junior congressman during midterm season. The sort who, late October, attends Sunday service with his Black constituents, poses for pictures, and reprises a Whiffenpoofian baritone for "Oh Happy Day" before coptering off to the next location. And just like that congressman, he flashed a Colgate smile to greet his colleagues of the court, the skirt-suited stenographer and officers in uniform, a few words to each that yielded smiles of their own and communicated without question that this was his domain. "*There* he is, the handsome young man," Walsh said when he finally approached Smith and shook his hand. "You look great in this suit, just perfect. You two sit tight. As I mentioned, today's just procedural. You're going to keep quiet and try to look sorry."

Senior nodded, scratched his ear with an index finger. "What exactly can we expect?"

"Best case? I go speak with DA Jones, and he's ready to strike a deal— some community service, some counseling, a few drug tests. I really don't think we're going to have a problem. The suit definitely helps. And it looks good to have Dad here as well," he explained, now speaking to Smith directly. "We've really got our ducks in a row. I mean, you got me, you got Dad, you got that suit. The story is clear: Here's a good kid who messed up, got peer-pressured into a onetime thing. Could've happened to anyone's son, and it *definitely* won't happen again."

Here he paused, and Smith wondered if he was meant to respond, to confess that this was in no way a "onetime thing," but his father chimed in just then. "Yes, of course. I don't know if we've mentioned, but David is, um, *clean* now," he said, stumbling over the foreign verbiage. "And we're very committed to keeping him so——"

"Yes, of course. *Good dad*," Walsh interrupted, placing his hand on Senior's shoulder with a Cheshire grin. "Let's just rap a minute, so I've got all my talking points in order. Remind me," he said to Smith. "Your dad says you work in tech? And where'd you go to college?" Smith answered these questions and then a few more, all of them about his background and résumé, the combination of which Walsh repeatedly called his *character*. So when the lawyer asked if he was open to treatment, "should it come to that," Smith was surprised; it seemed to go against the whole narrative the man had crafted—that this was a *onetime thing*, anomalous—to suggest that Smith might have a problem for which he needed help. But he could see from the lawyer's smile that this was not a matter of diagnosis but strategy; he would play whatever cards he was dealt. "Yes," Smith answered after a moment. "I'm open to it." And as the lawyer walked away, greeting the DA with a chummy handshake, Smith wondered if that was true, if he was genuinely *open* or reluctantly willing to play the game.

If body language could be trusted, Walsh began the conversation with a few minutes of chitchat—the DA's golf game or the Mets this season. It was apparent when the tenor had shifted because the DA's expression hardened. Everyone else in the room, the line of dozens who'd paused to accommodate them, watched as the two men whispered about the specs of Smith's case, the DA glancing over to appraise him. Here, the stagecraft in which Smith had been coached took full effect. He hung his head, eyes cast downward but observing the men peripherally. He could feel the heat of their gaze.

A heavy hand fell on Smith's shoulder. "Come with me," the lawyer instructed him gravely before escorting him back through the maze of chairs. Smith stared straight ahead, his father behind him as they trudged through the lobby and out the front doors, where they were blinded by the outside's vibrancy. They continued a heart-pounding fifty yards from the courthouse doors, through the busy parking lot, arriving finally at an empty stretch of asphalt.

Walsh turned around, beaming. "We've got a deal," he said. "And you know, I really had a feeling we would, like I told you. Because we had all our ducks in a line, all the dominoes. And now we've already got a deal. All we're gonna need from you is a drug and alcohol eval from a specialist, a couple clean drug tests, and we'll be looking at a full dismissal."

Stunned stupid, Smith tried to make sense of what the man had just said. Walsh observed his baffled expression and the matching one on his father's face, then clarified brightly: "This is the best-case scenario, no question."

Smith felt Walsh's hand beat firmly against his back, clapping it in congratulations; his body passed a wave of nausea. Otherwise, he felt very little. He heard his father's voice. "So, what are the next steps," the man asked in a pragmatic, neutral tone. He had no desire to celebrate this victory, which dangled still out of reach, beyond the legal contingencies listed as well as intangible ones (the judge's mood on the court date, her politics, her history) and one unspoken, without which the others were moot: Smith's continued sobriety.

Realizing there would be no Cabbage Patching from his audience, the lawyer shifted his tone. "Well, David will need to be tested once a month until his court date at an independent lab. Clients in the city use Quest; they're everywhere. And if these don't come back clean, clean for any- and everything, that's when you're gonna have a real problem. I can't tell you how many clients I've had arrested on possession who get rearrested before I can get them off. I remember one time—"

The reasons for Smith's own ambivalence in the face of the *best-case scenario* were opaque. In part, he mirrored his father's anxieties, though he controlled a greater share: There was no such thing as a guarantee. And of course, there was the lingering suspicion, on the memory of how close he'd come to using the other night at Inducio, that indeed he had a problem—some unnameable ache that would eat him alive.

"—and for treatment, there's a local guy I use," Walsh went on. "Dr. Meyers Mancini. Very well known, *very* well liked in the local courts. On name recognition alone, he's the guy you want. I feel bad for him. He's kind of—I try to send him work, you know? When I can. But, yeah, he's a bit of an odd bird. Anyway, you'll give him a call to get set up with those sessions," Walsh continued, taking a half step to reveal that he'd walked them to the door of his own Mercedes. "That's the only piece of the equation missing: the sign-off from Mancini. You get that, you're golden."

CHAPTER FIVE

The next day, Smith invented an excuse to leave work at noon, an obvious lie—*an ENT on the Upper East Side*—that was nonetheless permitted. By one p.m., he was sprinting through Grand Central's vast atrium, dodging hordes of headless torsos, their necks craned back to observe the domed ceiling, which drew the attention of tourists with no interest in train travel as the Vatican draws the damned. He arrived at track 10 just in time to catch the train easing into motion. On his phone, he confirmed the route: two hours east to mid–Suffolk County, Ronkonkoma, then a twenty-minute Uber through a neighboring town known for its unsavory smell. Emerging through the landfill stench into an odorless middle-class suburb, Smith unplugged his nose and observed the sprawl of unremarkable homes, low and weather-worn, the signage on their lawns communicating politics both immediate (*John Dade for Town Selectman*) and ideological (*We don't call 911*).

"We have arrived, mister," the driver, a formidably eyebrowed man, announced. It was just before four p.m. The house outside the car window was, like all the rest on the block, squat and low, muck gray like a pigeon's gullet. Its windows were dark. Smith thanked the man, opened his door, and approached the house with a sense of foreboding. He rang the doorbell. Beyond the thick wood, he heard shouting, then shuffling, then silence. Smith eyed his phone, realizing perhaps too late that it would've been wise to tell someone, his sister or Carolyn, that he was coming here. In the event of his disappearance (*We don't call 911*), his boss would be able to offer only that, as far as she knew, he had been having laryngological trouble on East Eighty-Third.

"Can I help you?" asked the young woman who answered, a bundle of mail in her arms.

"Yes," said Smith. "I'm here to see Mr.—or, um, *Dr.* Mancini." She wore a searching expression, as if she recognized the name but didn't see its relevance. "I have an appointment. David Smith?"

Recognition flared in her eyes. She shoved the screen door open and with a lopsided smile welcomed him into the dim foyer. Gingerly, she set the mail down on an antique table, then screamed at a nuclear volume: *"Meyers!"* A distant, muffled *"What!"* returned from the bowels of the house. *"Client for you,"* she wailed, then politely asked Smith to remove his shoes and follow her into the kitchen.

It was, in every way except one, an utterly unremarkable house. Other than the wide, worn sofa that lined the living-room wall and, even intact, seemed to advertise its ability to pull out into a mattress, the home was completely devoid of seating. The maple-colored dining table in the next room was unusable unless guests were keen to stand upright, prodding at baked potatoes with their index fingers. In the kitchen, where Smith was told to wait, there was a countertop without stools and a breakfast nook that contained another table at which a person could perhaps practice Warrior 3 over his or her cornflakes. Despite this, the room still managed clutter. Piles of paper claimed every open surface: sheafs of looseleaf, discarded mail, invoices, thank-you letters, death threats, save-the-dates, and funeral invitations. And glancing through them, Smith began to register also the mildewed, cat-piss smell of a home with many pets, which, as he walked over to a lemon-colored macaw beaking madly at its cage, he realized was precisely the case. A slice of the Lynchian domestic, conveying an ambiguous yet imminent horror.

Smith jumped at the groan of a motorized chair as it lurched into the room. In it sat a neckless man with a ponytail of gray hair and boxy black frames through which his gaze darted with reptilian alacrity from Smith to the macaw to the stack of paper his chair had toppled with its entrance, then finally back to Smith. "Step away or she'll bite ya" were the first words he spoke.

Smith flinched. "Sorry."

"Follow me." Dr. Meyers Mancini grunted. He executed an impressive three-point turn, toppling two more stacks of paper, then sped down the narrow hallway—swerving to avoid an Oreo-colored cat—around a corner, past two closed doors, and finally into a room that must have been his office: burgundy carpets and a leather-topped desk beyond which there was no chair for now-obvious reasons. Smith entered and, relieved to find a small stool, sat. He watched the doctor, flanked by a wall of numerous but at this distance illegible degrees, dig his nose into a manila folder.

After several painstaking minutes, the doctor finally looked up, pursed his lips for a moment, then howled the name "Gerta." A ginger cat leapt from behind his desk and retreated into the hall. "Diet cola," he barked when she arrived at his door. "You want anything, kid?"

Gerta glanced at him, not unkindly. "I'm okay," said Smith, and she scuttled away, then returned with a can and glass of ice.

Meyers clawed the aluminum open and filled the glass with crackling amber. "So," he said, smacking his lips with refreshment. "If I ask you to piss in a cup right now, that gonna come back clean?"

Smith stuttered. "Oh, um—"

"It's a yes-or-no question."

"Of course," he amended. "*Yes*, of course."

"Good," Mancini said sharply, looking back at the file. "'Cause Jimmy thinks it's a sure bet he'll get you off. Fifteen, call it twenty hours with me, couple clean drug tests, and we'll be looking at a full dismissal." Smith nodded—though twenty hours seemed, frankly, excessive. "And so the sessions, we'll want to do ten to fifteen, fifteen, maybe twenty hours of them, either here in my home or over Skype."

"Well, I live in the city, so Skype would—"

"Those Skype sessions are group sessions. Mondays, Wednesdays, occasionally Sundays. We've got a good group. Some nice guys, you'll like 'em. Lotta DUIs this time of year."

"Lovely."

Mancini paused to determine if he detected irony or insubordination, then, undecided, continued. "I'll have Gerta send over a link for Monday's session. That's Monday at six p.m. Not six oh seven, not six oh two. Six p.m."

"Yes, *sir*." The word stumbled; it seemed so odd a choice, this late in the conversation, to begin addressing the man as *sir*.

"Gerta will ring you up for the first few sessions," the doctor announced, setting down the file, which Smith now suspected had been merely a prop. And with that, it was done. Cautiously, Smith rose, wondering why he'd spent four hours and sixty-five dollars coming to a meeting that so definitively could have been an email, then followed Meyers as he zoomed back toward the kitchen.

Perhaps she'd been listening the whole time by monitor, perhaps her ear had been pressed to the door, but by the time the two reentered the kitchen, Gerta was already making out an invoice for the $1,523.87 that Smith realized he owed and would not be allowed to leave without paying.

He winced, handing over his card. "*Thank* youuuu," sang Gerta, shoving into her headphone jack a Square, through which she slid his Amex and pivoted her screen to sign—all in one swift and seamless motion. Smith dragged his finger across it, feeling more than slightly hustled.

"Remember," barked Meyers, gazing upward with disdain, "six p.m. You will *not* be late. You'll come at six p.m. or you won't come at all." With that, the yellow macaw cawed, and the doctor whizzed away, back into the hallway's darkness.

That Monday, Smith was summoned to an editorial meeting, the purpose of which was unclear. Rather, he understood its purpose—to discuss the end-of-year "emerging artists" feature—but not his presence at it, as generally he had no involvement in day-to-day operations. This slight annoyance was compounded by the fact that his first Skype session with Mancini was in less than an hour. And as the minutes trickled by, he realized he'd have to take it from the office. *Not ideal*, he thought as he studied the self-serious expressions of his colleagues—the executive and managing editors nodding along as a waifish staff writer droned on about a "re-*nay*-sance in queer abstraction," all of which was dutifully recorded by their social media intern, a mustachioed twink drenched in Aesop product. His boss's dark eyes hardened.

"Smith," she said, perhaps for the second time. "You'll need to be involved in the promo push, as we'll want to make sure we're targeting the broadest possible pool of *qualified* readers." The word *qualified*, which she pronounced with relish, was one of her preferred euphemisms for *rich*, or at least rich enough to afford artworks generally priced between five and ten thousand. But it was more than that. From a data perspective, it was also a matter of interests, tastes, and demographics. A *qualified* reader was not just one capable of placing an eight-thousand-dollar hold on their credit card without so much as seeing the work in person but someone who understood this to be a virtuous—and, to her mind, *political*—act. Someone subscribed to certain publications, a graduate of certain schools, an eater of certain grains, and a wearer of certain denim—such a person no doubt would have liked certain meaningfully adjacent pages or conducted certain searches, which was how Smith would find them.

"And, given last year's missteps, I'd like to also have you tag along on a few of the studio visits, as we could use your help navigating the *cultural* dimension." Ah, so there it was, the second and probably truer reason he was here: the shitstorm that had descended after last year's list had gone live with only four nonwhite artists out of fifty. Though, ironically, it was the inclusion of the sole Black artist—a figurative painter named Naomi Adefope—that had most incited vitriol, a now-fired staffer having written in the accompanying text that hers was an "intuition for the raw, unsung beauty of her subjects," implying that these figures—Black folks mostly cast in the street—were so unsightly that simply seeing them was a talent.

"Sure," Smith said sharply. Of course, it hadn't really been a question but a poison chalice, a lazy act of insurance. Blythe smiled, and as the meeting returned to a Rolodex of unfamiliar names, Smith diverted his attention to his laptop, where he refreshed the page to find the link for Mancini's meeting beneath a news alert. Its headline appeared as the bolded subject: ***Manhunt Begins in the Case of Elle England.***

Immediately, he stood and, mumbling, excused himself from the room. Having opted into these alerts, he was surprised by his own surprise. After all, it had been in that same conference room—at CNVS they were called "studios" and this one was Picasso's—that he'd learned the particular penchant of unwanted news to barge in at inopportune moments, like a sent-away houseguest with nowhere to go. But since that day, weeks prior, each update had been news of no news, until now.

In a locked bathroom stall, he reopened the email and clicked the hyperlink. *Police*, the article's first line read, *are seeking help in identifying a man who appears in surveillance footage leaving a downtown club alongside socialite Elle England on the night of her death*. He held his breath, eyes scanning the cascade of text and landing on the embed below, an image so grainy it looked like an artifact from a bygone digital age. Flip phones, Blu-rays—he hit play.

In the video, barely visible at first, two figures emerged from a neon doorway onto a busy nighttime street. The shorter of the two, a woman—no, *Elle*—was in a slip of indiscernible color, brown perhaps, or orange, though Smith remembered it red, the same shade as her lipstick, so immediately, he distrusted the image, its crudeness corrupting his memory. She accepted a light from a man whose face was obscured by a wide-brimmed Yankees cap. His skin was brown and he was wearing dark clothing, too heavy for the season. The two stepped toward one another, close enough to kiss. Then, strangely, the man looked up for a moment to the sky, as if expecting rain, and his features were briefly rendered. And here, whoever had edited the footage had slowed time so that this glance—probably, in reality, no more than a second—dragged on with excruciating languor. Still, it did little to make him legible. A police sketch by a blind man, he was a murky, inarticulate haze. As Smith's eyes strained for clarity, the man took a step back and disappeared. An accident of framing, it appeared as they smoked and she replied to him, *smiling*, that she was speaking to herself. And when she paused to listen, looking not at him but the road, where passersby were spilling out from their parties with a palpable frenetic revelry, she looked entirely alone.

Smith scrolled back through the text: A summary of the established facts—*the banks of the river, the ruined red slip*—its last line asking *anyone with information on the unidentified man* to call a tip line, 1-800-something. Smith examined the abstract face, attempting to match it in his mind— every half-remembered night, every drunken memory—but came up empty. The face was a void. Though, in the video, a familiarity was evident in their manner. Even through the grain, Smith could sense an ease in their touch, her laughter. He wasn't a stranger to her.

Though how could that be? She, who'd had him check moles on her back and told him thrice about her lifelong fear of Al Sharpton; she, who'd described the cast of her youth in exquisite detail, the children of Black Hollywood with whom she'd had beef or young love or everything in between—how could she not have mentioned someone she knew so intimately?

And who would such a person have been? He didn't look like her usual type: Black Ivy grads with designer sneaks and jobs in the "culture" industry. No, he was another breed. Someone she'd met in New York, no doubt. She was always picking up strays—cokehead dreamers, aspiring comedians she'd met in Uber Pools—and bringing them back to the apartment, so that some mornings he'd had to wade through a sallow-eyed circus en route to the door. But no one like the man in the video. Probably the police had obtained it some weeks prior and even with every resource at their disposal had been unable to identify the man. So their public appeal, while prudent, was equally an admission of failure.

In an era where one's every movement was tracked, surveilled in cell phone footage and the ledger of digital transactions, it was strange for someone to disappear so completely. The kind of person capable of such a thing, not just the cruelty of dumping her still-breathing body but the resourcefulness to erase himself overnight, would have to be someone prepared for the possibility, a person typically engaged in illegal acts for which he knew he would have to pay. That was, if he was ever caught. The police, the text said, suspected the unidentified man might have fled the city, so they were now *working with colleagues in neighboring states*. They *doubted he'd gotten far*, having had only hours until morning, especially since he himself appeared *inebriated*. Wobbling, woozy. It struck Smith as a fool's logic, ill-attuned to the nature of panic, that derangement of animal senses which must have fueled the man, however prepared he'd been for the possibility that he might have to pack and run. Perhaps he'd even done it before. It would have allowed him, after that initial ruthless act, to perform others, running blind with the rage of desperation.

Seeing the time, Smith stumbled into an open studio, Manet's, which faced southeast and the downtown tip of Manhattan. In the dimming late-afternoon light, the river unwrinkled her dress.

Despite Mancini's insistence, the session did not begin at 6:00 p.m. It did not begin at 6:01 p.m. or at 6:07 p.m. or even at 6:15 p.m. Instead, at 6:00 p.m., Smith and one other boy appeared in the virtual room, silent as they watched Mancini attempt to fetch the others from the digital ether. The second boy wore gamer headphones and a self-satisfied smirk as he observed Mancini's incompetence, dramatized with grunts and murmurs and occasional outbursts like "But I just *did* that" as Gerta attempted to instruct him just off-screen. At 6:11 p.m., suddenly and without an explanation, his video went dark.

Smith focused on breathing. No matter what else was on his mind, it was essential that he remain focused in these sessions—that he appear measured, cautious, sane enough to secure the vote of confidence that his lawyer had said he would need. A ticket to freedom. Quickly, he closed all the open tabs on his laptop and stared at the second boy, who appeared to be in a basement, the exposed lead pipe on the opposite wall glinting like a more precious metal. He had sleepy eyes and sallow skin and a *Shut up, Mom, I'm playing COD* look about him, which Smith pictured paired nicely with the prescription painkillers to which he was likely addicted. Immediately, in this way, Smith drew a line between himself and the boy. They were in completely different boats. The boy's glazed eyes and immovable sneer seemed evidence of his lack of remorse for whatever had landed him here, in discount virtual rehab. By the looks of him, he'd piss green the next time he was tested, worsening his present predicament, a deepening spiral of out-, then inpatient treatment, an inevitable stint in jail. No, no, the two were nothing alike.

Nonetheless, together they waited another twelve minutes as Mancini, appearing back in his quadrant, added the remaining participants, six in all, a sea of beige and receding hairlines, the sole exception being a brunette woman who called from what appeared to be a kindergarten classroom. A cartoon frog hovered behind her. And at 6:24 p.m., they finally began. Disarmed by his own ineptitude, the doctor had lost his mafioso acerbity and now adopted an avuncular air. "Welcome, and welcome back to most of you," he said before meandering into an explanation of his treatment philosophy—reliant on tenets of "accountability," "tough love," and, apparently, meaningless aphorism. By the end of his two-minute speech, he'd repeated the phrase *the beginning of the rest of your life* no fewer than six times. "So, how are we all today," Mancini asked as he opened conversation to the group. The seven men and one woman shifted in their seats, gazed off camera toward houseplants and air-conditioning units.

"Good," the doctor replied to himself. "So today we're talking about consequences. What they are and what they mean in our lives. You know, what we can learn from 'em," he clarified. "Who's first?" Again, his question went ignored—a full minute of silence, before: "How about you, Ronny?"

Ronald Patterson, as his Skype name read, sighed theatrically, mussed his dwindling hair, then answered that he had been *all right*, though work had of course been *tough* since the DUI, for which he blew a 0.2 after totaling his 2006 Lexus. No one but him had been harmed, but "it made the local news, so everybody knows," he explained of the *consequences*. "I lost my license, so my wife has to drive me to the shop every day. Can't help but think the boys are all talking about me behind my back. Saying what a *fockup* I am."

Mancini paused to ponder a response. "Well, you *did* fuck up. Bigtime," he decided. "But whether you *are* a fuckup remains to be seen."

Ronald nodded somberly. "I just feel so ashamed of myself. Sick to my stomach to think I could've hurt, or even killed, someone."

"Lucky it was just a lamppost," Mancini quipped, again missing the mark on the conversation's emotional hue. The woman in the classroom snorted, then quickly muted her mic.

"Yeah, um, I've been having lots of thoughts about all the shit's come out of my drinking. Losing jobs, friends. And I know it's too late to take any of it back, so now I gotta figure out what to do with the guilt, how to hold it, so I can keep on living."

It struck Smith as a rather poignant concern, one that might, in more capable hands, be spun into an affecting meditation on the human condition, the cruelty of time, and the regret that all of us share. Mancini cleared phlegm from his throat. "All righty, let's hear from someone else," he said, charging on. "Jake, how about you? Let's discuss the consequences of *your* actions."

Jake, it turned out, was the basement gamer about whom Smith was not far off. He'd been expelled from high school his junior year for selling pills, mostly Adderall, but only after becoming the most prolific dealer on the mid-Island circuit. He'd been referred to, in the bread-crumb trail of teenage texts that were collected by mothers and that served, in his trial, as evidence against him, as the *ampheta-maestro*. Mancini's leading questions as to the "consequences" of these actions—"How did your single mother feel after you were expelled for your *crime*"—were answered only in grunts. *Fine, good, bad*—a strategy so foolproof that the doctor soon surrendered, asking Jake to repeat the phrase *I am the sum of my actions, I am the architect of my consequence* thrice to satisfy his weekly participation. Despite himself, Smith admired the boy's refusal to earnestly engage, though it struck him also as a youthful lark. A punk naïveté unavailable to him.

But even with more willing participants, the results weren't much better. Cycling through, each client-patient-customer received three to five minutes of individualized attention, during which Mancini weaponized the details of their case to club them into submission, divulging in sober tones the casualties of their actions. Among them were four DUIs, two drug possessions, and one intent to distribute (downgraded from a felony, as Jake was still a minor)—offenses of some severity, some of which implied flatly that the participant suffered from a dependency that would not soon be solved over Skype. But here, in the acute absence of trust and anonymity, their candor had a hostage look. They searched, against the nondescript backdrops of their unfinished basements, for the words that would satisfy Mancini, his desire to *remind* them of the consequences in which they were presently embroiled. His philosophy, insistent on individual responsibility, seemed uncoupled from any notion of addiction as disease, treating it instead as a series of poorly made decisions.

With tearful eyes, the second possessor of drugs described how his opiate arrest had led him to be let go from a real estate firm with a mandatory report policy, to which Mancini, with all the tact of a drunk at darts, responded, "Bet you'll think twice before getting loaded, huh?" An arpeggio of tears alerted the doctor that Trevor's turn was done; he searched the grid for those remaining. "Who's next, then?" he muttered. "Mr. Smith, how about you?"

If Smith had an addiction at all, it was to a feeling.

His was an unspecified malady, a desire for the night. He loved anticipating it all day with an eye on the clock. He loved preparing for it: the hot shower, the mound of discarded clothes on his bedroom floor, selves shed or decided against. He loved the huddled musk of bodies in a crowded restaurant, the slink of a martini glass, and even the look of an olive, though the taste he found revolting; he loved the girls in their barely there dresses, faces meeting over a flame; how there was always another party, an address sent without context by one of his bad-influence friends. And afters, those glimpses into real estate and interior lives, made public after dark. If you lingered with the speedsters at close you'd be eventually siphoned off into a cab headed *somewhere*, which was never as expected—the fish-scented walk-ups and Bond Street palazzi, the three-knock Ridgewood basements that kept the night in, morning's call gone unanswered beyond a black window.

He hadn't always been this way. As a star student at his Southern prep school, Smith had been so single-mindedly focused on achievement that the words *sleepless* and *night* conjured only images of lamplit textbooks and science projects come undone. Even then, he idolized characters sprung from the minds and memories of Paolo Sorrentino and Evelyn Waugh, bon vivants who lived with abandon, but understood these to be enchanting fictions, glamorous mirages that resembled no one he'd yet met.

Then college did as promised, unearthed an elaborate, unknown world—of coastal prepsters and the spawn of oligarchs trailed relentlessly by rumors of wealth so vast, it necessitated security detail; grease-haired bohemians who refused beef but took peyote; bell hooks beliebers opining hazily as they circled a spliff around a dorm room; puff, puff, you could pass the night away—as a visitor to a self-contained universe with customs and styles and syntax of its own, a version of one's undefined self.

Elle was the first person on campus whom Smith had seen exist comfortably in the in-between: a glittering presence equally welcome at the divest rally and the pong table. For months, they circled each other in disparate scenes with mutual interest, recognizing that chameleonic thing they had in common, but their friendship failed to extend beyond the duration of a shared cigarette. That was, until sophomore year, when they embarked upon a two-week course in New York called Art in the Metropolis—its syllabus espoused lofty ideals around art and urbanity, though it amounted, in practice, to a private tour of the Basquiat-filled sitting rooms of white-haired collectors. They knew only each other and so attached immediately, the refusal of their request to room together leading Elle to declare that she'd be "staying elsewhere, with family." Nonetheless, in those first few days, a friendship commenced between them: whispered jokes and drinks at intermissions, prolonged eye contact as their professor, a gay art historian poached from Yale, described Mapplethorpe's thirst for Black cock as "an elevation of the African American body to the aesthetic standards of the renaissance Madonna."

On day five of the excursion, there was a boozy dinner: Professor Sidorov, sozzled, recounted stories of his twenties in Manhattan to amuse old friends—the mixed-media artist and MoMA curator he'd promised drinks on the university dime—while the rest of the table stayed silent. With a glance and a hand gesture, Elle compelled Smith outside for a cigarette. She lit her own, then stepped back beneath the neon signage, a wash of red falling onto her cheekbones. She looked luminous and otherworldly as she exhaled a kerchief of smoke, then smiled in a way he would come to know: the Cleopatrian features of her modelesque mother tugged back in a grin that tempted toward you, uncontent with the confines of her mouth, overbitten and lightly gapped and seeming to relish a humor so total, you were desperate to be in on the joke.

"You're coming out with us tonight," she announced.

So that was it, why she'd disappeared each of the previous nights after showing the bare minimum face at whatever organized fun had been pinched into the day's relentless schedule—*9:15 to 10:15 p.m.: Drinks at Trattoria Dell'Arte*—with all the joyless tedium of a root canal. Yawning, she'd excused herself, offering only that it had been a "long day" before escaping into her second night. Smith was exhausted, but he could tell there was no denying her.

The food was finished, the check swiftly paid, and as cabs were being hailed by their slurring professor, violet-mouthed and mumbling something about *the lobby at nine a.m.*, the two absconded in a car of their own. Elle redirected the driver to Chelsea. *Dre's apartment*, she explained, assuming correctly that Smith would know who that was: her lifelong best friend, the influencer son of a rap mogul father whose lavish lifestyle and high-femme wardrobe had been tracked by the tabloids since he'd emerged from what they called "the closet" several years prior. So that's where she'd been staying.

As in a movie, the elevator opened directly into his high-ceilinged loft, where a few were already gathered: a coterie of gays and fashion girls in fur stoles, neoprene, and thigh-hugging leather. A gaggle of black swans, they awaited their host, who, emerging from his (literal) closet, seemed to gasp all the air from the room. The stocky build of his gangsta rap father cinched into an onyx bodysuit whose neckline plunged to reveal a hairless, nut-brown chest.

"What do you think of the hat," he asked in a clipped, heightened affect that would prove to be his voice. Under a wide-brimmed San Diego, he stalked the room like a makeshift runway, recalling images of Naomi in corseted Dolce on her final day of court-ordered community service.

"Bitch, you look like my great-aunt Agnes," cracked Elle, and Dre glowered for a beat before breaking into room-quaking laughter, inviting the rest to laugh as well; one girl, her delicate dreads clipped back in a metallic barrette, couldn't stop her own giggle, a light and lovely sound.

Dre sent the hat fluttering to the deep-set couch he fell onto, the gaps between his neat cornrows refracting the light overhead. He looked up at Smith beside him. "And who are you," he asked.

Elle answered. "Smith's a friend from school."

"Oh, is this the one—" Dre began, a look of recognition falling over his features.

"Yes, my protégé," she confirmed darkly. And despite the strangeness of the statement, Smith felt himself grin as he offered Dre a hand to shake—a move so oddly corporate that he and Elle met eyes.

"Make yourself a drink, then; there's stuff in the fridge," said Dre. "I need to borrow Elle for a second." With that, he stood and the two disappeared from the room. Smith walked to the kitchen island, where the others were picking at a sushi platter. They'd all grown up together out west, he learned, were a part of that annual crop of Angelenos who, opting for East Coast colleges, arrived to sample New York, where they continued to hang, like colonial settlers, with exclusively their kind.

Elle burst back into the room and said in an effervescent murmur, "I see you're all getting acquainted." She circled the island to the fridge, rummaged through takeout containers, and finally surfaced with a bottle of half-drunk champagne, from which she poured two glasses.

"That's old," said Dre as he drifted back into the room. "Open a new one."

Elle ignored him, handing Smith the second glass. "It's from this morning," she explained. Dre snatched hers, sipped, then declared that the champagne was *burned*, prompting a riff between them—"If the champagne is too *burned* for your taste, Ms. Deveraux, don't drink it. The caviar, I trust, is not burned"; "I really wouldn't know. This is osetrova, and I prefer Petrossian beluga" (a reference to an episode of *Dynasty* that Smith had never seen)—which eventually devolved into debating the relative *laidness* of Dominique Deveraux's wig. To Smith, it seemed the two spoke in a language of their own, pulling from a murky gumbo of pop culture obscura, references haute and homegrown. Even when they'd dispensed with characters, their curious diction oscillated between Beverly Hills High and New York ballroom, both Black and queer in its references yet prone to a poshness that seemed neither learned nor affected. Smith sipped, passing the brut champagne over his tongue, and wondered why he found the scene so unnerving—a vision of unapologetic Black wealth, of excess, which seemed alluring and impossible at once, the veil of modesty in which he'd been schooled sloughed off as a snakeskin boot, if only for the evening. He swallowed.

That night, he was anointed in a curious politics. The ritual arrival: a town car that dropped them not outside but down the block, from which they could occasion a proper entrance; the obligatory tour, once inside, before settling into any one spot. They danced and drank and spoke, loudly over hip-hop, to strangers whom Dre seemed to know, one group subsuming them into a table over which he then presided, a benevolent empress, periodically beckoning Elle and Smith back to the smoking section from which they could survey the whole scene as nightlife zoologists; something as simple as the bag a club girl carried revealing something essential about her stratum in the social milieu. The two cracked with biting wit—their shade, observed minutely—and Smith clung to every word.

The night wore on in pounding melody, verse-chorus-verse, the looming faces like funhouse reflections. "Let's dance," Elle exclaimed as the opening taunt of Jay-Z's "Ride or Die" bled in from the next room. They pushed through writhing bodies, feet gliding across the liquor-wet floor, hoisted themselves up to the wide banquette on which Dre was already dancing madly in mounting heat. From the opening line, they rapped every word in tandem, relishing especially that lyrical interdiction on which most of the room rightly stumbled. A pair of syllables that fit them, a pet name in the right mouth.

They spoke it, sang it, screamed it.

By the time Smith awoke the next morning, his phone had nearly vibrated itself off the side table's edge. Charged just 9 percent, it announced, with polychromatic panic, how late he already was—a flurry of texts from Elle, from his hotel roommate, and from their professor, all demanding to know why he hadn't shown up for their morning tour of the MoMA. He shot out of bed, rattling the concave boy beside him, who flipped onto his side and asked, in an unplaceable accent, "What is gone wrong?"

"I'm fucking dead," Smith mused, riffling through the scattered clothes on the bedroom floor in search of his jeans and T-shirt. There was no time to charge his phone, Smith realized, as he scanned Elle's messages.

9:14 a.m.: *Oh no! U overslept*

Then, at 9:46 a.m.: *text immediately when u wake—and meet at moma!*

He didn't reply, but, opening Maps, found his blue dot hovering somewhere incomprehensibly deep in Brooklyn. Had they been in the cab for more than twenty minutes? Smith couldn't recall through the brain fog that was his hangover's sole symptom, the mercy of youth and pounding adrenaline. "Where the fuck are we," he asked loudly, now panicked; the boy rolled over but didn't open his eyes, answering with a word that Smith, in 2013, had never before heard but understood with a grim intuition: "*Bushwick.*"

The phone fell to 6 percent as Smith emerged onto a desolate street— an industrial hellscape dotted with sullen, arty types in daytime leather. He took off at a sprint, his partially tied Dr. Martens pounding concrete as he lurched toward the subway a half mile on, from which—if his phone could be trusted—he could take a single train to his destination; it fell to 5 percent as he arrived, leapt up the stairs to an aboveground platform, vaulted over the unmanned turnstile, and managed to catch the M train like the last plane out of Saigon. *Stand clear of the closing doors, please*; his phone fell to 4 percent. Smith sat and heaved loudly into the crook of his arm, looking up only as the train careened across the East River, the city's skyline like a chandelier mid-collapse. Then black.

He couldn't think of a single excuse. Twenty minutes late, thirty— these could be blamed on train trouble, on getting lost, but by the time he arrived, he'd be at least an hour and a half behind. A laughable delay. Sickness wouldn't do, as it might explain his sunken eyes but not his absence from the hotel bed that morning, information his roommate—an Am Stud major whose blond hair and cheery disposition tended to suggest a Mormon morality—would have volunteered gladly. He would have to come clean: say he'd gone out, fucked a stranger, ended up in some hell at the other end of the city. Surely their professor could appreciate that, and if not, what could he do, *really*, beyond removing him from the course or failing him or, Smith supposed, taking some further disciplinary action. His thoughts spiraled as the train barreled into Manhattan.

Finally, Smith emerged, phone at 2 percent, onto Fifty-Third Street. A man-made waterfall flushed the Midtown cacophony, the cab-honking, cell phone–talking, coughing, wheezing chaos through which Smith stumbled, poring over his phone map; realizing he was just a block away, he dipped into a pharmacy to buy some Listerine, which he stood on a corner and gargled. The light changed, and he spat, then jogged the remaining avenue to the museum doors.

"Hi," he huffed at the front-desk woman, attempting to catch his freshened breath. "I'm late, um, meeting—"

"Sidorov's group?" she asked. Sweat dripped from his forehead onto her desk. "Do you need a towel, honey?" From her bag, the woman pulled a pack of makeup wipes and handed Smith several, then directed him calmly to the second floor. American Modern—Hoppers, O'Keeffes, and fellow icons from the front half of the twentieth century. Smith found their group clustered around a familiar painting, a gray-skinned woman reaching longingly out toward home. Their professor paused his grandiloquent musing in the middle of the word *sublime*.

"You're here," he said.

Smith felt his chest constrict. He hated, had always hated, being admonished by authority. It took every ounce of his willpower to resist throwing himself to the polished wood paneling, like the polio-afflicted girl in the painting: "I—"

"How was she, then?" Sidorov asked with the toothy grin of a cartoon predator. *She.* She, she, she. Who was she? The girl in the painting? Or perhaps Elle, whom Smith allowed his eyes to find as he searched the scene for clues. She looked almost unforgivably put-together: a body-hugging sheath she'd paired with a chunky sweater, her hair pulled back in a pristine pony, not a flyaway in sight, and her skin with the healthful Californian glow used to sell face creams and green juice, never parties in smoke-filled rooms. Her eyes gleamed knowingly, and he remembered himself.

"She?" Smith questioned dumbly.

"Elle mentioned you were having breakfast with your great-aunt Agnes in Harlem. Rather, she *reminded* me. I confess it took a second for me to recall your asking at dinner—all that red wine, you know." Through the fog, Smith finally saw the sky: She'd covered for him. A not just good but great lie—the fictive breakfast, sufficiently vague and harmless, but paired with the detail that Sidorov himself had approved it. Inspired!

"It was excellent," said Smith.

Like that, it was dropped. The tour, which by then was nearly done, continued; the pastoral juxtaposed with the urban, lamplit windows and their quiet intimacies. American modernism was dying, falling swiftly out of vogue, and, with the atom bomb, collapsed altogether. Expressionist ashes, Sidorov mused, his words turning lyric. The abstract. In the shuffle, Smith tried to catch Elle's eye, but she seemed to be avoiding him. A new fear bloomed: Was she angry?

The exhibition ended, and they were released, instructed to take another hour in the museum's many galleries tracing the influence of the modernists on everything after. The school loosened into untethered fish, and without a word, Elle grabbed Smith's hand and tugged him toward an escalator headed up. "Where are we going," he asked once they were out of earshot.

She flashed a smile, and he knew that nothing was or could ever be wrong.

Up two floors, down a hallway, they escaped the fevered masses, entering a dim, quiet corridor where she paused to consult her phone. "My friend from high school is an intern," she explained. "Says there's something we have to see." They delved further into the darkness, detaching hands to track the wall. The corridor spread into a larger, lightless room where were staggered two freestanding screens on which spectral elephants roamed the polished concrete. A majestic sight but hardly *must-see*. Elle craned her long neck around the gentle mammoths, paused, then approached a square of distant light.

It was a white cube, curtains drawn across the far windows, the light haint blue. Empty but for two guards, stationed at the door by which they'd entered and in the corner opposite. And at the room's center, the presumed attraction—an elevated glass box in which what at first appeared to be a marble sculpture revealed itself as a lily-white corpse, then a living, breathing woman. But not just any woman. They circled the body, supine and still as a lake, and Smith recognized the face of the famous actress, her straw-colored hair cut short, clad that day in a linen blouse that fell open across her clavicle. He crouched to get a closer look and on the opposite end of the prism, his friend did the same, brown blurs beyond the looking glass. They watched the actress sleep. Her rising, falling chest.

"Thank you, by the way," said Smith, glancing up through the glass to catch Elle's gaze. Like a throuple in a twin bed, just feet between their faces and yet a somnambulant universe built from the bone-white contours of her sleep.

"Of course," Elle answered, shedding a grin. "*Ride or die, my nigga.*"

Both laughed and her eyelids opened.

CHAPTER SIX

"So today," Mancini began, clearing a wet cough from his pale pink throat, "we're gonna be talkin' about forgiveness: how to ask for it and how to offer it. Now, in my *extensive* experience with addict-alcoholics, I can say conclusively that you bunch are basically incapable of letting petty grievances go. And the matter with all that resentment is that it builds up inside of you, clogs your arteries, and that's no good. See, the danger of this *nasty, nasty* habit is you start to think the whole world's against you when, really, it's you the one's fucked up. So you need to learn to forgive and move on! Got it? So that's what we're gonna be learning today: *forgiveness*. Now, who wants to go first?"

In the murky image, Mancini's jowls hung loose. He appeared dumb-founded that his clients weren't leaping from their seats, doing cartwheels in their unfinished basements, at the prospect of learning, during the day's two-hour-long session, *how to forgive*. It was a Monday, Smith's third session. The previous two had indoctrinated him in the group etiquette, a dearth of enthusiasm that felt funereal. It wasn't that the participants were necessarily charmless but that they had all learned to be stoic in these sessions, as Mancini tended to fixate on those who showed a shred of vulnerability, devoting agonizing stretches to the details they surrendered about custody battles and workplace disputes. "Ronny," he predictably decided. "How about you?"

Ronny grunted. Again he'd been the last to join, having experienced the myriad technical issues expected of those his age, mid-fifties, and engaged only in the kind of labor for which a computer was not required. "Yes, Doc?" he asked without irony. Smith again wondered if Mancini had any medical authority to conduct these sessions, and if so, where exactly he'd earned it.

"Tell us about someone in your life who you've got a grudge against."

Ronny, his face beet red, his single brow furrowed in thought, searched his garage, its cobwebs and hammers, for hints. "No one's really coming to mind," he confessed.

Mancini was prepared for this answer. He leaned into his camera so that the cerulean glare against his glasses disappeared and one could see fully the whites of his eyes. "How about a situation that still *plagues* you with regret?"

Jesus, thought Smith, glancing back at poor Ronny, who strained to recall the foibles, fights, and failures that in Mancini's view had all led inexorably to his car crash on that unforgettable night. "Um," he finally said, his resolve weakened. Mancini leaned in ever closer. "I suppose I'm still holding on to some resentment toward my ex-wife, Valdosta."

A smile of vindication appeared on Mancini's face. "And what exactly are you begrudging her for?"

"Oh, I dunno," the man said, sighing. "Tons of things, I dunno."

"For instance—" Mancini advanced.

"Just the way she treated me toward the end, how quickly she gave up on things, you know? I'm raised Catholic, which she is too, you know?" he asked again, though how could they possibly. "So, growing up, we didn't believe in just quitting a marriage whenever you felt like."

"So when she *quit* on you, as you say, how'd that make you feel?"

"I dunno," Ronny said, though he must have understood by then that this was a futile exercise, that resolution or some semblance thereof would be extracted by any means necessary. "I guess, um, worthless," he confessed, adding, for good measure: "Like, I wasn't worth anything."

"Good, good. And where is she now, this Valdosta?"

"She moved back to Vermont a couple years ago with the kid. We're both remarried, actually. I got together with my second wife about—"

"Let's stick with your ex," Mancini insisted, so close to the screen at this point that his face took up the full panel, a cosmetician's view of the pores that dotted his bulbous nose. He gazed directly into the camera and went in for the kill: "Do you think that your drinking, your drunk driving, might've been a subconscious attempt to recapture her attention?"

Ill-equipped to refute such a neat diagnosis, Ronny shifted his weight in his chair. "I suppose that coulda been part of it?"

"That's *very good*," Mancini affirmed. "Very good. And so, to avoid any further self-destructive catastrophe, do you know what you gotta do to her?"

"Um." The question, so menacing in the abstract, hung in the virtual ether. "Forgive her?"

"Bingo," Mancini said archly, the consonants *b* and *g* ringing like pinball-struck targets. He allowed the sound to settle. "I think this is a real breakthrough for you." Ronny looked relieved; his flushed face assumed a more natural shade as Mancini drew back from the camera and attended to his notepad below, on which Smith imagined the word *Breakthrough* was now written in a childish scrawl. The note, presumably, would reappear in the files of Ronny's lawyer as evidence of his newfound virtue, a fact which lent the otherwise comic theatrics a heft not lost on the others. Mancini's words came down like a gavel. "All righty, who's next?"

Next, luckily, was not Smith but the kindergarten teacher, Clarence. Like Smith, she'd been busted while weekending out east, Montauk, though on charges—already dropped—of drunk and disorderly after throwing her full one hundred pounds at the doorman of a beach club, whom she'd spat at and called a "butt muncher" after being refused entry on the Fourth of July. The sole stipulation of her charge's dismissal was that she enroll in fifteen hours of drug and alcohol treatment and never so much as *think* of returning. Scowling, she fended off the doctor's attempts to ascertain against whom she harbored such rage. No, she was not angry at her mom or dad—their divorce ten years prior had been amicable—nor at her friends or students or boss or even God, in whom she didn't believe, not that she *cared* much either way. "I don't need lessons in forgiveness," she spat in a tone that implied such lessons, which as a teacher she must have doled out daily, were clearly beneath her. "I don't *resent* anyone. I just got too drunk on the friggin' Fourth of July."

Disappointed, Dr. Meyers Mancini shook his head. "Things are gonna get *much* worse for you, Clarice," he pronounced gravely.

"It's Clarence," she corrected.

All righty, who's next? One by one they were brought up for slaughter, offering tales of jobs lost and love gone wrong, the people around whom their little lives revolved, though the names never seemed to come to mind at once and so had to be Tased out of them, which left them weary, having followed whatever line of questions led them without exception toward self-immolation. It was always, in the end, *themselves* they were mad at, themselves as reflected in the eyes of another: an ex-wife, an ex-friend, a butt-munching bouncer.

By the fourth person of six, Smith had decided that he wouldn't be opening up today in front of these weirdos. He was reluctant to lie, but any truth he told would need to walk a narrow line, offering the appearance of vulnerability while being so neutered as to reveal essentially nothing. Childhood bullies, work drama—none of that seemed enough. And then it came to him: a prime-time tale of adolescent resentment. "*Yes*, I have something," Smith offered eagerly when asked. The others quieted. It occurred to Smith then that they seemed uniquely attentive whenever he spoke. The newest addition to their group, he was probably the character on whom they were least decided. He was difficult to place. They knew that he lived in New York, had been busted on a charge of cocaine, but otherwise, they could glean only the information available from his clothing and affect.

"So, um, growing up I was a total mama's boy," Smith began. Mancini nodded knowingly—one's mother, according to the pamphlet he would've skimmed for his degree, was the original source of all resentment—while the others remained opaque. Smith continued his story with the zeal of a comedian testing out new material, attuned to individual shifts in micro-expressions as well as the mood in aggregate. It was one he'd told on several dozen first dates when stumped for conversation, the beats of which he'd mastered—how he'd been a late bloomer who'd often slept in her bed, one of the "maybe thousand signs" he was gay—but in the absence of any audible response, they landed like birds shot out of the sky. A minute in, Smith watched eyes flit downward, reflecting second screens, and sped to the story's crescendo. "But I didn't bother coming out to her until the night before I left for college."

That night, they'd gone to dinner at an upscale Buckhead steak house, a strategic location, as he knew she was unlikely to yell or weep in public. They were shown to a two-top in the corner, just beyond a jazz trio and the middling singer they accompanied, who struggled through standards (the "best" of Ella Fitzgerald) as Smith and Nadine shared a frisée salad, a porterhouse steak, and a lively conversation about her own college days, the best of her youth. It was only after the peach-walnut crumble arrived that Smith recalled why he'd asked her to dinner, the conversation he'd put off all summer. Impulsively, he blurted the words just as the singer's own emptied into a scat solo of such distracting intensity that Smith, seeing his mother's stone expression, repeated himself in a shout. "Yes, *gay*," he said as the aphasic woman shoo-be-de-doo-op'd the house down. And finally, Nadine nodded, then flagged the waiter to ask for the check.

It was only after the bill was paid, the valet summoned, and they were ensconced back in the car's quiet that Nadine began a performance of her own, one as scattered and histrionic as the caterwauling musician's inside. Her objections began toothless, general (he didn't *seem* gay, was only doing this to embarrass her) but soon grew more specific (another *good Black man* down: gay, imprisoned, or married to a white woman) before circling back to denial (*You just haven't met the right girl yet*) and finally, as the early-morning hours arrived and his departure became imminent, distilled to a darker hue (*Don't you go getting sick in San Francisco*).

"I want to say I forgive her," said Smith, tugging free of the memory. "But something between us broke." His performance had been an eight out of ten. Other than Jake the Basement Gamer, who had lost interest mid-story (being Gen Z, he was less susceptible to the emotional manipulations of the "coming-out" genre), the whole group appeared affected. Observing their expressions, Smith stifled a laugh. The tale had been true, yet filled with omissions. Redacted details, emotions. The fact that he'd mostly been amused by his mother's response, saving his best ammunition for the final hour, when he'd snidely revealed he'd been sleeping all summer with a college boy who worked in their house. The fact that her response had been peppered with the frequent assurance she loved him, would always. And that, by Christmas break of that year, she'd undergone such a startling reversal, it was as if PFLAG had performed a lobotomy.

On gay shit, Mancini was unsure how to proceed. "That sounds very *difficult*," he pronounced slowly. "And your father? Was he around?"

"Oh, no," Smith answered, thinking the doctor sought to pin down his father's whereabouts on the night in question, when he'd been preparing to deliver the invocation at a Floridian HBCU. But Mancini's response, cheeks flapping back and forth as he shook his head in anguish, revealed another intention entirely. The doctor was asking if his father had been *around*-around, as in present for the whole of his childhood, and now, with Smith's denial, he was incorporating this fictional fact into a working narrative: the gay Black boy with the absentee father. The contemptible single mother. He'd seen the trailer for *Moonlight*, he knew all about this. Suddenly, the whole of Smith's life was revealed to him in a supercut of troubling snippets. Paternal abandonment, emotional abuse—all had cal-cified into a heavy brick he'd learned to sink with substances. The only problem, of course, was that it wasn't true. Even as the misunderstanding revealed itself plainly, Smith couldn't bring himself to correct it. It would be awkward, for one, now that Mancini had compelled him to "find a way to forgive her, *and him*, for your own sake," then promptly moved on. But Smith felt pleasure also, having pulled a fast one on Mancini and therein claimed control. Even as he realized that he'd merely submitted to a nar-rative that flattened his humanity—that this lie was fragile, undone with one call, and therefore dangerous—he felt pleasure.

And also a measure of pain. Because with that lie and its attendant undeserved sympathy, he relinquished fully the hope that this recovery might be more than an act. Though as acts went, it was one for which he was prepared. A lifetime of reading the room, intuiting what it was people wanted from him, what they needed him to be. He could play the fuckup reformed for the judge, the tragic Negro for the doctor to heal. But if he had a problem—with booze and blow, *sure*, but also with a performance so constant, he often felt worn to a fetal, half-drawn thing—it was worsening.

"I'm so thrilled," said Carolyn. "I feel like your mum dropping you off for your first day of school." It was a bright, brisk day—early October. The damp smell of last night's rain and a chill hung in the wind. Past Christopher Street, where a brood of rowdy bachelorettes sipped daytime martinis, the whole of Seventh Ave was abuzz. Hats and scarves, the first coats of the season—trenches in beige and leather nipped at the heels of their wearers as they headed for drinks or the park with the chin-up expressions of subjects waiting to be pictured, if only in their minds.

Carolyn wore high-waisted jeans, a patterned silk blouse, and an oversize blazer she'd "borrowed" from her boss—and indeed looked a bit like a mom, or a *mum*, as she called it, though more of the Paltrow-brownstone variety, minder of a bespectacled toddler named Timbre, and certainly not his. "Are you coming in?" Smith asked as they idled at the corner of Eleventh Street.

"God, no," she replied. "It'd be ruined for you if I came. The whole point is to be among strangers. Besides, it's a men's meeting, isn't it?"

"It is, yeah."

"Right. I'll just bum around, have a coffee, wait for you. Besides, it's lovely out."

It had been three weeks since Inducio's opening, when she'd tumbled so spectacularly off the wagon, then awoke the next morning pummeled by shame at losing more than thirty days' sober like a purse in a cab. The subsequent weeks had offered perspective. In fact, she'd explained on the phone last night, she felt almost relieved at having fucked up in precisely the way she'd known she eventually would. Nonetheless, she had suggested Smith try Twelve Step, after he'd relayed in lurid detail the farce of his first few sessions with Mancini, gripes to which she listened intently before sighing and saying, *Well, duh.* He hadn't needed much convincing beyond that. Her suggestion had affirmed his desire to probe the fit of that double-A diagnosis, *addict-alcoholic*, applied to him by Mancini, and he'd found his initial resistance eclipsed by relief, realizing that the words could be useful to him—a cask to hold his trouble. That same night, he'd begun sifting through the seemingly infinite options on Intergroup, comparing them across a number of metrics. There was the neighborhood, of course, as well as the physical building and even the room in which it was held; the type of meeting, grouped both by identity (Women's, and Russian, and Trans) and focus (Beginner, and Speaker, and Step). There were ones that laid on more or less thickly the religious undertones of the Big Book dogma, some named after Bible verses, others espousing a Unitarian ethic, their attendees encouraged to envision their higher power as an Instagram guru or a pulsing wave of light.

And so, for his very first meeting, Smith had decided on a men's group at the LGBT Community Center, a grand edifice he'd always admired but never been inside. Smith and Carolyn veered toward the rainbow flag, which billowed above Thirteenth Street like the beacon it was, nominally of pride, though it induced in Smith something more akin to nausea. He knew that the boner-killingly keen symbol—red (for life), orange (healing), yellow (sunlight), green (nature), indigo (serenity), and violet (spirit)—was a simplified redesign of Gilbert Baker's original, which had included two additional colors that proved untenable: sex in hot pink and magic in turquoise. The flag they approached, however, was yet another redesign. Subbed in just weeks prior, this one added, to some tragic corner, a cluttered triangle of black and brown along with turquoise, pink, and white to denote the inclusion of Black and trans people in a resistance movement they'd founded and an urgent call for advancement (the new colors' rightward direction evoking an arrow), an oblique nod to the failure of this same resistance movement, fifty years on, to have produced much observable progress for those too brown, too poor, too dead to savor the fruits of joint 401(k)s and the prime-time depictions they were told had something to do with them. These new colors joined the old ones in an unhappy—and ironically hetero—marriage of discursive literalism and lyrical metaphor. The cruel irony of a symbol that pointed brashly, with an arrow, to the inadequacy of symbols had been raised online in response to this flag, which, to its credit, managed in its tortured design to embody the strain of the cluttered and essentially impossible representation with which it was tasked. It called to mind the joke that older people, thinking themselves very original and clever, sometimes made about the ever-expanding acronym: *LGBT . . . Q . . . I . . . A . . . X . . . Y . . .* Of course, Smith's own reservations were principally aesthetic; he wondered, arriving at the open door, whether collective liberation came always at the expense of good taste.

"So I'll be back in an hour to fetch you," Carolyn said as she sidled into the lobby, still playing the mother well. She hugged him tightly, and he could smell her rose perfume. "I'm really happy for you," she whispered into his ear, then turned and disappeared down the sunlit block.

In the linoleum-floored lobby, Smith walked past a desk adorned with buckets of NYC Condoms and followed a sign directing him to the third floor, where, through a labyrinth of aging gays and beige decor, he found the door in a dank, inauspicious corner. He was five minutes late and the room was full—*full* of gay men, twenty-three of them precisely—their chairs arranged in concentric circles so that the first ten claimed the innermost, while late arrivals rippled outward. Were it not for the sign reading *Saturday Rainbow Realness: Gay Men Alone Together*, the crowd could just as easily have belonged to a CrossFit class or a Chelsea bar, peopled mainly by attractive white men in their thirties. About half wore gym clothes and signaled with their musk that this was but a stop in a weekend routine: from brunch to Barry's to baring one's soul for a bevy of unwashed strangers. Smith shuffled toward an open seat as the steps were read by a blond man in a pink polo through which his delineated abdomen showed. He was reciting step six—"To have God remove all these defects of character"—when Smith jostled a chair, inviting glances from his neighbors. Could they tell he was new? Smith wondered. Not just to this meeting but to this lifestyle, to sober as an identity—did his uncertainty show? He eyed a scruffy brunet in Levi's 401s who nodded along to the eighth step as if to a pop song, so comfortable was he with the notion of making amends to anyone he'd ever wronged. Had he once wandered into this room, quietly doubting he belonged?

The steps concluded with that crowd-pleasing twelfth—"To carry this message to others"—and the day's main speaker was introduced. Mike wore skinny jeans and spoke with a Cockney accent. "Thoinks, mate, for the introw." Mike had celebrity teeth, meaning fake, too big and too white—which gave him the amusing appearance of a man transforming into a horse—and a big belly veiled barely by a vintage Fear T-shirt. He struck Smith as the only person more out of place than he—at least two decades above the median age and undisposed to the implied step thirteen: "Invested tirelessly in the maintenance of our hot bods." Mike had been a punk, was still, though he was now well into his fifties. As such, he dispensed with the pleasantries and got straight to the good stuff: the booze, opiates, and eventual meth, which he'd tried for the first time on Avenue A. Heroin had a sensual sheen, but Mike favored uppers, whatever would extend the spiral from club to bar to bed, which, jobless, had turned into a life on the streets, bouncing between flophouses and strangers' beds, hustling, stealing from lovers while he was still charming. That was before his teeth went gummy as a child's and he plucked them one by one. He'd done other things too, dark things, cruel things, like knowingly given HIV to his boyfriend of three years. Robbed liquor stores, old ladies, and lied to anyone who'd listen. Then, after ten years, which had passed like mere months in his mind, he'd gotten clean. "It was loik I'd fucking doid, passed through hell, 'n' came out the other end."

The grisly details of the first act made the second feel earned. Past jump cuts of jail cells and disease diagnoses, past blood-drenched T-shirts and pockmarked skin, he'd happened across something like peace. It was a tale, in the style of the genre, of redemption, but one so gnarly as to ingratiate him to the group. All of them were comforted by the pulsing presence of someone who'd gone much further than they—minor menaces at wedding receptions—toward the edge, then off it entirely, yet clawed himself back to the land of clean teeth and the living. They clapped.

The pink polo stood and took over with a winsome smile. "We'll now open the floor," he said. "Just a reminder, please keep your shares to a minute. Hear that, boys? *One* minute. And if you need *help*, my phone alarm will play you out."

The minute-long shares were all different but in some ways the same. Repeated themes, phrases, canned jokes to which they nonetheless laughed. Smith realized, as he listened, that these men were *not* anonymous, at least not to each other. That probably this same group, plus or minus a few faces, gathered weekly to recount the same stories, making myths of their lives. And these myths were precisely what they needed to remember, to repeat like mantras, to keep themselves from swarming across Manhattan like a dropped nest of wasps, gulping and gasping and fucking, an endless mélange of booze, uppers, and anonymous sex that seemed to be what they all had in common, why they favored this meeting, free of wine moms and frat boys, a judgment-free communion. Still, there were levels. The former tech exec who'd gotten drunk at an off-site and come on to an intern was not exactly the same as the mop-haired Angeleno ten days off a bender, booze and meth, which had ended with him ass-up in a motel off the freeway for a train of the truly anonymous—a hunger which had withered to boredom. But that boredom, they knew. That ache. They had all found new ways to be lonely.

Each minute's end was marked by the *brrring*, then the next volunteer. In some of them, Smith saw himself, and he longed to say so. But he thought that if he spoke, he would have to attempt a truth not played for sympathy, shock, or melodrama. His neighbors had the same stories in shades more extreme: serialized arrests, dozens of friends who'd died by OD. "We have time for one more," the pink polo announced, and Smith's hand shot up as if caught on a line. "You, in the turtleneck," he confirmed, then started the clock.

The whole room pivoted, physically shifted in their seats, to face him. Forty-six eager eyes. Petrified, Smith cleared his throat. "Hi, um, I'm Smith. Addict-alcoholic, I guess," he said, pausing as they echoed his name. "I'm a bit nervous, this is actually my first one of these." A few smiled knowingly. "Even though I've been going to this other group that's, well, kind of bullshit." A few laughed. "Um, I should've said that I have, I guess, like, twenty-two days clean and sober? And, well, what else? I guess, until recently, nothing bad had ever really happened to me. Like, I've led a super-lucky life, where every time I've fucked up, I've been given another chance. Another chance, another chance. Until this summer, when . . . well, it feels like a dam broke or like a switch flipped, and now all of these, um, *consequences* are pouring out." He laughed. "Mixed metaphor, I know. But sometimes, I guess, sometimes, I feel——"

The sharp mechanical *brrring* arrived to stop his halting momentum. "One minute," the pink polo said. It had been impossibly brief. Smith thought of his mother, who, back in the days of his debate and oratory competitions, would use a red pen to tally the tics—*like*s, *um*s, *I guess*es— wreaking havoc on his speech. "Um, thank you," Smith said in conclusion, now feeling wrung dry. "I guess that's all I wanted to say."

The air thinned with articulated silence. Perhaps it had been this way with everyone, and he hadn't noticed, or perhaps, as struck Smith with a pang during closing announcements, they'd found his share evasive, entitled. They resented him, the fact that he still looked years from the last rung, that notorious bottom called *rock*. Smith stood and took the hand of a notorious bottom called Stanley as the room joined in the reading of the Serenity Prayer: *God, grant me the serenity to accept the things I cannot change, the courage to change the things I can, and the wisdom to know the difference.*

The meeting ended in a moment of silence—*serenity*—then a rumbling thrum: full-bodied embraces, kisses planted on cheeks. The hot air filled with a faintly erotic scent, and almost reflexively, Smith retreated to a corner. No one seemed to notice. No one appeared at his side and demanded his number, as Carolyn had told him they would, elders rushing in to champion newbies. That would've bugged him, no doubt, but its opposite was immeasurably worse. Indeed, it confirmed that his share had cast him in an unflattering light, that they thought of him poorly or, worse, not at all. Like an urban anthropologist, he recognized this scene from wading through dance floors of lewdly named parties: Horsemeat Disco, Battle Hymn. Nights that began always with the intoxicating promise of casual sex but inevitably, as the hours wore thin—even if he met someone with whom to tangle tongues, then detach after "I Feel Love" in search of another—confronted him with the hideous fact of his own invisibility in these temples of narrow desire.

*   *   *

Smith left the room alone. He retraced his steps down the narrow hallway and remembered only then that he'd picked this meeting in part out of a desire to check out a mural in the disused bathroom on the second floor: *Once Upon a Time*. Cocks out, they were everywhere, disembodied yet anthropomorphic, sprouting legs to lead lives of their own. One overlong shaft bobbed gently beneath its head's weight like an herbivorous dinosaur, an army of faceless men attempting to climb it; others squirted viscous, dribbling streams; and amid these cocks, humanoid blurs—men—jacked or sucked themselves off. An ecstatic, irreverent rebuke of what had been called the "gay plague," painted by Haring in '89, when he himself was just nine months from dying, having witnessed his loves, over the course of the decade, picked off like wilted petals. Smith was transfixed. Being of that generation for whom HIV/AIDS was not a death sentence but who carried some ghost of its terror, he found it difficult to imagine any whimsy in sex. The notion of pleasure without consequence would of course have been a fantasy in Haring's final days and, thirty years on, struck Smith as a fantasy still, though for the same *and* new reasons. Cruising had become, like all things in the internet era, a series of transactions with the self as sole commodity. The throbbing iPhone pulse, which had kept him up so many nights, strung out on the promise of real sex at the other end of a negotiation. *Pix? Yea, u?* The frenzied thrill that at any point, his phone might go silent, then, minutes later, resume. *Into sucking, fucking, kissing, rimming.* But by the time it ended, in sex or lost interest, the physical act was burdened always with the anticlimax of its being but the result of an agreed-upon contract.

And what of belonging—wasn't that also the point? On the walls, humanoid forms collapsed to their most basic—two-dimensional, phallic, monstrous—yet seemed seduced by this abstraction. Too little distinction to stratify their bodies, too little power to fight for, no real hope at the happy end. They were a people at odds with the mainstream, their sex vilified, their blood believed poison. And in that alienation, a word like *community* must have seemed a revelation, vast and sturdy enough to hold them, a ship on a rising tide. A word like a totem, like a tower, like a flag.

"*There* you are," Carolyn exclaimed as Smith entered the lobby, where she was propped against the front desk, leafing idly through syphilitic lit. "Where on earth have you been? The other gay alcoholics descended ages ago," she said as they stepped through the door and started east. "I've just had the most magnificent stroll. You'll never guess who I ran into." She'd seen Ollie, a college friend of theirs. Now a second-year PhD candidate at Cambridge, he had apparently returned to New York for a while to attend to his "affairs," which Smith took literally. Ollie was always good for romantic melodrama—a raconteur of great betrayals, dinner parties turned to shambles with revelations of infidelity.

"He wants to have us over for dinner tonight," she continued. "Is that okay? I already told him yes."

Smith answered that it was. He was hungry, and Ollie was always a good time. But it wasn't even six p.m., so the two kept walking, selecting side streets for optimal sun and lowest likelihood of running into those they preferred to avoid. They could not take Bleecker because that would mean walking under the indigo awning of a former friend's restaurant; nor could they take Prince between Broadway and Sixth for fear of running into Smith's ex, who walked his fawn pug and new boyfriend up and down the stretch thrice daily. Having lived there for three years, Smith saw the city like that: potholed and land-mined and littered with old lives.

And as they walked, Carolyn compelled him to tell her everything about the meeting. Smith was reticent at first, not wanting to confess outright that it had been a bust. Nonetheless, she understood. "Some meetings just suck, though. That's AA," she replied. Hearing about his share, she grinned, then remarked offhand that it also had taken her "months to learn not to subtly brag," which even now could be difficult. "That'll wear off, I promise, you'll just have to find a group that's more our vibe." Smith averted his eyes as they walked into the park, and beyond the glittering arch, a sunbeam briefly blinded him. In her statement was the presumption of shared experience, which underwrote most conversations between them, was the unsteady bedrock on which they stood. It suggested a likeness in how people perceived them, how each entered rooms, and therefore that his feeling of alienation was somehow mutable, perhaps in his own mind. He felt a vicious swell of contempt but swallowed it; it wasn't fair. And anyway, he was tired of talking.

CHAPTER SEVEN

Probably, were it not for him, Carolyn and Elle would not have become friends at all. On the face of it, this seemed strange, as the two had a great deal in common. Both beautiful, both glamorous, both from elegant coastal families entrenched in the arts—they had about them a kind of symmetry. Nonetheless, in college, they'd only come into occasional contact and, even in New York, seemed to pertain to variant slivers of the same milieu. That first postgrad summer in the city, Smith had zealously architected their distance: dinner with Carolyn and the friends with whom she'd grown up, graduates of Spence and the Lycée Français, then drinks with Elle, Dre, and the sleek, swart set to which they belonged. And on the occasions that the two did interact, he'd watch their polite conversations from afar with a sense of mute anxiety, fearful that theirs would be a combustible union.

One day that first autumn, Smith awoke to rain, its soft patter percussive against all the city's cars. He checked his phone and saw that it was nearly two p.m. Last night had been a late one, celebrating Dre's birthday at a Manhattan nightclub that felt right off the Vegas Strip, all bottle girls and oil barons and shitty EDM. His head was still pounding from it as he wrapped his comforter around him in a downy cocoon and moved from bed to the couch. Elle was still asleep. Faintly, he could detect the whisper of her breath from beyond her closed door. Saturdays, he often rose in the late afternoon to a flurry of immediate motion—workouts and lunches to rehabilitate his body before yet another night—but today, the rain offered relief. It removed the obligation to do anything but this: lie still on the couch, eyes closed and windows open, listening to her breathe.

Eventually, he stood and looked around the room. Having moved into the apartment six weeks before, they were still accumulating decor, slowly, recovering items from curbs and from wasteful, wealthy friends who disposed of perfectly fine furniture like pit-stained T-shirts. It had a collage effect—decades and styles, coherent only in the lens view of their taste. He walked to Elle's record collection, which sat alphabetized atop an old diner table they'd salvaged from a nearby café's closure, and flicked through the titles. Diana Ross, Marvin Gaye, Whitney, and Sade, then paused at a record he'd never noticed. *Nat England, Live from the Songs and Souls Tour, 1999.*

In truth, he'd never listened to much of Elle's mom's music other than that one song everybody knew, one he'd encountered in vegan soul food restaurants and massage parlors and the kind of Black-owned boutique that left one's clothes rank with lavender incense. He examined the cover image. She must've been, in 1999, a few years older than Elle was today, and the two shared a face: the same honey skin and full lips, though her mother wore her hair in a mane of locs. And there was a discord, Smith thought, between the earthiness of her mother's image and the designer glamour of Elle's own, one characteristic of the children of Black Hollywood with whom she'd grown up—progeny of athletes and rappers and prestige actors who'd ascended from their humble beginnings on the wings of a commodified *realness* and whose children, as a result, would never learn to park their own cars.

Smith removed the black disk from its emerald sleeve and held it in one hand. He put it on the turntable, lifted the needle, and placed it gently against the onyx surface, then watched as the record spun. A crooning sound emerged—a mystical, magical sound—as Nat's textured alto climbed the scales. He closed his eyes, and he was in the front row watching a hand beat against her hip to keep rhythm, her metallic bangles jangling along her slender wrist.

"See, now I know you're fucking with me," he heard, and he opened his eyes to find Elle in her doorway, a wide grin warming her face. "I almost had a heart attack, thinking my mom had shown up here without warning."

"Sorry," said Smith, smiling; on some level, he'd known this would wake her. The one time they'd been together when one of her mother's songs came on, he'd watched her violently jam her pointer fingers into her ears. Yet now she came and fell beside him on the couch, helping herself to half his comforter. She closed her eyes and said softly, almost as if he weren't there, "I love this part," as Nat's voice trilled upward and, at a note just beyond her range, suddenly failed. An indelicate rasp that was surprising, and human. Likewise, that morning Elle seemed stripped of artifice, of the larger-than-life persona she managed to uphold in public. Her voice was hoarse and quiet, her face completely bare. "Were you on this tour?" Smith asked, and she considered.

"I think," she said, locating the tour in her memory. "I was in school, but I joined for the European leg that summer."

Already, he'd become fond of these stories, tales that often appeared apropos of nothing of being christened on the road in a one-room Memphis church or receiving sage advice about a fifth-grade crush from Prince—snapshots from Elle's girlhood on her mother's endless tour, her home a bunk on a tour bus or a hotel bed or, later, in Los Angeles in the care of her father, a music producer who'd retired once Nat's career had taken off. It seemed she had experienced so much more by ten than he had at twenty-three—and he was eager to make up for lost time.

It was on that tour, she remembered, lying against the couch's other arm, her wavy black hair wreathing her face, that one of Nat's backup singers had given her a camera—her first—with the not-so-subtle suggestion that she amuse herself and stay out of grown folks' business. It worked. She took hundreds of pictures: of the tour managers and sound engineers and set designers and of her mother onstage or lining her lips in a lit vanity, her feline eyes ablaze. "I remember we got them developed in Brussels, and when they came back blurry, I wept," she said, laughing. "But I didn't stop, because I was totally sprung on the feeling. Watching people transform for the camera, take on a persona or, sometimes, *rarely*, become more themselves—it felt like I was learning the truth about them."

Smith refrained from asking, *Which am I, a performer or a person who becomes more himself when seen?*

Hour to hour, room to room, the day drifted by sedately. They went about their cooking, and showering, and reading, and eating, bound by an orbital gravity. Weeks in, they were still learning each other's rhythms—the clockwork cadence by which Elle would step outside for a cigarette or Smith's energy would wane and he'd retire to his room for a spell—but on the couch, the apartment became a living theater as Elle acted out some memory from a high-school summer spent in Lyon, a crush doomed, from the start, on a French host brother who only spoke English in aphorisms. And when she asked Smith about his own first love, he confessed he wasn't sure he'd yet had one—a fact that sometimes made him feel stunted and unlovable—and strangely, she laughed at this, and even more strangely, he did too. The day grew fat in its middle, then burned off in crimson wisps—the surprise of sunset arriving through a far window and engulfing every ordinary thing in gold.

And then it was night, the room blue-black. Smith heard his phone begin to ring. "Answer it," said Elle, smiling, though the effect was rather like a magician's fumbled trick: the day's illusion ruptured. Smith stood and walked to his room.

On FaceTime, Carolyn appeared fully dressed, wearing a beige turtleneck sweater into which her hair had been tucked so that it all seemed to form one continuous surface. "So you're alive, then," she said by way of greeting.

"Against all odds," he answered, glancing at the time: half past six.

"And yet, you haven't replied to one of my texts all day," she continued in a tone of mild reproach—they were both of the belief that texts were mere suggestions. "Are we still on for dinner?"

Smith racked his brain but came up empty. "Dinner?"

"Jesus, Smith—you lush. We spoke about it for twenty minutes on Thursday—we told Raf we were going to try her place tonight." Some edge of the memory surfaced—out Thursday night, running into some ethereal, elfin friend of hers who'd opened a natural-wine bar in Brooklyn.

"Right," he said. "What time?"

"Eight, and try to be prompt, if possible. She's doing us a massive favor with the last-minute reservation."

Some favor, Smith thought: the privilege of paying a hundred dollars for miscellaneous flora and a few sips of funky wine. He glanced at Elle, lit blue by the phone screen cradled above her face—her hangover subsided, she would no doubt be making moves as well. Suddenly greedy for her company, he looked back at his phone and asked Carolyn, "Can they take three?"

The place was decorated with the self-conscious taste of all Americans enamored of Japan—craft-wood tables adorned with arrangements of in-season flowers set against white walls with simple, geometric paintings. "I'm sorry we're late," said Smith, stooping to kiss Carolyn's cheek as they arrived at the table.

"It's all my fault," said Elle, beaming as she claimed the seat across from him. "I'm having one of those weeks where I hate everything in my closet."

"Very noble of you to take the blame," said Carolyn, looming closer to Elle in a conspiratorial lean. "But we both know Smith has to be forced, practically at gunpoint, to show up anywhere on time." Both of them laughed, and Smith adjusted himself awkwardly in his seat as an attractive woman with a blunt bob arrived and suggested an "earthy" red. Carolyn ordered it for the table, then turned back to ask about their day.

"We barely left the couch," Elle answered swiftly, explaining that they'd been out late last night celebrating the birthday of her best friend, Dre—"Who you'll have to meet"—first at a club in the Meatpacking District and then at a string of afters, from which they'd only sent themselves home at six a.m.

"My God, I remember my Meatpacking days," said Carolyn, Smith thought a bit patronizingly. "Chasing Leo DiCaprio all over Avenue."

"He was there last night!" Elle laughed as the wine arrived and was opened. Soon, Smith found himself barely speaking at all as the two flitted through a Rolodex of mutual acquaintances—not from college but their girlhoods on opposite coasts, the wayward western branches of prominent East Coast families, the handsy husbands and anorexic heiresses—with a rapport that at first relieved and then unnerved him as he understood finally that he hadn't been keeping them apart out of fear that they would not get along but rather fear that they would get along so well that they would have no use for him. Worse still, he wondered—as they finished that bottle and ordered another, their smiles aglow in the candlelight—if the easy intimacy he'd attributed all day to magic was, in fact, a trick Elle could pull with anyone at all.

They were at the bottom of the second bottle and Carolyn was in the midst of a deliciously scandalous story about a secret affair conducted on a sailing trip with the youngest son of a family friend when Elle caught Smith's eye—a spare, sidelong look, probably meant to convey no more than affection, though as Smith glanced back at Carolyn and saw the dissolve of a wounded expression, he realized it had been read as an insult, a private joke at her expense, and despite himself, he took some pleasure in her hurt.

And then it passed, so quick it seemed unworthy of mention. Carolyn's story came to a climax—being caught mid-coitus by the boy's frigid mother somewhere off the coast of Antibes—and they all burst into horrified laughter, but Smith could detect a change in the night's tenor, Carolyn's manner almost imperceptibly altered. She was colder now, more guarded. A version of her that remained as they finished their wine and asked for the check, then wandered out to the sidewalk, where they conferred over the prospect of a party just across the bridge.

They agreed to go, but as the car careened into Manhattan, all of them were silent. From the passenger seat, Smith asked the Uber driver for the aux and played a dance track at low volume, watching the girls' reflections in the rearview. He turned the music up. On the bridge, Carolyn cracked her window and flooded the car with the dank scent of wet concrete. She leaned her neck against the frame and tilted her face up to the stars. In the mirror, Smith watched Elle watch Carolyn, wondering what she saw in her then: haloed, headless, her hair iridescent in the headlights and violet wind. He watched Elle pull the camera from her bag and bring it up to her eye to train the lens, then take a picture.

CHAPTER EIGHT

The official court date, Walsh informed the Smiths, was set for October 31. *Halloween,* he wrote in his subsequent email, in case the coincidence escaped them. It seemed to Smith a bad omen, but he was eager to have it done so replied enthusiastically with an update: ten hours complete with Mancini, adding that he'd been going to AA as well—a move that Walsh affirmed would "look good" to the judge, as if it were a PR stratagem of little to no personal significance. He wasn't wrong. Over the two weeks that followed Smith's first foray into Twelve Step, he sampled the city's offerings. In the East Village, in Brooklyn Heights, in Bed-Stuy, he approached recovery like a cautious buyer at an open house. Occasionally, he'd hear something that stuck, a well-put feeling that matched his own. But most days, he balked at stock sentiments echoed relentlessly. Hearing yet another stranger remark how *one was too many and a thousand never enough*, he questioned if he belonged. He *could* have just one, he knew (didn't he?), so why was he here? Was he a tourist, a poseur, a leech?

The days were already shorter. The trees that lined the streets erupted in fits of vibrant color: marigold, crimson, plum. It should have been, usually was, his favorite time in New York, but walking along the raked beds of leaves in Central Park where new loves lay, hair tousled by hats or hands, he felt alone.

On Seventy-Seventh and Lex, he examined the pale pate of a med tech's bald head as he crouched to crotch-level and watched Smith piss in a cup. "You wouldn't believe the shit people try to get away with," he offered, eyes fixed to Smith's urethral meatus. At home in the evening, Smith nodded along as Mancini's bilious face appeared on his laptop screen and posited that a great deal of his issues arose from his lack of "basic impulse control." And in the morning, at a meeting on Church Street before work, he listened as a young woman, a Chinese American doctor, explained how an affair with an opiate addict had accelerated her own descent—which, after she lost her license for writing bullshit narcotic prescriptions, plummeted to a rock bottom in which she was left for days as collateral at the apartment of his fentanyl dealer.

Sometimes, Smith went in the middle of the day to a meeting across from Film Forum, refreshing Slack to ensure no one had noticed him gone. Matinee meetings were more sedate and more desperate at once. Creative types without a fixed schedule, the elderly and unemployed. "It only became a problem when I moved to New York," a middle-aged man proclaimed in his share one Wednesday afternoon, fifty-five days off dope. Afterward, Smith wove down Crosby, peering through shop windows and wondering why the man hadn't left. All around the city, there were people for whom the answer was obvious—leave, go anywhere else—just as it probably was for him. Yet here they remained, trapped in a collective delusion: that to leave was to slip toward obsolescence, a life barely lived. And at these meetings, after them, he thought of Elle.

Cocaine had appeared in her life in a casual way—just as it had in his—so it was difficult to pinpoint when it became a problem, the inflection past which a descent had begun. She'd arrived in New York a few weeks after him, having secured a position as the photo intern for a magazine known, in the hip milieu to whom it was targeted, for delivering "bold fashion content with a feminist edge." Already she seemed overqualified, having amassed a sizable following online for her photographs—mostly portraits, taken with the film camera she always brought on nights out—but the prevailing opinion at the legacy media companies was that she had yet to *pay her dues*, a sentiment her boss expressed directly, along with the assurance that interns would be regularly assessed for full-time positions. And so she began with enthusiasm not even at the base of the pyramid but a subterranean stratum, not offered a salary sufficient to live, just some pittance in exchange for what was then called experience.

That first year in the job, she'd often come home smiling, voluble about a shoot she'd assisted, having photographed a member of Congress or a happening designer who'd launched her own line. Elle's bosses weren't immune to her charm, the access she afforded them. She had ins with young designers, actors, socialites. She could get Dre to appear in a story, *gender-fluidity in high fashion*, without going through his agent, without paying him his rate. In reviews that arrived periodically, as long as Elle was sure to demand them, her managers applauded her can-do, down-for-anything attitude. And once she was granted the go-ahead to shoot her own spread, it seemed a foregone conclusion that she would be promoted in a matter of months to a salaried position. She waited, culling metrics of social engagement for meetings with managers, then waited some more. Lucidly, Smith recalled the day she'd told him that another intern had been promoted, a blond girl with an aunt on the board. Still, she saw this as good news, evidence that her turn would soon come. And when, after months, it didn't, something shifted. She began to make liberal use of the company's work-from-home policy, holing up in her room's meager light. Some nights, Smith arrived home to find her still inert. It seemed impossible, the most vibrant person he knew rendered immobile for days. There was no outward anger, no resentment. What he saw in her, as those days became weeks and her initial optimism warped with confusion and then soured to a bitter acceptance, more resembled heartbreak.

And then, just as he was beginning to worry, she was back to her usual self: out every night, a fixture on the downtown scene. He'd go to the bodega, the afters, sometimes just on the street, and strangers would speak of him in relation to her: *You're Elle's friend, right?* A question he would've found unbearable in relation to anyone else. All his life, he'd been Senior's son, Nia's brother, and despised it, but somehow he felt flattered by the shadow of Elle's inexhaustible light. Hers was a disorienting duality. A public persona predicated on glamour, yet she was sometimes so broke that she ate a sleeve of Ritz crackers for dinner—he began to understand that it was costing her something to be here; that asking her mother for help wasn't an option, either because she would not or could not or because the ask itself would be an admission of failure. There were other things, too, that concerned him—inverted baggies piled up in the bins, a certain look in her eyes. Once, running into their dealer in the middle of the day, Smith had been startled by the sallow-eyed boy's expression as he said, "And tell Elle I haven't forgotten she owes me"—then, with a wicked smile—"though I know she's good for it."

But when she'd disappeared a few weeks after, Smith wondered what kind of company she'd begun to keep. The first of May arrived, and he covered her rent, then waited anxiously for days until she returned, stumbling in on a blank afternoon. Her bearing alien, she could barely assemble her limbs. It was the only time he spoke to her sternly, asking where she'd been for six days and why she'd ignored his calls and messages. Her voice had become a hoarse whisper, almost inaudible as she lied about a check on the way. He followed her to her room, where she collapsed into bed.

Around her, the space was squalid, cluttered with dozens of crumpled-up gift bags she'd brought home from work, the cosmetics within them discarded—a veritable apothecary of copper- and cedar- and onyx-cased dusts, muck-colored liquids and creams—alongside feminine products in gaudy pastels, pocket-size sex toys, and the promotional galleys of books that tracked the career-hungry lives of the girl CEOs who'd penned them. The grotesque and glittering refuse that had been her only payment, it produced a chemical scent that mingled with her own sweet perfume, the one he'd so long savored but registered now with faint nausea. It was all too human. Her musk and the milk-fed expression with which she replied to her name. *Later*, she mumbled as she begged off to sleep. *Let's talk later.*

He awoke to find her gone, this time for weeks. *I've legit never been treated like this by anyone*, he wrote after days attempting contact, trading the language of worry for rage. Other friends confirmed they'd continued to hear from her in manic spurts. Several times he texted Elle that he didn't care about the money, only wanted to know she was alive. And when she finally returned, like Persephone in a dress for spring, her hair was neatly pulled back. She wore a Calvin Klein trench, draped exquisitely. She was lucid and tearful and told him everything about the embarrassment she'd felt after losing her job and realizing she could no longer afford to remain in New York. The debt on her credit cards mounting as she attempted to maintain a public face. The secret shame, for which she'd found no place, and so she'd disappeared to the house of a friend with no connection to what she called her *real life*. In fact, she'd referred to him just once and not by name but borough: *the Bronx*.

"And with the drugs?" Smith had asked, recalling the visions he'd had of her on loop. "I mean, do you need to get help?"

She considered the question, then a familiar, wry smirk appeared on her face. "I mean, I don't think I need to, like, *commit* myself to a facility."

And what if she had? Would she have said this? People almost never do, relying instead on the looks in the eyes of those who love them, which Smith understood he did. Because he didn't *have* to, had never been wronged in any meaningful way, and yet had forgiven, and wasn't that love? And wasn't it, then, his turn to save her? *Ride or die, my nigga.* Still, he wondered, in meditative moments in recovery rooms, someone's share insistent on the moment of grace that might have damn well saved their life, if the day she'd returned, evidence of whatever not yet cleared from her eyes, had been his one chance to love her not in the way she asked but needed. He'd missed it.

The Fourth Precinct station sat at the corner of Canal and Varick, a mere six blocks from Smith's office and two from the nightclub where they'd been on the night of Elle's death, so that the three points seemed to form a scalene of sinister significance. It was strange: she'd traveled so far that night, uptown, where she had been found, news of which rippled out to the city's distant reaches, only for the matter to come to rest essentially next door from where she'd started. Smith had attempted to express that strangeness in his first conversation with the police—he could think of no reason why she would have gone so far, no *known associates*, he'd said, though after a week in AA, he began to question that assertion on the basis of a surfaced memory, that man she'd referred to once as *the Bronx*. Still, it seemed a kind of *too-too* detail of the sort found in a mystery novel; the clue marked *clue*. Probably it was mere coincidence. But, because the central premise of an active investigation is that there is no such thing as a coincidence, and because the fact, once remembered, began to burden his psyche with a tremulous, pestering weight, he decided to call the tip line, on a Wednesday, ten weeks after his first conversation with the police. Curtly, a woman answered. An entry-level paper pusher, she took her sweet time tracking down the case file, then wrote a report with audible disinterest. Her patronizing tone and pregnant pauses—she was a woman well suited to the trade of sifting through streams of irrelevant information—confirmed he'd been a fool to think this detail significant. *Basically, all you're saying is that she had a friend who lived in the Bronx.* Yes. Yes, he was, and hanging up, he was sure that would be that. Days passed, a week. And then a voicemail arrived, on a Tuesday in late October, informing him that a Detective Janelle Clement had taken over the case from her colleagues and would like him to come back in.

While he'd gathered from the voicemail that Clement was a woman, Smith was surprised to discover, on arriving at the station and being escorted into her nondescript office, that she was also young, early thirties, attractive, and Black. She wore her short hair slicked back in a style that seemed to accentuate the taut mahogany of her skin, a mark of queerness, pragmatism, or both. She was affable and polished, firmly shaking Smith's hand as she asked him to take a seat.

"Thank you for coming in, I hope it wasn't inconvenient," she said in the same steady tone she'd used in her message. The ability to recognize another Black person's voice no matter how impacted it was by the modifications necessary to survive prep school or the police academy was typically a given, and it was only in rare cases like this that Smith found himself deaf to that particular richness.

"Not at all," Smith replied. "My office is around the corner."

Clement smiled in a way that suggested she knew this, and Smith wondered what else she knew, if somewhere in that bulky PC there was access to his every address, thought, error. Biometrics on the width of his nose and the cut of his chin. No doubt there was a record of his arrest and pending criminal status, which even unspoken seemed to clot the air between them. "Regardless," the woman said, allowing the silence to express her gratitude before advancing in a procedural tone, "I'm not sure how up-to-date you are on your friend's case, as I know it's been reported on at length."

"I don't read any of that," Smith replied; a lie.

"Of course. I can't blame you," Clement continued. "They haven't been very sensitive, the tabloids, and besides, most of what they've reported these past weeks has been patently false, or at least misleading. That's part of why I've taken over the case: to stop these leaks from obstructing our progress in figuring out what exactly happened and bringing justice for your friend."

The way she kept referring to Elle as "your friend" was disquieting, too personal for the context yet somehow dehumanizing both to Elle, who'd had a name, and to Smith, who resented the implication that he might break down at its mere mention. Still, he intuited from the particular verbiage that, on some level, she'd been brought onto the case precisely *because* she was thought a more suitable face: a Black woman to "bring justice" in the case of another. It was not such a different logic from the one at play in Smith's own office and in thousands across the city: that the general lack of progress would be resolved if only the subject and object, the elected and served—or, in this case, the detective and victim—had in common the core marks of their identity.

Smith waited for the woman to continue, and eventually she did. "Of course, as much as the press can be a nuisance, they can also be useful to us. It's more a matter of controlling the information to which they have access." So that was her pitch, how she'd wrangled control of the case from the white men who'd initially owned it. Perhaps she was the one responsible for releasing the CCTV—a clean, tactical shot after months of misfires, sustaining public interest while derailing efforts to make an arrest. She was *taking control of the narrative*. Smith wondered if this desire for justice was indeed out of some identitarian fealty, or simply a careerist drive to prove her own competence. He wondered if—had Elle been found alive, the drugs still on her person—any commensurate effort would've been deployed to help, or if her humanity had been articulated only in death.

But Smith could not deny that Clement seemed capable, more so than the men she'd replaced. She asked the right questions. Having clearly pored over the report he'd left on the tip line, she unleashed a barrage of questions about the man he'd called the Bronx. When had Elle met this person, she asked, and what was *the nature of their relationship*—that was the word she used, *nature*, signifying both its intrinsic character and its biological phenomena, whatever confluence of factors drew these apparently disparate personalities together. The doorman of the nightclub had described him as "rough," the kind of person he'd been instructed not to allow inside. Elle had to come to the door to receive him.

Smith answered her questions frankly. "All I know, really, is that she stayed with him for a couple weeks at the beginning of summer, so they must have been close."

"So she never mentioned his name," Clement said. She'd been taking meticulous notes, but now paused and looked at Smith directly. "How well did you know your friend, Mr. Smith? Was she an evasive person?"

Smith paused to consider. His instinct was to say no. In some ways, he'd known her better than anyone; over the years, they'd become capable of communicating entirely by intuition, a correspondence of glances unintelligible to those outside their private world. She was just *like that*, he thought to answer, not evasive but full of play, liable to speak in a language of inside jokes and invented phrases. Calling this man the Bronx was just another bit. But then, was anyone—anyone even remotely interesting, at least—ever entirely knowable?

"I ask," Clement continued, and now it was clear that she'd stopped writing in part because her questions had been leading somewhere, that it was *she* rather than he who would supply the day's most crucial information, which she'd held to deploy at this opportune moment. "Because, well, did you know that your friend was pregnant?"

For a moment, Smith caught his breath like a fish midair. And then it was flailing, headless, desperate for return to the blue from which it had come. Smith cleared his throat as if to speak but could not, and his confusion, though felt, barely showed on his face until he shook his head.

No, he did not know. Elle hadn't told him.

Clement continued. "Nearly five months." A strange sound emerged from Smith's throat, not a laugh or a gasp but something guttural, conveying disbelief. It was impossible. Nearly two trimesters in, she would've been showing, surely, and she hadn't been. On the night she died, she looked lean as ever.

"I don't," Smith began. "I don't see how that could be possible."

"We were surprised as well, given none of her family seem to have known either, but these tests"—she gestured with the file in one hand—"they're more than ninety-nine percent accurate. Do you think she knew?" Smith felt a vertiginous shift, not unlike the momentum gained when one slips from a stair and fails to immediately recover, as Clement's questions took a tumbling rhythm. *Of course she hadn't known*, he thought. Beyond the basic material concerns—time would've been running out for her to decide what to do about it—there was the simple fact that she'd been partying ever harder in the months preceding.

"No," Smith answered. "I seriously doubt it." Clement's face strained with disbelief, though surely she understood there were ways, modes of contraception that could fail so that even mild symptoms (*symptoms* was the word that occurred to him then, as pregnancy at their age still seemed a kind of disease) like morning sickness or fatigue could be written off as the usual irritations of having a body. Smith recalled an old anecdote of his mother's: a patient, on the pill, who'd come in with bad period pains, then was rushed into labor hours after.

"You must've seen the photographs—she wasn't showing."

Clement nodded. Yes, of course she'd seen them. She would have studied them like all the other voyeurs who'd flocked to Elle's Instagram in the wake, tripling her following to make her a kind of undead influencer. A diary of her days—film portraits of the characters she encountered in clubs, at delis, and on street corners interspersed with iPhone throwaways of herself in the mirror, like the one she'd posted on the eve of the day she died. "Was Elle seeing anyone," Clement asked. Another impossible question. She was seeing everyone, always, such a social enigma that, in the days after her death, Smith had encountered dozens of people online of whom he'd never heard referring to her as one of their *closest friends*. But of course, Clement had intended the colloquial meaning: a romance.

"Not that I know of," he answered.

"No one?" Clement asked, again dubious. "She was such a pretty girl, there must have been *someone*." The detective said this with no mirth, no sweetness in her voice. It was apparent that she considered the information to be of grave importance, not merely circumstantial but indeed *motive* for a death that would look to the untrained eye like simple negligence—a bad batch, a body to ditch—but might prove, under her scrutiny, to be a crime of passion.

Smith thought back on the summer in flashes. Elle in tan leather and silken separates and sundresses made of see-through synthetic, cropped faux furs and gaudy costume jewelry, T-shirts dressed up in archive Alaïa; every time she'd opened the door, saying she was going out, or disappeared at the club for an hour, chatting to God-knows-who in line for the restroom, all of it echoed. He felt an urge to give the woman what she wanted—a name, a narrative—if for no reason other than that it would mean he could leave and never return. But the pearls were all unstrung.

"Really," he said. "She never mentioned anyone by name."

It wasn't much, but the detective seemed satisfied, as suddenly she stood and thanked Smith for his time, then shuffled him toward the door. Her lips formed a smile. She was pleased, then, perhaps because the little information he had was useful, supporting her working theory. That indeed, Elle had already known the man with whom she'd left that night; he was the one she called "the Bronx." They'd been seeing each other in secret—he wasn't the kind of person she could bring around—and she'd become pregnant, which no doubt had upset him. And that night, once her friends had all said their goodbyes, she'd called him, told him to come meet her, then returned with him uptown, where she'd taken drugs, tainted either on purpose or by some unhappy accident—something that was happening all across the city, kids collapsing in euphoric asphyxia—so that his decision to leave her for dead was an act of self-interest in more ways than one. One couldn't underestimate the cruelty of men. If the detective had spoken her thesis rather than implying it with her questions, Smith would have said it *could have been* but was *not necessarily* true. Coincidences did happen; things were often as random as they seemed; people surprised themselves with their capacity for malice, which was every bit as tragic.

Someone she'd known, someone she'd trusted, had decided that she was disposable. That much was clear. And the idea that such a man might have been a lover, even father to her unborn child, was unthinkable, yet Smith *did* allow himself to think it as he arrived home to their wintry apartment. It was no longer prudent to leave the windows open, but it would be weeks before the heat was turned on, so the intervening days would be marked with unease. He closed the window in the kitchen, then fell to the couch, registering Elle's waning scent in the throws. *How well did you know your friend?* The question echoed in the silence. It was impossible to answer now, in her absence, whether she'd fitfully guarded her secrets or if they were unknown even to her. People so rarely saw themselves clearly.

Smith stood, walked to her door, and cracked it open. Inside, the chaos was perfectly preserved, a crypt for a queen. All her earthly effects entombed and gemlike in the dust-strewn darkness: silks and furs and books filled with her illegible hand. He'd been saving it, he realized, for a time not far in the future when he would begin to forget. He picked up a framed photograph of her and Dre as overglammed teens and tossed it, then began ransacking the room in search of something—a love letter, a clue—though as he riffled through the bins in her bathroom, finding tissues in lieu of tests from Clearblue, it became evident how little of her remained in these objects. And with the gravity of that realization, he fell onto her unmade bed, unearthing a cloud of her scent. He breathed it. Every flaring memory—it burned and darkened just as quickly, like a school of fish dispersed.

CHAPTER NINE

The studio of the artist he was to visit the next day was in a section of Brooklyn that took an hour to reach from the office, so Smith had told his boss that he would meet her there, opting for the considerably briefer commute from his apartment. Exiting the train, he checked his phone to find an email from Blythe: She was running behind and he should go in without her. *Mona would be a big get, so work your charm*, she instructed him earnestly. But Smith did not feel very charming. The night in Elle's bed had been fitful and restless. Kaleidoscopic, lurid dreams—the neck and the noose, the vein and the needle, the deer and the wolf and the field through which they sprint—images of violence so vivid he awoke several times in a breathless terror, her moonlit sheets soaked through with his sweat.

Smith buzzed the bell by the artist's name. Mona Ali—known, according to her bio, for creating "virtual-reality experiences that gesture toward a postcolonial futurity"—answered the door at once. Small, with a mostly shaved head, she wore a simple smock and a look of bemusement. "You're not this Blythe person, are you," she asked in a soft and lilting voice.

"No, she's on her way. I'm Smith. I'm on her team at CNVS." Mona assessed him carefully, then, without words, turned and led him into a large industrial space. It was spare, a wide desk in the corner with an Apple desktop and several stacks of books, not Taschen titles Twombly to Ernst but menacing scholarly texts, *Digital Architecture* and *3D Animation*, along with several graphic novels with lavender binding. In the back of the room, between two windows that siphoned light from a narrow alley, was another table topped with VR headsets, some embellished beyond recognition.

The once-sleek body of an Oculus had been painted tangerine, then beaded ornately and embroidered on its sides with towering synthetic plumes so that the person wearing it, Smith's height and clad in pleated purple, became a Crop Over queen, a calypsonian drunk on sugar's harvest.

"My friend," said Mona, gesturing to this bird of paradise, "was just leaving."

"Pleasure," the friend offered warmly. Without ruffling any feathers, they removed the extravagant headset and set it on the table, providing a flash of their face, its strange, illusory beauty.

"Okay, that was major," they said. "I mean, bitch. You've come a long way since that group show in the laundromat. This was just transcendent, and the colors. Like, *wow*."

Mona turned to Smith, her scowl unsettled by flattery. "My biggest fan," she said.

At this, they smiled big, baring cluttered, spotless teeth. There was something hypnotic about them, their unblemished skin of burnt umber— the poreless result of good luck, good genes, and expertly matched foundation. "Your turn," they declared, gesturing to the headset. Smith shook his head no. He knew he'd look a bit silly and had no wish to do so in front of these L-train androgynes. He had a vague sense that these were the sort to whom culture writers referred when they spoke of Afrofuturists: the deep-Brooklyn-dwelling, jewel-tone-wearing, natural-hair-having beneficiaries of the Solange industrial complex. "No, no," Smith insisted. "I should really wait for my boss before I—you know, this is really her visit. I'm just here to observe."

But the friend was resolute. "Nigga, if you don't put on this headset—"

Inside was only black, an abyss through which he could make out the distant glimmer of stars. He turned his head, allowing the illusion to overtake his senses, the reality of the brightly lit room. In one direction, it was nothing for miles, but, turning, he saw that his drift was not aimless, was not a drift at all but a descent into the maw of some red planet. And then he was surrounded by color, an atmosphere of Martian dust he could not smell or feel but in which he was engulfed like a saffron storm until it lifted. And then he was running through an arid landscape. The sky red, the ground red, his body black. It seemed he'd been running a long time, though of course he had not moved at all, when he rounded one of the horned ruby mountains and, coming toward an inlet, saw bodies. They were bathing; they were nude. They were Black. But the substance through which they waded was not water. It was dense and viscous, mud-like. They emerged slathered in it and planted themselves on the shore, then stared up at the sky as if inspecting a faraway mirror. Smith tilted his head and saw, against the red opaque, a video being projected. The show had just begun, and the sky dimmed for it. It was a familiar scene, one from the world he inhabited: archival footage from *Soul Train*, collaged together in an elegant edit of ecstatic bright gyrations. A flurry of bell-bottoms, wingtips, berets, and Afros. Smith looked again at the inhabitants of this strange future, who watched the show with reverence, as if it were all that was left of them, of us, the sole survivors of an abandoned planet.

This was what they knew of their history, and it was joyous.

*   *   *

Smith felt a soft shake, his arm. Immediately, he removed the headset and reentered the room, blinking back its unbearable brightness. He noticed, even before Blythe's arrival, an absence: That dazzling stranger had disappeared in the time elapsed. "How long was I in there?" he asked.

Mona laughed. To her, it was the highest compliment, to have accomplished that thing only art and sex can manage: to obliterate time or to render it useless. The work was just one of three "futurescapes" Mona had developed for an upcoming show, her first solo exhibition, at a small institution that offered grants to those making work at the intersection of art and technology.

"That's why you're perfect for this feature," explained Blythe minutes later after Mona had brewed a pot of tisane—hibiscus, elderberry, and sunflower blossoms—which they drank standing up. "We're really bullish on artists, Black artists especially, creating digital images that advance the social imagination." Despite her tardiness, or perhaps because of it, Blythe was in fine form; she had her pitch face ready and was relentless in the repetition of key bullet points, the benefits of the *mainstream reach* the CNVS platform could offer—though, of course, unspoken was the fact that CNVS would benefit equally, if not more, from the association, Mona's image used to burnish their corporate reputation even as it eroded her own.

And wasn't that why he was here also? Smith thought as Mona began to speak directly to him. "I want to ask, with my work, how do we shed the pain of our past while holding on to its legacy? Slavery, colonization, incarceration—these atrocities are intrinsically linked to what's so beautiful about us now," she said, her eyes on his. "But they're also modes of extermination that plague us still, threatening our survival. So the landscapes, they're art, but also a kind of radical therapy. Because, like, I'm not sure we survive if we can't envision possibilities beyond this."

Smith took careful note, as she spoke, of her use of the plural first-person, *we* and *us*, so that when her tone shifted and she stated pragmatically that she didn't see "working with y'all" as "possible," it was more the syntactical shift that shook him. "It's not even about the incident from last year," she continued. "Though y'all did fuck up." Smith glanced at Blythe, who wore a look of practiced empathy. "It's just, like, your whole thing is art as commodity," she stated plainly, and the honey in her voice grew cold. "And I'm trying to make something more."

Without a pause, so quickly that the two statements formed a continuous stream, Blythe responded: "But we're completely committed to access, innovation, pushing the bounds of what people understand to be art," she explained with still-extant hope; perhaps she really believed in what she was selling. She turned to Smith for confirmation, and he looked away, at the floor.

"It's a no," said Mona firmly. "I'm sorry you came all this way."

Claiming a seat on the train, Smith watched heads become midsections: crotches, stomachs. Nearby, a pearl-eyed infant in the arms of its mother examined him closely. Smith smiled, then, embarrassed, looked away. The next stop saw a modest influx, forcing those already present to shuffle. A thick-necked man who'd been near the door moved inward and, standing directly before Smith, raised his arm to catch the metal bar above. His T-shirt—a gray, unremarkable thing—lifted up to reveal his soft parts. The pillow of his bulging stomach, testing the elasticity of a visible band, was covered in a scatter of chestnut hair. It looked prickly to the touch and grew denser just below his belly button. His scent was a mute but intoxicating blend of sweat and off-brand deodorant. Smith gazed up at his face and felt a pang of want.

It wasn't fashionable to admit, but Smith sometimes thought that—given the right place and time—he'd fuck almost anyone. The few times he'd actually said this, usually to gay strangers after an ocean of chemical cocktails, he'd watched their faces stiffen before asking follow-ups: What about this guy? That guy? Eventually, he'd confess the limits of his own supposition—in truth, he'd said it mostly to provoke—but stood by its underlying logic: that he was not so much interested sexually in gratification as in being desired. This undiscerning sexual appetite was ironically countered by a toxic rigidity in his standard for whom he'd claim in public. He cringed, in particular, at interracial couples in which the Black partners were observably more attractive, presuming without so much as a morsel of context what this said about their psyches, how they viewed the value of their bodies in the sexual marketplace. Like the time, years ago, when a friend from college—a stunning golden creature—had shacked up with his goon-faced partner. Smith had gotten blind drunk at their housewarming party and, in response to two strangers commenting on the couple's collective beauty, remarked that, in his opinion, they were "hardly the same species at all."

At the Myrtle stop, the crowd loosened, opening seats on Smith's either end. The hairy man slouched into one—his musk now overwhelming, top notes of armpit and gym sock with base of cedar. The hairs on his meaty arm bristled Smith's skin, and he found himself contemplating just how long it had been. Months, certainly, since his last great fuck, his libido not so much subdued as deprioritized, background noise to an enduring psychic torment. Pleasure of any kind since the arrest, since Elle, had seemed an unearned indulgence—and sex was always tricky.

Though with A, his first, things were easy. A blond Californian with a swimmer's build, he was hot in an obvious way, like summers by the beach—tan lines, riptides. An aspiring playwright, he'd bonded with Smith over Beckett in the dimly lit garden of a frat house that was hosting its annual Ode to Foam. A did not smoke but didn't mind that Smith did, on occasion, and so when they kissed and he tasted the mix of cheap liquor and tar, he said nothing but "Come home with me." *Home* meant the housing complex across from Smith's own, where A shared perhaps the largest freshman dorm on campus with a Venezuelan plutocrat whose father had been recently smuggled in a suitcase to an island in the French Caribbean without the burdens of extradition. They fell into an easy rhythm, sleeping at A's most nights and building a romance on the soft foundation of things in common—Ben Lerner and the National. They ignored everything else.

A was a good kisser and practiced at sex, having had three boyfriends in high school with the grace of his parents—two centrist Californians, both public-school teachers, to whom he'd come out at twelve. Nonetheless, Smith put off the inevitable act, opting for everything else in his arsenal, the litany of sex acts which for him were still new. It was new to suck a dick and call someone his boyfriend, to meet this boy's parents, to claim and be claimed. A was understanding at first and then restless after many months' effort only loosened Smith's sphincter enough to accommodate an additional finger. So finally, in the first-thought way of teens, they scheduled the act for Valentine's. The plan was this: Dinner in downtown Palo Alto at a restaurant that served savory crepes. Two straight couples would join them, friends of A's, and after dinner they'd all go to a kegger at one of the dorms. Smith would eat light, and, following a brief appearance at the party, the two would abscond to fuck.

Dinner was fine and uneventful, its sole friction being the moment the bill arrived. The two straight boys predictably tossed in their cards, then A did the same, insisting on covering Smith. The kindness of the gesture obscured its regressive politics—the implication being that it was a man's job to pay and that A, who planned later to be the penetra*tor* and not the penetra*ted*, was the man—but not a measure of guilt, which Smith felt often with A, for whom money was exceedingly tight. He earned a laughable pittance at the student store at which he was required to work as a stipulation of his financial aid. "I insist," said A with a forbidding look. "It's a special night."

The party, by the time they arrived, was a chaotic blur—handle pulls and keg stands, punch bowls near radioactive with the neon of plastic-brand vodka. Everyone was being single and annoying about it. Sticking their tongues down each other's throats as Ke$ha compelled them all to go "Har-har-har ha-ha-hard." Quietly, Smith envied them and sipped his drink, wondering how he'd found himself in such a conventional romance. Some gay YA. The wrong book, the worst film. The music in the hall was loud—Flo Rida, white girls attempting to twerk—so he was relieved to find A in a quiet room. There, he sat atop a friend's bed beyond a poster of Kobe Bryant. He was now slurring his words slightly, having gone for the punch, his tanned skin red with passion as he argued with the boy on the bed opposite, a bespectacled nerd whom Smith knew to be the son of a prominent Black tech CEO. The subject of their debate was affirmative action in college admissions—a topic so played as to be of no interest to Smith were it not his own boyfriend on the opposition. After twice reiterating that he was an "unbiased" party, A invoked the case of his elder sister, a straight-A student and decorated diver whose many accolades had not earned her admission to the elite school where now they sat, her spot having presumably gone to someone browner and less deserving, though A was quick to clarify that he didn't mean any of the Black students he actually *knew*. "It's just ridiculous that her race would work against her, because we grew up, if not poor, then certainly working class. And both of *you——*" he began, eyes flitting between the wealthy Black sons of wealthy Black fathers with an oozing liquid rage. He'd forfeit the point without speaking it, though of course he'd said plenty, enough to sour Smith into a dissociative fugue as he endured their slow and labored sex hours after. "I just think," A had continued, "it's an *insult* to Black people."

Years later, Nia would observe a familiar pattern. "You always date guys, white guys, who you know will disappoint you. And it's avoidant, really, because it makes you invulnerable. You just wait for the thing that disqualifies them, then you get to hate them for it."

By then, she had a string of examples to admit into evidence. B, the boarding-school WASP with the clandestine stockpile of Ayn Rand. C, the slender ginger whose time in Teach for America had taught him not only how to Dougie but to speak in drunken patois. D, E, F, G—and between them, an unknowable sum of first kisses, first dates, and mornings-after.

In New York, sex seemed to Smith like a game. Scan the room for the hottest stranger. Take him home, rough him up, or, if he wasn't interested, move on to the next. Never dawdle, don't obsess. Nights spent this way, he struck gold on occasion. Weeks became months in the heat of another: conceptual furniture designers and experimental-phase sk8ers and brainy engineers who resembled JFK. Boys for whom he felt real affection, who proved themselves over time to be kind and essentially harmless yet who bore the brunt of his resentment nonetheless, their bodies surrogate targets for a seething rage—toward the parade of acquitted cops and off-color comments. The meth head on East Eighty-Third who'd asked, unprompted and in the throes of their drug-fueled sex, if Smith liked getting his "nigger hole stuffed," then expressed confusion once they both came shortly after and Smith called an Uber home. *That was fun :p*, the man had texted, a pulse in Smith's lap, as he watched the wintry city wake beyond the window.

By the time Smith met N, he had an undeniable *type*: handsome, clean-cut WASPs whose boyish charm offered only temporary reprieve from the burden of their stripped-down personalities. Ivy League pretentiosos with corporate jobs or family money to buttress their unrealized creative ambitions—they could talk the talk, were often fluent in Baldwin, but revealed themselves in subtle, analogous ways.

N struck him as different. An Australian in town for a year on a J-1 visa, he met Smith at a rave in deep Ridgewood. He didn't check any of Smith's boxes. Hadn't gone to a fancy school, didn't have a fancy job. He tended bar and seemed to lack any ambition beyond that. But he had a verve that silenced those concerns. And yes, probably he drank too much and used too many drugs—they both did. But he was a thrill, a treat, a belly laugh at parties. And he was kind, forgiving of Smith's many faults, the ways he could be cruel. So the fissures and flags—the time N recalled his friends on "gap yeah" making fun of the fact that he was hit on often by Black guys, or his penchant for petty theft—did not ignite Smith's ire. If anything, his candor was refreshing, making visible a lack others hid. Carolyn liked him. And even Elle approved, though she did let loose one comment, drunk at dinner with Dre: "He's no great mind, but it's okay because Smith likes to be smarter. An intellectual dom. Or emotional, if you wanna get dark."

When it finally came, the proverbial straw, it was typically small. A stray, nothing comment. N had overheard Smith's mom on a family call, held rudely over speaker as the two sat to lunch, and after it ended remarked offhand that he hadn't expected her to talk "like that." Smith paid the check, and they ambled back to his apartment through the stale summer air. Smith thought to, but did not, ask the obvious question—*Like what?*—because of course he knew. That his mother's cadence, the density of her twang, was misaligned with N's grasp of his background. This wasn't the woman he'd conjured from the information offered, a Harvard-educated surgeon, the debutante daughter of a lawyer and businessman.

They'd arrived home to an empty apartment—Elle was out of town that weekend—and drifted about the doubled space in silence. It was just large enough to lose one another. Smith picked up a book to read on the couch, while N, restless, went from bedroom to kitchenette, attempting to reclaim his attention. Finally, he went into the bathroom, turned on the shower, then eventually emerged nude in a cloud of steam. They were, four months into the relationship, past the need for foreplay. When Smith saw he was hard, he knew they would fuck, so he followed him into the bedroom. They barely kissed. He slid into the boy on a palmful of lube, flipped him onto his back, and watched the crest of his head beat softly against the headboard. They met eyes. In that moment, Smith felt toward him only malice, a malice he knew he would never express. N would never know why things ended, weeks later, after a dizzying agony of days in which Smith would inflict all the subtle and incisive hurt of which he was capable, drunk on the memory of what had that day broken.

The train rattled on like the bed in Smith's memory, its headboard creaking with the heft of each thrust. *Like what*, it creaked as he emptied into him.

Like what,
like what,
like fucking what, bitch.

CHAPTER TEN

Out of either superstition or routine, the David Smiths held to a nearly identical schedule ahead of their second court date. At four p.m. on Wednesday, October 30, Smith left work and headed back to his apartment, where his father was already waiting in a rental car outside. They set out on the road, speeding east on the Long Island Expressway, and arrived in Southampton amid a gust of golden light. They proceeded to Citarella, where they purchased more or less the same items and ate them again in twin beds fit for brothers, sitcom reruns lulling them into an uneasy sleep. Their morning routine was the same, their suits. And though neither acknowledged this ritual, each understood its grave importance.

It seemed too good to be true that they would, in a matter of hours, be released from this nightmare, which had worn on the psyche of each with a growing, gestative weight. Even the return of Smith's lab tests, clean and clear, and a letter confirming he'd completed twelve hours to Mancini's hard-won satisfaction had offered no comfort. Too soon, it seemed, would they be able to seal this experience inside of that record, *Mistakes*, and move on with their lives. And so it was with an almost comforting sense of fate that the Smiths, pulling up to the Southampton court, found a scene of utter chaos—hordes of enraged and bewildered defendants loudly demanding entry and answers.

"Ma'am, do you know what's going on?" Senior called out to one such woman. There was *no judge, no judge,* she explained in heavily accented English, somewhere Caribbean. And as she did so, more turned-away litigants encircled their car, a boulder in a rushing river. From here, they could see the dwindling legions at the courthouse doors expressing their grievances—they'd missed work, they'd come all this way—to the chagrin of two cops whose message was now clear: *Go home, get out of here, get.*

Through the fracas, Smith glimpsed his lawyer in a dry-cleaned suit, craning his neck to find them. "*There* you two are." Walsh beamed as he ambled over, then crouched beside the passenger door. "I've been calling you. What a mess! I'll tell you, in twenty years, I've never seen this." The lawyer embellished the young woman's account, explaining that the presiding judge had, not thirty minutes ago, left due to a family emergency, which would have been inconvenient but not catastrophic were it any day but today, when the on-call judge was undergoing a procedure—nothing serious, he assured them pointlessly. "Anyway, this shouldn't affect you or your outcomes at all, I've already confirmed with the DA. You'll just need an up-to-date drug test, that letter from Mancini, and we'll still be good to go. And I've filed a request already for a new court date. It's going to be a real headache, rescheduling everyone from today, but I'm hoping we can get in end of November, mid-December at the latest, and—"

"Wait, um," said Smith, now startled, "you mean this could extend all the way to December?"

"Well." Walsh clucked his teeth and exhaled brusquely. "What you have to understand is these small-town courts only meet every few weeks in the off-season. And now they'll have *all of today's* cases to reschedule. I'm telling you, in twenty years, I've never seen this."

"So how long?"

"I'm not a betting man," said Walsh, eagerly employing his catch-phrase. "But I've seen August dates pushed back to the week of Thanksgiving, then pushed back again to a snowy day in February . . ." He trailed off, seeing Smith's crestfallen face. "You have to be patient, hold tight. We're going to get this handled as long as you keep up with your testing, your meetings—the AA's gonna look really good, by the way, I've already mentioned that to the DA—and maybe we throw in a few more hours with Mancini as a show of good faith. Show them this isn't all bullshit; you're a good egg, reformed. The most important thing is that you stay out of trouble. As I've said, your piss lights up with so much as a whiff of oregano, and the whole deal's out the window. You understand?"

"Of course," said Smith.

Walsh leaned in, locking eyes for a beat. He winked. "Bye, Dad," he said to Senior before disappearing into the parking lot's swarm.

While the news had, on Smith, the effect of melancholy, Senior seemed in high spirits. As they pulled onto Main Street, he went on and on about what a glorious day it was, brisk but clear. A blessing, he affirmed—though the worst kind: in disguise. Having both cleared their schedules, they could spend the rest of the day together. And they could be grateful for that: the "quality time," the "weather," and the fact that Smith hadn't gotten arrested in a less idyllic locale, Newark or Reno or Gowanus.

They landed at a café in Bridgehampton that was known during summer for its scene, the see and be-seen, a watering hole of chic patrons fraternizing over steak frites. But today, the room was almost empty, just three other tables for breakfast. Near the entrance, an elderly woman in a cream turtleneck hunched over the Thursday crossword, a Montblanc pen perched above.

Their waiter arrived. He was achingly handsome, thirty-something with shoulder-length hair, coiffed back with natural oils, then tucked behind his ears, which were large and, like the rest of him, a surfer's golden brown. The last time Smith had come to the restaurant, the man had been a topic of frantic conversation, a lengthy debate over which way he swung. "Hello, gentlemen, my name is Terry," he said, his pink lips parting. "I'll be taking care of you. Can I get you two some wine or cocktails to begin?" The offer seemed, at first, like a joke—it wasn't yet noon—but looking around the room, Smith saw that indeed there were other tables enjoying weekday mimosas and sad morning wine.

"We'll just have water," said Senior forbiddingly.

"Still or sparkling?" Terry asked. Senior ordered still, and Smith nearly spoke up to clarify that he meant *tap*, but by then the heartthrob had exited stage left, soon returning with an indigo bottle. No harm, Smith figured; *he* wasn't paying. His prior visit to the restaurant, mid-July, had been memorable precisely because he *had* been paying, if only his even share, which had mounted swiftly as a friend ordered bottle after bottle of marked-up rosé. Smith had watched in horror as what was meant to be a casual lunch devolved into a $150-a-head affair. Initially, Smith had made use of game theory, deciding it was best to abstain in an effort to curb the grand total, but seeing his prudence was of no import to the others, he caved and began to drink with a vengeful indulgence, ending the meal so slurring drunk that he'd written his number on the bill for Terry. The next day, crippled by dehydration and shame—a supercut of every clumsy pass he'd ever made at a beautiful boy—he hadn't left bed until noon.

Terry returned to take their orders, and Smith caught his eye, attempting to discern if there was any recognition. But the man wrote down his order with a neutral expression before turning to Senior who, owl-eyed, examined the menu, then asked a few questions about the provenance of the salmon and the preparation of the lobster flambé. His enthusiasm for fine dining was amusing to Smith, who'd always found it a tedious grift. Lured once into a tasting menu for Carolyn's birthday, he'd choked down the opinion, along with each of the seventeen courses, that he found nothing more offensive than flavored foam.

The food arrived, and as they ate, Senior spoke about life in Atlanta, the ways he'd been filling his time since leaving his post as Whitley's president two years prior. "This Christmas, you ought to come home for more than a week," he said between bites of grilled homard du Maine. "It would mean a lot to your mother." Smith smirked at the sentence, its construction implying that it would mean nothing whatsoever to him, though he knew they both wanted him home. Over the phone, they'd mentioned it often, attempting a casual tone each time. But Smith was resistant to the idea on principle—a betrayal of himself at sixteen, locked away like Chekhov's Irina, listening to sad indie songs and yearning for a bigger life. Terry returned to shill another bottle of still. And Smith pivoted the subject to the one grad-school course that Senior still taught in his semiretirement, its focus on the Black church and how it had functioned as an organizing body in movements from civil rights to apartheid: a technology of resistance unintelligible to those outside.

Terry collected their plates and recommended a Key lime pie. "I may step outside for a second," said Smith when it arrived minutes later, delivered by a second server. He'd had two coffees with lunch and was now visibly trembling. Emerging into the mum afternoon, he closed his eyes and breathed deeply, the scent of sea mist and diluted smoke in the wind.

He walked toward it, rounding the corner to find the handsome waiter propped up against the wall. Smith stared a moment, taking note of the cool-guy way he caught the filter between his teeth to accommodate texting, but feeling observed, the man looked up and let his cigarette fall. "Something wrong?" he asked with apparent annoyance.

"Shit, sorry," Smith fumbled. "No, I, I was just wondering if you have an extra."

The man hesitated, then pulled a pack of Parliaments from his back pocket, thumbing the cover to offer them. He tugged a second one out for himself, then kicked off the wall to share a flame. Up close, Smith saw his skin had a shopworn quality.

"Thanks," said Smith, watching the man's mouth inhale. He worried for a moment that his dad would smell the smoke on him but decided it was worth the risk. This flirtation, this breath. "I was wondering, um, do you remember me?"

The man smirked. "From table six?"

"No, I mean, I came here during the summer." Lines spread about Terry's seafoam eyes like hairline fractures. "We were a five-top, all got pretty sloshed."

"Lotta drunk people here in the summer, man." He laughed, the high-pitched bleat of a cartoon pothead. Relieved, Smith felt the urge to walk away and leave Terry to his break, but figured that would seem all the more bizarre. He took a step back and leaned against the wall, as Terry was doing, staring out at passing cars. They breathed in tandem. "That dude you're in there with," the man said suggestively. "Is he . . ."

"My dad," Smith answered, cringing at the implication.

"Cool, man. Yeah, you never know." Again that bleat. "Though you don't really look alike."

"So I've heard." Smith smiled. "So, you live out here full-time?"

"Half the year. I'm heading out in a week, actually."

"Where to?"

"Colorado. Aspen," he answered. "I've got a winter gig out there, waiting tables at an après-ski." Smith nodded. He'd heard of these types, people who bounced between beach and ski towns, filling seasonal demand for bartenders and bottle girls. He imagined the same muumuu-clad leisurelies in midwinter Moncler recognizing the man and thinking to themselves, *Well, what are the odds*, as if they weren't tethered by the merciless demands of the marketplace. The ship and the barnacle.

"And you make good money doing that?"

"Dude, you wouldn't believe. I made like forty K this summer."

Fuck, Smith mouthed. It didn't seem like a bad life; good money, year-round spent in scenic locales. Surfing, skiing, fucking the tourists. "How are the people?" he asked.

His cigarette thinned, the handsome waiter lit another with the first's amber end. "Most are pricks, obviously," he said. "You know, poor people, or even middle class, they think of eating out as a luxury, so when they're at a restaurant, they're on their best behavior. But to rich people, it's just another night, so they bring their bullshit with them. But bright side? Most have never *worked* in a restaurant, so they don't know the game."

"The game?"

"Vegas rules, man. The house always wins," he offered by way of explanation. Smith raised an eyebrow. "Come on, can't you see? Everything's set up to work you for every dollar you got. Like the menu—when you go to a nice restaurant, what do you think the house wants you to order?" Smith guessed the obvious answer—the most expensive thing. Terry smiled. "Nah, they want you to get whatever's got the best spread between what *they* pay and what *you* pay, which is usually the fish. Ten dollars a pound and they charge thirty-five, but they'll put it right beneath a fifty-dollar porterhouse that costs the house thirty-four. Gets you thinking, *Oh, the fish is so affordable.*" Smith made a *huh* sound. "Tons of small things like that. Plus, the good waiters, career guys like me, we know how to work a table just based on personalities. It's all in the body language, the conversation. You read who's the alpha, who's calling the shots and gonna order share plates without asking the others. Or, if someone looks out of place, got the wrong shoes and the wrong bag, made their rez a month ago on OpenTable instead of just calling ahead, you know they're here to prove something—it's a big night for them—so you ask if they want another bottle loudly, not *rude*-loud but loud-loud, make 'em feel like the whole room's watching."

"And that works?" Smith asked.

"Like a charm, my dude. That's the game in these towns. We figure out what you're after, then make you pay for it."

In the car, Smith asked to head back to the city, but Senior suggested the beach. He didn't mention the cigarette stench but kept the windows down all the way to Montauk, where the lush state parks fell away and the island thinned to a needle. Smith thought of Terry. His mouth. What it had said. How the whole economy of this island, that great natural beauty extending into the Sound, trafficked on profitable illusions: that proximity to the thing was the thing itself—all the share-housing debtors at the end of America—that freedom was something for sale. Somewhere along this road lived his lawyer and, miles back, Mancini, and somewhere else the DA and the judge who would decide his fate—all of them understood this logic and served it in their way, even as they played on opposite sides. The state fed the lawyer who fed the counselor, symbiotic organisms bound in orgastic synergy. They reached the beach. It was quiet. A great gray sky stretched out across the ocean like the fat underside of a whale. They took off their shoes and felt the sand on their feet. Pebbles, shattered shells. The water washed them clean.

CHAPTER ELEVEN

November yawned wide and blew leaves to every corner, padding parks in beds of dying yellow. It was almost charming, but the days were too short and the weather too brisk. The news cycle surrounding the manhunt had gone eerily quiet, like a dead-end night, though once, twice, Smith ran into an old acquaintance—some club fiend whose name he could barely recall—who'd demand an update, couched always in the careful language of condolences—*I was so sorry to hear about*s and *Did they ever find the motherfuckers*—reminding him that vast swaths of the city were a captive audience to his grief. So he pared down his rotation, from home to work to home to work to AA on occasion, where he'd sit there in silence, then leave minutes early to avoid the coffee-and-Oreo chitchat.

And soon it was Carolyn's birthday, a date that generally landed right before or even *on* Thanksgiving. Just as Scorpio season bled into Sagittarius and the city emptied, she found herself in the unfortunate position of having to assemble a dinner from those who remained. Her grandparents had decamped to Long Island, so she decided to host at their empty apartment, the three-story loft she had occupied for her first year back in the city, her parents having sold their place uptown.

"Wow, I've missed this," said Smith as he entered the foyer, where Ann kept her studio. While her canvases out in Southampton depicted beach scenes in gauzy pastels, those she worked on here tended toward the urbane: Degas-inspired dancers whose limbs she sometimes studied through a window at Joffrey; sullen, rosacea-prone aunts and cousins; and a number of evening scenes, cocktail hours awash in flesh and color. They continued toward the living room, where Smith gazed up at his favorite of these: a frame from Ann's memory, a wedding, its suited guests imbibing heavily in the foreground while a blurred stroke waltzed behind them. The impressionistic lines offered the illusion of bodies in motion, mid-laugh, mid-kiss—a kinetic revelry which seemed to seep from the canvas and into the room surrounding it.

Smith glanced down at the table. "Just five of us," he observed. In the kitchen, Carolyn continued to grind fresh pepper over a pot.

"I told you I wanted to keep things small."

Smith studied the names in her looping scrawl: his own, Fernanda, Lacey, Oliver. Last year, she'd had her twenty-fifth in the very same room, a dinner to which she had (in an uncharacteristic bid at cuteness) planned to host twenty-four, which quickly swelled to thirty, thirty-three; a full restaurant's volume, for whom her friend Raf was expected to cook. She'd pulled it off, narrowly, not that it mattered. By the time the skirt steak and roasted rosemary potatoes were served, most of the thirty-three guests were sated, drunk, a few having already begun their darty-eyed trips to the restrooms. It seemed as soon as they all sat for dinner, some had begun standing, delivering toasts of increasing belligerence—to their host's *grace* and *joie de vivre*—excuses to glug through the bottles of wine, then move on to liquor. More were invited. Those more invited more, and soon the dinner devolved into a house party attended mainly by strangers who, *thank God*, didn't steal or destroy any artworks but did manage to drain the vodka bar like moths at a silken seam. The next morning, prepping frantically for her grandparents' return, Carolyn had called it her *best birthday yet*.

"Lacey, how long are you in town?" Smith asked Carolyn's cousin an hour later over dinner. She bore a striking resemblance to Carolyn. Raised in New York, she now lived in Los Angeles but made frequent trips home on the pretext of client meetings and gynecological appointments, mere alibis for checking on Carolyn. Both only children, they were each other's keepers. Lacey was also twenty-six but seemed both older and younger than her cousin. She worked in entertainment in some impressively adult capacity and rented a house in Santa Monica with her long-term boyfriend, their sex life predictably vanilla—based, at least, on her scandalized reactions to Carolyn's exploits, which she insisted on sharing, just like when they were girls, newly bloomed.

"Just for Thanksgiving," she said. "Figured I'd come a few days early for C's birthday."

"You're from here?" Ollie asked, leaning in so that the hollows of his cheeks took shadows. The room was almost dark, lit by a single lamp in the kitchen and the long tapers that crowded the table.

"Westchester."

"And is that where you'll go for Thanksgiving?" he continued, now propping his whole torso up on his elbows to loom even closer.

Carolyn answered: "No, the whole Astley clan is headed out to Southampton to stay with Dad's parents—everyone other than my mum, of course." She said this brightly, as if her parents' divorce and her mother's subsequent return to London just a few years ago hadn't been the torture it was. As far as Smith knew, she hadn't forgiven her father for the cruel and seemingly arbitrary way in which he'd ended his thirty-year marriage and even now agreed to see him only on special occasions.

Tactically sidestepping the implications of this answer, Lacey asked Ollie the same question. Ollie was voluble, answering that he was back in the Village—the rent-controlled two-bedroom in which he'd grown up—having taken a leave of absence from Cambridge on the grounds that he had lost interest in his dissertation topic, Lovelessness in the Literature of Early England. He made no reference to the catastrophic breakup he'd suffered at the hands of another doctorate of philosophy candidate, the subsequent depressive episode from which he'd only just emerged—he'd practically showered and headed straight to dinner—though it still showed in his eyes faintly. "Medievalism, that's fascinating," Lacey replied, her voice taunting slightly. "You don't meet nearly enough medievalists in Los Angeles."

"And for good reason," said Ollie.

The meal—pappardelle with slowly braised lamb and rosemary-garlic focaccia—was tasty and rich, and the combined effect of the kombucha's caffeine and copious sugar offered the illusion of a buzz so convincing that conversation soon enlivened. Perhaps there was also some pressure, because of their abstinence and the evident downsizing from years prior, to summon their most buoyant selves, their best stories. There was Lacey's, about the time Carolyn had persuaded her in customs, at age ten, to swap passports, which they hadn't switched back until fifteen. And Carolyn's, about the girl in her freshman dorm who'd stolen that passport and held it hostage for months in retribution for a crush kissed; and Ollie's, about being chased out of a wedding last summer after drunkenly coming on to the bride; and Ollie's other, about being chased out of a bar on the rue de

Jouy for soaking a love letter in absinthe, then lighting it on fire. Smith jumped in to tell his about the only time he'd dined and dashed, with Carolyn at a bar in San Francisco. How obvious they'd been, shuffling toward the door and speaking loudly of cigarettes, but once outside, they'd ripped through the plate-glass evening, booking it up, up, up and then down, down, down one of those steep slopes that marred the city's landscape. Carolyn said she'd gone back, months after, and tipped twenty-two dollars on a Diet Coke; Smith never had.

Finally, Carolyn stood to deliver her toast, the night's sole surviving tradition. "What can I say," she began. "It's been a year. Kind of a nightmare for most of us. Who'd have thought, a year ago, that I'd be bullying you all into drinking gingerade on my birthday?" She tossed her head back through the flicker. "I'd be remiss not to mention that we're down a guest tonight," she said, pausing significantly, and Smith felt his heartbeat quicken. He pictured Elle at the table, just there, catching his eye across the distance; she smiled, stood, and turned to smoke. "Tonight, we're only five," Carolyn continued, "but somehow I feel the warmth of a full room." She took her time to lock eyes with each. "My reasons to breathe."

A beat passed and Smith lifted his glass. "Hear, hear." They clinked. And conversation resumed with levity.

Fernanda had just stood to assemble dessert—strawberries in freshly whipped cream—when the room startled at the sound of a loud, low buzz. "Are we expecting others?" asked Ollie, grinning at the prospect. The candlelight dimmed his teeth and made him look ugly.

Rune, when he entered the room, wore a look less of surprise than mild disgust. His brown eyes were focused and cruel, his full lips pursed. It was an expression of such coldness and barely concealed contempt as to deflate the night's good humor. But Carolyn appeared to take no notice as she stood to embrace him. "You came," she said, planting a kiss on his cheek from which he pulled away swiftly. "Meet everyone. This is——" She introduced them one by one, ending with Smith, "whom of course you've met."

Rather than respond to the names with his own, Rune nodded and lifted a hand to show what it carried: a white paper bag printed with the name of his restaurant. "Dessert," he said simply.

"*Our hero*. We were just about to resort to eating strawberries with our bare hands."

They all laughed loudly at the slight—white noise that Rune tuned out completely as he placed the bag on the countertop and leaned in to whisper in Carolyn's ear. Out of the corner of his eye, Smith watched them, pondering the source of Rune's stiff formality, so at odds with the sex haze in which he'd been enraptured at the opening. Yes, affairs were generally conducted in secret, but that didn't explain the sudden shift. And why come to a party only to ruin it?

"We'll be back, just a minute," Carolyn announced, pulling Rune by two fingers toward the balcony. Through double doors, the two emerged onto a slim stone structure that looked past a waist-high banister onto Lafayette, a black-and-white billboard of a gloomy, mop-haired model in the distance. Just a windowed wall separated them from the rest of the party, who could still see but not hear them, so their arc was a silent wide shot: an asymmetry of bodies spliced from different films.

"Who is that morose man," asked Ollie, casually inspecting the contents of the bag, a hefty box bound in twine. With a steak knife, he ripped it open and lifted its lid to reveal a cake of spectacular beauty: a pristine half-moon encased in a dark chocolate shell, its surface encrusted with gold flakes and topped with six slender candles that flocked together like fasting nuns. Smith and Fernanda locked eyes, each willing the other to answer.

"Rune McKittrick, the chef," said Lacey. "My mom has his cookbook. I didn't realize C knew him."

"Looks like they more than *know* one another," Ollie retorted. Outside, immune to observation, the couple made language of their bodies. Rune's posture slackened; he now stood with a visible hunch, his face angled downward in the guilty way of children unable to lock eyes as they lie. He was speaking at a manic cadence, making great use of his hands—they moved as if unattached to a body, circling rhythmically, swift as a wind turbine. Carolyn's was less legible. Her chin tilted down to diminish her height, arms crossed in an attempt at warmth or protection. When finally she spoke, her breath bloomed in a cloud from her lips.

"How long has this been going on then?" asked Ollie, eyeing Fernanda, who looked away. He turned to Smith. "Come on, you two. Give up the goods."

"I don't know exactly," said Fernanda. "Smith, you met him?"

Again, Rune was speaking, though less frantically now. He stepped toward her as he did so, halving the space between them. His ungloved hand on her body, he rubbed one spot gently as she glanced over the banister at the thrill of cars beneath.

"Yes, briefly, at the opening of Inducio."

"Right. So, early September."

Frowning, Lacey asked the obvious question—"He's married though, right?"—in a tone so artificially neutral it writhed with discontent. "To that fashion editor woman, Amy . . . *Something*—I remember she kept her own name. Does she know?"

"I don't think they're the ethical-nonmonogamy types, if that's what you mean," answered Fernanda, intuiting the question's subtext. Smith grimaced, remembering the woman he'd met: Her pallid intensity. The way she'd allowed Rune to roam but, like a beachside mother, kept him always in view. Her liberal use of the first-person plural. *We love. We do. We are.* She was undoubtedly the sort who, confronted with the idea of open relationships by fashion gays at brand dinners, crinkled her poreless nose and said, "Well, that sounds fun, but not for *us*."

"She doesn't," Smith confirmed.

Lacey replied, "*Oh*," then glanced left. The two had moved into one orbit, a shared and visible breath between them. In heeled slides, she had him by an inch, so he angled his chin upward to examine her face, whatever there appeared. And finally, he made his request, the reason he'd come: what big or little thing he feared like death she'd dare deny him.

"We're ready for cake," Ollie blurted as the door closed and the two reappeared by candlelight.

"I can't stay," said Rune. "I just came to drop this off." In his tone was the hint of a joke, an awareness of the absurdity of that alibi, which appeared on his face as a tight-lipped smile. His pink lips parted for clean, square teeth—he *was* handsome—and he imbued his goodbye with a surfeit of charm as if to negate all behavior before it. "It was a *pleasure* to meet you all."

Carolyn escorted him out, back through Ann's studio, then reappeared at the living room's entrance. "So, what are we talking about?" she asked coyly.

"You," Smith answered. "Obviously."

"Her favorite subject," said Ollie.

"It's not like that," said Carolyn, aware of how it looked: another engineered drama with herself at its center. She approached the table but continued to stand. "I *like* him," she explained, placing a hand on Lacey's shoulder. She was the one at the table most likely to interpret infidelity as saying something about one's character. And perhaps, having coached her cousin through years of such dramas, Lacey had hoped that sobriety would mean she was done. With her touch, Carolyn tried to communicate something: She was the same girl who'd chopped, at Lacey's request, ten inches of hair with a pair of blunt scissors after a *Parent Trap* matinee—then, after tears, cut her own to match it. She knew her core, her pink insides.

"We should slice this," said Lacey, "the cake." She took her cousin's hand as she stood, then dropped it as she fled toward the kitchen.

Fernanda pressed for the story, everything said outside. From her greedy smile, it was clear that this excitement had made her evening, and Smith thought cruelly that this was precisely Carolyn's value to her, these tales of misadventure adding texture to her plotless life. "Well, he called me earlier to say happy birthday," Carolyn began. "And I mentioned dinner, just in passing, said he could drop by after work if he wished, but I didn't think he would actually *come*."

"Yes, he seemed shocked to see us."

"Not at all. It was, well, driving here, he got a voicemail from his wife—I suppose he'd texted her some vague excuse about a work thing that might go late. Which struck her as suspect, or whatever, so little miss Nancy Drew did some sleuthing on his desktop: iCal, emails, messages."

Barely suppressing her glee, Fernanda mouthed the word *no*.

"Luckily, he's not a complete dinosaur, so he'd had the good sense to delete our chats, but then—God, the woman *is* clever—she went to the fucking *web* version of Instagram and read his DMs." Ollie gasped with warped delight. "And I'd messaged a few days ago asking where to meet him for lunch. Otherwise, our correspondence was nothing damning. In any case, he's managed to convince her it's just a flirtation, that it hasn't gone anywhere yet. I guess she's not so clever after all," she said, her tone darkening. Finally, she took a seat at the table, her back to the canvas on the wall. The light reattached to her features: her cheeks, still pink from the wind, her eyes searching flame. "He's pinned it on me, made me out to be some fangirl he's indulging—the whole thing is absurd. And what's worse is that he agreed to call me tomorrow, in front of her, on *speaker*, and ask, or, I suppose, *tell* me not to ever contact him again. And I'm meant to actually *participate* in this performance, their marriage, affect disappointment that our *flirtation* can't continue." Flanked by the scene of a more lively party, she stared at her cake, its lacquer shell. "If he thinks I'm going to give some Oscar-worthy performance to save him, he's delusional," she resolved, plucking a candle from the cake's center and sucking clean its wickless end. "I don't know where on earth he got the idea that I have his best interest at heart."

CHAPTER TWELVE

There is always a degree of artifice in firing someone. One must choose the right place and time to do the firing, then direct the to-be-fired person *to* that place *at* that time, all without them picking up on the fact that they're about to be fired. Given terminations are generally decided upon several weeks before their execution, the interim can prove difficult, a time in which one must attempt to treat the terminal person typically, or as typically as possible. One must speak about *long-term goals and priorities*, while knowing fully that this person won't be around to pursue them, all in the service of what is essentially an ambush, a blitzkrieg.

In usual times, Smith might've been attuned to these machinations, the gentle ripples that signaled the wave, but as life lately had been highly unusual, he emerged from the elevator bank into his office on a Tuesday in early December thinking of nothing but the cold and the Christmas music he'd heard for the first time on his train ride over. Things changed, as they do, rather suddenly, when he arrived at his weekly "professional development chat" and found his boss accompanied by the "head of human assets." He opened the door, apologized for his lateness, and in the three seconds it took for him to glimpse their stone expressions and take a seat, he knew what would happen next.

"We have some difficult news," Blythe began, her eyes misting faintly. She handed him an envelope, then paused as he opened it—*Memorandum for employee dismissal*—so that she wouldn't have to say it aloud. Summoning the poise of someone who had already held two such meetings that morning and would have four more before noon, she did not attempt apologies, just explained that this was not "performance-based" but "a strategic decision, a financial imperative." Even now, in the most human moment the two would ever share, she hid behind a script.

"Don't worry, I understand," he said, interrupting her. And he did.

He took his tote bag and left, failing even to gather his things from his desk. Downstairs, outside, wind passed through the gaps of the mountainous buildings and whipped his skin. He turned onto Canal and kept walking, approaching a curious calm: He'd been released not just from his job but from his last material tether to New York. He passed the tourist shops with their junk, *New York or Nowhere* T-shirts, glittering fanny packs and sunshades and vapes. He knew, sooner or later, he would have to call his parents and admit this latest defeat. They would want him home where they could watch him, fearful that unemployment would be an accelerant in the spiral they'd witnessed from afar. But for now, on Bowery, time was a door left open. He passed onto the bridge and slowed at its middle. The pedestrian path was desolate. In recent years, the waist-high banister had been reinforced by a tall metal fence. Evidently, others had dreamed of falling. He hooked his hands through the grid and considered the blue beneath.

That first summer, before everything, the biggest problem they faced was AC. The first unit Smith ordered on Amazon had shorted a circuit by the window, and the second one they sent for never came. So all that summer, they'd simply sweat, slipping languidly in underwear from bed to kitchenette, waking up to soaking sheets. Heat rises, and so the sixth floor became a dense bog by June, so comically unlivable that when their fancy friends visited, trudging up six flights of stairs in stilettos, they'd arrive at the door with cries of shrieking laughter. *You live here? How could you possibly?* they'd ask. *And why?* There was no reasonable answer, none beyond the simple fact that they were rarely home and, anyway, were both more adaptable than others gave them credit for, impudent sweat glands that allowed them to emerge sleepless midsummer with a faintly dewy look: one of the advantages of being twenty-three. Besides, they had each other.

They had, between them, an impressive wardrobe, items inherited and bought at consignment, hanging shapeless on hangers like skins; they shared them, their dissonant contours making old items new. An oversize Whitley blazer that had belonged to Smith's father became a structured dress, and Smith slept every night in one of Elle's mom's old tour T-shirts. They had secrets, ones not easily kept in close quarters and nights too hot to sleep—on one of which Elle slipped into his room and woke him, beckoning him up toward the roof and the stars. They had traditions. Friday nights, coming home after work, they'd blare rap songs and shake ass in the kitchen, shedding the workweek in favor of another endless night. They had each other and, corny as it may sound, they had New York.

Here, it was easy to think of home as storage, a room to rest one's head. There was air-conditioning in restaurants and nightclubs and other people's apartments. And there was a faint breeze on Fifth. If you paused at the corner by the park and closed your eyes, you could listen as the honking traffic and heaving bodies swished and spun with laundromat rhythms and imagine that, when summer ended, all of this would again make sense—how you lived here, indeed, and *why*.

II.

Down South

CHAPTER THIRTEEN

G ale was used to seeing the men she loved destroyed.

At fifteen, she was a stringy girl with maple skin and kinky hair that took an hour beneath a hot comb to lay flat. Known around the neighborhood for her smarts and headstrong personality, she'd been called bossy since learning to talk, three months before her elder cousin Tom. Just shy of sixteen, Tom came by most days to help with chores around the house: haul pails of water or snap the necks of chickens clean in half to be plucked and cooked for dinner. Both sets of parents worked until dusk on neighboring farms—rather, on the neighboring *plots* they rented from a white landowner in exchange for the bulk of their crop. That was the trade down in Brazos, one of those deep Texas towns where screen doors keep more mosquitoes in, where nights are black as your blackest stretch of skin.

Tom was a handsome, lean boy. Pink gums between ivory teeth— they showed when he smiled, which was always, often with a honeysuckle pinched between; its nectar sweetened his spit. A track star in school, he was popular and defensive of his "little cousin." Everyone knew talking shit about her would mean dealing with him so kept their mouths shut whenever she did the insufferable things to which she was prone, like correcting the teacher's spelling. And even if the other girls had spent all day exchanging glances meant to convey the 1940s equivalent of *Who does this bitch think she is*, they couldn't help but envy Gale when she was escorted home by the handsomest boy in school.

He was fast, had promise. His mile times were good enough to get him out of Brazos, out of the unpayable debt his family were told they owed and into a paid-for college somewhere else—TSU, TC, maybe out of Texas entirely. Gale was happy for him, but lonely. She had few friends and more and more, as the season sighed toward summer, saw Tom retreat into a life of his own. Into running, and girls. Nonetheless, he continued to appear at their door daily, often jogging the three miles home. Sometimes Gale would join him outside, looking up from her book to ask him questions as he picked the fowl clean. She knew he had secrets. One day, given money to buy new bathing suits at the colored department store, he remarked offhand about a nearby stretch of the river where he loved to swim, many miles from the land they tended. And when Gale asked him how he knew it, he just shrugged and, inscrutably, smiled.

Then June came: the rumors, the whispers, pine-scented evening air. At Wednesday worship, one of the church ladies said she'd seen Tom down streets not meant for him, making googly eyes at girls with whom he had no business. Sentiments expressed always in vague euphemism; no one had anything like proof, just a feeling. It was in his eyes, which looked suddenly as though they'd seen inside life's fleshy edges; in his body—where months ago he'd been a fledgling bird still learning the use of its limbs, he seemed now to understand the jokes of the men who smoked Black and Milds outside the A&P, and if he understood those, and not by way of any of their daughters, then things were bound to rot by end of August.

The night he didn't come, they ate red beans for dinner. No one spoke, not wanting to confirm out loud what they already knew. Forks screeched across plates in chorus. And after, Gale sat on the floor of her room, the lights off and windows open. She'd never heard that kind of quiet. Fat mosquitoes drifted in and hung low in the quivering air. They landed against her skin, but she didn't bother swatting them.

Overnight, news traveled to their side of town, a warning to all the boys who looked like him. She'd heard, with the others, that white folks sometimes salvaged bits of the body—fingers, teeth—as souvenirs. She wondered who now had his gums. At the funeral, staring into an empty hole, she choked back the tears that seemed expected, as if this small restraint was an act of resistance.

But that was justice in backwoods Texas: a limp body, a taut rope.

The next week, they loaded up the Model A at sunrise and passed all day through rain. Buckets of the stuff came in through the gaps of the car's flawed body, bloating the seats with the threat of mildew. But on they drove, afternoon into evening, reaching Houston at dusk. It was a migration not so much "great" as "good enough"; the girls—Gale and her eight-year-old sister, Lula—would be safe with their aunt when their parents returned to Brazos. The owner whose land they worked would be unlikely to notice missing girls, still too young to be of use to him.

And Houston was another world. In 1942, they'd just finished the Espersons, exquisite monuments to the extravagance Texas oil could afford. Gale had never seen such a thing: a building so tall it dwarfed the pines back home and seemed to prod at God Himself. She enrolled in a big school with several hundred kids per grade, where other girls made fun of her country accent. Still, she excelled, kept her head down and achieved with a kind of vengeance. Memories of bike rides down dirt roads still textured her sleep. Skinned knees, the din of a night that hums.

It was in college, at Texas Southern, that she first learned there was a whole system of rules by which society was meant to be governed, a way of living based in law, and that these laws could be questioned, even changed if one knew how. These laws could be used to protect the ones she loved. She knew that the way to those laws was books, so she read them. She'd seen property burned, assets seized; she'd seen bodies roughed up and bloodied. So she knew that books could always be taken but what was inside them was hers.

This drive took her through college, soon after which she met and married a dark-skinned merchant marine and began to bear his children, nursing her first with *Nicomachean Ethics* at her side. It took her through their young years, the domestic tedium of feeding, bathing, and clothing two sons and two daughters, who were soon in school with lives of their own. It took her through law school, part-time evening classes, and the Texas Bar, soon after which she became one of the first of her kind.

In the sixties and seventies, she took on any case that came her way: family law, divorce. She cut her teeth representing unruly women. One, a white debutante with a psychiatric disorder, got picked up for shoplifting. Forgetting Gale's name, she referred to her in an official court document as "that rich Black bitch" on the memory of watching her arrive at a meeting with a thin gold chain atop a blouse of cream chiffon. Gale had been *Black* all her life, had gotten *bitch* more times than she cared to count, but *rich* was a new one. She framed the document and hung it up in the office of her independent practice, smiling each time she remembered the wild woman she'd gotten out of jail and into treatment, where weeks of psychotropics brought her trembling down to earth.

There were men also. And boys. And boys tried as men, for whom she assumed the hybrid role of lawyer, parent, and probationary officer. She'd call every day of their cases to ensure they stayed out of trouble. By then, her own boys were gregarious preps, popular in school. By contrast, the boys she defended sat stoic in courtrooms, lost in rhetoric yet attuned to what it obscured: that they were meant to be tagged—now, in their teenage years—then tracked for the rest of their lives. She wouldn't let that happen; she would fight what she could.

Then the 1980s arrived and her children left home for Harvard, Cornell. After her youngest, Nadine, left, the once-cluttered house was empty and quiet, Gale's husband often out in the evenings. She watched one night, from her perch at the kitchen table, a White House announcement on CNN. In it, Nancy Reagan wore a cherry-red blouse, gold earrings, and a misty-eyed expression. Lamenting her five years observing the devastation of street drugs (and a new one, called crack, in particular), she declared drug use to be a moral issue, one for which there was "no middle ground." Crack was on everyone's mind, on everyone's lips. Distinct from powder for its cost-efficiency and attendant inner-city clientele, it seemed to pose the greatest extant threat to the much-eroded fabric of the American family. Adopting a look of pained maternal concern, she compelled America's youth toward abstinence with a catchphrase for which she, and the era, would come to be known: *Just say no.*

That same year, a man by the name of Len Bias made headlines. A small forward at the University of Maryland known for his dynamism, his *raw and explosive* talent, Bias was found dead at the age of twenty-two in his college dorm mere hours after the announcement of his draft by the Boston Celtics. The rumored, and later disproved, cause of death: overdose by crack cocaine. When Gale saw his smiling picture in the *Post*, she saw her elder son. She saw Tom. Every boy for whom she'd cared who, on the cusp of something—maybe life—met a violent, undignified end.

When the first drug case came across her desk, it was March 1987. A boy barely eighteen caught for possession of a stem-full of crack, which he claimed to have used *a few times*. Nonetheless, the law was unyielding. He couldn't be wriggled out of jail and into treatment. Addiction was now a criminal issue and the quantity with which he'd been found bore a mandatory minimum of two years in prison, followed by parole. It was a devastating blow and would not be the last: four more in April, five in May. She observed, at the courthouse, a disquieting trend: the white boys caught with powder got less time than her clients, less by orders of ten, which a colleague explained had something to do with the chemical composition. The disparity in sentencing was, he claimed, commensurate to the disparate potency—a statement that struck Gale immediately as having the wan shimmer of something counterfeit.

The country's prison population by the end of the decade had swelled to the greatest size in human history, its disproportionate share made up of Black men convicted on the back of Len Bias. Gale's own children went to grad school, became doctors or lawyers, and had kids of their own—the youngest of whom, David, was born with Tom's same mahogany skin. She lost track of the many she'd defended, the teen boys for whom she'd served as a surrogate. She lost track of the unwell woman who'd called her a *rich Black bitch*. She settled into a new life entirely, one defined by its relative leisure—so far from herself at fifteen, fleeing terror in the snarling South.

Smith's dream was troubled by a distant sound, the rhythmic drum of his name. *Where am I*, he thought, blinking rapidly. The room reassembled into a ten-by-ten of zebra print and elephant headboard, a stack of Harry Potters teetering at the edge of a weary bookshelf. The artifacts of his youth—collecting dust, losing color.

"*David!*" he heard again, the urgent call of his mother, apparently at the base of the stairs.

"What?" he croaked hoarsely.

"We leave for church in ten minutes," she announced, then silence. Smith closed his eyes but stayed awake, standing by to see if she'd forfeit. He tried to recover the shape of his dream but found the effort futile. Its faces were opaque, darkly shrouded.

"*David!*" Nadine howled again after a minute.

"Can't you just go on without me?" he asked. It was not an unreasonable request. When Smith was growing up, his church attendance had often been negotiable. He could recall many months during which his parents had excused his Sunday school truancy, in part not to call attention to their own, scandalous only because Senior himself was ordained and called upon to deliver the occasional sermon at churches city-wide. As such, the Smiths were lifelong floaters. Denominationally promiscuous, they'd alternated, over the years, between a Methodist chaplet a mile west and a Pentecostal megachurch ten miles in the other direction where congregants sweat and swayed and burst spontaneously into tongues. Occasionally, they sampled a more Universalist sect downtown, where a youth minister named Pastor Darrell wore boot-cut jeans and peppered his sermon, frequently and with flagrant self-congratulation, with hip-hop lyrics.

And when you ain't right with God, it does indeed ALL FALL DOWN; can I get an AMEN?

Never declaring a "church home" allowed them to often attend none, to eat brunch at home over CBS's *Sunday Morning* while maintaining the appearance of the hopelessly devout. But today, it was obligatory, since— Nadine explained to Smith as he slouched resignedly into her passenger seat and cleared gunk from his eyes in the rearview mirror—his father was preaching. "That's a nice shirt," she remarked of the navy button-down, neglecting to note it was wrinkled. She sped out of the driveway and onto the open road, eager to shave off the lost time. He yawned.

"You'd have never survived my mama's house," she said, weaving be-tween slow-moving cars on her way toward the interstate. A teen in an Audi honked. "She used to wake us up at six a.m. every day when we were home from college, and not gently like me," she explained without irony. "Used to walk down our hallway and just *baaaang* on the walls"— she thumped her hand loudly against the dashboard in demonstration— "yelling, 'Get up, get up, get up.'"

"Get up for what?" he asked, picturing his grandmother Gale in a silk robe and head wrap stalking the length of her hallway in Houston.

Nadine shrugged. "For nothin', usually." She caught his eye and laughed, then, in her mother's Texan twang, said: "'I won't have no lazy kids in my house, now, you hear?' We'd have just gotten home from Cam-bridge, Ithaca, exhausted from finals, but you know, months of reading books in fancy libraries sounded like a cakewalk to her, so the very next morning she'd be at our doors, six a.m. like a hound, banging on them walls. 'Get up, get up, get up, *get up*.'"

Smith took a sip from his mother's thermos. "Where's he preaching?"

"Ebenezer," she answered, the last church in their rotation. Of them all, it was the grandest and most conservative, famous for having been helmed, in the early middle of the twentieth century, by the Reverend Martin Luther King Senior. As such, its storied reputation drew a flow of tithing tourists in addition to the usual congregants who pulled up weekly in Beemers, Benzes, dressed to the nines and eager equally to praise God and brush shoulders with the crème de la crème of the Black bourgeoi-sie. In fact, it had been there, following a humanely timed sermon clearly penned by a Presbyterian, that the Smiths first met Obama.

They arrived late and so had to sneak slumped down the aisle to the seats saved for them in the second row. Senior wore a closemouthed smile as he watched their approach from the pulpit, their impossible attempt to go unnoticed drawing side-eye from more prompt, put-together congregants, self-satisfied in Chanel. Any face they'd lost Senior recouped with an easy joke—"I see my wife and son caught the Holy Ghost in the parking lot"— which drew a big laugh before he returned to his sermon. It was, that Sunday, about resilience, a theme for which he interwove the Book of Job, the narrative of a runaway slave, and the story of the year prior during which he'd lost his younger sister to breast cancer. There was a lithe elegance to his theological approach, typified by the five-hundred-page thesis he'd once penned on the moral authority of revolutionary politics. He managed to, in the seventeen minutes for which he spoke, make a personal tragedy universal, microcosmic of the whole human history of loss, then narrow the word's relevance to the Black American context before collapsing again to the personal. It was storytelling, essay, and proverb—theater and poetry. *We do not choose the ways we grow*, his sermon urged, *for growth within the bounds of our volition, in the absence of pain and heartache, is none at all.*

The (good) word led into a (mediocre) prayer, then the choir's final hymn, a round that comprised only rhythmic intonations of the word *amen*, sung like *Aaaamen, aaaaaaaaamen*, looping and eventually coalescing into one final—and, if the arrangement was at all successful, affecting—*amen* in which they would all join. And as they sang these *aaaamen*s in anticipation of that final *aaaaaaaamen*, Senior was led away into the bowels of that church, beneath the choir stands, where offices and a small greenroom revealed the similarities between his and any other stadium performance. Like Bono at sixty, he'd down a bottle of Evian and a few M&M's to recoup his energy for the encore. Nadine placed her hand on Smith's and, without looking over, offered him a mint from her purse. And the church said *Amen*.

* * *

A lively tune commenced on the organ, and everyone was standing, hugging, greeting—a social free-for-all. Senior reappeared, having wiped his forehead clean and readied his smile for the liturgical fanfare. In the insular world of which this church was a central part, Dr. David Smith Senior was something of a celebrity. Even when he hadn't spoken, it customarily took him at least an hour to make his way from where he sat to the exit, wading, as he went, through church ladies in church hats— honey-tongued aunties in peach-tulle confections, pastel wedding cakes of layered polypropylene, Carmen Sandiego slashes, Jackie O. pillboxes, and the occasional fascinator built to resemble a bird (a raven, a blue jay, a toucan). Then there'd be the Whitley grads with their extra-wide smiles, introducing themselves by graduation year only. "Class of '88," they'd croak, their meaty hands in his, obliging him to chitchat about the Lions this season or Spike's latest film.

Meanwhile, Smith was himself passed around a carousel of older, indistinguishable women—crepe-skinned AKAs bragging of beautiful granddaughters not in attendance. The few whom he actually knew engaged in a greater violence, not taking his *This and that* as an adequate answer for what he was doing, what was his plan, and when, *oh, when* would he be attending grad school. On this last point they were relentless. After all, their sons and daughters were all at HMS, at HBS, at CJS, at Stern. They were all busy becoming orthoneurocardiosurgeons with two sets of twins on the way, and here was Smith, who'd once shown such *promise*, wasting his youth in a dingy walk-up. While bohemianism might suit white kids or the children of Black celebrities, those whose success seemed a foregone conclusion, it was not for their own—they who'd so recently reached the grand ballroom of the leisure class they'd forgotten to tuck their tags. To grow complacent now was to threaten slipping, to spit in their faces one by one when they'd only offered a kiss.

Amid this flurry, Smith spotted his mother, her made-up face slightly taut as she extracted a smile for a pair of women known as the Squawkers. These two, a macchiato-skinned mother and her cortado-skinned daughter, were infamous among the Smiths for their flamboyant comportment, their Creole mysticism, and their borderline-inappropriate obsession with David Senior. Since his presidential tenure, they'd seen it as prudent to keep themselves close, drawn by whatever access, erudition, and power they believed him to represent. Nadine didn't trust them. They were not exactly attractive but both possessed a confident command over what some would call wiles. Normally in plunging blouses and second-skin denim, they were today in poorly fit brocades of cloying Easterly shades. To see them in church was to see two drooping flamingos in a box at the opera. And their laughter . . . a kind of hideous belch best produced by tilting one's chin toward the sky and applying staccato breaths to whichever note's highest. Only then could you begin to imagine the sound they produced, which attended them everywhere and always and inspired, in even the most *Christian* of observers, a sense of bitter misanthropy. In his mother's eyes, Smith recognized a look he saw rarely, equal parts boredom and panic, as they squawked on and on about her husband, on how good *the Lord's word* had been today and how they longed to *pick his brain* sometime over gumbo.

"Mom, are you ready to leave?" Smith interrupted them graciously. "Sorry to, um—"

"Oh, Nadine, is this your son?" said the mother, in pink. "Isn't he handsome?"

"He surely is," answered the daughter, in yellow. "And what is it you do, *young man?*"

Smith didn't particularly appreciate being called "young man" by a woman not ten years his senior. He considered, briefly, the ways he might answer. He could skirt the truth, say that he worked at a *start-up* in *Manhattan*, where he was *learning a lot* in a *high-growth environment*, implying with these ambiguities some imminent, Zuckerbergian ascent. He could say something glamorously vague, like *I work in the art world*, or he could attempt to be honest, confess that he still didn't know. Surely any answer would do, any besides *Well, since my felony arrest and recent termination, I just try to get through each day without swan-diving into the East River.*

"I'm, um, I live in New York," he finally answered.

Brows arched and lipstick smudged slightly, the two women shared a moment's glance and then—with forgiving, *All God's children* sorts of smiles—remarked in eerie unison, "How fun."

Arm in arm, he and his mother left the Squawkers, who redirected their attention to a former ambassador, and advanced through the crowd in search of Senior, the flash of his broad forehead like a billboard beyond traffic. "I see him," said Smith.

"I'm going to use the ladies'. Ask Daddy if he wants us to wait," Nadine instructed him, reprising the role of the dutiful wife. "Tell him we're happy to."

Fat chance, Smith thought, but he nodded. "I'll meet you by the door."

His father's smile—a packed congregation of teeth whitened beyond the threshold of naturalism—was beginning to wane. To the flock surrounding him, which rippled in concentric circles, he'd look affable, charming. But to the trained eye, his expression had a pained, hostage look, evident in the wrinkle of his brow, the downward turn of his plump pink lips. Smith kept his eyes on his father as he *Excuse-me*'d his way toward him, now observing a mild tic: Each time Senior finished with a congregant, having shaken hands or brushed cheeks, he would allow his face to go slack for a moment before reclaiming that smile as he cupped the palm of the next with renewed astonishment and glee—an act of tedious precarity, like juggling knives. Smith would have laughed were it not so unnerving. It occurred to him that, all around, these sorts of acts were fraying at their ends, masked emotions peeking through.

Back in the car, they pulled slowly from the parking lot out onto Auburn Ave. Sweet Auburn, once dubbed the "richest Negro street in the world," had seen better days. All up and down the broad thoroughfare had stood dozens of Black-owned storefronts; girls gussied up for their dates, the dresses they themselves had sewn more inventive than the couture in magazines faithfully hoarded, came on downtown to meet dapper dandies, slack suits who haunted the marquees of nightclubs where James Brown and Little Richard once lit up the night. But in the intervening years, as a result of whatever bad luck or insidious policy determines the winners and losers, most storefronts had been gutted. Boys from the block now shot shit on corners amid the faint scent of piss and sound of sirens. Smith rolled up his window and asked his mother, "What'd you think of the service?"

"Oh, it was lovely," Nadine answered, her eyes on the road. They kept quiet, edging onto 75 South from Bell Street, slowed by Sunday traffic, stop-and-start as they merged onto 20, where it loosened and flowed. They careened westward, crossing Ralph David Abernathy onto 285, a short five minutes before they pulled off at Cascade Road. What had once been Muscogee territory, canopied with towering oaks, had become a test site for the sundry violence of the American South. A battleground through which Confederate generals had marched their battalions, fighting for their "way of life" on plots where Smith later learned to play T-ball, and, losing, they'd returned to the city and left these woods alone. That was, until the 1920s, when the land was purchased and developed over decades into affluent suburbs. It was the 1960s before, amid the tremors that would soon become seismic shifts, its residents were forced to contend with *the Negro problem*. A young surgeon named Dr. Clinton Warner, who'd braved the beaches of Normandy only to come back down south to find its reception of him unchanged, purchased a plot on Fielding Lane. The neighbors wouldn't have it. Trading landlines for land mines, they plotted their defense, compelling the mayor, Ivan Allen, to erect a literal wall on Peyton Road to curtail any further "intrusion." For seventy-two days, it stood. Petitions were filed, picket lines drawn. Black professionals barricaded city hall, crying chants and flying signs that decried "Atlanta's Berlin Wall," a dark mark on the city's growing reputation as a *separate-but-equal* haven. And when it fell, ushering in a blitz of white flight to Decatur and Marietta, affluent Blacks rushed in to replace them, sunning themselves on the lawns of their McMansions, golf courses and country clubs where Negro ladies dared to lunch. Mayors, entertainers, artists and surgeons, prosperity preachers and Sunday-school teachers all found their way to this curious corner of the American South, which seemed to defy all traditional notions around race and the standard of living.

Smith and Nadine eased into the subdivision through an arcade of tinseled maples. Smith watched a young mother in sisterlocks pushing a stroller and, farther down the street, a pair of boys playing war in their front lawn. One, shot dead, fell to the grass with an audible yelp, then leapt back up with glee as Nadine pulled off the road into the driveway. The house itself was a modest thing, its sole distinction being the manmade lake by which it sat. When they'd toured it in the 1980s, the view had inspired visions of the pastoral: a life on Walden Pond. Now caked in a thick fur of algae, it was habitat to an animal ecosystem—deer that scampered through lawns and ducks commuting in daily. The inside mirrored this inchoate charm. Each Christmas, like clockwork, Smith and Nia came home to find some element radically altered. Last year, it had been a whole bedroom eclipsed by a slick white wall to accommodate Nadine's closet expansion. Such adaptations were necessary. It had been three years since the Smiths had moved out of the presidential residence, a grand neo-Georgian built of pecan brick and Doric columns, and back into Smith's childhood home. There had been the issue of clutter, of collapsing two homes into one, but there was the existential matter also—what was the *point* of all this stuff? On the walls of the modest dining room now hung two portraits of equal size—Nadine and David Senior—that had once graced the ovular foyer of the house at Whitley, the kind of space that could accommodate such grandiose gestures. But here, their likenesses looked listless, their gilded frames gauche. Past these, Smith trudged upstairs to his boyhood room, where he shed his clothes into a wrinkled pile, then slid back between his sheets—pained to think he'd run so far only to end up right back here.

The smell of fried fish poured in through the walls. It was a rich, mouth-watering scent—one of grease and spice and marbled fat—that got onto one's hands, then into one's skin, and excreted through pores in the subsequent hours, staining one's pillows faintly. On the grounds of health and personal taste, Senior refused to eat Yasin's, but Nadine nonetheless went weekly. It reminded her of girlhood, Sunday fish fries in Fourth Ward parking lots, while it reminded Smith of hunger—his chubby tween frame bingeing leftovers, still cold, in the glow of an open refrigerator.

By the time Smith was lured downstairs by the scent, Nadine had set two plates at the kitchen table, so he knew there was no escaping; they were going to have, in her words, *a talk*.

"About what?" Smith asked when she said this.

"You know what," she answered. Sipping Perrier, she cleared the tartar-sauce taste from her tongue, then paused to collect her words, workshopped and rehearsed as they were, yet faltering still as she said them. "We haven't had a real chance to discuss *everything*," she continued vaguely though in-tractably. It was a conversation she'd put off for months, preferring to have it in person. "I want to know how long you've been *using*."

Awkwardly, Smith smiled. "I'm really not sure what you mean."

Evident in her tone was the fact that she had pictured this conver-sation precisely and, with the nerdish zeal that had carried her through med school, had studied how to conduct it. She was determined to do so with tact, but the two had a tendency of speaking past one another. So when she amended her question, asking where he'd first tried it, Smith was genuinely unsure what she meant; if she was asking about his drug of choice specifically or his history of use in general. Perhaps she wanted the play-by-play common in recovery rooms, the greatest hits dating back to a distant first, his in high school, bumming finals-week Adderall from a friend dubiously diagnosed with ADD.

"Freshman year of college, I guess," he answered, opting for brevity.

"Okay. And who gave it to you?" she asked. She couldn't even say the word *cocaine*. Coke. Blow. Dust. Sneeze. Sniff. Snow. And like a novice at cards she had revealed, in the question, her strategy of play. What she wanted, more than anything, was to shift the blame. To recast her only son as the victim of a milieu she distrusted, these "friends" of his whom she imagined sprinkled the stuff over their morning Cheerios, kept rocks inside solid-gold lockets. She'd warned him so many times that he wasn't like them, really, and that any delusion otherwise could prove fatal—a lesson she herself had been taught, time and again, by her mother, so intimately acquainted with the graveyard of history.

"I have no clue," he answered frankly.

"Okay." She sighed, took a sip of water, then asked her next question. "So when did you notice that you had a problem *using*?" With a napkin, Smith shielded his smile at her choice turns of phrase, so clearly borrowed from some tragic blog on confronting your addict son—overly casual, unspecifically hip, yet spoken with Shonda Rhimesian drama, as if delivering a deadly diagnosis. What exactly had he been *using*? And, indeed, what *use* had it been to him?

"I guess—" he began, then paused for what seemed a long time. "It's been bad for a while." Bad. *From good to bad to worse. From magic to mania to chaos.* Those were the words he'd heard in AA, spoken by people who'd rehearsed over decades the narratives of their lives. He wasn't like them, he feared. Hadn't yet lived long enough to know his patterns beyond randomness, the strikeouts at parties. Without the arrest, would it have ever occurred to him, amid bleary-eyed mornings after nights of regret, blacking out at some tweaker's apartment, to say that he had a *problem*? "I'd say it's more . . . I've needed a distraction," he confessed, ignoring her labored look of empathy, one he'd seen on so many faces and found now filled him with rage. "Not because of Elle or whatever, just generally. I've needed a way to quiet my mind and fill time. Or not even fill it, like, negate or *obliterate* it somehow."

Her questions, however obliquely asked, had followed a formula—the who, the what, the where, the when—and now arrived at their logical conclusion. "*Why* would you want to obliterate time?" she asked. It was a good question, perhaps her best. Her expression was cautious and expectant, anticipating a big reveal. The trauma event recounted, the place on the doll where he hurt. The truth was more dull, yet difficult to articulate. How does one express a fundamental difference in relative concern with time, a neurotic fear of its fleeting? How even the best nights, drawn-out dinners with friends, their smiles mirrored in palms of wine, struck a note beyond the range of a healthy ear's hearing? How soon would those smiles dip like setting suns, leaving blue, then black? When would a moment's silence linger too long and be met with the good-night kiss of death. That *Well, I'd better be going, be gone.* Those whose brains were tuned to this frequency understood that the party's height also signals its end, when cheeks would be kissed, cabs and nights called, then the rush of unbearable quiet. Drugs helped. They did the work of making a fleeting feeling seem forever, a rare good mood seem replicable and true. They quieted that nagging, that warning, that *nothing lasts.* The trouble was that to remain where it seemed you were just a minute ago (or was it two minutes? An hour?) required careful observation and regular intake. The trouble was that, for those who understood time on those terms, chasing the feeling was itself a trap, one that ate away hours and youth in years.

He spoke with his mouth full, as she'd taught him not to. "Why wouldn't you?"

CHAPTER FOURTEEN

Mondays, Nadine left at eight for Grady, David at nine for a graduate lecture at Emory, so by the time Smith rose around ten, the house was empty. He made coffee, then planted himself in the living room, its domestic trappings made uncanny by time. In a family portrait above the mantel, the boy who once was him wore a cream vest and khaki trousers, his cub-like body wrapped around his father's arm.

His decision to come home had been sudden. After a week of puttering around his apartment, leaving only to pick up the takeout he was ordering thrice daily, he'd decided to return because of an email, which had landed in his inbox like a bomb. *I am a journalist*, the email's first line read. Or perhaps it had been *I am a reporter, a writer*, Smith couldn't recall. He'd deleted the message as soon as he'd scanned it, though certain phrases stuck.

This was to be a "feature" story, one for which the writer hoped to "speak to Elle's closest friends" in order to convey a "longer reported piece that would recenter her humanity," everything lost to "the public spectacle." Smith hadn't needed even a minute to consider. After all, he'd been asked by the Englands, via the crisis PR person they'd retained, not to speak to the press; they themselves had abstained. The early tabloid blitz had proved a bloodthirst—for clicks and for traffic, for *exclusive interviews* and *shocking new details*—that shouldn't be fed lest it grow more relentless. It *had* rather shocked him. He hadn't thought of Elle's family as all that famous—her mom had retired from the music industry in the early aughts—nor of Elle as the descriptor now commonly assigned: a socialite. And although this *journalist, reporter, writer* insisted in the email that this story would be *different*, and although Smith deleted it on receipt, the request still shook him: the renewed interest in the story, the wolves at the door. And while there was a kind of ursine peace in the idea of holing up in his room all winter, he'd quickly realized that this would be a death wish and booked a ticket home.

Smith stood from his chair and walked the length of his parents' living room, finger trailing the built-in bookshelf to gather a dusty film. Of everything accumulated, the books were the most astoundingly plentiful. In addition to the ones on display—leather-bound classics and alphabetized *Britannica*s—there were several rooms whose sole purpose was to house Senior's collection. Smith remembered his horror at being told, at thirteen, that he was expected to read all of those in his father's home office, books which together formed the basis for Senior's studies. Probably the man had meant it as hyperbole, but Smith had taken it literally and violently refused, put off by their tedious titles, books by cultural critics and art historians, biologists and obstetricians, Black feminist anthologies curated by MacArthur geniuses and sheet music for slave songs. Downstairs, Smith thumbed their faded spines, marveling and occasionally laughing aloud at the specificity, from those of immediate relevance (*The Black Woman* and *Black Childcare*) to the more distant relations (*The African Ancestors*); the carnal (*Understanding Black Sex*); and philosophical (*The Negro Dilemma*). He wondered if there were also, buried among these stacks, books of equal length dedicated to the undying importance of *Dapping Black Acquaintances* and *Lotioning African Elbows*, so extensive was the array, yet devoted to a central, shared condition. Skimming Frantz Fanon, he took note of Senior's annotations, so dense they disguised the words beneath, on weathered pages soft from time. He paused on a single line.

The Negro is comparison.

In his old Hyundai Sonata, Smith headed for the highway, passing, as he wound through the neighborhood, a handful of homes he knew. There'd been a whole group of kids from Cascade who'd attended the private schools across town. They'd known each other young, their mothers having met in Jack and Jill and decided early to be allies. In practice, this meant carpools in ever-shifting permutations, permeable always to whichever mother couldn't get out of a meeting or an appointment or bed and whose child, as a result, would need to be driven home. They'd all pile in, three or five or seven in a crowded Escalade, donning varicolored prep-school uniforms or the activewear of after-school, smelling of sweat, jojoba oil, spearmint. They'd head southwest, and, stalled in rush-hour traffic, the deputized mother would attempt to inspire conversation between them: "Davey, you know Terrence throws discus as well," she might offer, only to be met with eons of silence before a chirping prepubescent "Oh, that's cool." That they had nothing in common seemed self-evident to them but eternally mystifying to their mothers, who imagined them some kind of United Negro Justice League. Some, of course, *were* friends—claimed the back seat to trade gossip or play games on their phones—but most never transcended the politesse of occasionally shared space. Catching each other's eye in the cafeteria, they'd nod and say nothing, so insistent were they on how little they owed one another.

Most had gone on to success—elite colleges, then graduate school or careers in corporate America. Some had married young and borne brown children, moved to Brooklyn or Baldwin Hills to reproduce the conditions that had gilded their leisure. Because of this, the casualties among them were all the more scandalous. "Whatever happened to DJ?" Smith recalled asking his mother about the boy whose house sat at the corner of Moncler and Niskey, red brick with cream accents, its windows now quiet. "He went to prison for stabbing someone," she'd answered brusquely— then, quickly regretting her tone: "I feel just *awful* for his mother." Smith remembered the boy for one particular instance, a birthday party at which DJ, then ten, had pinned him down and threatened to kill him. "That's a shame," Smith had said in response. Down Danforth, he passed the tall gate of another. The girl who'd lived there, Alexandra, had been expelled their junior year for stealing cell phones from lockers. Even then, it had struck Smith as odd; they'd driven her home many times, dialing the code at this wrought-iron gate before snaking down the drive to arrive at a home of palatial beauty—her parents were both corporate attorneys—so *why* did she need the seventeen phones she'd (allegedly, though certainly) stolen? Of course she didn't, did not even know what to do with them. She'd been so easy to find, in part, because she'd never resold them, so searching her locker on an anonymous tip, the administration had found her shoeboxed spoils. As rumor had it, she'd *wanted* to get caught, kicked out, had wanted, a not unusual teenage compulsion but one she no doubt overindulged, to embarrass her parents, and she saw her own damage as collateral. Smith zoomed north on 75, wondering about all the others— Black kids who'd grown up as he had, with professional mothers and ever-present fathers, lessons in lacrosse and piano, who'd bottomed out young on some compulsion to self-destruct. Where had they all ended up?

On the road, Smith found himself retracing the path most familiar, pulling off West Paces onto West Wesley, where he passed streets with antebellum names: Margaret Mitchell and Old Plantation Road, extravagant homes tucked into wooded groves. Through an ivy-covered brick gate, he cruised onto a sprawling campus, often mistaken for a college by athletes bused in from Nowhere, Georgia, what people at his high school had referred to with disdain as OTP, *outside the perimeter*, thinking themselves a different breed of white southerner, moneyed and genteel, entirely unlike these *bumpkins*. It was no mystery why he and his cohort of prep-school Negroes had wanted out. They'd faced, each in their way, a lifetime of dissonance, of alternately stunted and impossible expectations to which they could respond in one of two ways: adopt the twice-as-good ethos of their parents' generation or rebel and in that rebellion sacrifice themselves. Even some of the popular ones, football stars whose names were chanted Friday nights, found quiet ways to burn it down. Like the star quarterback Kwame, who'd always wanted to act but found his request met for years with mocking and outright refusal from his coaches; he had managed to get the lead in *Othello* senior fall, but only after breaking his wrist in a "golf accident" whose timing and severity (recovery would take the entire season) struck many on the team as convenient, though it would have required an act of incredible will, which Smith had seen in his eyes as he took to the stage on opening night and proclaimed, *I kissed thee ere I killed thee. No way but this.*

Smith had fallen without question into the opposite camp: try-hards, gluttons for whom *good* was not enough. He wanted it all and always right now. An adolescence guided less by passion than pedigree, the pursuit of whatever it was others wanted; he would take it from them and thereby prove his worth. But of course, once he'd gotten the grade, the role, the letter, he startled at the vacuity innate to getting whatever it is one most desires.

*　　*　　*

Drifting through a grid of manicured lawns, Smith charted a map of personal meaning: the lamppost he'd crashed into, the Starbucks where he'd cried. And by twilight, he emerged through a green crush to see the sun, like a yolk burst open. Sophomore year, someone had figured out that the gates to a nearby deck were closed at night but never locked, so it had become a tradition for dozens from the surrounding schools to gather, circling their cars on the roof like wagons on a new frontier. Beneath a watercolor scrim, they splayed out on hoods and passed spliffs from mouth to mouth, unconcerned with the threat of arrest—whoever owned the lot would've locked it had they cared; surely they'd seen the crop circles of ash and discarded beer bottles each morning.

Smith remembered the first time he'd gone, thrilled by the invitation to mar the *good boy* reputation by which he felt stifled but, arriving, was racked with anxiety. He said nothing but startled at sounds from the depths, a SWAT team awaiting their moment. Inevitably, the headlights were just kids, not "invited" but welcome nonetheless, as at any lovers' lane. The *real* parties were down the hill in Buckhead mansions, normies high on the peaks of their lives. Those who gathered here were literally above it: a mélange of chain-smoking queers and bong intellectuals.

It was only senior spring, after years of anxious, occasional visits, that Smith began to bask in the danger. By then, he'd gotten into college, checked every box, so he set to work amassing the nights he'd missed. His life splintered in two. Soon, water bottles of tepid vodka piled up in his trunk, reveries of other worlds, accompanying a light-skinned friend who played bass in a ska band to strips on the edge of town, where OTP kids with less to lose played noise shows in gutted storefronts, got too fucked up to drive and just fucked up enough to fight strangers. You could always tell when these brawls were about to begin, in the hour when the music was done and the venue had emptied, when the kids had mostly finished their beers, their packs of clove cigarettes, and were now just leaning on cars waiting for something to happen. In the end, it'd be something simple: a wrong glance or a bad joke that, like a fuse, lifted. Their concave, wanting bodies; their sweat-congealed hair. Kids would spring from their cars to watch the boys—and they were always boys—ignite with the passion and fury that had made them mosh inside, a way to touch with longing. They'd beat each other senseless or at the very least tired. It was why they'd all come, to taste the edge of violence. Smith watched them with a thrill he'd never known. To beat oneself down just for something to do—it seemed inconceivable. How would they explain to their mothers their moony eyes and blood-wet lips? Or would they not bother?

He never found out because, most nights, he was the first to send himself home, a little woozy from the drink he'd timed strategically. Whatever happened didn't matter much as long as he made it home before curfew. He'd shed his jacket in the garage before heading inside, gargle mint, and then spill into bed, visions of drug-sick gutter-punks still moshing in his head.

CHAPTER FIFTEEN

It was in the next few days that Smith discovered, for the first time in his life, the pleasure of driving. He'd always been an anxious motorist, untrusting of a body that could neither catch balls nor change lanes with any confidence, but lent the use of his father's car, by far the nicest he'd driven, he acquired an ease. In unfamiliar neighborhoods, he observed the local custom. Two Virginia Highland gays tandem-biking in the late afternoon; they turned and yelped, easily startled by his engine's silent hum. He carried on to East Atlanta, where a line stretched outside a fast-food restaurant, everyone in it brown-skinned but otherwise bearing no resemblance. At the door, two Deltas with silk-pressed hair picked up their orders, flanked by boys in baggy sweats, a pair of suits, then a rowdy crew of skaters in fresh-dropped Fear of God, their friends kicking flip tricks in the distance. "Girl, you sure this is vegan?" one asked the other as they clicked around the corner, where the line continued, sustained at its end by a DJ whose booth was a collapsible table. Driving on, Smith caught a whiff of spice and rhythm and the sight of somebody's grandmama, in a royal-blue sweatsuit on which a church name had been stitched in rhinestone, shaking ass in his rearview mirror.

Georgia's winter was a deciduous jumble—days oscillating between fifties and sixties in the illusion of other seasons. The trees kept their leaves; cheating death, they shed them slowly, until one night, they fell at once. Smith drove west, drove south, as days set and began again. In parking lots, at vistas, he'd watch the view or read, sometimes as little as a page of whatever book he'd pilfered. Frazier and Fanon. Hooks and Hartman. Westbound on 20, southbound on 75. He drove to the market, the mountains; he turned the music up loud and imagined that the lyrics meant something, not just in a general sense but to him in particular. The trees grew more spectral by the day, looked now like fingers splayed out to the sun.

One day, early December, Smith received another email from the writer whose name he had forgotten but whose forthright diction he recognized at once. *Dear David*, the correspondence began. *I'm not sure you received my earlier email. I'm a journalist, finishing up a feature story about Elle England for* Vanity Fair. *I know you two were close, so I want first to offer my deepest condolences. I'm writing because I hope you'll be willing to speak, as soon as possible, about Elle—who she was beyond the tragedy of her death. I've spoken with several others, but I would love to include your voice as well.*

Smith hit reply and began to write back, no doubt this person intended to keep contacting him until he did, but he wasn't sure what to say. He typed the words *Fuck off* as a joke. He knew he wouldn't send them—not just because it *wasn't very Christian*, as his grandmother Gale would say, but because this writer was an imprecise target for his ire. A staffer at a legitimate publication, she was different already from the legions of tabloid vultures who'd descended upon his inbox and DMs those first days, requesting comment, then went ahead and printed their salacious swill.

Probably this writer had seen that coverage and been equally unsettled by its leering speculations and casual racist misogyny; that was why she'd decided to write this story, to *recenter Elle's lost humanity*, or whatever it was she'd said. A virtuous goal indeed.

Still, Smith didn't trust it. Writers needed a story, and this was a good one: money, glamour, drugs, death. Writing it well would demand some artifice, the act of centering not Elle but the journalist herself, her politics or narrative aims, and, through no fault of her own—it was, after all, an impossible project, to capture in five thousand or so words the essence of a total stranger—she would fail.

Smith closed but did not delete the email. He got in his car and drove. Midafternoon, the roads were empty, so he accelerated well beyond the speed limit to get far fast, still thinking of the email's last line. The writer had spoken with *several others,* presumably friends of Elle's who'd broken their tacit vow of silence. He wondered who they were and what had been their motivation. No doubt it was pure, a desire to reframe the narrative by doubling down on the PR-approved lines: That this had been a *tragic accident,* a *night of celebration gone wrong,* something that *could've happened to anyone.* It struck Smith as the same logic his lawyer had used in court, framing his drug use as a *onetime thing* in an effort to distance the act from his notional character or whatever could be displayed thereof by his mannered appearance in court. The lawyer had understood from experience that this was essential—for any client, perhaps, or for Smith in particular.

Identifying him as an *addict* and therein making an appeal to the DA's compassion was a last resort, for the psychic weight of that word in relation to his body carried the burden of history. Imagined landscapes of urban Black squalor, inured to the rock or the needle—images so pervasive in the American subconscious, they were the oxygen it breathed. They underwrote policy and inspired art. Just yesterday, or perhaps it had been the day before—they'd all begun to blend together—he'd been reading bell hooks and was startled to see a typically sordid portrait of an addict buried in a book of leftist sentiment. *Addicts want release from pain; they are not thinking about love*, hooks wrote of the archetypal addict, depraved and concerned only with scoring, including and especially at the expense of their relationships, secondary always to their *greedy search for satisfaction*.

The line had vexed him. Because, for Smith, drugs had always been less about relief from some intangible pain than an altered relationship to time and to his body—these things by which he felt bound but could un-think in inebriate moments. Intimacy, too, had often been a motivation, as substances tended to offer access to an alternate plane for those who took them. Just the act of absconding from a crowded dance floor, escaping upstairs to a room with its own music, created a camaraderie that often gave way to conversations that seemed more honest, whether because of the forgone inhibitions or the establishment of a mutual trust. Of course, any intimacy forged in an altered state was arguably counterfeit. The good folks at AA had often called these sorts of single-use friendships, born ten to a stall in a discotheque bathroom, the bonds of "lower companions"—but in this reasoning, they came up against the prevailing wisdom of Brooklyn rave gays, some of whom Smith had witnessed firsthand exalt the ineffable power of dance drugs to strip away barriers to a deep and in-tuitive knowing. And if nothing lasts forever, why should intimacy shared for the duration of a pop song's chorus be any less extraordinary?

Smith thought of Carolyn then, how the first few times she had called herself an addict, often in a tone of wry brutality, her audience had been taken aback. They never thought she had a problem using because of her elaborate disguise, the projections her body carried like a petticoat of smoke. It had taken time, but Elle's had come undone. Smith recalled a friend who'd called him once after meeting Elle for breakfast and, seeing that she hadn't slept, expressed concern. Memorably, he'd remarked that she was different from their other friends, who consumed the same drugs and patronized the same parties, because she lacked "that thing in her brain that tells her to stop." Smith considered whether that was a better definition of an addict: *one who has never had enough*. But it was a quality he had never read as a lack, the product of some interior erosion and essentially bankrupt condition, but something else entirely: a desire inescapable, and often ruinous to those who possess it, to scrape with fanged nails against the marbled flesh of being—arriving finally at bone, then marrow.

Recovery had words for this. *Too many and never enough*. Words that scratched at the gossamer shell of the ineffable. They summoned a mythos that both drew and repelled him. He was intrigued by the poetry, the sensual threat of being *built different*, but questioned its relevance to him. After all, were it not for his arrest, wouldn't he have continued drinking and drugging without much social consequence? That was the norm for his set, upwardly mobile urbanites who'd come to New York to devour it. But losing control, spiraling downward, *no*. The hunger in the eyes. *Addict*—that word meant something different when applied to him than it did when applied to Carolyn, just as it would've for Elle. She would not have been blind to the distinct impression that, for those who looked like them, that word was a moral failure, a confirmation of society's worst fears. A forfeit of all the tenuous advantages given.

"Mom says you've just been driving around," said Nia from across the booth of a dimly lit restaurant. She'd come home that morning, ten days until Christmas, to modest fanfare. The very bones of the house seemed to sigh with relief.

"Oh, yeah?" Smith grunted.

"Yeah, she says she's barely seen you." Having this sort of conversation, which Smith suspected she'd been put up to, was precisely her function in the family: to interpret, to take their mother's grievances and translate them into his tongue, though even her casual tone couldn't quite defang the comment, "She says it's all very *mysterious* where you go."

"I've told her," Smith snapped. "I just drive."

Seeing she'd gone a stroke too far, Nia was silent. Smith recognized the look of caution on her face, a hiker encountering a wild animal. Bared teeth, this was how he kept his pain private. For a moment, Smith thought to tell her everything—about the emails and the police, his mounting anxiety about the story the writer would tell and what role he would play inside of it—but their parents arrived just then and put drink orders in with a chipper waitress before asking Nia about her journey home; she brightened.

"I hadn't done my laundry since October, I kid you not. The machine's broken in my house and the nearest laundromat in Cambridge is a *trek*," she explained, exasperated, though one could tell that this was a story of triumph. "You should've seen me at check-in, lugging two gigantic duffels, each twenty pounds over. The Delta attendants were trying to make me pay an extra hundred, but you know me, I opened them up right there—" Despite himself, Smith grimaced. He could see the scene clearly, one he'd witnessed frequently throughout their shared youth, each time she'd moved, which was often: to and from dorms in college and, after, to DC, then Cairo and Beirut and Ramallah for stints at NGOs dedicated to human rights, and now to and from Boston between years and even semesters. She'd overpack her bags beyond belief, beyond any reasonable person's understanding of the airline guidance, then, at the check-in counter, summon every tactic in her arsenal—beyond the offer of actual money—to get her way. Maybe 70 percent of the time, this worked; she got her unyielding wish through argument, cajolement, and tears. But the rest of the time, it resulted in these displays, her zipping open the packed duffel in the middle of the terminal to remove its intimate contents, her underwear on the unclean floor, and find the jackets and sweaters she could layer onto her person to make weight, an act that never failed to mortify Smith. By contrast, she relished the shock of passersby and the horrified desk attendants, who always, after watching for a while, relented, telling her now mesomorphic frame that it was fine, they would take it, just as she relished telling the story to them now. "I guess the Christmas spirit was in the air because I swear, the whole check-in line mobilized behind me, cheering me on and heckling the attendants. By the end, they were practically *begging* me to give them my bags and get on the damn plane."

"My daughter the revolutionary," Senior joked, smiling. Their waitress returned with two glasses of Malbec and a vodka martini, the latter of which she set in front of Smith, then apologized profusely when it was pointedly claimed by his father.

"So how did your semester end up?" asked Nadine. It had been Nia's second to last—a time, she explained, when corporate firm recruiting had come to a fever pitch. Every night another dinner, shanks of prime rib and copious wine charged to the company card at the toniest haunts in Boston. She'd attended at least two dozen, she recalled, though of course she had no intention of joining a firm. It was yet another instance of her defining trait: a desire to pull a fast one on the corporations and institutions whose rules and very existence she found meaningless. She was always on the make, eager to prove their idiocy—a desire that sometimes led her astray. Smith thought of the Delta staff then—just doing their jobs—and how, in fact, they were a great deal more inured to the system whose arbitrary rules they upheld than she, able to defect so brazenly against these structures precisely because she was comfortable within them. Other than these dinners and her usual schoolwork, she continued, most of her time was devoted to the *Law Review*, on which she was an editor, and to working as a nanny ten hours a week for a pair of Black Am Stud professors. All in all, it was *manageable* as long as she talked fast and slept very little.

"Do you have time to see your friends?" Nadine asked with shrill concern, though she'd been the same way as a med student on that same gothic campus. "And to date?"

"Well, yes to friends," Nia offered, a given; her elastic time had always stretched to accommodate them. "And I go on dates occasionally, but no one special. Y'all know any eligible bachelors you can set me up with while I'm home?" Nadine laughed loudly, sipped her wine. "Dad, any Whitley guys?"

"I'm sure there will be some next Sunday."

"Of course," Nadine affirmed. "That's perfect."

At the mention of Sunday, Smith perked up. Listening for context clues, he recalled the masked ball they'd attended annually when he was in high school but for which he hadn't been in town since. He didn't bother asking if he'd be expected—he knew that the answer was yes—and tuned out again as the conversation returned to Nia. There had been a time when he would've felt competitive for his parents' attention, but now he felt nothing more than relief at their eyes directed elsewhere.

He thought again of the writer's email. He trusted that no one from Elle's inner circle would talk, so he wondered what narrative the writer would spin from the meager information on offer. Sophisticated readers would want something more than a retelling of the graphic details, the doom and gloom of the tabloid's tragic Negress, but if the writer was a serious person, she would also see through the counternarrative, the lie of sanitized perfection that elided Elle's flawed humanity. A *tragic accident*, indeed, it had been, but wasn't it also tragic to suggest that she was only deserving of grief if her bones were immaculate?

"David—" He focused in; his father's face was slack, jowled and hanging, as it always was when angry. "Your mother asked you a question."

"Oh. What was it?"

She was smiling, slightly buzzed. "I just asked what your plan is for after Christmas. If you'll stay home, or—"

"I have to get back to New York," he announced.

"Well." She paused, frowning. "*Why?*" She had a point. He did not *have* to get back to New York. Without a job, New York was all liability, a hemic wound of cost. And if he wasn't even happy there, as he'd foolishly confessed he was not, there was no benefit to rushing his return.

"I have to attend to my affairs," he answered, intoned as a joke. He hoped she would drop it.

"You mean your *court date?*" she clarified, whispering the words *court* and *date* as one might *vaginal* and *discharge*. "When's it rescheduled for?"

"Not until the twenty-third of January," Senior intercepted, and then, decisively: "You'll stay here until then, and we'll fly up together."

"No, I have to go back, and—" He faltered, then grew suddenly furious with himself and his father, his voice raising as he blurted, "I have to interview for a job!"

Senior frowned, then looked at him appraisingly. "I didn't realize you were applying."

"Yes, it's—" Smith scrambled to think of a position, one sufficiently impressive yet vague, something boring and behemoth. "It's in analytics at—"

"Dr. Smith!" boomed the darkness just then, and out of it rose a man in a Whitley sweatshirt, who, ducking slightly, became visible in their table's pooling light. "Class of '09," he offered along with his outstretched hand.

In the time it took Senior to turn his head, his expression had already shifted. There was that second face Smith had observed. "How you doin', brotha," he heard his father ask, a hue Blacker than his usual cadence.

He was beaming now, a mall Santa, as if they'd been waiting all night for this stranger's arrival, which had stalled but not derailed the conversation. Smith knew it would return swiftly to the question once he'd gone, which, after beckoning over the Spelman grad he'd met in college and to whom he'd recently gotten engaged, evidenced by the spectacular diamond displayed on her manicured hand, he did.

Senior took just three seconds to regain his cool composure and relocate the dangling thread. "You shouldn't be applying right now, with this arrest and pending case hanging over your head. What if they run a background check?" he asked, a question to which Smith had no answer. He was right. "You'll stay home. There's nothing for you right now in New York."

CHAPTER SIXTEEN

On the morning of the Candlelight Cadre, Smith realized he couldn't locate the black suit he kept at home for such occasions. After careful questioning as to the last time he'd seen it, Nadine concluded that the tux had never made it to Cascade and was likely still in the cedar storage of their former basement—a hunch she confirmed midday with a text to the college's current first lady, Denise. The two went back decades, were old friends from med school, though these days, Nadine spoke to her only when she realized she'd left some item, a bracelet or book, in one of the considerable nooks of that house, as if it were still somehow hers, put in the temporary care of another.

Having been told he could pick up the suit that evening, Smith arrived downtown around six and, pulling onto campus, rolled his windows down. Slowly, at an almost crawling pace, he examined the familiar surroundings—the Whitley quad covered in a brochure-ready litter of leaves, hemmed in on all sides by pillared redbrick buildings. Just a few days until Christmas, the few people remaining were harried-looking faculty and security manning gates, guards of the uneasy silence that now reigned in a place most often abuzz with sound.

It had been 1971 when Senior first arrived on campus, a fact Smith had learned from the inside cover of his father's copy of Franklin Frazier's *Black Bourgeoisie*:

David Alexander Smith
Freshman, Whitley College, October '71

On the heels of the sixties, this place that had produced so many of the movement's leaders must have called to him like a siren: a haven for Black political thought, scholarship, and action. The man—or, Smith supposed, he was then just a boy—had excelled in high school, played in a rock band with his brothers, and taken an interest early in the radical politics alive on Chicago's South Side, where Fred Hampton was making strides building a working-class coalition that cleaved racial lines then collapsed after his murder at the hands of police. When alive, Senior's mother had often told a story about having to plead with the principal after her son was expelled at sixteen for dressing as a Black Panther every day for a month—a tale that was now told in jest, as if to say *how naive he was then*, but it was Smith's preferred image of his father: at a bus stop in 1969, flat-topped in a leather jacket and a face of unmasked ire, years and many miles from the man he would become who, in the dispassion of his late middle age, wore golf shirts to bed. Smith often wondered when that shift had occurred, and what exactly had comprised his *education*.

Idling along the quad, Smith pictured his father as a young man, loafing hall to hall in threadbare loafers, reading anything he could. Having escaped the clutches of urban poverty into the very cradle of the Black elite, he would've embarked upon an education as much social as intellectual, one inextricably bound to class. Indeed, in that book he had marked a line that distilled this: *The Negro student should strive to be respectable.*

It was unclear whether he'd underlined this sentence in anger, agreement, or both—if he'd picked up this book, rife with bourgeois critique, and read in it a manual—but by the time Smith and Nia were born, he'd certainly internalized that logic into a regimen of elocution lessons and pressed hair and fresh clothes laid out for playdates. Smith had been a freshman in high school when his father, during his first year as president, had helped champion a dress code that demanded Whitley men don "appropriate attire" to class—banning, among other things, do-rags, pajama pants, and dresses. This new policy was quickly denounced for what it was, a thinly veiled crackdown on what the administration referred to as *cross-dressing*. Smith recalled with an eidetic precision watching through his bathroom window as a protest formed on the quad. It was a Sunday, and the lurid blur of queer brown bodies was soft with rain. From his distance, their signs were illegible but their chant came clear through the walls, decrying the flagrant femmephobia of an administration that had deemed their identities *inappropriate*. It had struck Smith even then, at fifteen, as a policy unlikely to pass at the Ivy League, disguised as it was behind the insidious veil of respectability. According to the press release: "A necessary means for preparing Black men for their professional futures." Within hours, their numbers dwindled, chants fading beyond the murmur of wind, but Smith had kept watch until the very last two, towering beauties in rain boots and skintight neon dresses, surrendered—for the day or for good, he couldn't be sure, though he never saw them again, at least not in the style of dress by which he would have clocked them. He watched to the bitter end, as the damp night arrived to taunt their wet bodies and they stomped home through the thickening mud, just as he had watched other rituals play out on that lawn: debutantes in white dresses and pledging Ques howling mad in formation—the love and battle cries of their ecstatic humanity.

What Smith had never known, and what he wondered now as he arrived and gazed up at his old stone balcony, was what these students thought of him as he came and went from the high-gated mansion perched like a stage for their view. Smith parked the car and, as instructed, texted his mother that he had arrived, then waited as she relayed the message. From here, the house had a Camelot quality—its lawn lush and manicured, forming a crisp rectangle around the grand neo-Georgian. Its sheer size blocked the view beyond it, but Smith could still see, as if by x-ray vision, the untended green plot past which sat a series of low and run-down homes, rented not by students but those in the sort of squalor one rolls up one's windows to avoid. A "bad neighborhood" in aesthetic opposition with the quad the house faced.

Tonight, its windows were bright with activity. If Smith wasn't mistaken, there was an event, a cocktail reception before the Cadre. In a pillar of light between the drawn calico curtains, he could make out the flurried silhouettes of waiters with trays in hand. It was the sort of event that had occurred here near nightly in his youth, through which he'd passed only sullenly and by obligation before escaping with a plate to his room.

The house, all lit up at the center of campus, betrayed its own intent. It was indeed a stage on which to project a kind of life. While the presidents of other colleges lurked like distant specters, gray-haired animatrons wheeled out for donor dinners, his father had seemed to have a more immediate role. Tactical, to be sure, to separate the rich from their money, but also deeply symbolic, he and Nadine held up, like this house, as the embodiment of that Du Bois–ian notion, *the talented tenth*. Models of what intellect and hard work could offer. But like any great symbol, it was at least half a lie. Were the house not freely given, they could never have afforded it. Not the house, nor the full-time staff, nor the black car with the university driver of whom Smith had been so embarrassed in those early days that he'd described the man to a friend, exiting the back of an Escalade outside her sweet sixteen, as his "pop-pop." It was the same apparent logic of any system that relies on illusion, a vision of achievable wealth blocking an uglier view, the unsavory realities beyond and within.

But Smith had bought it entirely. The adjustment had taken years, getting used to living in a house both private and public, passed through by an endless parade of academics, celebrities, and donors. To them, he could be rude, resistant to his new reality—even its perks, which Nia enjoyed unabashedly—but at some point, he'd come to accept this life as his, one whose edges were sanded silently down by people disposed to his comfort, and in him brewed a quiet sense of entitlement. By the end of high school, when Nadine had swooped in last minute to host his prom-picture party, he'd allowed himself to savor fully the perverse pleasure of watching his guests, well-to-do white kids and their parents, enter the grand foyer with its carnival of costumed waiters, their faces blooming in astonishment at the house and those who inhabited it.

Denise opened the door and peered out. He waved. If any question remained, her appearance confirmed without a doubt that she was hosting, her treated hair swept back in a nest-like bundle and her supple frame sheathed in a satin gown. Folded over her bent brown arm was the suit bag, with which she walked briskly to the gate. With youthful vim, Smith leapt up the steps to greet her. She offered no smile, no expression at all, telegraphing that *this* was an imposition; already he didn't like her, her large green eyes frightening against her high-yellow skin. But when she opened the gate, these eyes widened with recognition, and her stern composure fell away as she asked in a low-pitched warble, "Is that little Davey?" Smith answered that it was, and the woman began to explain that she'd thought he was a messenger. She hadn't seen him in over a decade, not since he was a chubby tween nearly half his current height, so it was surprising—in a way he was unlikely to understand until he was older and had witnessed this phenomenon in the faces of friends' children—to see the man he'd become. And as she explained, the warmth swelling to cover the coldness that had preceded and dampened it still, like mixing liquids of disparate temperatures, he thought only of his mother, her face, the second self she'd left hanging in there.

The night was warm, even for a Southern winter: fifty-three degrees with clear skies in which the faint suggestion of stars still shone. Still, the temperature could not dissuade party guests from recycling jokes about "Black folk and the cold" as they huddled around heat lamps, swaddled in coats and furs. Soon, they would spill indoors from the terrace, cutting the imprecisely named cocktail hour—actually two, in observance of CP time—short. Within seconds of their arrival, Senior and Nadine were pulled into conversation with a nearby couple, and Smith watched them transform into elegant social creatures. Surely this breezy woman in the beaded mask could not be the same who, not thirty minutes prior, was nipping at his ankles with the trunk of a portable steamer, shrieking that he couldn't leave the house *like that.* "Shall we get a drink?" Nia asked, then, with a look of sudden alarm: "Just like soda or whatever."

Smith smiled. "Sure."

They moved briskly through the guests, about half of whom were masked. Most had opted for simple designs, onyx bat-eyes from Party City, but the more committed among them had run with the theme, purchasing or having made custom veils of lace and feather, jeweled beaks that disguised them entirely. This operatic drama was heightened by a sharp, low strum. At the opposite end, Smith could make out a six-piece orchestra, all Black like the party they accompanied and dressed in black as well.

The progression of chords struck Smith as familiar, and his ears perked up to identify it, not as some Ludwig van Wolfgang but a contemporary number, a top forties hit dressed up as concerto, which brought conspiratorial smiles to all the party's young while their elders remained oblivious, swaying stiffly to a Young Thug they'd called "trash" on the radio.

"So what do you think?" Nia asked as they sidled through the crowd. Smith shrugged. It was a strange question, considering they'd attended this party before, along with hundreds interchangeable—Whitley homecomings and garden parties in Oak Bluffs and galas filled with night-black boys in tailcoats—scenes of leisure which always seemed to thrum with neurosis, all the pretense like a bid to be seen.

"I need a mans," said Nia, leaning back against the bar and removing the sequined mask she'd worn for all of twenty minutes. Her tone was playful, but it was not really in her nature to play, so Smith took the words sincerely. Often, she'd lament her lack of a partner, which he interpreted not as an antifeminist regression but a symptom of her immense demands from life; if hers was to be a Gesamtkunstwerk of achievement, it could never be realized without that final prize. "You can help, Davey."

Smith rolled his eyes but agreed; he could think of nothing better to do. The two took their seltzers and reentered the crowd, orbiting those who looked around their age. "What about that guy," Smith whispered even as he was openly pointing with the knuckle of his index finger. "He's cute."

"Wedding ring," she said simply.

"Well, that's not a very can-do attitude," said Smith, a joke she apparently—a *tsk* sound emerged from her lips—did not appreciate.

The scoping stage of flirtation continued for several minutes, during which each of Smith's suggestions was nixed—one boy's complexion looked jaundiced, another's suit was ill fit; one was too young, yet another too pretty. "Oh, look at him," Nia said, zeroing in on her target like a craft toward the moon. His name was Malcolm, they learned. He'd gone to Georgetown, Yale Law. He was handsome, mocha-skinned with an unreceding hairline and a mouth of the most perfect American teeth orthodontia could offer. After the usual pleasantries—Smith, by way of introduction, had simply walked up and said, *Meet my sister*—they moved on to debating "qualified immunity" and "Chevron deference," subjects on which they agreed fundamentally with only the sorts of divergences that lent to healthy debate.

Smith excused himself to the bar.

"Vodka soda, right?" the tender asked, proud of himself for misremembering.

Smith smiled and began to correct him, but something in the man's expression, along with the strain he was evidently under, compelled him to affirm the order, which the bartender prepared in a lime-garnished glass. The orchestra swelled in a lush bloom of strings, "All of the Lights" in B minor. "Thank you," said Smith, staring into the drink, which could pass for water. He pictured getting roaring drunk so that the whole scene would amuse him, but Nia arrived at his side just then.

"Where's Miss Malcolm?" Smith asked.

"You noticed too," Nia deadpanned.

"I notice everything," he said, and left the drink, untouched, on the bar.

Scanning the crowd, she tugged him again by the crook of his arm toward another group where she'd recognized an older boy from school. Enthusiastically, Stefan enlisted in their game, introducing Nia to no fewer than four of his former Whitley classmates, three of whom stuck around, encircling her. Smith observed their hetero pageantry. With her body language and time, she balanced each of these suitors with the roving focus of a reality-show contestant. The three boys—Alphas, in both senses of the word—adopted a competitive air, interrupting and subtly cutting each other down with snipes that were amusing to them but did little to endear them to her, Smith could see in her pained laughter. There was something uncanny, even threatening, in the intensity of their focus. It was unclear if they were genuinely interested or saw the situation as yet another joust in the way of so many men who, no longer sent to wars, sought their drama and petty victories on whatever fields they could.

The Negro is comparison, Smith mused with a grin as they were beckoned in for dinner.

Goat cheese croquettes, fresh figs wrapped in Parma, variegated lettuces, each dressed in vinaigrette. A braised shank of lamb bathed in rosemary, garlic, fennel, and thyme. A sad bouquet for the sole vegetarian. And, after nectarine tart, a toast for which all members of the Cadre were asked to stand, one by one, in spotlights of rousing applause. Briefly, they lifted their masks, and Smith recognized friends of his father's—the time-speckled faces of judges and surgeons and titans of business—along with the man himself, whose smile at this distance did not appear forced or flagging but full of felt emotion. Pride, perhaps. Relief. No doubt all of these men had seen others eaten alive—by their politics, their ire, their inability, or perhaps it was a refusal, to graft the mask onto their face.

So they were, indeed, miraculous. And like all of the others, Smith clapped.

CHAPTER SEVENTEEN

Crossing three lanes of traffic, Smith pulled to the side of the road. He had the strange apprehension that this email, the writer's third, would be different. *Hello, all*, it began, addressed not to him but in the plural second person. His eyes flitted over the address line, where he saw that the recipient's email was the same as the sender's—an anonymous list in bcc. And in the copy line were two additional addresses, representatives from the fact-checking and legal departments. *Thank you all for your thoughtful participation in helping me tell Ms. England's story, particularly during this trying time.* Having ignored her previous emails, Smith wondered why he'd been included. Perhaps it was a mistake, he thought, though the diction of this email was so precise, its construction so intentional, that he doubted the writer was prone to such inelegant errors. *Given the sensitivity of this material*, the email continued, *I have received permission from my editor to share an advance proof so that you may read through and confirm the quotes and facts included. If you do feel that any information is inaccurate or has been misrepresented, please let me know as soon as possible, as the issue will go to print next week. Thank you and happy holidays.*

The timing of the email struck him as odd, a bit tacky. Just days before Christmas, people would receive it in airports and train stations, amid holiday parties and family meals, and would be blindsided again by the tragedy. But evidently, this could not be avoided; she was in a rush to close the piece and go to print, fearful that pushing it even a month would mean losing some critical advantage in the media cycle, for which primacy was everything—or perhaps that, by February, there'd be another beautiful dead girl and the world would have swiftly moved on.

Smith clicked the attached PDF, and the story swallowed his screen.

The Charmed Life and Tragic Death of Elle England

At the top, they'd printed a photograph that, strangely, Smith had never seen: Elle, impossibly chic in a fur stole and full beat, seemingly outside a black-tie gala. He zoomed in on her face for a moment, then began skimming through. At first glance, it appeared that the writer had kept her word. The piece was thoroughly reported. Swiftly, he identified a number of the interviewees, a motley crew that included a former boyfriend, two sorority sisters, and the doorman of a nightclub called Jungle, none of whom would have been called upon to deliver a eulogy, but Smith supposed that the writer—Anna Clark, according to her email signature— would have been forced to make do as Elle's inner circle closed ranks.

She opened with "the tragic death"—she had to get asses in seats— described in a series of time-stamped events played out in the dusky metropolis. At *3:38 a.m., England was seen leaving the downtown club in the company of an unidentified man.* And by *8:13 a.m., she was found on the banks of the river, clad in a red silk slip, then rushed to Lenox Hill, where she was declared dead at 10:15 a.m.* But after this lede, the writer stroked back toward Elle's Californian beginnings. Her pace and diction changed, her sentences lush as she described a girlhood of prep schools and Baldwin Hills' Black elite. It was heartening, in some sense, to see Elle's upbringing made to mirror his, but it was disquieting also, how easily its specificity had been flattened into a factory backdrop of extravagant privilege.

College was touched upon briefly—sorority sister clichés about her *style and infectious smile*—and then it was New York, which the writer took time to render as a psychic space. A Fitzgeraldian green light that year after year beckoned new hopefuls, eager to make themselves known by sheer force of personality—though style, beauty, and the last name helped. Cade from Jungle, that crew-cut troglodyte with the Darger tattoos, had offered a quote: Elle was *just one of those girls who everyone knew. She was in here most nights last summer*, he'd said, and Smith could confirm that was true; he'd been with her most of them, running half mad about the cavernous room on their own adventures, which they'd recount on the cab ride home. Still, the combined effect of these quotes was not to render her particular but archetypal: an aspiring *it girl*, daughter of privilege and sampler of the demimonde, balancing on the razor's edge of romance and tragedy.

Skimming, Smith could see clearly where the gaps remained. For the descent the writer described, from this vaunted ingénue to her lifeless shade, was rendered quickly and without nuance. It was all a speculation: an ex from college who'd expressed concern, gossipy colleagues of whom Smith had never heard. Drug debts were postulated and her love life flayed open, autopsied in minute detail, until the writer arrived, finally, at the man who'd appeared in the CCTV. *When NYPD footage was released in early autumn, friends of England's were startled to learn that she seemed acquainted with the suspect, whom many had assumed was a stranger.*

Here, the writer luxuriated in subtext, legible to anyone who'd seen the footage and recognized their manner as too intimate to be that of total strangers, people who'd met only that evening. In probing the shape of their history, the writer had dug up useful information, far more than the police had yet shared. Though she still didn't offer a name—perhaps because she didn't have it or perhaps because printing it would've opened up a world of liability; the man was innocent until proven guilty, after all— she filled in details that refined his abstract picture. Interviewing Cade about their interaction at the club door that night, she'd asked not only for a physical description but one of vibe, the *type* of guy he seemed. *Six feet, dark-skinned, with a native New York kind of fuck-you attitude*, the bouncer said, stumbling over a few more euphemisms before arriving at what it was he really meant: *Like, hood.*

The writer had followed the story from the nightclub downtown up to the Bronx, where she'd interviewed neighbors of the man in question. Requesting to remain anonymous, one described certain behaviors— inebriated young girls leaving his apartment midmorning, the wads of cash he'd seen him slipping the super—which alone were not damning but in context deepened his sinister air. He was a man with no shadow. Even the fact that the neighbor had asked not to be named was telling, suggesting that he considered the suspect a credible threat. Even in hiding, even in custody, he might still have contacts in the city capable of retribution. An unmarked car beyond a window, a gloved hand on a neck.

Though the suspect's exact relationship to England remains unknown, rumors that she was five months pregnant—Smith stopped cold. He reread the line, then read it a third time, his vision blurring. Though he'd feared for weeks that it might, seeing that fact appear in the piece was an almost convulsive shock, derailing his attention in a barrage of frenzied thought. Unattributed, these "rumors" might have come from anyone: Clement or one of the others she'd no doubt questioned before or after Smith. Perhaps a nurse at Lenox Hill, who'd done with the information what little she could, taken cash in exchange for the tip. Smith kept reading, his breath hot and quick, though now the words were barely registering. The writer was cunning; she'd sent this proof not as a courtesy but to see what response it would yield from a private audience before its wide release. To the gossiping hordes downtown, starved for months of new details; the panting internet voyeurs who'd read this or one of the follow-ups it was sure to spawn—now that it had been covered by a prestige publication, it might be picked up anywhere—and would form their solemn judgments based on half-heard information. Certain facts had a habit of overwriting truer truths, and one so salacious would hijack the narrative, rerouting it, irrevocably perhaps, from a story of random misfortune toward one of recklessness or even cruelty, painting her as yet another *type*: the addled Black mother, undone by her addiction.

The writer had gotten her story indeed.

Though she had, as promised, attempted a complex portrayal, it was in the end a story of symbols, cultures, and their collision—Baldwin Hills, the Bronx, fentanyl, cocaine. It was a story so innately of New York, in which the uneasy proximity of excess to inconceivable tragedy was a daily animating tension. A story of the opioid crisis and the ravages of privilege, and as Smith read its last line, he grew numb, knowing that its publication would mark a second death. The beaten hope that she might still be unearthed from the thrown-dirt of spectacle, stripped of the mask she'd learned to wear as her face, and underneath—in the tendon—be rendered human.

CHAPTER EIGHTEEN

Christmas came. Rain streamed through the open windows, dewed bedsheets, collected on countertops, and filled the rooms of that house with the damp and earthy scent of everything outside. With cooking, and presents, and music, it could become merry, but the soft patter imbued the air also with languor. Smith woke and, still robed, drifted downstairs with the quiet care of a coal-fearing child, arriving in the kitchen to find Nia hunched over her laptop.

"Are you seriously working right now?" he asked.

She didn't answer but asked a question of her own. "How did you sleep?"

"Poorly as ever," he said, and, in the Keurig, deposited a morning blend. "Merry Christmas, by the way."

"Merry Christmas," she replied.

For a while, the two sat in comfortable silence, attending to their respective screens. Then, suddenly and with sitcom broadness, a woman entered the room. Smith turned to find his mother's sister, a brittle woman in a doobie wrap and bone-hugging Luon, charging toward the refrigerator. "Hi, Sonny," said Nia, then repeated the question *How did you sleep?* to a vastly different response.

"*Horribly,*" the woman pronounced, the first syllable lilted to a Texan *haw*. "I don't know how anyone could sleep on that mattress."

She'd arrived late the night prior, having driven all day from Dallas, where she practiced property law, through Houston, where she'd picked up her mother and headed east. Smith had strategically dodged their arrival, sending himself to bed at eight p.m., and now felt a mild nausea at the anticipation of his grandmother striding into the room and greeting him with a look of disapproval. Sonya stalked to the Keurig, with which she fiddled for a moment before announcing that she couldn't drink Starbucks—*Your mother has such haw-rible taste*—on account of its burned flavor and, arriving at the breakfast nook, placed a hand on her own lower back. Again, she sighed. "I'm serious about that mattress. I can't take another night," she said, announcing her plan to move to a hotel downtown at which she would not be subjected to the injustices she had last night endured—the space heater malfunctions and low-thread-count sheets— complaints to which Smith and Nia paid little mind. Her love language was and had always been complaint, her first and only recourse and the sole lens through which she viewed the world. She had been dealt, by decade, good and bad hands by life and was now, in her sixth, eager to make her many resentments known. But what had in her teens, twenties, and even thirties been called "attitude" now registered only as bitterness. "We'll miss you," Nia replied, barely looking up from her breakfast.

Sonya planted herself in the chair next to Nia and, shutting her laptop for her, began to ask about school—with whom she was studying and what she was learning over at *that dump*, she joked—as Smith returned to his phone's many feeds. After a moment, she glanced over and, sneeringly, added: "And I already know what you've been up to, you little felon." An agonizing pause ensued, then she snorted, and all three of them burst into laughter, cracking the room's stale air like an egg for frying. Within minutes, perhaps summoned by the sound, both David Senior and Nadine appeared, each dressed in what they'd worn to bed, and then, finally, Gale drifted in also, looking stately and slightly mystical in a floor-length muumuu of Princely purple, embroidered on its arms with a pattern of sequins that matched the silver turban atop her regal head. "Good *mooorning*," she sang, and Smith felt a flood of relief, seeing nothing but warmth in her eyes.

Per tradition, the presents were not opened that morning, or afternoon, or night. The mostly regifted items sat untouched throughout the day as a fire roared and a marathon of Christmas films played. The cooking would be protracted across seven hours and not without drama: bickering and land grabs for counter space. Sent out of the kitchen—his melancholy so total, it seemed transmissible and, to the vibe, deadly—Smith sank with his phone into a brown leather chair.

And again, he opened the email. *Thank you all for your thoughtful participation*—he reread it quickly, as he had dozens of times since receiving it. In the corner, there was now a scarlet prompt, nudging him to reply. For three days, he'd considered it and second-guessed; he'd drafted, then deleted. But he didn't see the point. The faults of the story were not in the facts but their assembly—the picture, incomplete, looked nothing like the girl he knew.

Smith closed the email and opened a new message. In the address line, he pasted the only email address he had for Elle's mom, one cc'd years ago on an exchange about the lease. He hadn't used it in the wake of Elle's death, unsure of what to say. While Elle had met his parents, joining them for meals and matinees the few times they'd come to the city, she'd never introduced him to her own, so Smith was unsure if the contact would be welcome. Or if Nat would read it as he had so many of the condolence texts he himself had received—as an inconvenience and a bid for unwanted intimacy. Grief was its own celebrity.

Dear Mrs. England, he wrote, then paused. She would know his name, of course, but he wasn't sure what else she would know about him or the depth of his friendship with Elle. He thought back to his one mention in the story—"from a modest two-bedroom apartment, which she shared with roommate David Smith"—so minor he'd missed it on first read. Another fact, and yet a wounding omission, a casual reduction of everything they'd been. He typed: *I'm sorry it's taken me so long to write.*

The twin portraits of Nadine and David Senior loomed large above the dinner table as conversation soured, Sonya recalling her first impression of David as *stiff and pedantic* when Nadine introduced them on the Christmas of 1986. "What is it you said, Mommy?" she asked Gale, already cackling about her response to learning Nadine planned to marry an academic. Gale's smile widened with the memory. "Must've been something like 'Well, how much money can he make?'" The whole table erupted in laughter, and even Senior grinned, though his portrait still glowered behind him. Over the years, he'd mastered the skill of resisting these provocations, so typical in Nadine's family. Each time conversation began to orbit a sensitive topic, he'd lob it back to greener pastures. Like this, they'd made it through the climate, queer politics, #MeToo—subjects on which Sonya's conservatism tended to show. By contrast, over heavy pours of wine, Nia renounced her usual penchant for peacemaking and embraced her underlying love of mess, the fun of coaxing politically explosive commentary out of her aunt as she grew drunk and voluble, but Senior was resolute, shepherding them through dinner without any irredeemable outbursts, after which he determined his duties complete and retired to his bath for the evening.

The rest stayed seated. Nia asked after her grandmother's health, if she had any plans to retire from the practice she'd now run for half a century. "Retire?" Gale cried as if propositioned. "My work keeps me going. My work, church, and meetups with my sorors."

"Mommy's never going to retire," Nadine explained to her daughter. "We can't even convince her to hire someone to help out with those apartments."

"Well, I shouldn't be hiring any stranger, that's family business," she said. "I've told Brandon and Davey they ought to come down to Houston for a few months and learn the ropes."

Smith forked a bite of cake and stayed silent. He knew that by *Brandon and Davey*, she meant himself and his one male cousin, an out-of-work video-game designer who lived in Santa Fe. He also knew the apartments to which she referred, the dozen or so properties in Houston's Fourth Ward that his grandfather had acquired over decades and managed until his death. He glanced up, surveying the women. "The ropes," Smith repeated.

"Working on plumbing, installing appliances, collecting rents," she explained, though that was hardly the source of his confusion. "That way, at least someone in the family will understand what it takes to manage these properties."

"I think that's a wonderful idea," said Nadine, a yellow glint in her eye.

Gale continued. "And that way, at least you'll be able to earn a decent living. You know, I'm not going to be around forever—and the apartments will go to Nadine and Sonya's generation, but they all have *careers*," she said, wielding the word with an incisive flourish so that Smith saw what kind of conversation they were actually having beneath the rhetorical surface, one about the sacrifices she'd made and he'd squandered. Smith looked again at his mother, whose chin was raised so that the whole of her brown face was daubed with the light above. She looked calm and resolute. He glanced at the chair where his father had been and realized then that this was not an impromptu discussion but something decided upon in his absence—this stern suggestion that he move to Houston and, under his grandmother's tutelage, learn the family trade of earning a passive income. The realization struck him with humorous absurdity, *As fucking if,* matched by an equal anger that this was what they thought of him, as a liability to be managed, prodigally incapable of earning his own, and then a fleck of relief. In a breath, he watched a future bloom in which he never went back to New York, even to retrieve his things; he left them there, all of his belongings, and his friends, and the version of himself he'd been, tossed his phone into the lake, and moved to Houston, where he'd disappear into the dust of Gale's home.

The pause endured a beat too long, and Nia gave in to the tension. "Yes, Davey Wavey would make a great landlord," she joked, then asked their grandmother, "Were you ever able to fix all that damage?" Smith remembered last Thanksgiving, in Houston, driving down the stretch of houses that amounted to their dwindled inheritance. Descending the hill on which they sat, each had been in worse shape than the last. At the bottom, where flooding from Hurricane Harvey had forced residents out for months, two houses stood, inside them the squalid aftermath. They'd spent an afternoon emptying one; its former resident had relocated to higher ground, having realized that even climate and its attendant disaster would not be exactly shared. On the walls of his gutted apartment, purplish stains spread like bruises across a meaty thigh.

"We were able to renovate, yes, but that other one across the way, where Shanie and them live, can't do a thing about that one until she pays some rent. They're about six months behind, and I've already been in telling them, soon as you pay your back rent, maybe I can get someone in here to—"

"But that house isn't livable," Nia interrupted. "She shouldn't pay *until* you've made those renovations."

To this, Gale bristled. "She hasn't got no right not to pay."

In fact, the legal line was dubious, pliable to the interests of the opposing counsel, but it came down in the end to the question of habitability: Could a person really live here like this?

"They should take you to small-claims court," said Nia, topping off her glass with a swish of Nebbiolo. "Hell, I'd represent them."

"Um, how, Miss Three-L?" asked Sonya. "You realize you have to actually *pass* the bar to give legal advice."

"Obviously, that was a joke," she said, rolling her eyes. "But that's exactly why I'm going into public service, to stop greedy people like y'all from taking advantage of people who—"

"Take advantage!" Gale exclaimed, letting out an ugly laugh. "They're the ones taking advantage of me! No chance in hell she'd have ever tried this while Bobby was alive. He'd have put her on the street."

This elicited a visceral response from Nia. "That's despicable. And not something to laugh about. You realize eviction is one of the most traumatic events a family can go through."

"Then pay rent," Gale replied archly. An uneasy peace resumed.

"Nadine, remember how Daddy—" Sonya began after a few seconds' silence bled into a girlhood memory: The times they'd gone with their father to the apartments on Holloway, a teetering building which had seemed vast and filled with a mythical squalor, screaming babies, and the gutted silhouettes of barely dressed women guarding doors. Children raised in rooms of smoke. "He used to carry his gun in his holster like a promise," she recalled of him fondly. Nadine, for her part, stayed silent throughout this account; if she recalled the image to which her sister referred, two primly dressed girls hiding behind the pants of their father, she didn't acknowledge it. "He rented to people who couldn't have gotten another apartment, no way. Didn't matter, long as they paid their rent on time."

Smith watched Nia's face as she absorbed the information with evident consternation. "So he was a slumlord," she stated plainly, as was her wont.

You could see, even in the mocha hues of Sonya's face, a sudden loss of color. The room lost wind, like a sail set empty. "How dare you," she spat. Nia was now smiling faintly. "How dare you call him that," their aunt repeated, this time louder. Her expression was stone, eyes empty of the joke they usually carried. It wasn't the first time she'd heard her father called that, and the word held the devastating weight of all truths in dispute.

"From what I'm hearing," Nia proceeded, only slightly cowed, "that's exactly what he was." Smith looked at his grandmother, sitting still, with a weary expression. Her wrinkled hands were crossed like gloves in her lap. "I mean, call it what you want, but that's predatory."

"*Predatory?*" Sonya shrilled. "He was giving them a place to live, wasn't he?"

Finally, Nadine spoke. "Yes, what you have to understand is that a lot of these people were unbanked, unemployed. No credit, terrible housing histories. It's true that barely anyone else would've rented to them."

"I understand that," said Nia sharply. "And I'm sure he was charging them completely extractive rents precisely *because* he knew they had no options. That's what makes it so craven."

Sonya snorted, and the room again fell quiet. "Big words," she said, pointing her spindly index finger in a schoolyard taunt. She set her whiskey down on the table, where its melting cubes swirled with centrifugal motion. Her eyelids liquored heavy, her words came sharply barbed: "It's easy to spout big words when you grew up silver-spooned, but the fact is, you wouldn't be where you are without those apartments. Your mother couldn't have gone to college, let alone med school, without those apartments—none of us could have."

Nia cocked her head, searching the wall for an appropriate retort; there was none. "I take your point," she conceded. They returned to dessert, wine, coffee, and again attempted the politesse they'd managed all dinner— plans for the New Year, travel, and birthdays—but the cloth night had been stained by everything said. One by one, they excused themselves, first Sonya, then Nadine, then Nia with an impenitent look, but Smith remained seated, for some reason immobile, as Gale stood from the opposite end of the oblong and began to clear the plates remaining. So quickly her initial request had devolved to a music of inchoate rage. He'd never replied, and as she left the room, he wondered what he would have said.

Smith awoke to a faint dawn, pitched just beyond the trees. No one else would be up for hours. Downstairs, the thin hum of one collective snore passed from room to room, and in the wan glow of string lights left on, he could make out phantom shadows. Despite the calm, he was anxious, his heart keeping merciless time. A kind of burn unlikely to cure with chamomile. Nonetheless, he headed to the kitchen, where on the island, amid drying dishes, sat his aunt's fifth of whiskey. All night, he'd watched it in her hand, dwindling to this pool of amber. It wasn't even his drink. Still, the thought of it, its warmth and oaky flavor, clawed open an ache.

He walked to the cabinet and retrieved a glass.

Some part of him would've loved to lose control. To have a sip, then have guzzled the bottle. There was solace in this vision of himself, vomit-bathed on the bathroom floor. It would have been an answer, an explanation for everything wrong. But as he took his first sip, he knew that would not be the case. The whiskey tasted tart, and good. *One too many and never enough*. He took a second. It tasted tart, and dull. He knew he would have *just one*. He would not wake on the bathroom floor. Would not take the Tesla to score an eight ball or invite a stranger off Grindr to fuck in his childhood bed. He would drink this drink, slowly and without an excess of pleasure, then he would go back to sleep. And he despised this knowing, which threatened to unwrite the story he'd just started to tell.

With his glass, he stepped out to the porch's daylight. It was no longer Christmas. The sky was a formless, shifting gray—a brilliant and blinding luminescence. Smith gazed across the fungal tarp at the neighbor's house. A tan-colored Spanish colonial, stacked ornately into tiers beyond a sloping green, it had been inhabited for a number of years by a single woman. *Ms. . . . Something*. She had always seemed eccentric. While the Smiths' other neighbors embarked upon home-improvement projects with the usual suburban frequency, this woman had for many years been in the process of a never-ending gut renovation, attended to by legions of hard-hatted men whose pickups filled her driveway daily. As a child, Smith would watch them from the balcony: hammering, drilling, dozing, snacking, plastering, napping, painting. But the next day, the next month or even year, he would look back at the house, and it would seem, as if by magic, entirely unchanged.

The woman herself was a mystery, unintegrated into the social life of the neighborhood, which had centered a weekly prayer group and the communal raising of children she never had, but Nadine knew her personally. A brilliant surgeon who'd been top of her class at Howard, the woman had moved to the neighborhood alone and rebuffed any and all invitations in those early years. *Always*, she was busy, *had to work, work, work*. To build and then maintain a spotless reputation for skill and professional bearing, which had earned her, at forty, the honor of becoming the first Black chief of cardiology at Grady Hospital. She excelled, won numerous awards, and made good on that relentless pursuit of perfection those few who knew her admired, even as it continued to lay waste to her home. *It's not good enough, start again.* Then she'd hung herself, the winter prior. Construction had promptly ceased, and the house—not yet sold—had stalled in an interminable state of becoming. Smith downed the rest of the whiskey, sucked a cube of ice with his tongue. Finished, he washed the glass and went to sleep.

III.

In the City

CHAPTER NINETEEN

"So you've been a good boy, eh?" asked Mancini over Skype following several minutes recapping his holiday season in breathless monologue: the two-week stay at his sister's in New Jersey, the spoiled children and deadbeat husband of whom had reminded him daily why he (to his mind, volitionally) lived alone. "Staying clean, going to meetings?"

Smith affirmed that he had, though it had been over a month since he'd attended one and precisely two weeks since he'd relapsed on booze, though the word *relapse* did not seem to suit the situation. Since that one glass of whiskey, he hadn't had, or particularly craved, so much as a sip. "It was tough, you know, with the holidays and whatnot, to stay on the straight and narrow. But I did, and I'm proud of myself, really, for using all those *great tools* you taught me."

Mancini's face was so stiff and inscrutable that Smith wondered, for a moment, if he'd overhammed his part. Then the features glitched, the Wi-Fi recovered, and Smith could see he was smiling. "We'll know soon enough, anyways," he said then, sternly, invoking the purpose of this check-in, late afternoon the second Wednesday of January. Smith would need to submit to another drug test, the doctor explained, his third and hopefully final. If the results came back negative, which Smith had no reason to believe they would not, then the doctor would update his letter of completion and pass it on to Walsh. "Yes," Mancini said, and still he was smiling, though now the quality had somewhat altered, as if let in on a crueler joke. "You can lie to me with your mouth but not your piss."

The call ended, and the screen went dark. Smith closed his laptop and examined the empty room. He would not be able to afford to live here much longer—unemployed, in a two-bedroom apartment, a full third of its space cordoned off like a shrine. With the dwindling remains of his severance, he surmised that he could make it through March, then he would have to find a new roommate or apartment altogether. Two options which seemed inconceivable: waking up to the sound of a stranger's snoring, their hair in the bathroom sink—all of the carnal closeness innate to sharing space.

Since the *Vanity Fair* piece had gone live, three days ago, he'd protected his space with an almost animal intensity: space from Nia, who had clearly seen but refused to mention the story, so had hovered around him in rooms as if on permanent ledge patrol; from his parents, who'd expressed sadness at his sudden decision to leave Atlanta, though underneath, he sensed relief; and from all the others, friends and acquaintances who'd texted to ask if he'd *seen it*, or, more boldly, *if he thought it was true*, and all the internet strangers who'd descended to the comment sections of Elle's Instagram feed as to the cheap seats of the Roman Colosseum, hungry for blood.

In fact, his only contact since he'd landed back in Brooklyn had been an email from Elle's mom. She'd taken ten days to reply, so long he'd almost forgotten he'd sent it. *Dear David*, she wrote, her tone a bit cold. Making no reference to the "heartfelt condolences" he'd offered in his message, she'd gotten quickly down to business. *I'm sorry that, with every-thing going on*—she wrote, that euphemism a gut punch, though he confessed he had no better language to hold the heartache—*we haven't been able to send someone to collect Elle's things.* And of course, hers would be far greater, so immense that such obfuscations would be a necessary defense against the onslaught of unearned intimacy. She would've spent months fending it off, from friends and fans alike—people who felt that they knew her so could demand it, though their brazen attempts at connection were but daily reminders of the depth of her grief.

But in the email, her tone had lifted in the last line, a shift that had sealed his decision to return to New York, their apartment. *I'll be in town next week actually*, she'd written. *Perhaps I could stop by?*

Elle's room was in the same disarray he'd left it, clothing plucked from hangers and tossed to the floor, her bed unmade and trash bin emptied, as if looted by a thief. And Smith did feel a bit like a grave robber as he began to fill a duffel with the clothes he now carefully folded. And moving on to the books, the knickknacks, the records in the living-room corner, he wondered if any of these objects—which, for him, bore a totemic importance—were his to keep.

Crouching, he reached under her bed and removed one by one the shoeboxes in a Technicolor of designer shades: burnt mustard and crisp café crème and Lanvin eggshell blue. But when he lifted an onyx box behind them, it was eerily weightless.

Opening it, he found it was filled to the brim with film negatives in laminate sleeves. He grabbed one and held it to the light at her window, examining the images, or their opposites: shade-like and spectral, all translucent hair and empty eyes, as if wading back to the land of the living.

In the months before she died, Elle had begun to seek out a new kind of beauty. Relieved of her job's editorial demands, she was no longer interested in taking portraits of the professionally pretty but, increasingly, of strangers she'd met on nights out. Smith recognized a few, the ghostly twins of images uploaded online: a club kid with a *hood shit* face tattoo, a drag queen with a chipped and deadened tooth. A few old heads hanging out on the stoop across the road, throwing dice and shooting shit, lighting cigarettes and laughing. They all appeared in the light box of her room, hundreds of portraits, and Smith's pulse quickened as he realized that one might be him.

The Unidentified Man. The Bronx.

Having seen only a brief blur of his face, he found it impossible to say which, or even if, one of these portraits was him. There were so many men, crust punks and ravers, bankers and thugs—some of whom she'd no doubt spoken to for only a minute, the time it took to pose them for a picture, others of whom she might have really known—but Smith thought that if he got the film developed, he might be able to make an educated guess from the public information. *Six feet, dark-skinned, with a native New York kind of fuck-you attitude.* He could assemble his suspects and bring their photos to the nightclub bouncer or deliver them directly to Clement—or, better still, he could take matters into his own hands by uploading them online and letting the internet do its vigilante thing.

Smith ripped off a clear strand of tape, pasted one of these reels against the window, and examined as if under a microscope a shirtless man in baggy sweats before what appeared to be a laundromat. And for the first time, he thought he might be sitting on something that could crack the case open—a record of her private memories, stashed in the quiet dark.

One by one, he held them to the light.

CHAPTER TWENTY

The med tech barely flinched at the scent of Smith's piss, despite being mere inches away. After three days of total reclusion, there was something satisfying about this proximity—the skin-to-skin on a rush-hour train, eyes locked across a distance, all the people, people, people. Smith handed over the sealed sample and returned to the grim waiting room, where he watched—as the front desk charged his card—a tide of passersby through the window.

One paused, and for a moment, it appeared they were staring directly at him until he recalled that the windows had been mirrored to protect patient anonymity, so this person was gazing only at their own reflection. Smith studied their face, familiar and alien at once, and thought to himself that it was precisely the kind promised in the literature of a *post-race* America: caramel-toned, fine-featured, with substantial lips and eyes of teakwood hazel. But this face also courted other *post*s. For one, it wasn't an immediately identifiable gender. It was hairless and romantic, a pore-less pallor that was unnerving up close and would've induced in Smith an envy were its features less peculiar—but he saw, as they settled, that those lips were accompanied and arguably overshadowed by a protruding, beaklike nose and eyebrows so dense, they hooded the hazel with a thicket of constant concern. In this way, the face was both ugly and unspeakably beautiful. *Post*-speech, *post*-beauty.

"Would you like your receipt?" the woman asked.

Smith shook his head and, looking back, saw that the person had vanished—and only then did he recall how he knew them. Immediately, he strode out into the blue afternoon, where a soft snow had just begun. Squinting, he saw them down an avenue's distance through the cotton wisps midair and took off at a sprint, catching up as they paused on a corner. They glanced up with a startled expression. "I know you," they offered, beaming. Their bottom teeth were cluttered and the top ones were too big, everything about them overdrawn. "*How* do I know you?"

"From that studio visit," Smith reminded them, and they squinted, as if this explanation had roughly the clarifying effect of saying they'd met somewhere on the North American continent. "Mona Ali's, remember? I came in with my boss."

"Oh, right," they recalled. "The *emissary*."

Smith's face fell at the perceived slight.

"I'm playing," they continued with a grin. "I'm O, by the way."

"*Oh?*" Smith questioned. "Is that a name?"

They laughed obscurely, glancing down, but didn't answer. Just barely, against Smith's tote's thin canvas, one could make out the cover of the last book he'd looted from his father's office. "Adolph Reed," they observed in a tone that straddled approval and reproach. "So you're a class reductionist."

"Well," said Smith. "I'm no stan, just an interested party."

O nodded, grinned again, and a chemical relief filled Smith's veins. "My mom has about twenty years of the *Village Voice* stacked up in her closet. I used to tear through archives of his essays. You know the one where he calls bell hooks a hustler?"

"The nerve," Smith said, cackling at the comment's cruelty.

"Careful now," said O, still smiling big. "Jack and Jill–type like you reading Adolph Reed? The last thing Brooklyn needs is another Moët Marxist." Smith took a step back, slightly wounded. It was a clean read, a precise estimation of the distance between who he was and how he hoped to be seen. He felt embarrassed, realizing then that he'd dressed up for the clinic—as if a cashmere sweater and slacks would dispel any question as to why he required a drug test, implying that it was for a job in finance or the government rather than an imminent appearance in court. O glanced back at their phone, and their eyebrows convened in concern. "I'm late for a meeting with my thesis adviser."

"Well, what are you doing tonight, give me your number," said Smith, the run-on tumbling out of him like a drunken conga. His muscle for social nuance, he realized, had atrophied in the days (weeks?) he'd spent alone. O laughed and took his phone.

It was nearly eight p.m. when Smith arrived at the address he'd been given. Just a twenty-minute walk from his own apartment, on a desolate block, he found the door, propped open with a house slipper, and proceeded through the grime-slick lobby, past two shaggy-haired Mansonites with skateboards wedged under their arms. Cautiously, he shuffled through the dark, guided by shocks of laughter. In the laundry room, between the humming dryers, were piles of supplies—condoms, bandages—all grouped by kind and being stuffed into sacks like children's sandwiches. Immediately, the motion ceased and four sets of eyes flit toward him as in a crime bust, a meth lab. Smith glanced first at Mona, then the others: a heavyset dark-skinned girl with neon box braids that swept her sweatered back, a gap-toothed boy in a patterned silk bandanna, and of course O, whose cropped, glitter-toned turtleneck matched their evening eyeshadow. O leapt up smiling, then introduced him to the room, a flurry of *What's good*s and nigga nods that came without mention of names. "Thanks for having me," said Smith, regretting the bottle of wine he'd brought as an offering. He noticed, on the braided girl's face, a look of outsize reproach.

Swiftly, O replied, "Thank you, that's so kind," then placed the bottle in a corner where it was likely to remain. "But we're actually getting ready to go."

O apologized, as they walked toward the train, for not explaining the plan more clearly; frankly, they confessed, they didn't think he would actually come. Several times a week, Tia organized a group to distribute supplies to the unhoused, some dope-is-death harm-reduction thing that had begun in the hot summer months, when she'd been frequently joined by dozens, but as the months tattered on and the weather grew inhospitable, she'd seen their numbers dwindle with disheartening swiftness.

The elevated train rattled along its imperfect spine. Just a few others, bundled in Michelin puffers, exposed their wind-bitten faces to the clinical light. Placing Smith in her memory, Mona warmed to him quickly and began to catch him up on the months since they'd met: the success of her show and the major curators who'd expressed interest in its aftermath. It seemed that she'd been wrenched in a matter of months from relative obscurity, the marginal space of the avant-garde, into the luminous mainstream of the commercial art world. Smith pictured graying financiers in Patek Philippe watches slipping on her embroidered oculi, entering *the impossible Black future* from the comfort of their orchid-filled studies. "I'm so happy for you," he said.

"It *is* a bit strange," she confessed, shifting her weight toward him. "I mean, with a lot of these curators and critics, it's almost like the work is an afterthought." This had become apparent recently when her first major profile was published, a piece for which she'd spent three days in her studio with a rakish reporter, explaining the complex tech behind her practice and musing on its lofty aims. But in the final piece, there was just one paragraph, about two hundred words, devoted to the work. The rest traced her childhood in Barbados as the daughter of an English-educated functionary who'd been vocally opposed to the commonwealth, the country's allegiance to the queen, and the many other vestiges of colonialism that she'd learned to detest in her youth to her present life in New York, where, despite a *nontraditional background*—she had no related degree or connections—she'd become one of the year's *most exciting artists-to-watch*, staking a claim on an emergent medium largely helmed by men, *white* men, who often used it to play out their *problematic fantasies.* In this way, she felt that the biographical details of her life had been laid into bricks to be lobbed for the journalist's own aims, "which was unfortunate," she said with a waning smile. "But you know how it is," she mused. "You only get to play messiah if you're willing to be a martyr also."

"So I'll take Sixth with Luis, and y'all go east, a'ight?" said Tia as they emerged from the train to Mona and O and, Smith supposed, himself, though she had still yet to acknowledge him. He noted, as she spoke, the peculiarity of her accent—regionally unplaceable but unequivocally Black, a mélange of Southern roots and New York reeducation that suggested a circuitous path. And despite himself, he wondered about her history.

"How is it you know Tia," he asked as they ambled east. Mona answered, "From Church," and O let out a bright peal of laughter before explaining that Church was a party that had functioned during the week as a safe house for trans runaways but illegally and after-hours became a nightclub—the cover charges covering rent. Fats, freaks, femmes, they took the train to the end of the line, a converted convent on the edge of Ridgewood, where for months they built a thing holy—until others arrived, drawn in by loose-lipped scenesters and the Instagrams of those who'd ignored the forbiddance of photography.

"Tia used to live there and run door," O explained. "First time I came, I was on line for like an hour, and right as I got to the front, these Williamsburg twinks pulled up in an Uber SUV and tried to cut, *tal'm'bout* some 'I know the DJ.' She was like, 'I don't care who the fuck it is you think you *know*, you're about to *learn*.' That's how I knew she was that bitch."

Nights thereafter, once the door had closed around six, they'd find each other in the smoke, talk shit, dance. Their courtship played out in cacophonous rooms, their histories obscured but for the blips they let slip as the after-hours stretched into days, a kind of midnight family. "And then it closed, last June," said O. "The cops claimed for permits, but, well, I'm sure you heard, there was a lot of bad coke going around Brooklyn." Smith's attention sharpened. In truth, it hadn't occurred to him, the many others who must've met the same fate as Elle on a few grains of the wrong stuff. "And this kid Ari OD'd at one of the parties, which affected all of the regulars, of course, but it *really* soured something for Tia, because she'd always thought of Church as an Eden, a place where people would look out and show love in, like, a radical way. 'Cause that's how it'd been for her when she first got to New York and had nowhere to go, long before it became, like, a *scene*. And she felt a lot of guilt, I think, because Ari died alone, in the stalls, and wasn't even found for hours."

When it closed, an illusion shattered. Most of the people they knew then, saw weekly in those illusory hours, they didn't know much about their outside lives. If you clocked someone in daylight, it was with the vague recognition of a dreamy apparition. You didn't know who had money or who was crashing upstairs; they all dressed in baroque disarray. But it did close, did come to an end. And those cut loose were left drifting, making abundantly clear that what was amusement for some was survival for others. "So where did she go?" Smith asked. "*After*."

Immediately, he could see he'd struck a nerve. Mona locked eyes with O, who, in the glow of a Dominican deli, held the flicker of a pained expression. "Mine for a while," they said. "But that didn't really work, so she's been drifting ever since, you know, couch to couch and room to room."

At Tompkins Square, they slowed, looming toward a group of three huddled on Avenue A. Two men and a woman, who wore a lavender wig beneath her hooded coat. O greeted her by name and she looked up, lips parting to reveal scant teeth. She was older than at first she'd appeared—forties, maybe fifties—and frightfully thin, dependent on the body heat of the men who sat beside her. Immediately, she launched into an account of how she'd ended up out here in the park rather than at a nearby shelter, whose staff were always telling lies on her and stealing her stuff as well, though what stuff, she didn't specify, carrying on at a languorous clip. O nodded with polite concern but asked no follow-up questions; perhaps they'd heard this or some version before. "Tonight, we have everything. Test strips, wound kits," they added knowingly but with the distinct indifference of someone trained to remove all judgment. Smith examined the plastic sleeve, which read *Rapid Response*, knowing that its contents were just strips of paper but divisive nonetheless, in some states illegal, the implication being that drug use was a moral failure for which death was an appropriate punishment. Even in her condition, the wigged woman seemed aware of this. Her wide eyes darkened, but she took the pack.

Despite the cold, the park was alive. Tipsy postgrads passed between dives, speaking loudly over a chorus of buskers. Amid this bustle, it was easy to ignore the scattered, limp bodies splayed out on benches, pitched up against trees, sleeping bags and coats cocooned around them. In the lamplight, Smith scanned the faces of vagrant men—sullen, stoned, nearly all of them Black. They seemed so far from him, not the kind of people generally thought capable or perhaps *deserving* of rehabilitation, even as the opioid crisis had brought about a swell of newfound empathy. In congressional town halls and newspaper headlines, bipartisan calls for treatment were paired always with the accounts of college kids who'd gotten hooked on prescriptions then moved on to something harder so that even the meager supply of empathy was selectively applied to those understood as victims—of profit-seeking doctors and Big Pharma billionaires—rather than victims only of themselves, the agony of their lives and their own *base* instincts. In this way, Smith thought, the war on drugs had not subsided but undergone a branding shift, one with insidious echoes in policy. And what had these men in the park to gain from that redesign, the *fresh face of addiction*?

He had, though, hadn't he, benefited from that shift—addiction recast as a reaper who could enter any home, making crime-tough fogies adjust their timeworn tune. His lawyer had worked to ensure it. *Iron your suit, comb your hair*, all reminders of a lifelong lesson: that class and its comportment offered a proximity to whiteness that could make you a person in another's eyes, one deserving of a second chance. Perhaps that was what Tia saw in him, that hideous chimeric thing. She'd taken one look at his natural wine, his Saint Laurent boots, and clocked him as a spineless striver, one willing to dance when told. And so she had known that his presence here was essentially frivolous, the latest in bourgeois amusement. He would use this to feel good, then move on, as had so many others. He could tell, from those same subtle markers of dress and affect, that Mona and O were more of a kind with him. They were here out of fealty, good politics, but not need, not fear that they might someday end up on the other end of a cruel equation. But for Tia, *couch to couch and room to room*, the slip from that rusted last rung into the endless bottom would be so slight as to be silent.

CHAPTER TWENTY-ONE

The next day Smith called Carolyn, and they made a plan to meet. Arriving on Broome Street in Chinatown, he took a freight to the penthouse floor, then stepped out into what appeared to be a construction site until he realized that this temple of stark modernity was her boss's home—the expanse of polished concrete strewn with odd, misshapen objects not immediately identifiable for their function. "You're right on time, how awful," she said, appearing from an unseen hallway in a sherbet-colored robe, the only speck of color in that black-white-beige monstros-ity. Engulfed in her tight embrace, he could feel her words move through him. "*My God*, I've missed you."

She'd crashed here last night, and the one before that, she explained in a harried tone, absently picking up a few garments as she beckoned him past a long dining table of sleek obsidian into an area he'd hesitate to call a *living* room—a better room for *dying*, its couch an emerald slab topped with a polar bear hide whose petrified face was propped up on one end. She was looking after Dmitri's cat while he was in Los Angeles, she said. But Smith saw no cat, and though he believed she'd been tasked with its care, he doubted she'd been asked to stay, this being the kind of home in which a sock left out is a capital offense, most often inhabited by those to whom the idea would never occur. And already, there was the bright, fragrant proof of her being, of which she'd have to leave no trace. "Five minutes," she shouted as she slurred out of the room; somewhere, a shower sputtered on.

Like a forensicist casing a crime scene, Smith moved through the empty apartment, past the Nero Marquina marble kitchen, through a Rick Owens thicket, and into the bedroom, where he half expected to find an open sarcophagus. Despite the clinical sterility, he could detect the not-yet-loosened stench of smoke. A side table had been cleared, but not completely, and a number of still wet rings were fading into wood. She'd had guests, then, likely within the last twenty-four hours; perhaps she hadn't even slept. In a corner, he finally found the sphynx cat perched, sculpture-like, atop a stack of books: Tillmans and Goldin. The photographer's face, beat black by a boyfriend, gazed up like a warning.

"One sec and we can go, okay," said Carolyn, appearing in a Turkish towel behind him. Whatever she'd done, had been doing, it had not yet caught up with her. She was luminous, though now derobed, observably thin. Her clavicles emerged bluntly beneath wintry skin. In some way, it suited her, this angular face. It was a face too pale to accommodate blemishes, of which there were graciously none, and had about it the quality of anything won on a witch's bargain. A face of voiceless beauty. She dressed quickly in a sweater and slacks, and together, they descended to Broome Street, where the fish-scented afternoon came apart in Smith's memory: Some morning, some summer, stepping out of a pounding basement as the markets were opening outside, he'd bought a mango and peeled it with his teeth.

"Did you hear me?" Carolyn asked, her eyes wide. "Which way?" Smith answered, "Whichever," and she took off toward Allen, where curbside men shilled star fruit despite the season. As they walked, Carolyn hooked her arm in his and spoke feverishly on many subjects, the *everything* they had to catch up on, composed mainly of observations, comic anecdotes which she'd bookmarked to tell him and did so now in a voluble stream that more or less forbade interruption. She was sometimes speaking so quickly that zoning out for a moment had the effect of spinning out. She'd sped on to the next subject, the next street, along a conversational speedway that both heightened his desire and negated his ability to ask a simple question—*Are you all right*—much less to bring up more somber subjects.

On Leonard, she stepped without warning into a deli, where an ancient shopkeep hovered above the register, his yellow eyes unblinking as he glanced up from a magazine. Beyond him was a grid of every possible vice: cigarettes and cigarillos, swishers, skittles, starbursts, vapes, poppers and pills and probably weed, and after scanning them, she alighted on the one of her choosing. "American Spirits," she said, then, to Smith, "I've been smoking." Not an apology, exactly, more a test—no doubt it was the least of her indulgences—to which he gave no reaction. "Please," she said a bit curtly to the waxen Yoda, who closed the magazine and shuffled off.

Smith's face darkened.

On the cover was a photograph of a nubile actress who'd recently become a household name for her portrayal of an Old Hollywood icon. Wearing a white baby-doll dress, she held her plump, perfect face in an emotionless posture, as if told that to be a star was to be impassible, accessible only on-screen. "Yes, the blue ones," Carolyn instructed the fumbling shopkeep, whose spindly fingers reached out, tiptoed, for the pack. It was Elle's issue, he knew, January's *Vanity Fair*. Within those glossy pages, buried among starlets whose faces were all teeth, male models too frail to fuck, would be an image of Elle, the same that had accompanied the story online, printed now full bleed. It was the first to appear when she was googled, which meant it would forever be the world's first glimpse of her. Even at that moment, it must've been gazing up at strangers in waiting rooms, salons, and cafés across the city, indeed across the country, telegraphing that telegenic dream sold on the cover only to be punctured in the text. Some transformation was complete. In death, she was famous, and the work of fame is to be consumed.

With a tap of her card, Carolyn paid and stepped back into the cold. For a moment, they were silent, Carolyn lighting her long cigarette, then breathing smoke into the wind. Stealing a drag, Smith wondered if she'd also seen the magazine; how could she not have? He waited for her to speak, just as he had for weeks, wounded each time her texts arrived, speaking blithely of other subjects. Even if she hadn't read the story, hadn't scoured the comment sections and allowed strangers to rob her of sleep, she must've heard whispers among the downtown set. It was clear that she'd been spending all her nights out, collecting keys, running from something. And Smith wondered whether her mania was a means of avoiding this painful subject, but as they walked west and she plunged again into meaningless gossip, he resigned himself to the distinct possibility that she wasn't thinking about it at all. Already, she'd moved on to the next season of her life, wading back into that midnight world. *How well did you know your friend?* he thought as they crossed into Tribeca, and he glimpsed the faint crescent moons beneath her eyes, growing darker in the gloaming twilight.

In the neon blush of the Odeon, she paused. "Let's get some food?"

Smith considered his miserly finances. Here, he would squander a half week's budget on a burger and fries, leaping closer to the day when his life in the city would become untenable—like Elle, with her debts and secrets. His stomach growled. "Maybe a coffee."

They entered to find the restaurant packed, wall to mirrored wall. "There's no way we're getting a table," said Smith, though Carolyn had already stalked toward the hostess to present their names for the bar. He remained by the door with the other clustered hopefuls. From that short distance, he watched their inaudible conversation, a negotiation during which each of them laughed several times, Carolyn's cutting the din. The brunch crowd had overstayed its welcome and was joined by early dinner. Empty champagne flutes watched in fearful awe the sultry approach of the night's first martini, swishing seductively atop an upraised tray. Finally, the glass arrived and was drunk half empty by a haggard-looking mother. Screaming in its high chair, her baby demanded attention from parents who gave it none, the teachings of some woo-woo philosophy. They had the best table in the house and were making a real mess of it in the way of people used to such things, such tables. Eventually, the woman relented and, despite her husband's protests, plucked the infant from its chair and rocked it in her arms gently. It quieted. And only then, once the room's equilibrium was restored, did Smith realize that he recognized this woman, her husband. "Oh, fuck," he said aloud.

Carolyn arrived at his side. "I dropped my best names but it's going to be an hour; let's just go somewhere else," she said. Smith nodded, relieved. He pushed the door open. "I'm just going to run to the restroom," she announced, and by the time he'd turned to protest, all that was left was the bounce of golden hair as she stalked across the room, not along its periphery but a labyrinthian path that zigzagged through its center. It was too late to call her back, and shifting his gaze to the corner, where the wife remained distracted by her child, he saw that Rune had also taken note of her warpath through the room. He watched her as one hopes to be watched by any former flame, with ravenous fury and regret, and Smith realized that their presence here was not by accident. She had known he would be with his wife at their usual Sunday table. She had pictured this moment precisely and now savored it, returning—after a time in the bathroom barely enough to wash her hands—with operatic precision, her chin angled upward, a haughty look in her eyes as she gazed above her seated stadium at no one in particular, arriving at the door with a cruel, triumphant look. "Let's go," she said.

Go they did. And Smith said nothing as they traversed the half mile to her grandparents' apartment—they had been out east since Christmas, *Ann likes to paint the beaches empty*—and on arrival, she immediately poured herself a drink: just vodka on ice, ungarnished. Seeing the defiance with which she sipped, Smith knew this would be her sole admission.

"I'll, um, I'll have one as well," he said, figuring it best that they were both fuckups, at least then they'd have this in common. She smiled, relieved, and poured him a drink. In a sigh of pastel brushstroke, she blurred back into a softer animal, her blue eyes alive as she recounted stories of Christmas on Crosby. Her father had taken to bringing home girls half his age since the divorce: concave, birdlike women ill-attuned to social nuance who often hung around for family breakfast. Smith half listened, smiling meekly, while musing over everything unsaid: Not just Elle, the story and the rumor and the stalled investigation, but Carolyn's relapse and his own and the growing gulf between them. Emboldened, he took a sip of his second drink and interrupted. "Carolyn," he said. Her face fell. "I think, um, we need to talk—"

"About?" she questioned with a look of cervine surprise.

"Just, you know," he began. All day he'd wanted her full attention, but now that he had it, he wasn't sure what to say. "Um, well, my court date is coming up."

"Of course," she said in an ambiguous tone. She wasn't sure what to do with the information. She sipped. "When is it exactly?"

"Two weeks," Smith replied. "On the twenty-third."

She nodded. "Would you maybe want me to come with?" she asked.

Smith was surprised, both by the offer and the turn, how quickly he'd become the object of *her* concern. Briefly, he considered the optics. No matter how she'd been spending her nights, he knew she would show up on time, dressed conservatively, her blond hair swept back from her face to frame its beauty, projecting cleanliness and health. But her presence, its evident asymmetry next to his own, what story would it tell? That he was *of* this place—not an interloper, a tourist, but a person proximate to whiteness, wealth. And would that be a boon or a liability?

He was still deciding when her phone came alive. She tapped *Ignore*. "Sorry," she said, looking back at him, expectant. But then it blared again, flashing the word *Unknown*.

"Do you think it's, well—" Smith paused. "You saw him, obviously, at the Odeon." Her look confirmed that she had, and as the phone began to ring a third time, he raised his voice sternly. "Well, turn it *off* if you aren't going to answer."

With a long, exasperated sigh, she stepped into the open kitchen. "Yes, obviously I know that it's you" was her greeting. "Don't be ridiculous, it's a popular restaurant. Smith and I were just going for dinner." Her tone was convincing, conveying that she did not wish to speak. "I'm still with him," she said, then firmly, "*No*." Which, perhaps, she didn't. Perhaps, despite her earlier efforts, she had no wish to speak to the man but couldn't resist such an easy opportunity to ruin his evening. "If you do that, I'm calling the cops, goodbye," she said, then hung up the phone, her face flushed with drink and anger.

Smith stated the obvious—"You've still been seeing him"—and met her gaze across the counter. But before she could answer, the buzzer rang, and it became clear he'd called en route. Her face caught tightly.

She marched from the kitchen to the locked front door, Smith in tow. He leaned against the wall of Ann's studio and watched the watercolors mist in his slurring vision.

On the monitor, Rune's face appeared fish-eyed, his forehead vast and convex against his small frame. But his sound was not small. With the front door of the building just feet away, his voice carried. She needn't even press the intercom. "Let me in," he demanded, then waited a few seconds. "Carolyn." His voice was low and warped. "You need to let me in," he ordered. "What are you trying to fucking do to me," he asked. "What are you trying to fucking do?"

Another minute passed, during which he was silent as he considered his options. Most likely, he'd told his wife he had an errand. He didn't have all night. He buzzed again. "I know you're in there," he said, an observation or a threat, though the loft felt like a fortress: the fabled house of bricks that the wolf could not blow down. He stepped away from the buzzer, and for a moment, it appeared he would go, until the blur of another came into view. An elderly woman propped open the door as she exited, and in he came. Carolyn's face, when she glanced back at Smith, flashed panic. But there was amusement also. And as the pounding began, Smith braced for insults—*harlot, homewrecker, whore*—but when the voice came, it was quiet.

"Carolyn?" it asked with pillowy softness. "Carolyn," it repeated. "I know you're in there. Open the door, please, we need to talk." Carolyn glanced at Smith and mouthed the word *Sorry*. He shrugged, sliding down the studio wall, then cooling his hands against the wood. He could hear, in Rune's voice, pure desperation. Just inches between them now, a thin yet impenetrable distance, so the voice came clear and close. It desisted with demands and attempted to plead. *Please*, it said, *please*.

Carolyn's face, leaned against the metal door, was obscured. But from her quivering back, he could tell she was crying; the only logical conclusion to the chaos she'd been determined to create. It was clear that she had a problem, one which had accelerated in his absence, but it was not just one of substances. It might be years before the thick coat of glamour began to chip, before she struck out at parties and burned through bridges and slipped into the sort of squalor one is taught attends addiction. Or perhaps she would never—would continue instead to inhabit clean rooms in the company of beautiful people. Hers was a problem of substances, yes, and of pride, but also of something that was not her own. The passes she would always be given. And for that, Smith envied her with an ardor for which he had no words. It was an ugly thought, he knew, because he understood it was a hindrance to recovery, to be stalled at that first step, accepting one's *powerlessness*—how could she when her rock bottoms would always seem romantic in retrospect? Nonetheless, he envied her. For to be seen to *have* a problem struck him as a luxury, one that would give her the space and time to negotiate on her terms, to learn over decades its contours. It was a harrowing burden, and yet, *yes*, a luxury afforded to few. And with his envy came a wave of overwhelming resentment for which he saw no easy resolve. An audience of one, he watched her and thought darkly of a line he'd inked weeks ago in one of his father's Black books.

How does it feel to be *a problem?*

CHAPTER TWENTY-TWO

That night, the snow began to fall and didn't stop. The evening had ended in bathos, Rune's eventual forfeit after an hour at her door, and after, Carolyn had asked Smith to stay—the squall had begun and the trains would run slow—but he'd refused, braving the blizzard to be alone.

He awoke to a thick carpet of the stuff, layered atop concrete, dense as manna. He put on a pot of coffee, then spent the next hours in front of Elle's window, examining the faces in the film negatives. With a pigment liner pen, he moved systematically through the subjects, subtly marking those of interest with an *X*—menacing shapes that seemed possible matches for the blurred, behatted man in the video or the character conjured from the writer's description. Nearly every roll contained at least one of these; already, he counted eighteen he would have to get developed, at substantial investment, though surely no cost was too high for an answer.

A text arrived from O, and realizing that half the day was gone, Smith agreed to come meet them. On the car ride over, he closed his eyes and projected those images onto the movie screen of his mind—he brought them in, one by one, for questioning—such an immersive reverie that when he finally arrived at the address, a well-appointed brownstone with a single buzzer, he was certain he was lost until the front door opened with O behind it, and, forgetting all of his home training, he expelled the words "You *live* here?"

"Not really, my mom's," O answered with a frown—a sentence that didn't exactly scan until Smith entered the living room and, seeing a portrait above the mantel of two nude women entwined, realized they meant *moms*, as in multiple. "I'm house-sitting for a few months while they're upstate, helping build some sustainable sapphic commune up near Saratoga."

"How many mothers do you have, exactly?" Smith joked as he shed his puffer.

"Just the two. Want tea?"

As the kettle came whistling to a boil, O explained that their biological mother, Maureen—a curator of African art—had during graduate school become pregnant by a man whose name was glossed over in a way that suggested estrangement. The two had never married, and Maureen had raised O in a cramped one-bedroom apartment until they were twelve, when, by chance on a subway platform, she'd encountered a born-rich architect, Jess, who would soon become her wife—altering her and O's lives rather radically as they swapped a social sphere that had centered a conservative church in the Caribbean section of Flatbush for one, across the park, of the queer sophisticate set to which Jess belonged, a rotating cast of soft-butch artists, high-femme academics, and anarchist dykes. "I guess, in a way, I had far more than two mothers," said O. "We went from, like, a Spike Lee joint to gay, gay, gay all the way," they explained with a mischievous grin as they fell to the tufted couch. "High-key, I blame Jess and my mom for all my dysphoria. They made being *just gay* look so nineties."

It was a joke, of course, but Smith was intrigued. In that moment, he saw O's youth, their likeness and difference also. While he was a child of Barack, weaned on the myth of linear progress, O had come of age in another, albeit immediately succeeding, era—one in which that myth was upended, riddled with holes. They would have known, in their teenage years, that identity was neither destiny nor salvation but a kind of animal trap, useful only if one was deft enough to claim the bait without tripping the door to the cage.

Prompted by his questions, O told Smith about the years when their life was uprooted from a four-story walk-up to Jess's family home, a change of address which offered entry not only to a tony charter school but a class status they'd only seen on TV, all accompanied by the usual chaos of queer becoming. They recalled insisting, the week of their high school graduation, that Maureen reach out to their dad to invite him; the two hadn't seen him in a number of years, his most recent return to their lives accompanied by its fair share of drama, homophobic rants, financial and emotional manipulations. Nonetheless, Maureen had eventually capitulated, then begun the arduous process of tracking him down, a matter always of triangulation, disconnected phone lines and filled voicemail boxes, estranged family members and old Rastafari friends who *hadn't seent him in a while* but would *pass the message hizzah wee*. It was on the third or fourth of these calls that she'd encountered the voice of a woman cooing *Who wanna know* when asked if he was in.

Maureen was used to these kinds of responses, so typical were they of the women with whom he shacked up, each for three to six months before moving on to another, as if setting up franchises all over town. That wasn't how it'd been with her nineteen years prior. She had been a master's candidate, pushing thirty when they'd met, sexless and studious, and he'd struck her immediately as a bad decision. He'd actually whistled when she walked by and spoke with a Hennessy quiver that followed her down Ocean Ave., where he'd asked for her number. In the brilliant, blinding sun, his skin looked lineless, cheekbones like a baby's fists against a golden scrim. He was younger than her, to be sure, looked not a day over twenty, though he claimed twenty-six. She had known *exactly* what he was, that he would love and leave her, but she was no fool for love, and on that humid slog of an afternoon, the trash bags strewn in the sun and his tee clinging barely to his well-defined chest, it occurred to her that time was waning to make such bad decisions.

The day Maureen called to invite Akil to graduation, the small voice on the line had said that he was not home. He had been "picked up" on a parole violation and was now awaiting trial. Eventually, it landed him back at Otisville, another eighteen months for a crime committed at sixteen, felony possession of crack cocaine, for which he'd already served the mandatory minimum. O hadn't cried, hearing this. After all, they barely knew him. They'd only met a dozen times—Knicks games from which they'd been brought home two hours too late to the wrath of their night-dressed mother; then there'd been *the incident*, O's thirteenth birthday, when the man had turned up uninvited, soused on something brown, and angry without reason at all those nice white folks: tweens in velveteen robes and scarves in observance of the theme, Harry Potter, as their parents sipped sauv blanc and complained of co-op board politics. By then, his son struck him already as soft, odd, unreachable. It had taken several minutes for him to understand that the coiffed Jewish woman in work boots was Maureen's lover, not roommate, and that they all lived here, in this house, without him. He hadn't made a scene. Hadn't called her a slur. Rather, he stumbled, muttering, on the outskirts of the party, then eventually, without goodbyes, disappeared.

"I wasn't sad, I was angry," O recalled of the months that followed Akil's return to prison. "Being eighteen, seeing all the shit you see growing up here, going to grad parties where white kids were snorting eight balls off their MacBooks or whatever, thinking how he got locked up for less. And I had to learn to redirect that rage, because I wasn't actually mad at *them*. They were just trying shit, testing the boundaries of the playgrounds set up for them, these rooms I'd happened into that he'd never see inside."

A pensive look fell over O's features, and observing it, Smith felt a sudden urge to slip into their skin. They had so much more reason, or *right*, to rail against a system that rewarded privilege and exacted punishment along lines drawn at birth, to grasp that intricate knot of guilt, grief, and anger that Smith was still trying to untwine. And so he asked a simple question: "How did you get rid of it, then, the rage?"

The tension splintered, and they grinned. "I'll be sure to let you know."

That night, they shared a bed but didn't touch. Smith was so clenched that he remained awake for hours, well after O's breaths had bloomed into symphonic snores, their formidable nose mellophonic. For a while, he watched them, bathed in moonlight, trying to discern what about them drew him in, if the attraction he felt was sexual, romantic, or if he saw in them a mirror, though distorted, less whittled by the blade of expectations. Perhaps it was just a relief to be seen. He closed his eyes and woke up to the world in white. The sun peeked meekly from the clouds and with it, a few from their houses, stepping out with expressions of awe. In the park, children shot headlong down icy passages, occasionally flung from their sleds into beds of fresh-laid snow. Their parents took pictures. Some packed their own snowballs, then pelted their gleeful children. Others flung them at trees or signs or the sky.

"Where are we going?" asked Smith as they walked with urgent purpose past the botanical garden, where packed snow loosened underfoot. Eventually, they arrived at Mona's apartment and trudged up three flights of stairs in a cavernous building which looked more likely zoned as commercial. The windows in the stairwells were covered with swatches of spare, eroded fabric, so light seeped in, dimly colored. When they knocked, she answered quickly, hugging O and then Smith, smelling of eucalyptus.

"You came," she whispered, then raised a finger to her lips.

Silently, they followed her into the apartment, which was spacious yet cluttered and seemed to constitute some sort of commune: a hodgepodge of couches and street-salvaged chairs, murals and easels through which a steady stream of grease-thin roommates shuffled. There was one, on a hammock tied to wooden beams, reading a book by Jean Genet and another, in the kitchen, tossing an apple core onto a pungent compost pile. A congregation of fruit flies dispersed. To accommodate the extra bodies, lofts had been built and topped with mattresses, constructions that seemed haphazard at best. And it was to one of these scaffolds they strode, arriving at a soft drape of purple fabric that Mona pulled back to reveal a living space beneath her lofted bed: a maximalist collision of Tuzani tufted pillows and sateen scarves and a low wooden table covered in chenille, all sat upon an old Persian rug. A Sun Ra album played quietly in observance of the hour, charming the snakelike flame of a bodega candle emblazoned with a brilliant image of the Virgin de Guadalupe.

"Can we speak?" O asked.

"Softly," said Mona, smiling. "Sorry, it's quiet hours at the moment."

"Is this a commune?" Smith asked. "I peeped the chore chart in the kitchen."

"More of an *intentional living space,* " she said with mild irony. "I've been thinking of leaving and getting my own place, but all my money right now is going back into the work. With all the shows I've already scheduled this year and next, I'm going to have to hire an assistant."

Her work, O explained, was why they'd come. As they'd begun drafting their thesis on Afro-pessimism and futurism as dueling impulses in Black contemporary art, the simultaneity of hope and despair, individual triumph and collective collapse, she'd emerged as a central subject, exemplary of the speculative impulse. In an era where the imaginary could be indiscernible from reality, the virtual was an immaculate frontier. It could be used to sedate or enliven, manipulate or reveal. "A radical freedom," Mona agreed, though lately she'd watched that future darken in her mind as she found herself locked in a preoccupation with the past—images of scorched backs and urban blight infecting her liberated visions. "In truth, I've been having violent fantasies," she said, her face beaten by shadow.

"I can't see anything," said Smith once he'd tugged on the device and entered a world of black. Mona told him to wait. It was buggy, but when it began, he would know. And after a few idle minutes, he did. A room appeared. It was a bright, early morning. The pink-hued sun streamed through the open windows, pooling light on the pinewood floors. Before him was a desk, an oblong mirror behind it, though too low for him to see his own face. He was elevated, seated on a high bed covered by a floral canopy. Indeed, the whole room was an antebellum notion, robbed of its romance and terror by the absence of bodies. There were none. Not in the fields, which he could see in the distance through the window, their crop (cotton? Cane?) untended. The location unclear, the foliage equally at home in the Caribbean and the American South. His avatar stood and, entering a dark hallway, found the house eerily still as he moved languidly down the staircase and through a salle à manger in which all the house's silver—soupspoons and salad forks and footlong butcher's cleavers— were laid out for the weekly polish, into the kitchen, where a great feast had stalled in preparation, a slab of bone-in beef marinating in spice and blood, and finally out a screen door to the house's wraparound portico of blinding white. Nets of Spanish moss swayed tremulously in the trees as he walked slowly, passing column to column, toward a rocking chair in the distance where a body was slumped, not dead but sleeping deeply. He approached the man, whose peach skin had burned an overripe shade as he drew tortured breaths, incapable of sex or violence, incapable even of anger, and examined the tender nape of his neck.

CHAPTER TWENTY-THREE

The light in the room looked amber. Filtered through film, it cast eerie shadows across the floor, which was otherwise empty. Smith had spent all morning packing the last of Elle's things into boxes and bags, then moving them into the hallway. Her mother was due any minute, and though he'd rid the room of all of Elle's personal effects, he'd left these images up, as in a gallery or a detective's study. He thought Nat might like to see them. Lit from behind like that, the images were revealed; you could picture how they'd look once developed, could see the care in the composition, if not the color, the queer and alien beauty of her subjects. But beyond that, Smith knew that he needed to ask Nat for her blessing, perhaps for her *permission*, to do as he wished, making public this archive of Elle's private memories.

A rap came at the front door, and he flinched, then quickly closed the door to Elle's room, suddenly self-conscious; if Nat saw it immediately, she might think him a freak. He took a deep breath and, as he opened the front door, emitted an involuntary sound—because there she was, Elle. Though, of course, it was actually her mother. A radiant woman; her gently worn caramel skin clung to the high cheekbones of her face, Elle's face, its same depths and shallows, and it was eerie to see it again, aged beyond its years, like a virtual rendering of a now-impossible future.

Nat arched her eyebrows and said, pointedly, "May we come in." Smith stepped aside.

He'd been so shocked by her resemblance to Elle that he hadn't noticed her companion, a slender mocha-skinned man at least twenty years her junior who planted his many-ringed hand in Smith's and introduced himself as Ray. "Nice to meet you, brotha," he said, trailing Nat into the apartment.

Smith followed. Leaning against a wall, he watched her stalk the length of the living room, her heeled boots beating firmly against the hardwood. Near the coffee table, she crouched before an open box and began to leaf through Elle's records appraisingly. In this light, it was easier to make out their distinctions. Though their faces were similarly made, the sculptor had taken liberties with each. Nat's cattish eyes, light and narrow, were all her own. And though she still wore her hair in the mane of locs for which she was known, they had grayed, so that her ethereal beauty appeared accidental—she was not a vain woman, just one preternaturally untouched by time—and Smith could see why she'd once been undeniable. A luminous star of dark intensity; he found it hard to look away.

"I thought Elle hated Janet," said Nat suddenly as she examined the pop-art image of the eighties album. Her voice was low and melodious, entirely unlike Elle's, which in its California cheer had about it the quality of a summer breeze, while Nat's native Oakland timbre remained intact.

"She loved that one song," said Smith, though the comment hadn't been aimed in his direction. "*Miss Jackson, if you're nasty.*" Smiling, Nat caught his eye, and he felt a flood of feeling: a euphoric burst, tempered by guilt, at knowing something—even something so insignificant—about her daughter that she did not. Like many parents, like *most*, she had access only to the shreds of Elle's life she'd offered freely, all bleached a blinding white. Nat had never stepped foot in their apartment, Smith knew, Elle having insisted on meeting her at her hotel the few times she'd come to town. Perhaps it had never been a matter of convenience but a desire to mark the boundaries of the life she called her own. It would not have been easy to step out of such a cosmic person's shadow.

Even as an agnostic to her messianic stardom, Smith found himself weak-kneed and a little woozy in her presence as Nat stood and took stock of all the boxes.

"We won't be able to take all this today," she said, turning to her companion. "Will we, Ray?"

"Probably not, no," he said in a slightly servile manner, which made Smith wonder about his role. Who was he to her? To Elle?

"Well, that's all right," said Smith. "I can mail you anything you don't take today."

Nat thanked him and took a seat. Suddenly an anxious host, Smith offered the contents of his fridge—sparkling water, Diet Coke—and attempted to engage her in chitchat, though it clearly did not come to her naturally. She had a tendency to take an agonizing pause before answering even the simplest question, like "What brings you to town," which made him wonder if she, like he, was hiding something. Closing and opening her eyes with what appeared to be manual effort, she often looked to Ray for answers, which betrayed something else about her character—that beneath this enigmatic aura was something childlike, detached from the world of dates and facts and figures, and so allowed to remain entirely in the realm of art. Some of that had been inherited by Elle; often, Smith had had to remind her to do mundane things like take out the trash or file taxes.

Finally, after several minutes, Smith worked up the nerve to ask the question "How do you two know each other," and again, Nat looked at Ray.

"I'm her manager," he explained, though of all the available answers, this seemed the least likely.

"But I thought—well, Elle *told* me you'd retired," Smith said to Nat, aware from the pained expression on her face that he was dipping into territory too personal, demanding information she wouldn't otherwise have given.

"I'm considering," she began, he thought a bit mournfully, "one final tour."

This was news indeed. Smith knew she hadn't toured or recorded since the early 2000s, when she'd mostly disappeared from public life. He'd seen her refer to that decision in an interview with *Rolling Stone* as the "cost of mothering," lamenting the many moments she'd missed in the early life of her then adolescent daughter, but Elle had once told him this was only half the story, that in fact she'd retired at her height, at least in part, because of a fan who'd written her hundreds of letters, each more unhinged than the last, convinced that Nat's music not only mirrored the shapes of her personal dramas but took inspiration directly from them—an obsessive delusion that, filtered through her increasingly violent prose, had highlighted for Nat the danger of all that unearned intimacy. And despite herself, she'd begun to see all of her fans as vultures, circling bones.

"*Wow*," said Smith, attempting to imply in his tone that this was news of great personal import, though mostly it confused him. Why would she choose now, when her family life was already being turned into tabloid fodder, to make a grand return?

"Yes, the fans will be hyped," said Ray, his wide smile bleach white. A pause ensued, during which it became clear that this tour was not being undertaken entirely by choice. Perhaps she'd chosen this moment, in a year of paralyzing grief, to throw herself back into her work, but more likely, there was some other urgent need. If she spent as Elle did, with abandon, she would have chipped away at whatever she'd stockpiled in the endless tour of the 1990s and early 2000s. More than once, Elle had intimated that asking her for more money was not an option, and now Smith understood—the woman before him had likely spent years batting away the insistence of industry men like Ray, who saw with clear yet predatory eyes the deepening precarity of her extravagant life. It was not indefinitely sustainable. But she still had her name, that face. After everything, that was still a bankable commodity. Even more so in the wake of tragedy. All across the country, her fans would hear those old songs and, in them, new truths—about love lost and the "cost of mothering."

Nat stood and crossed the room. "Was this room Elle's?" she asked, placing a hand on the doorknob, and before Smith could remember what it was he meant to say, she'd pushed it open. In streamed that eerie light, and for a moment, Nat just stood, silhouetted in it. Smith had stripped the room bare, packing even the sheets, and spent much of the morning erasing every trace, but approaching from behind as Nat studied the collage on the window, he felt Elle's presence there.

"Are these—"

"Yes," Smith answered, interrupting her. *Yes, they were Elle's*—her memories, attempts to capture or create beauty, cut short before she settled on what it was she meant to say, that question artists gave their lives to. Coming up beside her, Smith watched Nat's eyes glide across them, transfixed, he thought, by the same realization he'd had: that somewhere among these faces might be the man who'd left her daughter for dead.

"*Dazzling*," Nat whispered, a prideful smile appearing on her lips. And Smith realized then that she wasn't looking at the pictures as he had, as data—as signs, or clues, or signals—but only as Elle had intended, as art.

He continued. "I did think, maybe"—stumbling over the words—"we should take them to the police." She stayed silent, leaning in and squinting to make out the spectral, obsidian face of one subject, smoking a cigarette on a fire escape, backed by the city skyline. "Because, you know, one of these men could be the one"—he waited, and when she still did not respond, continued in a wounded whimper—"the one she was with *that night*."

And this was her gift, what made her a magnetic performer and would sell out stadiums upon her return: She understood silence, how an absence is also a sound. She held it for what seemed an interminable time, and Smith felt himself lean in to hear her breathing. "David," she said, not cold, but low and firm and absolute. "You need to leave this alone." It seemed an inscrutable sentence. She must have known something he did not about the case, perhaps the real reason she'd come to the city—surely she did not mean to imply that he could simply look away, *move on*. He thought to clarify but found himself incapable of speech. Nat sighed. She took one last, long look at the images, the ghosts of Elle's life in New York, then said, "You should keep them."

CHAPTER TWENTY-FOUR

Every morning for the next few days, Smith rode the train uptown. He didn't care about the cold, its whip against his skin. He traced the same route, greeting it as an old friend: the street purveyors of "Bucci" bags and essential oils, breath-warming their ashen hands in Harlem; the mink-hatted older ladies walking their terriers on the Upper East Side; and down, down, in Midtown, where suits emerged from their gray-slat towers like tidal waves of minnows, their manic lunch-break motion some brief reprieve, though paced still to the demands of production. A glittering urban ecosystem in which he played no part. Even if his case was dismissed, Smith realized, it might be months, or even years, before his arrest was sealed. And in the meantime, he'd be stuck in this purgatory, unemployable in government, finance, tech—those heights for which he'd been bred—every day running down the clock on the time he could afford to remain in New York. Drifting, aimless. In search of what, he wasn't sure.

It was clear that he had to move *on*, as Elle's mom had so pointedly suggested, but on to what? New York was where people moved to make their lives happen, but here, he had stalled, like a car on a desolate shoulder. And this happened to people, he knew. They faltered and never found their footing. You could see it in their eyes as they passed, how far they'd strayed from the lives they wanted.

Yes, it was a paralyzing question—how to spend today, then every one after it—but as he moved through scores of people, most of whom he knew had far fewer options, it was clear that paralysis itself was a privilege. To live in the city was to keep moving. And he could not deny that, in some corner of his mind to which he scarcely had access, he felt relief. To have fucked up young and thus shed the unbearable weight of expectations. To be offered a clean slate to draw a life that felt more true. Probably, if he asked, Mona would at least consider him for her assistant position; just as probably, if he asked, O would let him crash for a while at theirs. He could build a new life in New York, one whose roots were entwined with people who would love him if he let them. A terrifying prospect indeed.

From the piers, a black curtain swept across the Hudson. Evening joggers tottered on. He watched their silhouettes darken until they were cleaving moonlight, then headed east. "Mona had to bail last minute for a gallery dinner," O explained when Smith met them in the Village, a McDonald's on Varick, where they were holding court with a group of punky derelicts, demonstrating how to use the test strips on a pack of branded salt. Outside, all the city's snow was being scraped into sculptural piles. And as they strode throughout the Village, O was voluble about the bars they used to frequent in their teens, when they drank like they wanted to die. "You have no idea," they said when asked if they'd been *trouble*. "I was six foot two and like a hundred pounds, but you could catch these hands any night of the week," they said with a throaty laugh. And Smith pictured them there, in a skimpy dress, stumbling out of the Julius. A razor blade in a bar of soap. Back then, they explained, they'd known all the queers who haunted the encampments on Sixth and Seventh Aves., the girls and gays who worked corners; they'd trade gossip or smoke. Some were barely legal back then. Big-eyed and from nowhere, they'd sloughed off their tortured pasts. Years later, the few who remained had a rangier look. And the others? O shrugged, glancing across the road, where a man lay splayed inside an ATM vestibule, dope-sick or just drunk, as another stepped over his neck. "You know as well as I do how this city eats people alive."

At the West Fourth Street Station, a man begging change held the exit door open. They passed through and, seeing their train's delay, collapsed onto the stairs. "I wonder where Tia is," said O, double-checking the time. "I told her we'd meet up." Smith shrugged. He wasn't particularly pressed to join her and was thinking still about what they'd said, *how this city eats people alive.*

"Did you hear that?" O said suddenly.

Faintly, Smith could detect the edges of a rasping, faraway voice. "Someone trying to rap or something," he murmured. O's eyes narrowed with recognition, then panic, and they sprinted down the staircase toward a crowd loosely gathered on the platform's other end. Following, Smith cut through the crush and watched a scene render: Tia's tangerine plaits swinging violently as she whipped her head between the uniformed cops and delivered a blaring screed, the words of which Smith could barely discern, though he heard her call one of them *a raggedy street rat with a God complex,* which the man, who indeed bore a certain family resemblance, took on the chin without a shift in expression, while his partner, a tall man with a fresh fade, continued to repeat the word *Ma'am* until he found an opening, when she paused to catch her breath, to say, "If you keep this up we're going to have to take you in."

"You think I give a fuck," Tia spat back, his words having the precise opposite effect intended. In a brief pause, Smith examined the crowd. Most had their phones upraised, as they'd been taught to, having seen the super-cut of Black bodies on the news and learned that it was their role in these dramas to witness. Tia continued. "And for what? I haven't broken any—"

"You have," the tall cop said, raising his voice to interrupt her, though she continued speaking so that their words battled for meager airspace. Nonetheless, Smith understood their subject: the vagrant man just beyond them, passed out on the platform bench. Dressed in an oversize polo be-neath a quilted coat, he appeared to be sleeping deeply, even as this drama played out around and about him.

"It's freezing, *where the fuck's he s'posed to go*," she asked with an audi-ble tremor. The cops had no answer; they were just doing their job, return-ing this man to the streets. Smith felt his breath catch as O broke through the crowd onto the stage of their attention, this theater in the round, and as Tia turned, her expression shifted.

"Excuse me," said O calmly but firmly, then explained that they'd been late to meet their friend and asked what had happened. For a moment the tall cop's expression suggested he would tell O to step back, but when he spoke, it became clear that he was relieved to have been offered a means to defuse this situation as he assessed the fabric of lenses fixed upon him.

"He can't sleep here," the cop said simply, gesturing toward the man.

"Okay," said O. "Would you mind if I try to wake him?"

The cops' eyes met briefly, and the ratty one agreed. O crouched and, using their phone's flashlight and a gentle hand, tried to rouse the man. It occurred to Smith then that they might be in for a grimmer end if it turned out he hadn't been sleeping but dying all this time as he was used as a pawn in a kind of political theater, but then his head fell from the bench and his neck tensed to catch it. His eyes fluttered open, alarmed; he took in the crowd and tried to stand but stumbled. It was evident he wasn't in his right mind. Not that night, perhaps not for some time. His eyes darted madly and some derangement there had taken hold—the siren panic of those who have no place so are hunted. He stood and lurched left, parting the crowd in a squeal of terror, then was gone. But the drama was not yet done because there was still the issue of Tia, who stood with a sullen look ten feet beyond the whispering cops; she'd insulted and belittled them; she'd obstructed their duty; she couldn't be allowed to just *leave*. The train arrived in a gust and dispersed the few remaining. "Officers," said O, taking a tentative step toward them. "Is it cool if I take my friend home? We've all had a long night."

"You're sure you can get her back without any more trouble?" the ratty one asked.

"Yes, sir," said O as Smith planted himself in the threshold of the waiting train.

The cops shared a meaningful glance. "We're going to let you go," the tall one said, now speaking directly to Tia; her irises glimmered. "You should thank your friend."

In the blaring silence, Smith could hear nothing but the train's machinery churning them toward Brooklyn. He watched O, who watched Tia, who watched the view beyond the window, a constellation of lights refracted off the river. "You good?" asked O as they eased into the station.

She paused, then shook her head. "That was just fucking wack, what you did."

They hadn't expected a thank-you, but they had not expected this either, that much was evident in their bemusement, eyebrows brooding at the center of their face. "What I did," they repeated.

"That 'yes, sir' house nigga shit," she said. It stung, both the words and the ease with which she deployed them—it was evidently not the first time she'd accused them of this betrayal, that perennial line walk that was second tongue to people like O, like Smith, an ever-shifting code which must have amounted in her eyes to a load of high-class coonery.

O's forehead wrinkled. "I'm sorry you feel that way," they replied casually, another bid at de-escalation, though after a beat, they reconsidered. "But for fuck's sake, Tia, what did you think was going to happen? You'd make a scene and—what? They'd give up, go home? Shit doesn't go like that."

"Oh, tell me how it *goes*, Omari," she said with an acrid laugh, still seething from that scene or perhaps some earlier tension, lugged like an overpacked bag through every conversation. Smith recalled the six weeks and three days O said she had slept in their bed, the daily frictions amassing with such speed that they'd eventually asked her to leave for the sake of their friendship, which had lapsed into resentful silence for months in the aftermath. Because what use was a boundaried love?

"Look, Tia, you're right. Like, politically, morally, you're right," they said, summoning a full decade of therapy to keep calm as they parroted a line they'd no doubt heard from their mother, the same taught to all little boys who were Black, so learned young the shrug between living and dying: "But being right's never stopped a bullet."

Tia considered this. Of course she would've heard the line a thousand times—she was all the more acquainted with her mortality—but still, she rejected its anesthetizing logic. "Best weapon they got," she said as the train slowed and her breath formed a cloud in the breach of wind, "it's not a nightstick or a gun, it's your fucking fear." Her words bore the strain of their relationship, the gulf between their lives: the hideous ease she'd glimpsed in theirs, which she could neither forget nor forgive.

At the next stop, they all detrained. They were going in different directions. And Smith began his long walk home through the blur of neon streets, the afterglow of their faces still burning in his mind. Love curdled to hate, and hurt, and resentment. Almost an afterthought, he checked his phone to find a flurry of messages, missed calls, and then a single news alert:

In the Case of Elle England, an Arrest Has Been Made

S mith felt his throat close and mind empty (*Red slip, river, ruin*) as he opened the link on a quiet corner. It was midnight. And the piece, which had been up for hours (*The Bronx man allegedly responsible for dumping the lifeless body*) would have made the rounds by then, passing from tabloid to group text through a constellation of anonymous strangers; even Nia had heard in Cambridge and texted to ask *Are you okay* (*was arrested today, coming off a plane at the Miami International Airport*). Jean-Pierre Baptiste, a stranger. A second-generation Martinician American raised by a single mother, or so claimed a paragraph of biographical details that summoned bile to Smith's throat, designed if not to humanize then to keep him reading. He nearly threw his phone into a gutter but kept it close (*Authorities can now confirm that the accused has a criminal record, convictions on narcotics possession and intent to distribute*); a dealer, a shill, he haunted shadows and could be found wherever people purchased powders. Smith might have even met him, he thought, if not that night then another. What if they'd shared a key in the back of a crowded club or swapped cash, palm to fetid palm, in the front of a stalled Subaru. He looked familiar, Smith thought, scrolling back to the top of the page where a mug shot glowered, though familiar in the way a street sign is familiar. In the way a pop song is familiar, even one you've never heard. The face of a million men. It was the kind of face one passes every day in New York without ever really seeing. So why had she seen him? Smith wondered as his heart's pace subsided and his breath returned, heavy in the wailing moonlight. He had big eyes of the sort some people mistake for kindness. Eyes which, in this image, glistened with remorse or maybe fear, whatever well of feeling leached from his otherwise neutral features—those plump, pink lips and the blade of ivory teeth beyond them; his wide nose, thick brows; his darkly luminous skin; and the snatch of twists pulled out of his eyes, those awful eyes, the last to see her living.

Smith stumbled into a dive and claimed a booth to calm his breathing. The texts kept rolling in: from Carolyn, from Kofi. He put his phone on silent, then reopened the image of *Jean-Pierre*, the name's consonance like a film on his tongue. It was an elegant name—distinct enough, Smith imagined, to be found easily online. After all, the writer had done it. With nothing but his name, fed to her probably by a contact in the NYPD, she had found the man's address. She had spoken to his neighbors, people who'd been—however peripherally—involved in his day-to-day life. It might even have been the shock of that intrusion, a flex of investigative muscle, that convinced the man that he had not escaped, and never would.

But when Smith searched his name now, only the news results appeared. Stories all published in the past several hours, pickups by tabloids who reshuffled the details in an effort to make their reports appear new; the search traffic would be enough that even the smallest fish would get their fill. Smith knew this, yet read each story with tense anticipation, retracing the facts of the man's heritage and broken home, his two convictions and three arrests echoed so relentlessly as to offer the impression that this alone composed a life. This was all a reader needed to know to fill in that abstract picture, now in blinding view.

But now that he'd seen his face, Smith realized he could find him in the somber gallery of Elle's bedroom. The image would be of no use to the police or to the public, but it might still be to him, illuminating that lingering question as to *the nature of their relationship*—so he trudged on, past club lines and drug deals and furtive, glancing men, arriving back to the dark apartment. One by one, he peeled the reels from the window and examined them by lamplight, tossing to the floor the still lifes and landscapes, the men too heavy to be him. And then one frame stopped him cold. Even in this inverted image, he knew at once that it was him, the same angular face and tendriled hair. Taken in what appeared to be a park, it was not like the others, posed portraits of grandiose personas—the masks people wore for the camera. This subject had not wanted to be pictured, had raised a hand to block his face, but between the slender fingers, one could still make out the spread of a dimpled smile. An expression of almost excruciating softness—like a verdict, like *proof*.

CHAPTER TWENTY-SIX

O n the third run, the David Smiths conducted their court-date ritual with mechanical precision, like stage actors weeks after opening night. Silently, they readied: washed, dressed, made themselves presentable. The only difference now was that Smith, as he moved through the motions, allowed himself the ambient hope that, in hours, this all might be over.

From the courthouse doors, they were escorted by the stocky bailiff to the lawyer section, from which they watched the usual parade of minor infractions. The DA was again at his post, grinning ear to ear as he closed a case with a pen stroke, then swiftly moved on to the next, filling the room with the pleasing whir of any workable machine. Walsh arrived and, looming toward them, shook their hands, then asked about the drive in, and as Senior answered, Smith thought, strangely, of his mug shot. At twenty-five thousand dollars—between the doctor and lawyer—it was the priciest portrait he would ever take, and if things went to plan, he would never even see it. Glancing around the courtroom, he tried to picture his own face but watched it blur into that of another, that man from the papers and the portrait in Elle's window. For days, that face had been appearing everywhere, on trains and through shop windows, in evanescing crowds, then disappearing just as quickly—it was him, *just there*, though of course it was not, Smith's rational brain knew, but starved for months of its fleshy detail, he'd been bingeing. Some nights, he studied it for hours. Some nights, he saw it in his sleep: elaborate scenarios in which, aided by machines or spells or serums, the accused was incapable of elision, so answered every question in lurid detail. *How long did you sit there, watching her fade, before you decided to run?*

Jean-Pierre's mug shot was like any other, definitionally generic, yet it still offered clues. Like the starched white shirt he had worn, as if he'd dressed that day to be arrested, which probably he had. The papers had reported that, after months of hiding out in Fort-de-France, he'd decided to turn himself in. No doubt he would have consulted his counsel on what to wear and what to say and how to seem and when. In the papers, they'd put out a statement—

> *My client and Elle England began a casual friendship last spring after meeting at a celebration downtown. Since then, they saw one another on occasion, initiated always by England. When she asked for a place to stay in early June, he graciously agreed. On the night in question, he experienced a state of shock, witnessing her reaction to contaminated narcotics, and though he had no hand in encouraging her to consume them, he regrets his actions deeply.*

—which even in its terse, evasive wording revealed so much. They could not claim innocence, which at this point would have proved an impossible burden—he had run, an admission of guilt in the court of public opinion—but planned an attempt to shift the blame. The diction was precise: The two had met at a *celebration*, meaning a party or, more likely, an *after*-party, some squalid congress of glamazons and dope dealers and hapless insomniacs, and begun a *casual friendship*, to be clear that even if it had at some point become sexual, it was not some torrid affair. He was not a jilted lover or a cold-blooded criminal. He was just a kid, scared shitless. That was their plea, and perhaps it was true. Now that he was in custody, the deck was almost insurmountably stacked against him. It would have taken a massive stock of resources to redirect the narrative away from one of certain guilt, and if even the basic details of the reporting were true, he didn't have them. No doubt he had pooled money from family and friends to afford a decent criminal attorney, and still, he wouldn't stand a chance. Which, even that night, in a "state of shock," he must have known. She was something made of porcelain; he was no one. Even the doorman had clocked their asymmetry; it would not have taken a genius to figure out what he was and what he'd done. If he'd brought her to the hospital, he would have left in chains. And with the stacks of cash in his apartment and the dark marks on his record, he would've been looking at a hefty sentence. Yes, from the moment her breath had shallowed and her limbs gone limp, he would have known that his life, too, was done.

The judge arrived. A terrifying woman. Stately despite her diminutive height, she wore kitten heels of a distinctly matronly shade. Her mass of immovable hair was dyed red to the root. Mounting the bench, she cast one panning glance around the courtroom, her eyes coming to rest on the suited defendants in the seated section. She was a bird of prey, to be certain. Her docket that day was full, so she wasted no time in calling the first of the probationers, each attended to by a small managerial team: an officer and a lawyer and, for the first to be called, an elegantly dressed older woman who appeared to be his mother. The client himself was well coiffed, wore a suit and a platinum watch peeking nervously from his ivory cuffs. His lawyer stood and, for several minutes, conveyed the pressing issue of her client's license, revoked several summers prior after a drunk-driving incident had resulted in the death of another. After three years in prison, the young man had been recently released. The Honorable Lisa Harrelson listened without questions to the urgings of the capable lawyer, who argued that her client had paid his debt to society, and as he was now sober and gainfully employed, deserved, in fact *needed*, to regain agency over his own transportation. The judge considered the argument, then addressed the young man directly, asking, or more demanding, that he stand. He did, and she spent the next several minutes excoriating him and his lawyer for the request. Did he not *realize* that his release from Dix Hills had been almost "*irresponsibly* premature," she asked rhetorically, before assuring him that she would not reinstate his license until she could be certain that he no longer posed a threat on the road. And as the young man shot a look of reproach at his lawyer, Smith saw clearly why this judge was the subject of such fear in these courts: her insistence that she could not be bought. Though, of course, the issue of a license was minuscule in relation to the many years' reduction in his sentence, which gave this refusal an air of rank vacuity. The boy's money, which he wore well tailored, had already insulated him from the law's full fist.

As the next probationer was called, Smith breathed and attempted to focus. For months he'd anticipated this day, this moment precisely, but now that it was here, he found his mind elsewhere, playing out that other courtroom scene.

Though Page Six had declared, just yesterday, "An End to the Tragic Story," Smith knew it was not an end but another beginning. There would be a trial, which meant more press, more investigations into Elle's life and person. Already, these had begun. On the evening news, Detective

Clement had appeared above a crush of hungry reporters, her kinky hair slicked back, and delivered a somber sound bite. "I hope this arrest will offer solace to Elle's family in California and her community here in the great city of New York," she'd said, as if this arrest would bring life back to the dead or peace unto the living instead of rippling ever outward, unsettling all lives in range.

How well did you know your friend? she had asked, and still Smith had no answer. Still, he might be called to court and asked, under oath, about her "secret pregnancy" or "spiraling addiction." A narrative forged by the press that would prove useful to the defense—she was not a perfect victim. Perhaps a lawyer as capable as Smith's own could successfully recast the accused from a low-life dealer, an archetypal thug, into someone *deserving* of sympathy. With his mug shot and public statement, that effort had begun: to mold his respectability from the ashes of Elle's own. Clement had concluded her statement, smiling: "I know they'll sleep soundly tonight now that the young man responsible has been brought to *justice*."

"David Smith Junior," the bailiff called, and Walsh swiftly stood to attention. "Please approach the bench." Smith followed his counsel, his heart pounding in his ears, and as he glanced back at his father, he suddenly regretted telling Carolyn not to come. It would have been a relief to see her then, her smile, her ease. He turned and watched the judge open a manila folder. Languorously, her eyes scanned its contents, then flitted upward toward Walsh, then briefly toward the husky DA. "*The People of Southampton, New York, versus David Alexander Smith Junior*, in violation of section 220.06 of the penal law of the State of New York," she announced for the cheap seats. "Criminal possession of a controlled substance."

"Yes, Your Honor," Walsh confirmed.

"Says here that the defendant has completed three evals, sixteen hours of drug and alcohol treatment," she continued, barely glancing at the results from the lab, the letter of completion from Mancini. Hawklike, her eyes narrowed on Walsh. His word, in the end, was all that mattered. "Can you attest that your client has completed these and indeed remains clean and sober?"

"Yes, Your Honor," Walsh confirmed brightly, winking at Smith, who studied his hands.

She continued. "And the DA's recommendation is full dismissal following six months' adjournment. What would be the reason for this rather than the usual twelve?" she asked, implying with her tone that this sentence was insufficient, a mere *tap* on the wrist.

"Statutory, Your Honor," Walsh replied, unflinching. He'd explained it all again that morning. The statute he planned to pursue would seal Smith's record in six months, provided he wasn't again arrested. "Pursuant to section 170.55 of the criminal procedure law of the State of New York."

"Oh, well, that's . . ." She paused, clearly cowed, bested in her knowledge of the book she'd been preparing to throw. "Yes, that's correct, 170.55," she confirmed, now flustered.

Then, for the first and last time, she looked at Smith, standing there in his pristine suit, big-eyed and thin-skinned and practically incontinent from nerves. She addressed him directly.

"Well, I hope you've learned your lesson."

For months and years thereafter, Smith would try and fail to recall his exact response, which emerged from his mouth as if by a ventriloquist's hand. Had he, as his father insisted, had the wherewithal to say *Yes, Your Honor*, or had it been *Yes, ma'am*, a curt *Yes*, a *Yeah*; had he said anything at all? What he could remember as he was pulled from the courtroom by his lawyer, past the front desk, where a guard couldn't help but jeer *Don't bring your daddy back here*, into the rush of cool air, was a single, lingering question: What exactly had he been meant to learn?

Hello. You've reached Carolyn Astley. I can't come to the phone right now, but if you leave a detailed message, I'll return your call at my earliest convenience. Smith hung up and tried again. *Hello. You've reached . . .* the simulacrum echoed. He tossed his phone to the unmade bed. His father had just left, back to JFK to prepare his notes for a morning lecture in Atlanta on Boesak and Tutu, so the apartment's eerie calm fell like a curtain around him. Smith tried to call her again. After everything, she was the one person he wanted to tell. To celebrate, or at the very least hear his relief echoed; only then would it begin to feel real. He tried her again. It was strange that she wasn't answering. Texting her on the car ride home, he'd assumed she was busy at work, but now it was evening. Was it possible that she was ignoring him? That seemed petty and absurd. The prospect alone enraged him. Yes, their last hangout had ended uneasily, a look of confusion and hurt on her face, but it wasn't really like her to harbor resentments, she who'd once told Ollie, after he'd cut contact for months on the request of a threatened ex, "You could probably kill someone, and I'd still forgive you." If she'd seen his calls, read his texts—and how could she not have by then—surely she would have been at his door.

"Hey, babe," Fernanda answered when he called around ten. "To what do I owe the pleasure?"

Smith laughed at the mock formality—clearly she, typical for their age, considered phone calls innately suspect. "I was wondering, have you spoken to Carolyn today?"

A pause. "Spooky," she said. "I was actually *just* thinking about her when you called. We were supposed to grab dinner last night—you know, loose plans—but she ghosted." Smith felt his stomach turn. "Is everything okay?"

"Um, I don't know. I've been trying to reach her," he explained. "But we actually haven't spoken in, well, a couple weeks."

"Seriously?" asked Fernanda with genuine surprise. She must not have heard, or rather Carolyn had not mentioned, that lately they'd been drifting. Perhaps she hadn't cared. Smith asked when last they'd spoken.

"Last Thursday," she said, scrolling through her call log. "She said she'd come for dinner, but then two calls yesterday and no answer."

"And how did she sound when you spoke?"

"Normal," she said, then reconsidered. "A bit scattered, maybe. Why?"

Smith set out on foot. To keep calm, he contemplated the innocuous reasons for her silence, though with each step, these seemed less likely. He hailed a cab, directed it toward Brooklyn Heights, and soon arrived at a tall stone structure. He buzzed *Astley*, then buzzed it again. He backed toward the street and craned his neck, attempting to discern if hers was the lit window or the dark square one over. "Do you need to get in?" a voice asked, a young man in leather, who held the door open in a neighborly gesture that the building expressly forbade. Smith thanked him and rushed inside, tapped the elevator button in time with his heartbeat, and, arriving at her door, banged percussively. "It's Smith," he said loudly, recalling with déjà vu the circumstances of their last encounter, the other man who'd banged on her door. *Had she seen him since? Did he have something to do with her silence?*

The next door opened, revealing an elderly woman with a sullen, cop-calling expression. "The girl's not in," she said, stepping into the hallway light. Her Florence Henderson hair was daubed with swatches of gray and clipped near its middle by a rhinestone barrette. "She's not been home for days."

Smith paused, unsure what to make of this statement, this woman, who continued to speak. "If you see her, *please* tell her, and I've told her this a number of times myself, but you know how young girls can get when an old bird like me tries to offer advice," she said, touching her hand to her silk-robed chest, "that it isn't very *becoming* to have guests at all hours of the night. It's like my mother always said, nothing good happens after mid—"

"She's had guests?" Smith interrupted curtly. "When was this?"

"Well, *that girl* has guests all the time, you know, but last weekend certainly. Friday and Saturday at ungodly hours. I finally had to write an email to Sadowski. I didn't want to—she *is* a sweet girl—but if I've told her once, I've told her a thousand times, nothing good happens after midnight." This second time, the old woman delivered her mother's advice more like a pronouncement, a condemnation, as if to say that those who failed to heed her words deserved whatever miserable fates befell them. Smith thanked her and left her there, bounding down six flights of stairs to the street.

He texted Fernanda. *No luck, I'm headed to Dmitri's.*

The night was, by then, a lake, streetlamped and quiet. He waded into it, three blocks to the train, then one stop to Grand Street, where he emerged and took off at a sprint toward the studio, then laid on the buzzer like a pimple for popping. One, two, three—"Hello?" Her boss's heavy accent sizzled.

"Hi, I just wanted to check, um, is Carolyn in?"

"No," the voice said sternly. "She doesn't come in this week."

The peculiar syntax eluded him. Did she not, as he said, *come in* because she had asked for time off, in which case an impromptu vacation might explain her radio silence, or had she not *come in* unannounced? Her boss's tone betrayed nothing more than impatience. Smith pressed the button again. "So, do you know where she is, then?"

The voice returned. "I have no ideas."

As Smith walked away from the door, he dialed Fernanda's number to relay the update, *No ideas*, his concern inciting her own. Swiftly, she dictated a short list of friends whom each should call, only after which would they contact Carolyn's family. Smith took a seat in a pool of lamplight and dialed his assignments, pressing each for information in a tone attempting casual. The first was a bust; they hadn't spoken in over a month—Mac had been *working a lot* and besides, they hadn't been *so close lately*. The second had texted her in the preceding weeks with some frequency, mostly memes, to which as recently as Sunday she had continued to reply, though without any hints on her whereabouts. The third, Ollie, proved far more fruitful. He'd actually seen her last Saturday, at a party in a suite at the Bowery Hotel. She'd been drinking heavily, though so was everyone, and had at some point disappeared in the company of two unfamiliar men. "Freaks," he described them. "But gay, I think." The combined effect of these conversations was to create a loose forensic map of her comings and goings, all of which had ceased promptly last Sunday; no one had seen or heard from her since.

"I'm calling her cousin," said Fernanda, then placed Smith on hold. Headed for SoHo, he ducked beneath a heated awning to counteract the wind. A gaggle of girls in heeled boots struggled down the street, belching violet laughter, swallowed by the din of a bar nearby. Fernanda's voice returned, asking Smith if he was there, then she asked the same of Lacey, who confirmed the calls had merged. Lacey hadn't spoken to her cousin since Christmas but was surprisingly calm, considering. *No*, she was not aware of any trips Carolyn had planned to Los Angeles or London. *No*, she was not at their grandparents' place on Crosby; Lacey had Skyped them just that afternoon. Nonetheless, this was not unheard-of behavior. Indeed, Carolyn had a "horrible habit" of losing her phone, going quiet, which each had witnessed over the years. They should remain calm, she insisted. Spend at least another hour trying to track her down before informing her parents, who no doubt would involve the police. Lacey would call family members to subtly discern when last they'd spoken, while Fernanda, marooned at her parents' anniversary party uptown, would call more friends, track their socials. And Smith would continue on foot, making his way to the downtown spots she favored, in one of which she was *sure to be* tucked, alive and well. Fernanda seemed convinced, unburdened, and in fact made a joke that Smith couldn't help but think she would later regret if things took a darker turn. Because he'd been here before, he recognized the crimson shade of panic.

Red slip, river, ruin. What words still open a sinkhole inside you, Smith thought, striding west and peering through restaurant windows en route to his destination, the café in the Village which had once been their watering hole. Their first year in the city, they'd gathered here nightly, permitted by the relative obscurity that the restaurant suffered in those early days, when the stylish friends of the debt-addled owners would descend without reservation, colonizing each of the tables from ten until close, after which they did not leave but were permitted to chain-smoke indoors. The barstools would clear and there would be dancing.

Entering now, Smith found that the place had, despite its surge in popularity, maintained its sex appeal. A small room, lit dimly and packed with bodies bumping knees and savoring Dover sole to the soft, dulcet moans of inoffensive jazz, which wafted sensuously between the tables like sweet perfume. He caught the eye of one of the owners, headed toward him, kissed his cheek.

"*Buonasera,*" the man offered joylessly as he went outside to serve a pair of martinis to a pair of brunettes, who were braving the cold to smoke.

A morose Italian known for his good taste and ill temper, he had—for a while—dated Carolyn, a relationship whose dissolution had been catastrophic enough to unstitch the social fabric that had governed those long-ago nights. Smith hadn't returned since but knew she did occasionally, late on nights when her ex wasn't working. She sat at the bar and drank vespers, mixed by the man who now looked up. "Smitty, my man, long time," said Ryan, beaming brightly as he rinsed, then offered his hand.

"Been a minute," Smith said brusquely, the circumstances inspiring a general animus. He hunched across the bar and asked, in his best take on film noir, "You seen Carolyn in here lately?" Ryan's dark-featured face went flush at the mention of her name, but he maintained his goofy smile. Smith was one of the few who knew that he and Carolyn still sometimes fucked, itself the source of the drama that had a year ago erupted. But both were hopelessly drawn to mutually assured destruction. It wasn't just their sex, which, according to her, was *fantastic*, but the copious drink each required to consummate without disabling guilt, along with a portion of the vast sums of cocaine he took nightly. Smith sometimes wondered if she even liked him or if his draw was somehow Pavlovian: his narcotic drip, her bell.

Without answering Smith's question, Ryan placed two glasses on the bar and filled them each with viscous yellow. "Limoncello," he explained.

"Thanks," said Smith, eyeing the liquid. "But I'm not drinking tonight."

Ryan rolled his eyes impishly. "Come on. We're celebrating." Smith thought to ask what he meant but recognized the irony. They were celebrating nothing in particular; today was a party, as was yesterday and the day before that. He took the glass, and Ryan lifted his own. *"Cin cin."* They clinked; a tart, saccharine punch. "You mentioned Carolyn," he said, pouring another.

"Yeah, um—her phone's off, and I'm trying to find her."

It must've seemed strange that he'd shown up here asking the questions of a hardened private eye—*the curious case of the missed call in the nighttime*—but if Ryan was concerned, his face didn't betray him. The man gestured to the second shot, and Smith sighed but accepted. It was in his best interest to play nice. "I saw her this week. She came in on Sunday," he said.

"And how did she seem?"

"Oh, you know." The man shrugged, typically noncommittal.

"I actually don't," said Smith. "It's been a bit since I've seen her."

"Really? You two have a fight?" Smith half nodded; it seemed half true. "She was fine, just sleep-deprived. She came in with that kid who throws the parties. Pablo?"

"Carlos?"

"That's the one," Ryan confirmed, leering at the memory. Smith wasn't surprised. She and Carlos were not exactly friends, but he made cameos in her grittier stories, a club kid whose life in New York seemed an endless bender and to whom she referred, a bit snobbishly, not by name but handle, *@gayforplay*, as if that were all he deserved. "Yeah, they'd had a big one the night before and hadn't slept." He snapped his fingers. "You know what? I bet that's where she'll be tonight. That party he throws, Club Gloom, at Chalet."

By this, Smith was satisfied, and, after taking the third shot offered, left slightly woozy and dumb with hope. Ryan had seen her most recently and could confirm she was alive. If she'd been with Carlos on a binge, that would explain her silence. And he was easier to track, prone to posting dozens of stories from his interminable blend of days, geotagged within an inch of their lives. Smith texted Fernanda an update—*Ry says she'll be at club gloom*—taking note of his phone's low battery. He passed the Padua church and headed downtown.

* * *

The night had deepened to a cryonic cold in which his limbs numbed quickly. And every step, he was falling through craters of memory, so potent they appeared undiluted: the exact cross-stitch pattern of the chair in which he sat when the vibrations began in his pocket, the smog and garbage smell of that marked summer day, the swarming heat, her face, her face in slivers on cell phones on subways and reposted by Instagram strangers; it was harder and harder to breathe, so he took off at a sprint at Canal, slowing to catch his breath only when Chalet came into view. The line stretched a full block. Club-kid wannabes crowded the concrete and affected impatience, though most would endure another hour in the cold to be offered entry to the city's best disco, alternately being declared a *private party* and *at capacity* by a bespectacled doorman in faux leopard fur. By day, Maxy was a talented painter and performance artist. An old friend of Elle's, he'd slept on their couch for a year's worth of weekends, crawling into Smith's bed on Sunday mornings to watch *Curb* as Elle caught up on sleep. He looked just the same—sunken-eyed with a mass of matted locs. "Angel," he sang in a monotone as he waved Smith in, much to the chagrin of a horde of panting Parsonites. "How are you?"

"I'm—have you seen Carolyn tonight?"

Maxy's face wore a searching expression. His eyes, through thick Warholian lenses, looked tired. "That's your blond friend?" he asked, and Smith nodded, thinking to himself how much this would annoy her; the two had met a dozen times. "Don't think so, but it's a madhouse, she might've slipped by."

"Well, if you see her—"

"Of course. Have fun, angel."

Past two bouncers in ill-fitting suits, Smith ascended the stairs. The carpet, patterned red with gold diamonds, was meant to look regal but beneath the bright fluorescents recalled the ballrooms of budget hotels, the sort that mistake Froot Loops and browning bananas for *continental breakfast*. By day, Chalet served lukewarm moo shu to a parade of fanny-packed tourists, an enterprise insufficiently lucrative to fund its FiDi real estate, so they'd years ago begun to rent it out for parties, first, bar and bat mitzvahs and middling corporate shindigs, until the gays and downtown set caught wind and, rebranding its tackiness as camp, descended upon the venue with the gusto of the Allies at Normandy. Inside were skaters and debutantes, nodels and models, socialites and celebrities, and a recently disgraced designer who'd emerged from several weeks *listening and learning* in a spectacularly public fashion, grease-haired and flailing atop a brown leather booth, belting out the bars of some Minaj interlude—all of whom were distinctly difficult to spot through a milk-thick haze of smoke. Indeed, this was such a crucial element of the place, this carcinogeno-sphere, that it inspired the looks of some. Down the center aisle stalked one of RuPaul's finest, seven foot two and corseted with Mugler cat-eyes and a gas mask.

Scanning the room, Smith was alarmed by its many new faces. He could remember a time, not even a year ago, when he would've recognized someone at every table, but it seemed that in those intervening months, the crop of cool kids had mostly turned over, as their elders, meaning those in their mid- to late twenties, moved to LA or stopped going out, leaving an opening for their perkier progeny: bony, beautiful teens whose fake IDs bore all the structural integrity of a Pokémon card. It was another of New York's many cruelties: a reminder of how little the city owed each of them. It would forget them soon, throttling on like an errant train.

Smith began his tour of the club's three rooms, though his intent tonight was not to find the coolest spot but his friend amid the youthful miasma. He stalked through the slinky silhouettes onto the dance floor, impenetrably black, until the lights picked up at the chorus and filled the room with writhing bodies. In the strobe, he caught glimpses of girls who resembled her. Her cheek, her lips, her hair, her eyes. They disappeared to the beat. And by the time the light recovered, they were transformed, looked nothing alike. She would never wear heels to a party like this, a fete at which they'd once watched a Yale MFA performing an ode to Gaga, his body covered in honeyed prosciutto to be picked off, and presumably eaten, by strangers.

In the next room, he was relieved to find a familiar face, a boy named Fai lounging on a barstool in an army-green bomber and flares. He'd once been frightfully handsome, was still, though ridges had just begun to set around his mouth, cementing his smile for always. "I haven't seen you in fucking forever," Fai said, his tone accusatory.

"I haven't been going out much."

"Word, well, what can I get you to drink?"

"I'm actually looking for Carolyn. Have you seen her?"

He warmed. "I asked her about you, actually, and she said—"

"Tonight?"

"A couple weeks ago. Anyway, what can I get you to drink?"

"Wait, so . . ." Smith paused. "You have or you haven't seen her, *here*, tonight?"

Silently, Fai held up the middle and index finger on his right hand as a signal to the bartender, who poured two shots of tequila, one of which he gave to Smith. "Not yet, man, but it's early." Requiring neither salt nor lime, Fai downed his own. "I'm sure she'll show." Just after midnight, it was relatively early. And as he hadn't yet seen Carlos, he'd have to wait. An hour, two—he couldn't be sure.

He sank his drink.

* * *

In the passing hours, everyone to whom Smith relayed news of his friend's disappearance came alive. They were transfixed. Roused from their vodka-ketamine stupor, they wanted details: last sightings, last words. Had she made any enemies or scorned any lovers? *Yes, and, well, yes*—if he had to speak to police, Rune's name would be the first from his mouth—but to these inquiries, he replied with a cagey dismissal, explaining that they hadn't been in contact, so he didn't know exactly when, or even *if,* she'd gone missing. Some had useful information: A ginger pixie said she thought she'd seen her at an after last weekend, where she'd been acting like a *twat.* And another, a man who worked as a director at her father's Chelsea gallery, had seen her crying on the street; he couldn't recall exactly when but did recall the shock of that intrusion, like a neighbor nude across an air shaft.

Often, after relaying this information, these people would offer advice—"If you don't report the disappearance to police in the first twenty-four hours, they almost *never* find her," parroting lines they'd learned from books and films, where the *disappearing girl* was cause for great alarm. Usually white, usually pretty, usually virginal and therefore *good,* she was a stand-in for all things worthy of protection, saintly in her absence and blameless for her fate, a trope that had been invoked, then inverted, in the narrative of Elle's death to drive engagement, so Smith felt a growing unease as he watched these faces bloom with interest, aware that their perverse desire for the cinematic narrative—the all-night search, the victim, and the villain—belied a duller, far more likely reality. *You know as well as I do how this city eats people alive.*

Already, he could picture the headshot they'd use in the papers if she were found bone cold in some dank apartment: the click-bait copy, comments, and condolences. Though he wondered if things would play out differently for her. If her family, demanding their *privacy at this time*, would be granted it. No doubt that was the case for most who died young in that tragic, increasingly common way. They were not turned into tabloid fodder, pilloried until the ink bled through. Of course, he thought, *Black* pain was always spectacle, was always entertainment. In viral videos and abstract paintings, in policy, medicine, and history, their humanity was so incidental as to be revoked at will—their bodies inseparable from their capacity to suffer, and bear it smiling. So Smith slurred from room to room, taking anything offered, his worry, hurt, and rage blending to one.

A flurry of texts arrived as Smith stepped out to the curb, where an armada of cop cars lined the block. They'd shut down the party two hours too soon, and the chaos was palpable. Partygoers streamed out and gathered in manic clusters, attempting to sort their next move. Checking his phone, Smith realized just how shoddy his service had been inside.

Any luck? Fernanda had texted twenty-three minutes earlier.

I've talked to like 10 people and no one's heard from her

I'm fucking worrid.
*worried

Lace thinks it's time to call her parents

Fuck, Smith replied at once.

Ok. yea

Do you need me to do anything? My phone is 3%

no Lace is about to call them

It was time to go home, Smith figured, now that the search party was being handed over to professionals. Go home, stand by. He glanced down the block, where the cops were attempting to disperse the crowd remaining, which splintered and then gathered again. One group caught his eye. Carlos, that Tampa-born wonder, had donned his signature look: a dizzying blend of camouflage, faux fur, and animal print atop a tank and Dickies. A Harajuku girl at Berghain, he married the austerity of techno with disco-cum-club-kid excess and was always, like those in his orbit, tweaking slightly, whether it was midafternoon or in these wee morning hours, when he was known as the plug for the afters: an endless Rolodex of hard-partying scions who trusted him to court the golden ratio of gays and gals for an all-night spiral.

Smith called his name thrice, and on the third, the boy whipped around. "Who the fuck keeps *caallllinng me*?" he singsonged, silencing his googly-eyed hangers-on. Languidly, he scanned the group like a cataract queen and, seeing Smith, squinted. "*You.*"

"Yeah, me," Smith confirmed, fairly certain the boy couldn't place him. "You haven't seen Carolyn, have you?"

"*Who?*"

"Carolyn Astley." Carolyn he definitely knew; they'd once holed up for days at a mutual's Midtown condo. "You must remember her?"

"Duh," he said with sour breath. Next to him, a boy in a cropped ox-ford tugged his forearm and asked about the Uber but, like a dog, was shooed away. "Why, where is she?"

"I don't know," said Smith, stating the obvious. "That's why I'm looking for her."

Carlos wobbled where he stood. "Why are you *looking* for her when she's right in there," he said, gesturing theatrically at the door of the club they'd cleared with martial swiftness. Those who remained on the sidewalk shivered as they monitored the inching progress of their surge rides home.

"*What?* You saw her inside?"

"Duh," he jeered, teetering on what Smith now saw were stilettos. It made no sense. When the lights had come on, revealing a gallery of sweat-warmed faces, Smith had scanned the crowd as he was pushed toward the doors—surely Carlos was mistaken. But as he opened his mouth to clarify, the boy's eyes lit up. In an instant, he pushed past Smith's shoulder toward a black Escalade, yelling through the passenger window to confirm it was his. He flung the door open and threw himself into the back seat. "Wait," said Smith as the others flooded after him, nine for a car with six seats. "Wait," he repeated louder, now screaming, as the car doors shut and the driver pulled away, leaving him on the curb with the others. He stamped the concrete and cursed.

"Girl, *chill*," said the cropped oxford, clearly embarrassed on Smith's behalf. "We have the address if you wanna come with." Smith thought to tell him to fuck off, but cooled. He glanced back at the club doors, the cops on either side; she wasn't in there, of that he was sure. And she might well be wherever it was they were headed; it couldn't hurt to check.

A stale beer stench, thick in the air as they entered, emanated from the walls. The suite must have been the largest and most expensive in the hotel, the cheap sort off Bowery, its rooms suited mainly to the desultory drug deals and squalid affairs there conducted. The front desk attendant, a Chinese teen playing Candy Crush on his iPhone 7, had barely looked up as they passed.

Maybe thirty guests filled the length of the living room, into the hallway that stemmed from it and offered entry to a bathroom, bedroom, and closet. Even in the dark, it was evident that the furniture was stained, both recently and long ago, everyone's general attitude being that this place should be honored by their presence, so a drink spilled or a cigarette ashed directly onto the carpet was not just permissible but the whole point of being here. The crowd was a grungier set, punks and part-time stylists, models better known for bad behavior. On the couch, between opie-eyed waifs, sat one greasy quadragenarian who had once been an indie icon, his hirsute mane now thin and brittle.

Walking through, Smith examined every face. Downers, drinks, they stared back blankly. Smith imagined himself again as the private eye, tugging back the hair of a drooping stranger to force him to look at her picture. *You seen this gyal?* he'd ask, and he'd shrug. *What's it worth to ya?* No, there was no point in asking. By now, the girls would've told Carolyn's parents, who would've passed it on to the police. Besides, any info obtained here would be inadmissible. She'd be everywhere, she'd be nowhere. She'd have slipped out, a girl with that hair, that coloring. *Same eyes but wider nose. Just here, now gone.* "Are you looking for someone?" asked a Rubenesque Madonna, catching Smith by the crook of his arm.

"Yeah, um, for Carlos," Smith answered. He'd come all this way. Probably the boy knew nothing, would glare at him sedately from the depths of his K-hole, but he'd come all this way.

The girl smiled; she'd guessed as much. "He's in the bedroom," she said, gesturing down the hall. "But has *company*," she added, intoning the word with a subtext that did nothing to deter him. Smith thanked her and, past a straight pair tonguing, arrived at the bedroom door. Ceremonially, he knocked before entering.

Atop the California king in the foreground was a curious sight. What appeared at first to be one overlarge creature of limbs writhing horribly revealed itself in an instant to be several nude bodies entwined, engaged in a sex act of Rubik's Cube complexity. Smith scanned their faces. But quickly, his attention moved elsewhere, beyond them, where three more were gathered in a small sitting area, two seminude boys who appeared to have split from the scrum and the third a poshly clad woman who stood out like a thumb.

An argument had broken out. Nearing, Smith realized that the tanner of the boys seated on the couch of shopworn leather, back to him, was Carlos—the glass-topped table before him covered in a mountain of snow, at least a thousand dollars being carved into lines by the second. Carlos himself was repeating, with increasing insistence, the word *No* in response to an accusation levied by the sleekly dressed girl, who sat on the sill of a window and seemed content to ignore both the Olympic sex act before her and Smith, though both were in her full view. It took just seconds to discern the subject of their argument. The girl—moon-white skin through which blue veins showed faintly—held a bottle of prosecco in one hand and an empty flute in the other; she was screaming, accusing Carlos of having stolen a watch, presumably hers, last weekend at her apartment. His outright denial did nothing to erode her certainty. After all, it had been him who'd spent the whole night, nearly, in her closet, doing his *disgusting drugs*—and it wouldn't be the first time, she reminded him, *the backpack and Gucci loafers*. "You lent me those," he shrieked, then bent his head to snort another of the seven lines before him. "And if you had any fucking class, you'd have known to return them," she retorted, now visibly red at his refusal to confess to the crimes of which he was certainly guilty—

stealing, yes, but also of *using her* on too many occasions to count. "*Using you?*" he bellowed with laughter; more like the opposite, she'd be nothing without him. She clenched her purpling fists around the neck of the bottle, the vein of the stem. Reason had done her no good, and so she reverted to cruelty. He was a *social climber from fucking nowhere*, a *literal piece of shit*. She was a *dumb, stuck-up cunt*. His friend cackled loudly. And just as Carlos bent to snort another line and send that euphoric burst through his scarlet insides, the girl stepped suddenly forward and struck him, not with her hand but with the blunt end of that bottle of prosecco—a gasping crack on contact. The boys on the bed ceased their frottage, dismounted, and, seeing the scene, began to yell like a pack of hyenas: "*Stop, you're hurting him, stop, you're hurting—*" as she drew back and, with renewed vigor, struck him again, then again—a gash near his ear, bringing his insides out. By the impact, he was incapacitated. He didn't fight back. "*You're hurting him, you fucking psycho bitch.*" The boys screamed out the obvious, what she'd wanted to do for some time; she struck him again, and again, and again. No one stopped her, nor did she stop herself until the bottle finally caved into shards in her hands. And only then, in the immediate aftermath, did others spill in from the next room—summoned by that horrible sound— to the sight of her standing over his limp and keening body.

Smith saw flashes of horror on their faces as he passed through them, back into the living-room darkness from which most, though not all, had come running, into the bright hall, and down the stairs. He found a cab on Bowery. Diving into it, he directed the driver away, away from that party, that past. The still-lit city gleamed beyond the East River, which, beneath the bridge, resembled not water at all but a dark amorphous expanse, perhaps a road, headed northward by roiling asphalt toward the Sound and southward toward the bay and on to the vast and invisible ocean.

CHAPTER TWENTY-SEVEN

"I had to get out or I was going to kill myself," said Carolyn bluntly as she examined her untouched breakfast. Her eyes were alert. They moved with a decisive fluidity through the liquid late-afternoon light, which streamed long and yellow through a café window.

She'd returned, from the dead, without answers.

It had been later that night, after he'd gotten home and charged his phone, that the texts came streaming in. Lacey, Ollie, Fernanda, Mac, then, finally, the only one that mattered, which proved the whole evening a waste: *My mum says you've been looking for me. i'm okay and i love you. talk soon xc*

Another six days of silence followed, during which the emotional carousel spun—worry, hurt, and rage, along with annoyance, sadness, and coy humiliation at his feeling these things about a person who could not be bothered to call. Until that morning, when she'd invited him here. He'd searched for her, online and on foot, in dark rooms and dance clubs, in his mind for the memories that might offer clues, and now there she sat, in front of him, but he was searching still.

From the basket between them, she plucked a piece of nut bread and used it to burst a yolk, over easy, flooding her plate in canary yellow. "It all happened so fast," she continued, her voice steady as she recounted the facts. Twelve days prior, a Monday, she'd plucked herself from a five-day bender, showered, and boarded a train at Penn Station, eight and a half hours to Waterbury, Vermont. "Not exactly a rehab"—not a rehab at all, but a meditation center at the base of the mountains to which she had checked herself in, surrendering her cell phone in exchange for the bamboo mat on which she would sit for ten days in consummate silence. Dry out, think. That was, until day four, when she awoke to a monk at the foot of her bed. "He'd been in touch with my mum. He gave me my cell phone back and told me I had an hour." She recalled the litany of texts and calls that had rolled so urgently in, demanding to know her whereabouts. "Imagine my shock," she remarked with a smile. "To go from days without saying so much as hello to my roommate to that."

"Imagine how it was for us," Smith said coolly. He would have laughed at the explanation—a meditation retreat, so typical as to seem like a punch line—were he not so angry. But exuberant expressions of rage seemed to him mere admissions of one's vulnerability, the power the other still held. He'd withhold them.

"I know," she said. "I should've—well, I do feel sorry for worrying you."

"Do you?" he asked, and now his voice was not louder but certainly sharper, a showerhead of raised pressure. "Seems to me if you felt so bad, you wouldn't have done something so selfish in the first place." Smith knew that Fernanda and Lacey would forgive her without question. She was an addict in active recovery and needed to do what was best—for *her*, never mind what that meant for the others. But he had no such intention. He was done with this, the constant and meaningless drama; he had to move on with his life.

"I don't," she began, then paused, glancing back at her yolk-soiled plate. She knew they weren't talking just about her, but the memory surfaced, a blanched corpse from a lake. She looked down, the peach corners of her lip upturned. Her face had dimmed from the days of asceticism; the meals in the ashram were described by her mother, who'd gone herself in the early eighties, as *plant-based*, a generous term for what amounted to a week of unseasoned cabbage, as if salt itself were a wanton indulgence to be renounced on the path to nirvana. "I don't think you understand how it's been for me."

How it had been for her. Spurred on by Smith's silence, she recounted the days in early December when she'd relapsed on Rune and booze at once— two vices which, by then, were entwined. Mostly, they'd meet downtown after Inducio's closing, sometimes well after midnight, and have drawn-out dinners at the restaurants of friends who kept their kitchens open. Of course, there was something romantic in this nocturna (the back rooms, slinking home through the dew-glossed streets) and also abasing (the waiting and late-night cancellations). She skipped her trip to her mom's for the holidays because he asked her to and also because she knew her mother would take one look at her face and know that she'd been using. Did she really like Rune that much? No, not really. But there was a freedom she'd never known in existing absolutely for another, in prostrating herself before him. She forwent sleep, and work, and even the possibility of plans for his company—the thirty-minute to three-hour stretches he could steal away, which she gave to him gladly. Their sex was familiar and reciprocal. It was good and secret and frequent and made sexy because of this secret, though often it was brief, had to be fit within the bounds of a believable alibi. It was obsessive and compulsive and delirious; he gave good head and compliments, brought gifts, and quieted always the question of what she was meant to do with her days, beyond this.

Christmas came and, with it, the bundled-up tourists on Broadway, the freshly laid snow. Rune went to Vail with his family. And her apartment, where she was often drinking a full bottle of wine before dinner, began to feel small, so she moved to Dmitri's downtown. Through a window, she observed the pantsuited women marching to their jobs, the stylish young mothers. Women self-possessed; she despised them, and as the year hemmed closed and another opened, just as she began to accept that this chapter was ending, her period was late. Rune was normally, about condoms, a regular after-school special but had weeks ago gone without just once in a fit of mild passion. She made an appointment to terminate the pregnancy the same afternoon she confirmed it but didn't tell a soul. Rune, she knew, "would be a total pansy," would freak and maybe blab to his wife. So she screened her calls, and after the abortion—in a reversal of feeling that startled only him—blocked his number.

In the new year, the ugly, cold city turned to stone. On curbsides, in restaurants, she caught herself crying. It wasn't about the abortion or Rune. It was that something big had happened, and now it was done, and it was crushing to be back in her body with nothing to show for it. Back in Brooklyn, she attempted to wean herself off the half gram a day she was by then using. She couldn't go out and she couldn't stay in. A compromise: Emerge just once a week and then stay out for days, keeping only the company of those in no position to judge her, an increasingly unsavory pool who used as she did, with a *vengeance*, staying up on whatever as the city was rising for work. And once, coming home to her empty apartment, she got hold of one of the barbacks from Inducio, whom she'd befriended on the after-party circuit, to get him to score her some heroin. "I didn't use it, but I knew that I could, in case—"

* * *

The waiter had stopped coming by to refill their drinks, sensing the conversation's solemnity. So Smith's throat was dry, his voice small, when he asked, "Why didn't you tell me?"

"I couldn't," she said without pause. "For one, you were avoiding me, don't you dare deny it."

"I wasn't going to," he said. It was true; he had wanted space, perhaps since Elle's death. In her absence, all the faulty seams of his friendship with Carolyn had shown themselves plainly, the fits too snug or too loose, and it had deepened his grief, seeing them and realizing just how rare it was to be known. "You're right. With my court date and everything—"

"I understand," she said, and still she was smiling—a docile, impenitent smile ill-suited to the words, "I just felt very alone."

Smith sipped his second coffee, contemplating the days he'd spent texting the void. "I'm still not sure that absolves you," he said, his dispassionate tone beginning to fray. "You're not a child. You can't light fires, then act surprised when they burn."

Her smile faltered, and as a reflex, he began to apologize, but held it. "You're right," she said. "That pattern, it's one I've described a lot in AA, how I use people's concern to feel seen."

"Well, congratulations, it worked," he said flatly. "I really thought you might be dead."

She was quiet a moment. "You know, I miss her too." *Her* meaning Elle. She didn't bring her up often. And now it was clear that this wasn't from lack of feeling but fear, fear that he'd grown too possessive of his grief to share it. He could see, in her eyes, how acutely they'd both been alone. "Do you remember that morning when you called and told me the news? I got off the phone and just stared at myself in the mirror for hours, thinking, *This is your wake-up call*. Like, if I couldn't make sobriety stick this time, I never would. But then, I don't know, time—" She took a deep breath as if the words had weakened her, and Smith studied her face. He pictured her there, in the ashram, a jade-limbed buddha for days, poring over her young life's rubble. "Sometimes I feel—and this isn't your fault but you *are* a part of it—I feel like no one wants me better, because better is *boring*," she said, pronouncing the word with grave derision. "It doesn't suit me or, like, this character I've created, who seeks out trouble and excitement and lives to be observed. And she's like a dead layer of skin I'm trying to shed, but it's hard, when that's who I see reflected back." Her voice held a tremor. "And it just kills me to think that's how you see me."

There was truth to what she'd said, and real pain in that face of unmasked anguish. Still, a part of him wished to say the worst thing, to hurt her in a way he couldn't revise. Still, he felt the rage; it was an insult, really, to complain of being trapped in a room of one's own making, inconsequential in the contest of pain, and yet—he took a breath, and she continued. "You know, when you're meditating, or *trying* to meditate, for that long, eighteen hours a day, ten days straight, it's like dying. Your whole life opens up in front of you, and you can see all these things you've forgotten, or repressed, memories you've cherished without understanding. It's like the whole universe you're trying to shut out comes flooding in, and even in that deluge, I found myself coming back to you."

He breathed and held her blue gaze.

"And what you're supposed to do is observe how recurring thoughts feel inside your body—*Don't judge, just observe*, that's what they say—and with you, I always tightened. And I think there was a lot of resentment there. And love, and sadness, but more than that, I felt guilt. Because even when I was at bottom, seeking the gnarliest rooms I could find, I always knew I would come out clean." Through the window, a sunbeam fell across her blank features. He didn't know her, he thought then, not beyond this glittering surface which had drawn, then repelled him like a party scene the morning after, the confetti and beer on the floor. But history, thick and rank in the air between them, could not be disavowed. It could only be endured. And in time, it would come to mean something.

He took her hand.

CHAPTER TWENTY-EIGHT

One of the best days of spring came in late winter, the kind of balmy, unseasonal surprise that conveys both relief and ambiguous dread—of warming, yes, but also something sour in the wind. News from abroad had begun to warn of a virus, damning those in recent health to hospital beds, hallways, graves, but in Prospect Park, they were out in great numbers. People from all surrounding zip codes descended in droves to the park's main lawn, where they laid out their blankets along the rolling dunes, a Seurat scene of flesh and color. It was O's birthday, their twenty-third, and in typical Pisces fashion, their sole wish was to feed their friends: pan-seared steak and potatoes au gratin, roasted rhubarb, and an olive oil cake inspired by a chefluencer of Condé Nast fame whom they described as having "call-the-cops-on-the-cookout energy" but whose recipes they loved nonetheless. Smith was just happy to be involved—though as they walked through the grid of tents, leafy produce, and pink meats on ice, he kept his distance, mind adrift.

Last night, Carolyn had left in an Uber for the airport. She'd had two bags, each the size of her torso, and although she had yet to sublet her apartment, he knew she was not coming back. She would spend the foreseeable future out west, beginning with a two-month stay at an inpatient on the coast, which she'd already taken to calling the "Hotel California." As the town car disappeared into orange smog beyond the river, Smith had felt—for her, for both of them—relief.

Back in O's kitchen, two hours to spare, Smith was assigned simple tasks— chopping, cleaving, the various mutilations that would make these items edible—while O began the careful chemistry required in preparing cake. Measuring a quantity of freshly milled flour, they spoke to Smith at an up-beat cadence about tonight's guests. Mona was coming, he knew, having spent the past week "trialing" as her assistant, a personal courtesy she'd offered him with apprehension, which he'd quickly allayed after a single afternoon spent rewriting her show texts had left her very nearly in tears. Then there were at least a dozen others, artists and academics and activists, coming together for this last communion. Notably absent was Tia, whom O had barely mentioned in the weeks since their rift, though the pointed si-lence suggested anything other than apathy. Rather, it suggested that they thought of her often, always, that her absence was the air they breathed.

Already, the intimacy he had with O was marred by distance. He hadn't told them about his arrest. About Carolyn or Elle. About the accused, his arraignment in two weeks' time. The whole nightmare of the past year, which Smith had redacted from all accounts of his personal history— out of a desire, he thought, to *move on*—though it reannounced itself in thoughts and pangs each minute so that every silence between them was weighted.

This would only grow harder, he thought, once the trial had begun. Soon, every time he checked his phone, he'd see that face: the accused, who, according to the papers, had not posted his extravagant bail. So at that very moment, he was seated in a cell somewhere in the sprawling city, awaiting trial. It would be a final torment, for Smith and Carolyn and Dre and all the others who would watch with rapt attention the attempt to grant them *justice*, knowing all the while that this was a flimsy proposition; there was no bringing her back. Still, Smith yearned for the trial. For the cool eye of reason to pore over the facts, uncover all of the truth-sworn secrets, and make a formal declaration as to how it had happened and who was to blame. And on solemn nights spent walking through lamplit parks or sitting on the banks of the river, this was the fantasy he returned to most often: gazing across a crowded courtroom into the eyes of the accused and offloading all of his grief.

"You good?" asked O, glimpsing his dazed expression. Smith nodded, and they took over for him in dicing the grape tomatoes. The blade slid without effort through the taut, ripe bodies. And as Smith admired the brutal and elegant act, rounding the counter for a better view, O saw he'd been left without a task and nodded to their phone on the counter. "Take it out when it looks like the picture," they instructed, "the cake." Smith crouched with the phone in his hands. From the screenshot, he scrolled through an infinite grid—sunsets, outfits, every angle of their face—and wondered if knowing someone was a matter more of data or intuition. He clicked on an image, one of the first in their phone, of Tia in a dimly lit room, her laugh so open he could see where a tooth had been filled. Years had passed. She was different. But still they'd kept this picture, the memory of who she'd been that night perfectly preserved. And though there was still so much to tell them, this was the urgent thing: that time was always wasting.

And dazed with the force of that fact, Smith opened O's texts and typed in Tia's name.

*   *   *

Within the hour, the guests began arriving, and because O had not had time to change, Smith played the cohost, welcoming in a radiant woman with a dark crown of curls, then a person whose epicene face was covered in fine-line tattoos. Mona arrived with a handsome young man, and then O descended, having covered their hair in a silken scarf too ornate to describe as a do-rag. Each time Smith opened the door, he felt his anxiety peak, then plunge, as he saw she had not come and probably wouldn't, even as he began to fear his impulsive act had been a betrayal as much as a kindness; he thought of O's father showing up to their thirteenth birthday at this very house, radiating resentment and rage.

Ten minutes passed, twenty. The vibes, otherwise, were immaculate—everyone being very *young, gifted, and Black* about it, uncorking bottles of sparkling wine and chatting with equal effervescence about all things under the sun, their pleated gem tones swaying to Sade. And then O's face went slack midsentence, and without looking, Smith knew she had come. No one else seemed to notice; she had let herself in. But Smith saw, across that garrulous sea, O's surprise wane to confusion, which no doubt conveyed to Tia that her invitation was counterfeit. And for the first time, Smith thought she looked truly out of place as she glanced back at the door through which she'd come. It was too late; the two locked eyes.

The last time Smith saw Elle, he remembered, had been across a crowded room. On the dance floor, her birthday, her guests had split in every direction. Anxious about his meeting in the morning, Smith had begun to make an Irish exit, not wanting to halt the night's momentum by announcing that he was headed home—he would see Elle there, anyway—but as he moved through the strobing disco toward the door, he'd spotted her, impossible to miss, all hips and hair and rhythm. The room spun like a track along her center spindle. She was always bringing him out, out of his room and his mind, into the world—and into people. She craved them in a way he never had, their beauty and chaos; she basked in it, and perhaps that had been her ruin but it had also been her gift. To be pulsing and open, *what a thing*. He hadn't gone then and pried her from that throng but had waited, watched, as she danced to one last song.

For a moment, after O arrived in front of Tia, the two just stood, examining one another like playground children. Something passed, without words, between them. They embraced. And the sight of it, their silent resolve to wade through the muck of their past toward an unknowable future, filled Smith with a crush of emotions: longing and envy and regret, and then an almost unbearable tenderness.

He left the room alone. On a table in the backyard, Smith laid out a checkered sheet, then the glasses, the plates, and the food in big bowls to be spooned out like they were family. The sky was beginning to darken, a mass of blue wonder. He cut fresh flowers and lit a mound of votives he'd found in the kitchen so that everyone, spilling outside, marveled at his artistry—grateful for the extra hour of daylight that the season had given them. Soon, it would again be summer, and the days would come hot and long and relentless. Smith wasn't sure he could take another in the city, nor where he would go if he could not. But for a few hours, the night's hum silenced those concerns.

The votives burned down to the wick and, because Smith had not placed them in holders, set the sheet aflame. It grew quickly and was just as quickly extinguished, gasped into smoke. Silence fell around the table. And then O began laughing and the others followed suit: a music of fevered relief. The sight of the bright black gash in the bedspread, a breathless howl that didn't remit. And because it was funny, Smith laughed as well. A gut-clench, sight-blur of laughter, full as a palm's clutch of fireflies. They swam out to the night. Into the warmth they knew was a gift that would someday eclipse them.

While this is a novel, it is inspired by true events. In the summer of 2018, a close friend of mine died by overdose, which led to a months-long media spectacle and police investigation. Years later, as I began writing a novel that followed a character named Smith navigating the projections placed upon him in court and recovery rooms and by society at large, I quickly realized that I was writing around, instead of *through*, my own unprocessed grief. In writing *Great Black Hope*, I brought in aspects of my friend's story as a means to unpack that grief, to look at larger cultural narratives around drug use and Black bodies—and to probe questions that, in real life, were never answered. The other characters, as well as all action and dialogue, are products of my imagination and not intended to portray any real people or represent any real events.

ACKNOWLEDGMENTS

I have never been the kind of writer who can wake up and immediately get to it. I generally have to get psyched up or tricked into it, so I want first to thank all of the artists whose work has helped me build and then return to the world of this novel, among them Richard Siken, Joan Didion, James Baldwin, Margo Jefferson, Hilton Als, Ben Lerner, Jay McInerney, Donna Tartt, Justin Vernon, Max Richter, Charli XCX, Solange, Lana Del Rey, Frank Ocean, Nan Goldin, Deana Lawson, and Lynette Yiadom-Boakye. Reading, listening to, and looking at your work reminds me why I write and, even on my worst days, brings me back to the page.

Thank you to everyone at Summit Books and Summit Books UK—Judy Clain, Suzanne Baboneau, Josefine Kals, Anna Skrabacz, Kevwe Okumakube, Luiza de Campos Mello Grijns—for entrusting this novel to relaunch the imprint and for the astonishing level of care you've shown me throughout this process. Thank you in particular to my editor, Laura Perciasepe, for seeing this book's potential, then pointing out my tics and asking the thoughtful questions that allowed me to realize it. Thank you to everyone involved in copyediting, design, and production at Simon & Schuster who had a hand in getting this story onto the printed page—

Tracy Roe, Kayley Hoffman, Amanda Mulholland, Lauren Gomez, Zoe Kaplan, Carly Loman, Beth Maglione, and Alexis Leira—and to Emma Trim for my author photo.

Thank you to my incredible agents, Audrey Crooks and Ellen Levine, not just for your tireless work and guidance in helping me navigate the publishing business but for being thought partners and sounding boards in the many months that this book was still becoming.

To all of my teachers, the first people who gave me an inkling that I might want to do this and, perhaps, that I *could*, thank you. I am so lucky to have found, at every stage, the mentors who I needed: In high school, Nedra Roberts, who taught me to be brave; in college, Kai Carlson-Wee and Nicholas Friedman, who nurtured my voice as a poet, who gave me books and suggestions, and who (rightly) looked at me askance when I announced that I was planning to become a consultant after graduation; and all of my NYU MFA professors—Joyce Carol Oates, Uzodinma Iweala, Jonathan Safran Foer, Alex Dimitrov, Hari Kunzru, Brandon Taylor, and Nadifa Mohamed—who took me seriously as a writer, who challenged my ideas and scrutinized my sentences. Thank you in particular to my thesis adviser, Katie Kitamura, who read this book in many iterations and was a fierce advocate and trusted mentor through them all. Having you in my corner has been the greatest blessing.

To my NYU MFA cohort, who awed me with your talent, thank you. Thank you to August Thompson, for your humor and guidance and gameness for midday celebrations at Bed-Stuy bars; to Sarah Lieberman, for your peerless kindness and generous feedback; and to Rapha Linden, one of my earliest readers, whose incisive critique and unwavering sense of self helped me learn when to bend and when to stand firm in my vision. And to all the other writers—Emmeline Clein, Hannah Gold, Cora Lewis, Makshya Tolbert, Ana Velasco, Joseph Charlton, Alexis Okeowo—who read my works in progress and allowed me to read their own and who graciously connected me to opportunities that have helped me grow as a writer, thank you.

Thank you to all of the friends, too many to name, but I'll try—Charlie Cockburn, Sebastian Mancera, Chiara Towne, Ziwe Fumudoh, Rob Noble, Kelly McGee, Tom Nye, Brandon Caruso, Robert Burns, Isaac Halyard, Allison Otis, Nika Soon-Shiong, Ian Malone, Clara Galperin, Camila M. Barshee, Patricio Galindo, and many more—who've cooked me a meal or given me a room or chased me across a foreign city to return my passport while my mind was clearly elsewhere. Your friendship makes life sweet.

Thank you to Cameron Norsworthy, my first editor, who at sixteen gave me a book that changed my life and who, in the sixteen years since, has been a collaborator and confidant.

Thank you to Charlotte Lansbury, the best friend a boy could ask for, who has taught me so much about life and love. It's been a pleasure growing up together.

And finally, thank you to my family, without whom I'd have nothing. No words for what you mean to me.

ABOUT THE AUTHOR

Born and raised in Atlanta, Rob Franklin is a writer of fiction and poetry, and a cofounder of the nonprofit initiative Art for Black Lives. Franklin holds a BA from Stanford University and an MFA from NYU's Creative Writing Program. He lives in Brooklyn and teaches writing at the School of Visual Arts. *Great Black Hope* is his first novel.